Lola's SUPER CLUB

"My Dad is a
Super Secret Agent"

PAPERCUTZ™
NEW YORK

MORE GREAT GRAPHIC NOVEL SERIES AVAILABLE FROM PAPERCUTZ

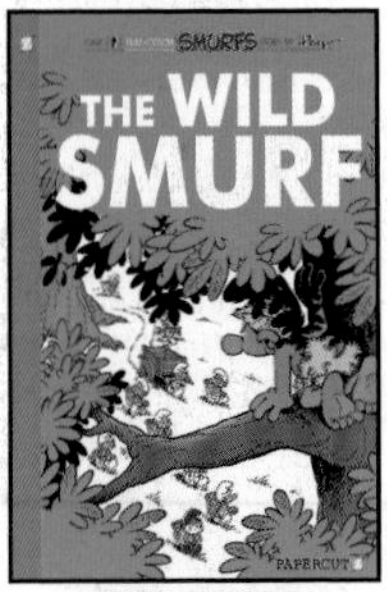
THE WILD SMURF
PAPERCUTZ

THE SMURFS

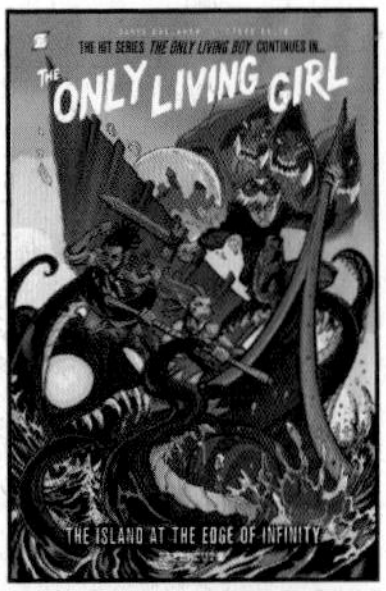
THE ONLY LIVING GIRL
THE ISLAND AT THE EDGE OF INFINITY
PAPERCUTZ

THE ONLY LIVING GIRL

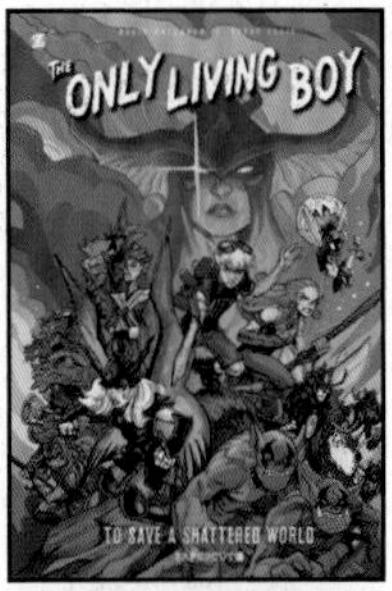
THE ONLY LIVING BOY
TO SAVE A SHATTERED WORLD

THE ONLY LIVING BOY

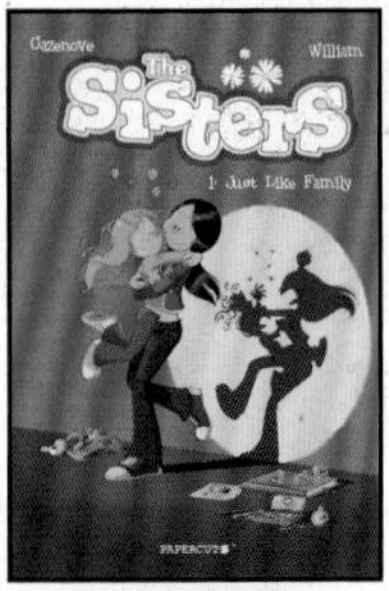
Cazenove
William
The Sisters
1. Just Like Family
PAPERCUTZ

THE SISTERS

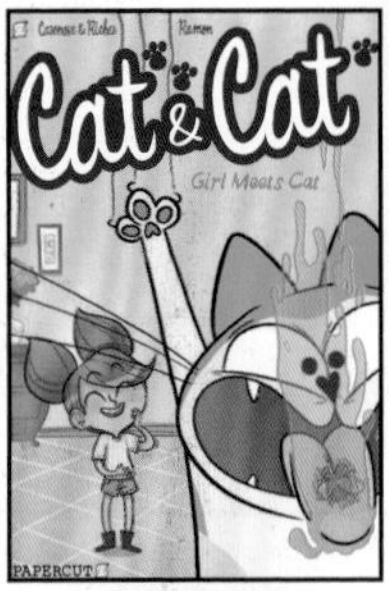
Cat & Cat
Girl Meets Cat
PAPERCUTZ

CAT & CAT

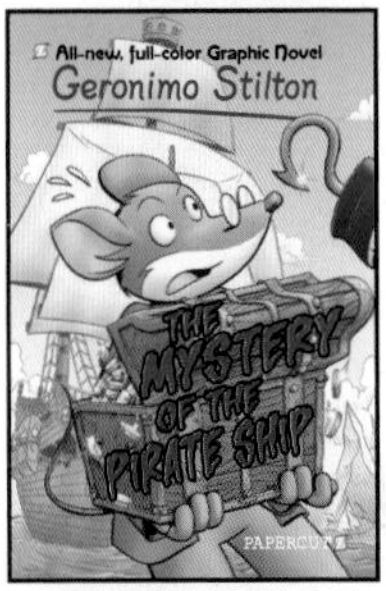
All-new, full-color Graphic Novel
Geronimo Stilton
THE MYSTERY OF THE PIRATE SHIP
PAPERCUTZ

GERONIMO STILTON

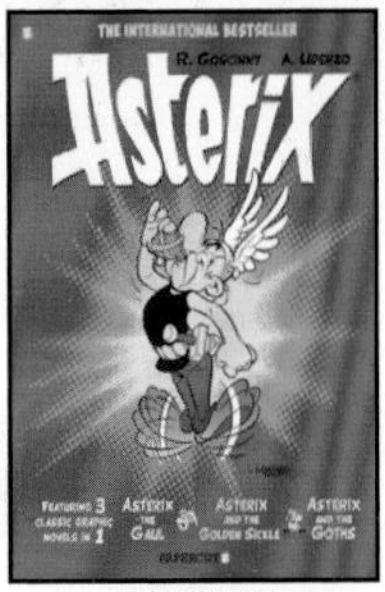
THE INTERNATIONAL BESTSELLER
R. GOSCINNY
A. UDERZO
Asterix
PAPERCUTZ

ASTERIX

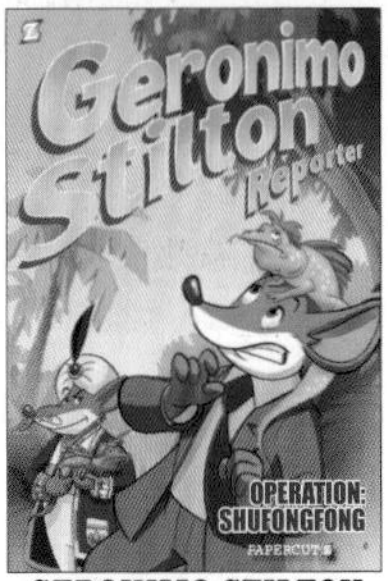
Geronimo Stilton
Reporter
OPERATION: SHUFONGFONG
PAPERCUTZ

GERONIMO STILTON REPORTER

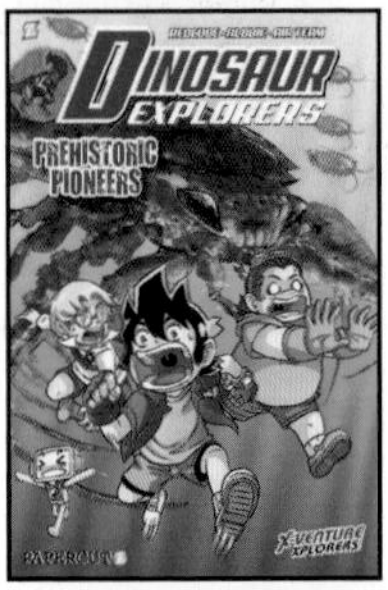
DINOSAUR EXPLORERS
PREHISTORIC PIONEERS
PAPERCUTZ

DINOSAUR EXPLORERS

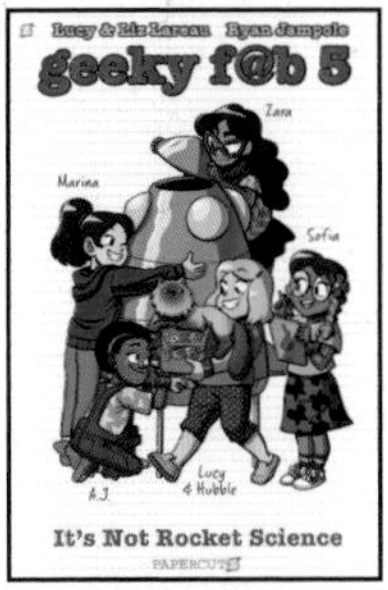
geeky f@b 5
It's Not Rocket Science
PAPERCUTZ

GEEKY FAB 5

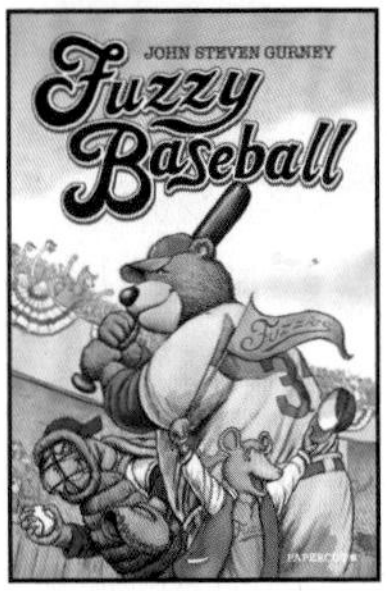
JOHN STEVEN GURNEY
Fuzzy Baseball
PAPERCUTZ

FUZZY BASEBALL

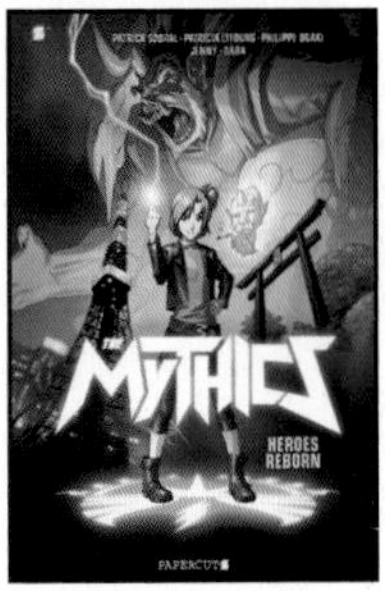
MYTHICS
HEROES REBORN
PAPERCUTZ

THE MYTHICS

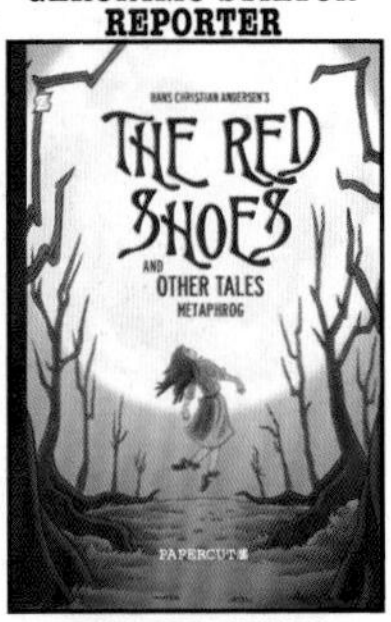
HANS CHRISTIAN ANDERSEN'S
THE RED SHOES
AND OTHER TALES
METAPHROG
PAPERCUTZ

THE RED SHOES

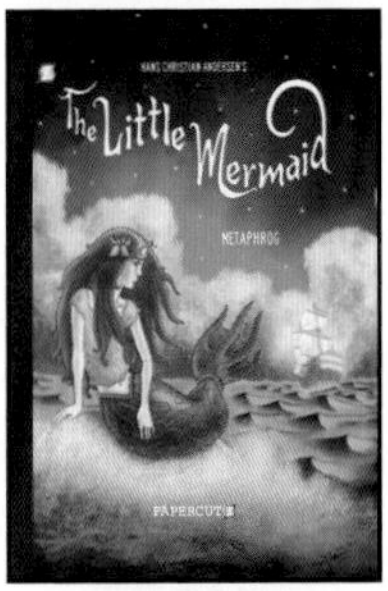
The Little Mermaid
METAPHROG
PAPERCUTZ

THE LITTLE MERMAID

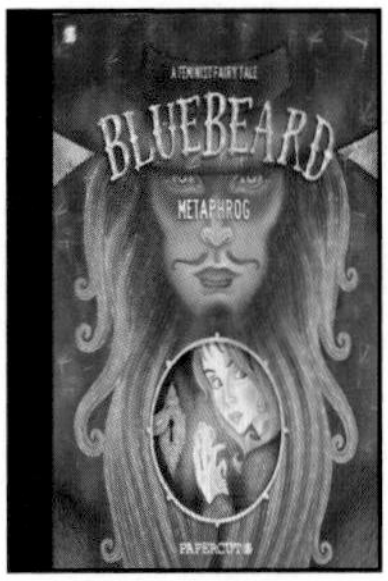
BLUEBEARD
METAPHROG
PAPERCUTZ

BLUEBEARD

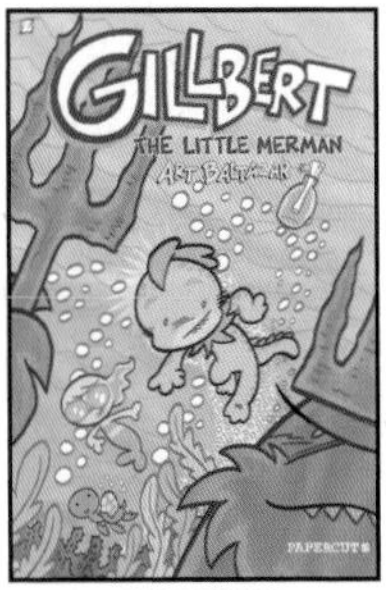
GILLBERT
THE LITTLE MERMAN
PAPERCUTZ

GILLBERT

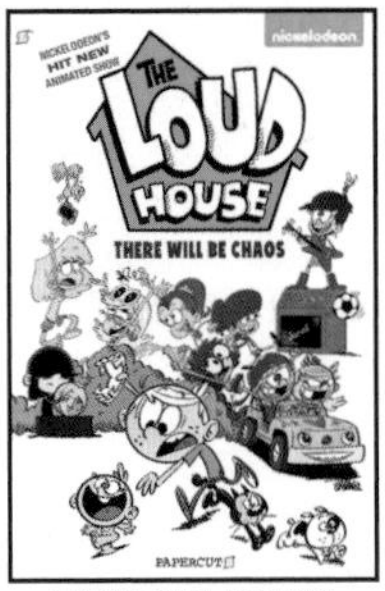
nickelodeon
The LOUD HOUSE
THERE WILL BE CHAOS
PAPERCUTZ

THE LOUD HOUSE

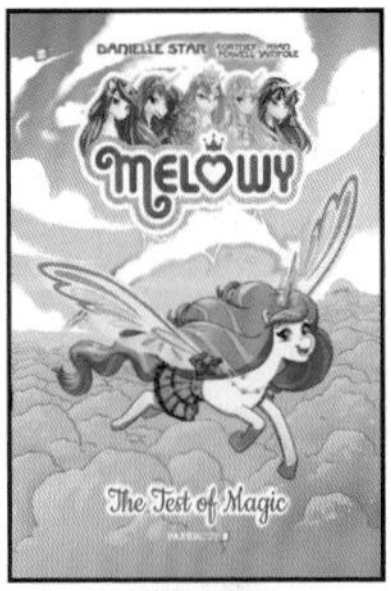
DANIELLE STAR
Melowy
The Test of Magic
PAPERCUTZ

MELOWY

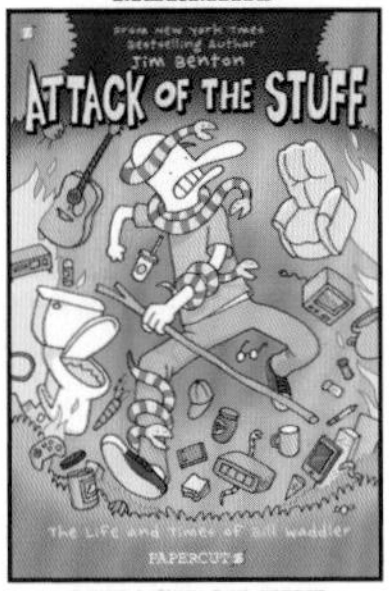
From New York Times bestselling author
Jim Benton
ATTACK OF THE STUFF
The Life and Times of Bill Waddler
PAPERCUTZ

ATTACK OF THE STUFF

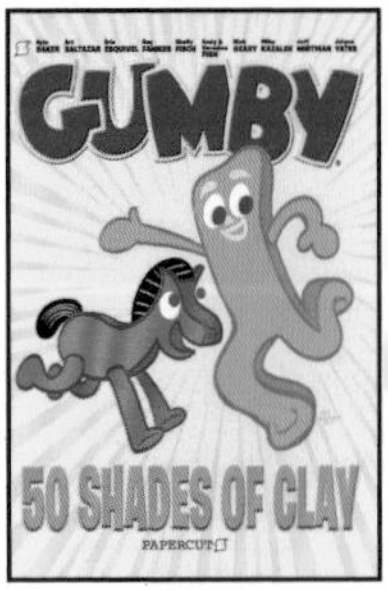
GUMBY
50 SHADES OF CLAY
PAPERCUTZ

GUMBY

PAPERCUTZ™

papercutz.com

Also available as ebooks wherever ebooks are sold.

Lola's SUPER CLUB

I - "MY DAD IS A SUPER SECRET AGENT"

Script and art
Christine Beigel + Pierre Fouillet

Original editors
Maxi Luchini + Ed

Original designer
Immaculada Bordell

© Christine Beigel + Pierre Fouillet, 2010
© Bang. Ediciones,2011,2013
contacto@bangediciones.com
All rights reserved.
English translation and all other editorial material
© 2020 Papercutz
English translation rights arranged through S.B.Rights Agency –
Stephanie Barrouillet

Paperback ISBN: 978-1-5458-0564-0
Hardcover ISBN: 978-1-5458-0563-3

Special thanks to Stephanie Barrouillet, Manu Vidal Ibañez,
and Eva Reyes

Papercutz books may be purchased for business or promotional use.
For information on bulk purchases please contact
Macmillan Corporate and Premium Sales Department at
(800) 221-795 x5442.

Jeff Whitman–Translator, Letterer, Production, Editor
Eric Storms, Ingrid Rios–Editorial Interns
Jim Salicrup
Editor-in-Chief

Printed in China
December 2021

First Papercutz Printing
Distributed by Macmillan

Lola's SUPER CLUB

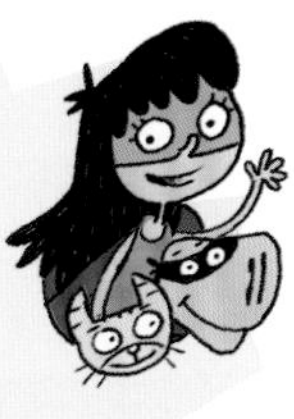

"MY DAD IS A SUPER SECRET AGENT"

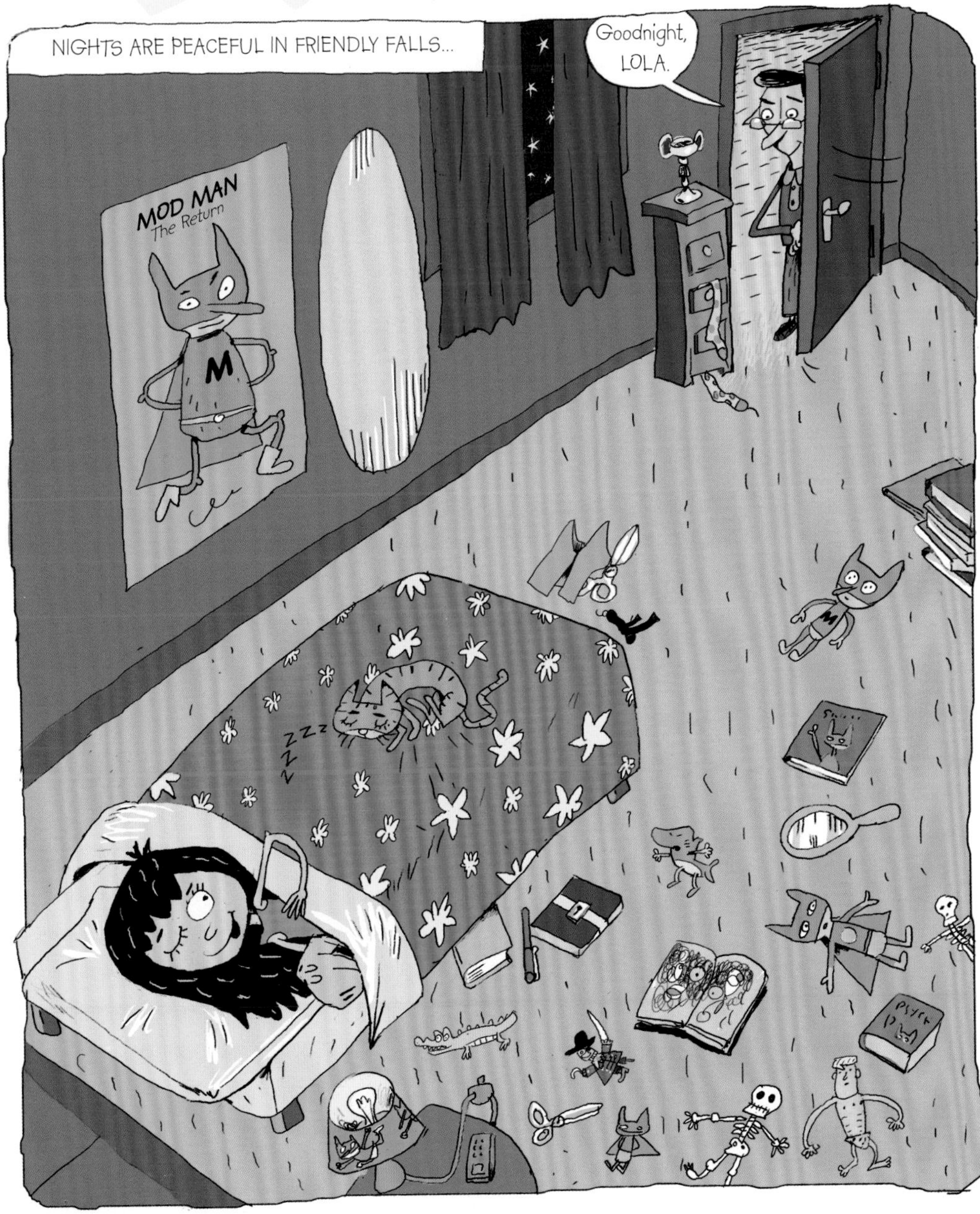
NIGHTS ARE PEACEFUL IN FRIENDLY FALLS...
Goodnight, LOLA.
MOD MAN
The Return
M
Z Z Z
Z Z Z

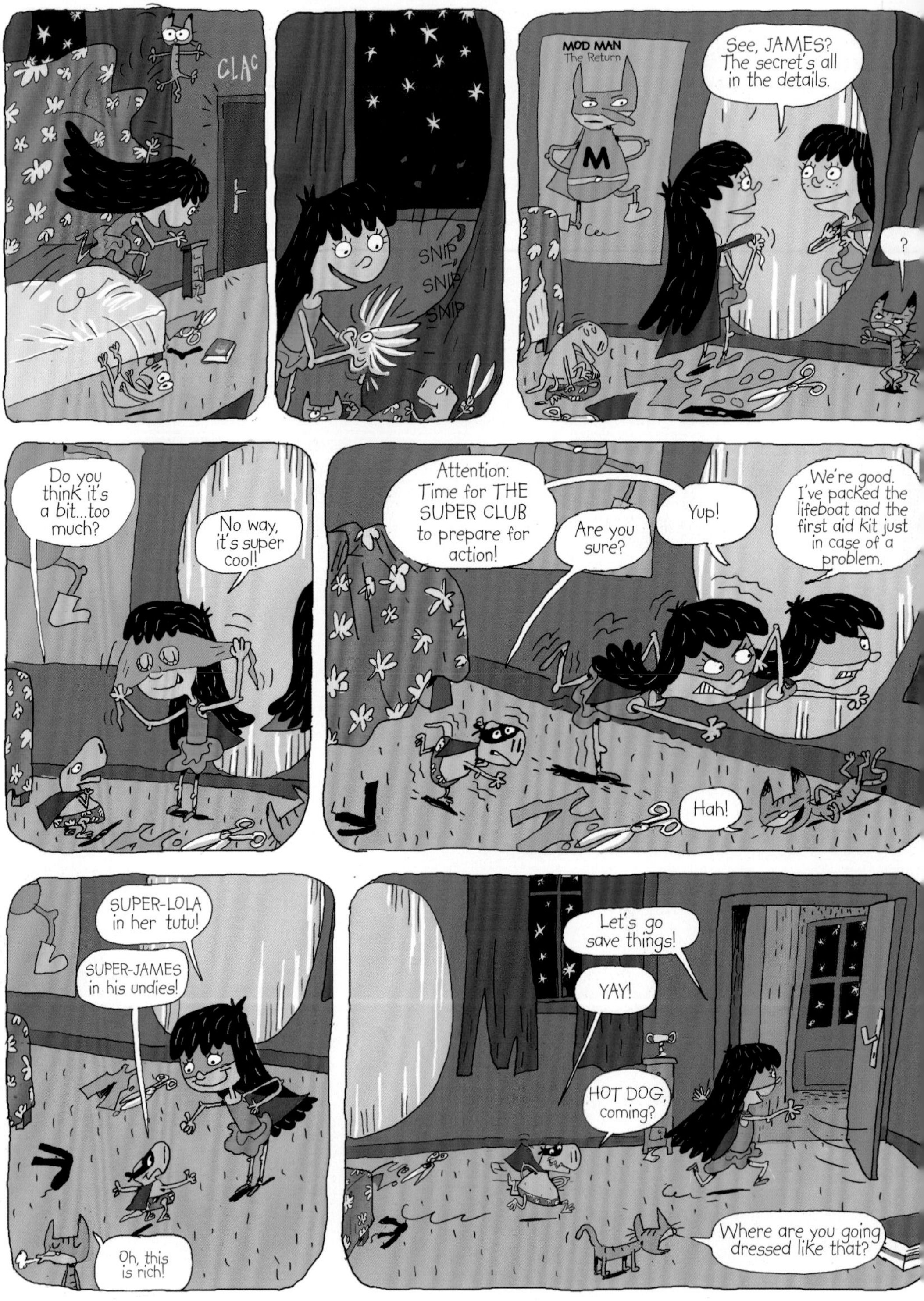
CLAC
SNIP
SNIP
SNIP
MOD MAN
The Return
M
See, JAMES? The secret's all in the details.
?
Do you think it's a bit...too much?
No way, it's super cool!
Attention: Time for THE SUPER CLUB to prepare for action!
Are you sure?
Yup!
We're good. I've packed the lifeboat and the first aid kit just in case of a problem.
Hah!
SUPER-LOLA in her tutu!
SUPER-JAMES in his undies!
Oh, this is rich!
Let's go save things!
YAY!
HOT DOG, coming?
Where are you going dressed like that?

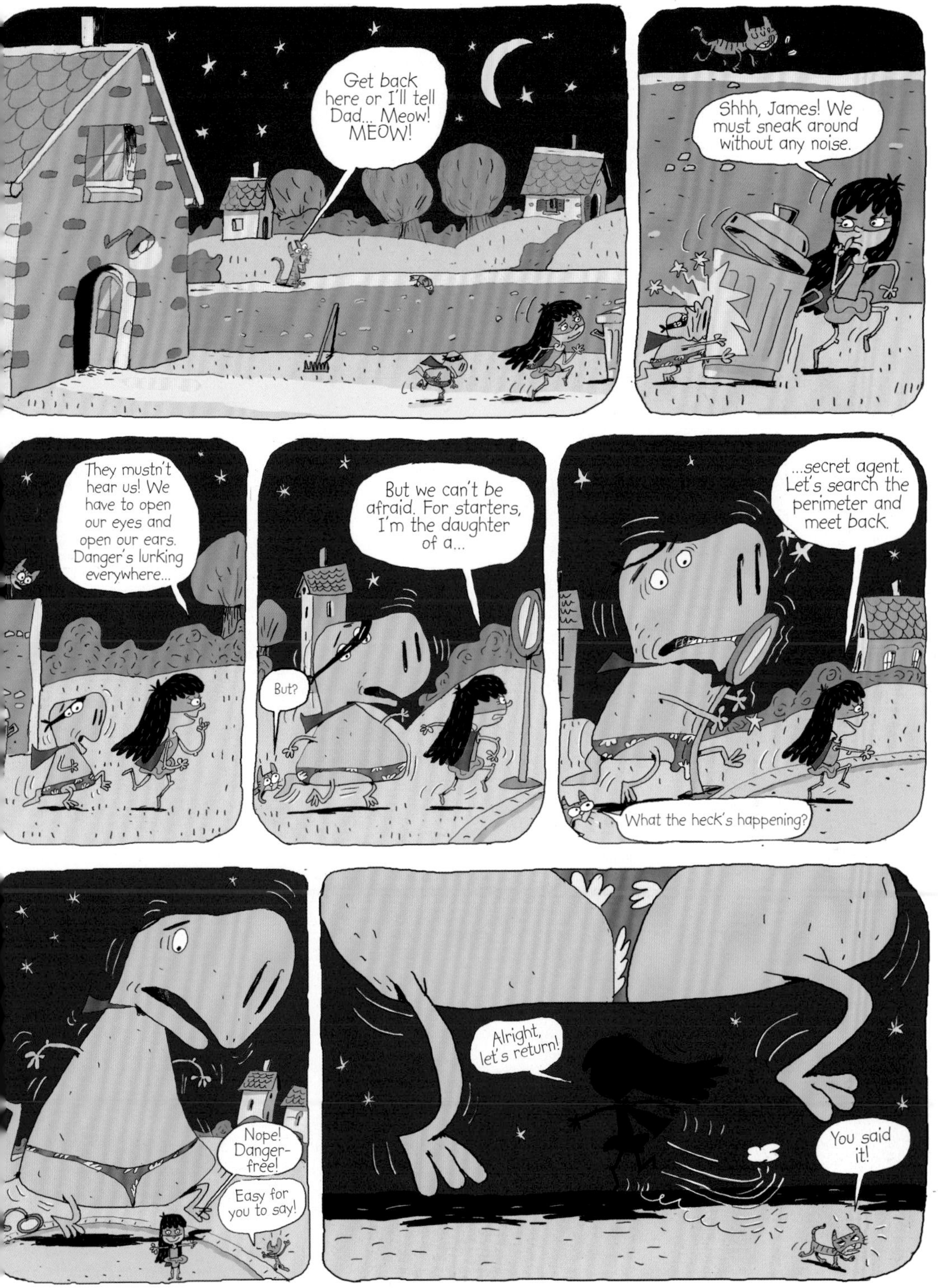
Get back here or I'll tell Dad... Meow! MEOW!
Shhh, James! We must sneak around without any noise.
They mustn't hear us! We have to open our eyes and open our ears. Danger's lurking everywhere...
But we can't be afraid. For starters, I'm the daughter of a...
But?
...secret agent. Let's search the perimeter and meet back.
What the heck's happening?
Nope! Danger-free!
Easy for you to say!
Alright, let's return!
You said it!

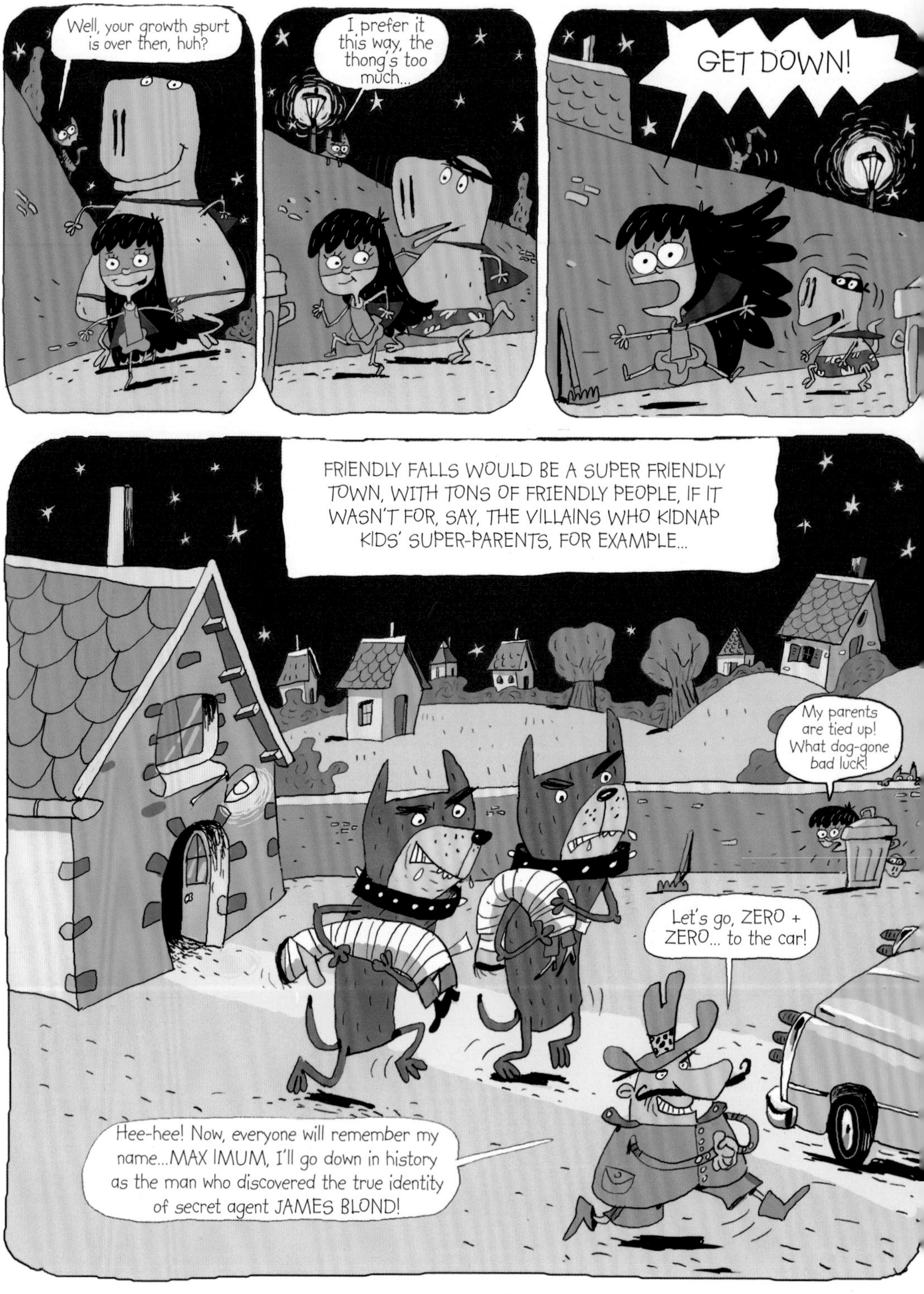
Well, your growth spurt is over then, huh?
I prefer it this way, the thong's too much...
GET DOWN!
FRIENDLY FALLS WOULD BE A SUPER FRIENDLY TOWN, WITH TONS OF FRIENDLY PEOPLE, IF IT WASN'T FOR, SAY, THE VILLAINS WHO KIDNAP KIDS' SUPER-PARENTS, FOR EXAMPLE...
My parents are tied up! What dog-gone bad luck!
Let's go, ZERO + ZERO... to the car!
Hee-hee! Now, everyone will remember my name...MAX IMUM, I'll go down in history as the man who discovered the true identity of secret agent JAMES BLOND!

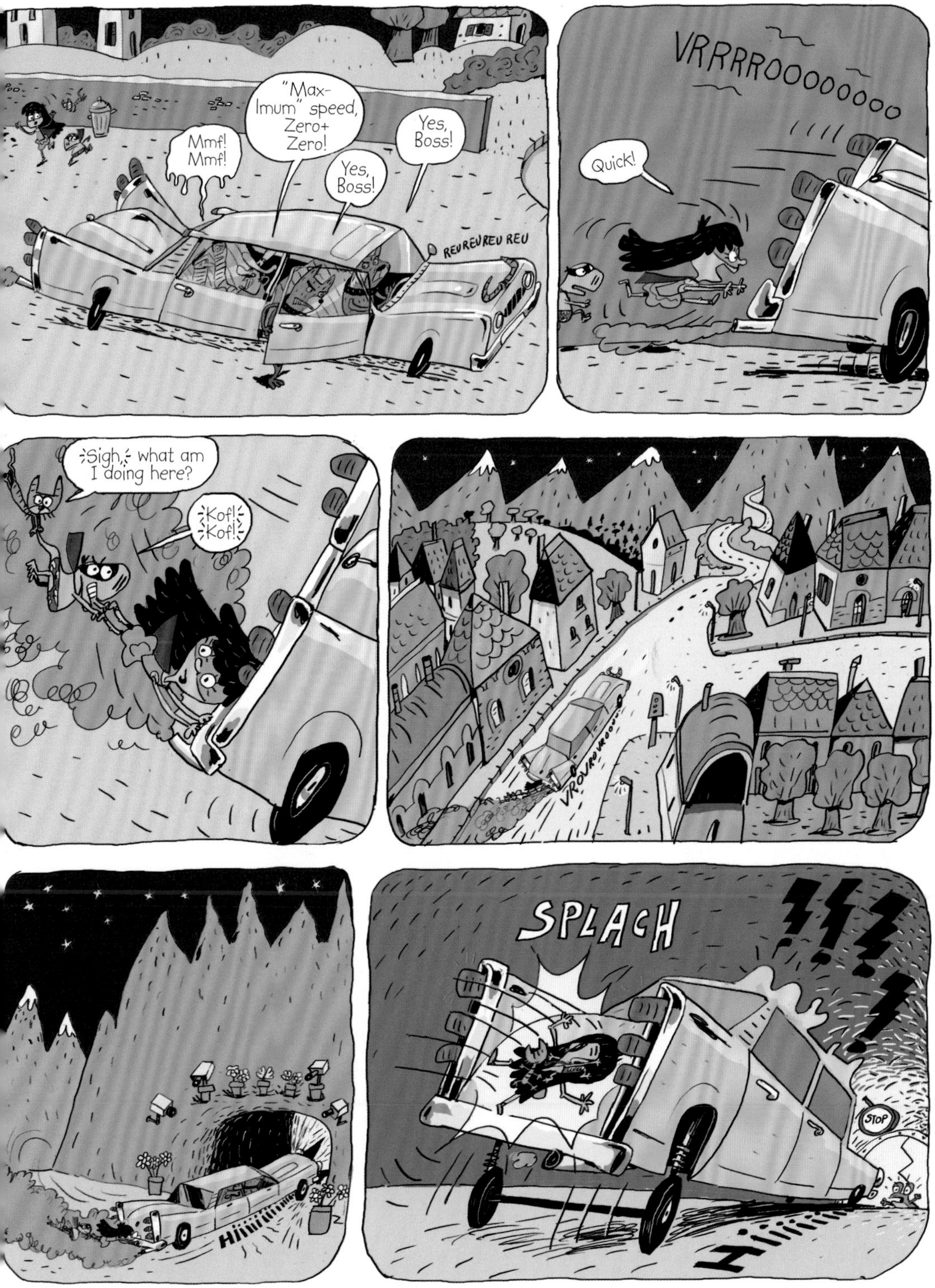
Mmf! Mmf!
"Max-Imum" speed, Zero+Zero!
Yes, Boss!
Yes, Boss!
REUREUREU REU
VRRRROOOOOOOOO
Quick!
Sigh, what am I doing here?
Kof! Kof!
SPLACH
STOP

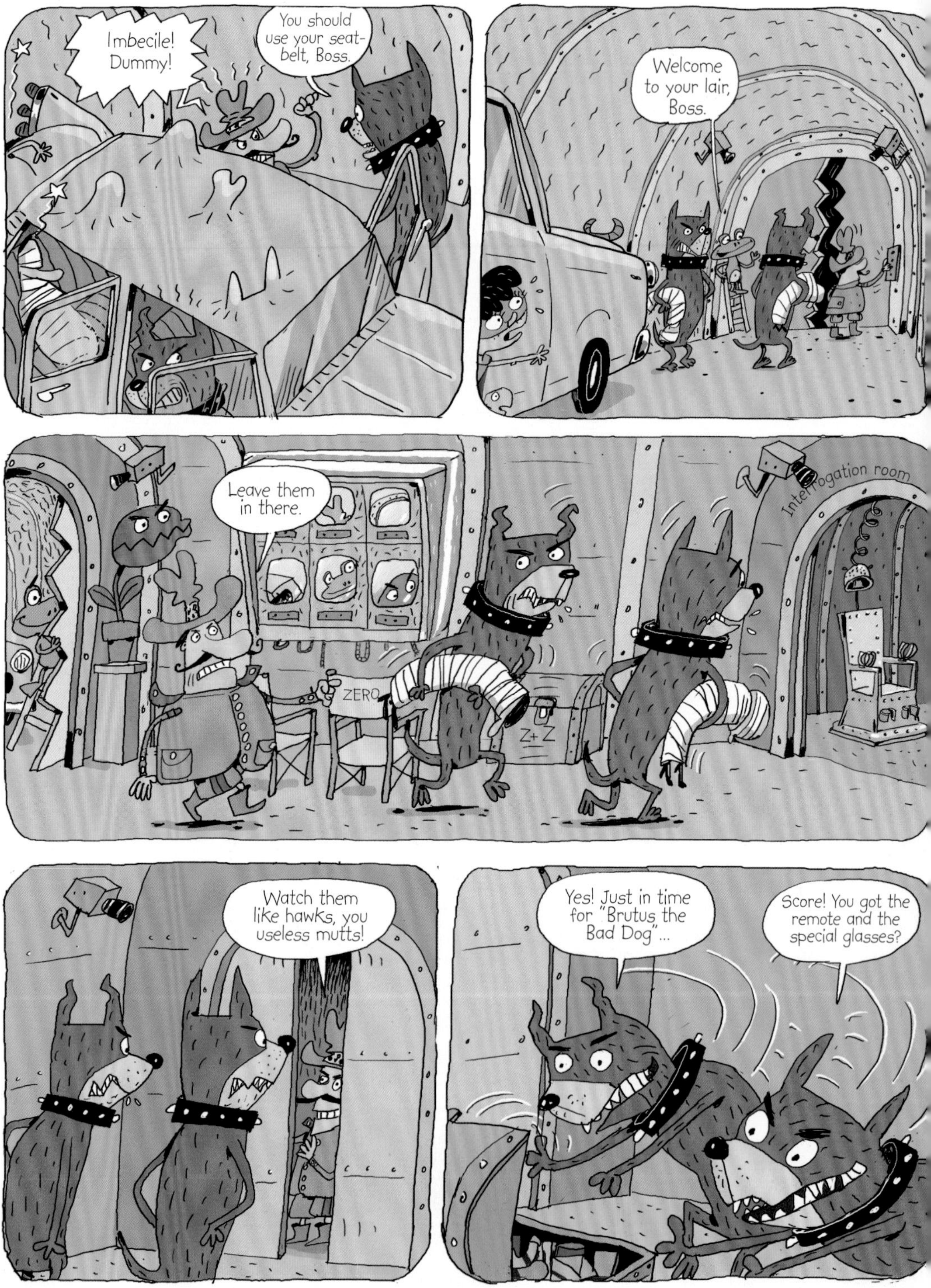
Imbecile! Dummy!
You should use your seat-belt, Boss.
Welcome to your lair, Boss.
Leave them in there.
ZERO
Z+Z
Interrogation room
Watch them like hawks, you useless mutts!
Yes! Just in time for "Brutus the Bad Dog"...
Score! You got the remote and the special glasses?

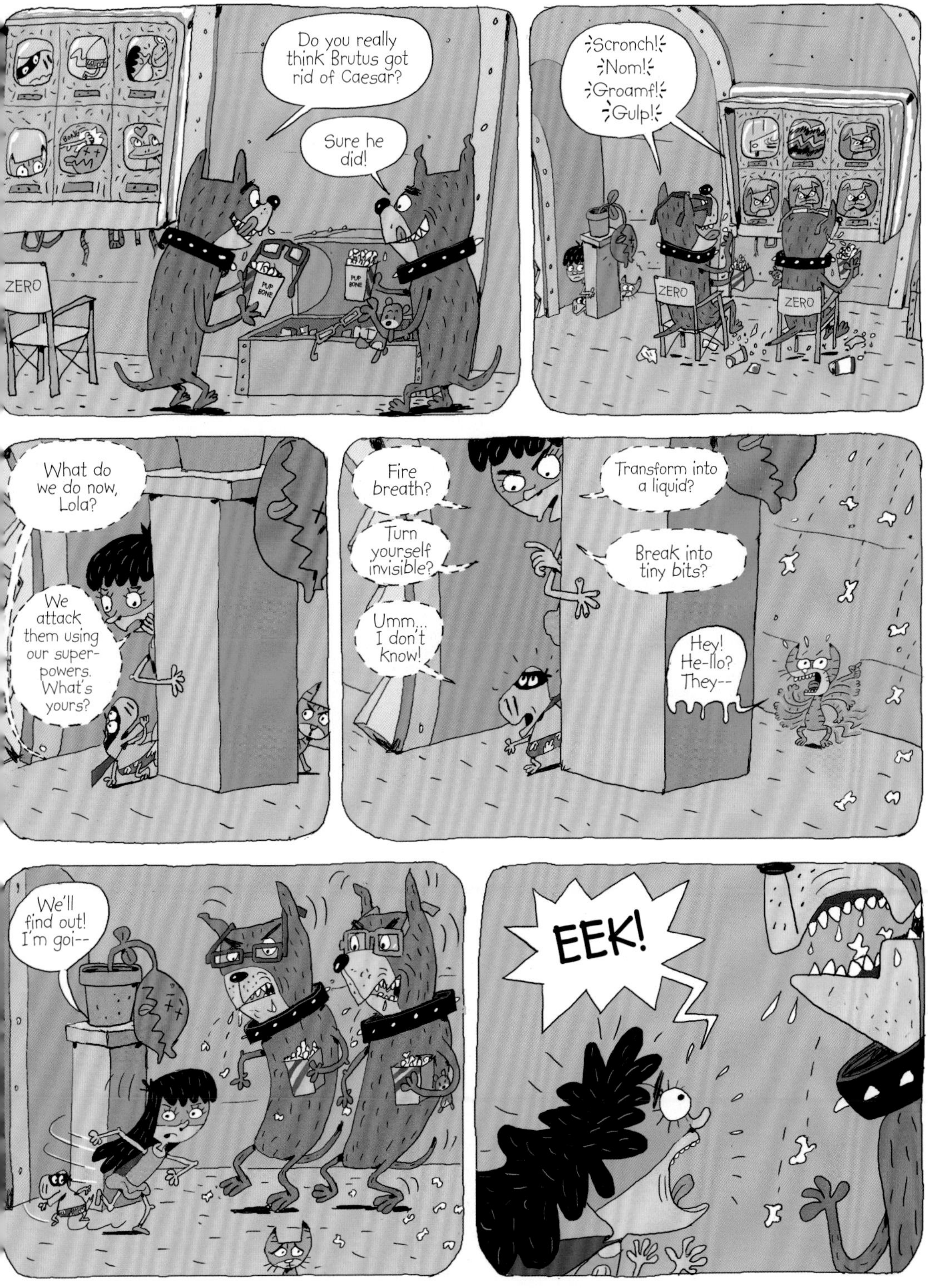
Do you really think Brutus got rid of Caesar?
Sure he did!
PUP BONE
PUP BONE
ZERO
Scronch!
Nom!
Groamf!
Gulp!
ZERO
ZERO
What do we do now, Lola?
We attack them using our superpowers. What's yours?
Fire breath?
Turn yourself invisible?
Umm... I don't know!
Transform into a liquid?
Break into tiny bits?
Hey! He-llo? They--
We'll find out! I'm goi--
EEK!

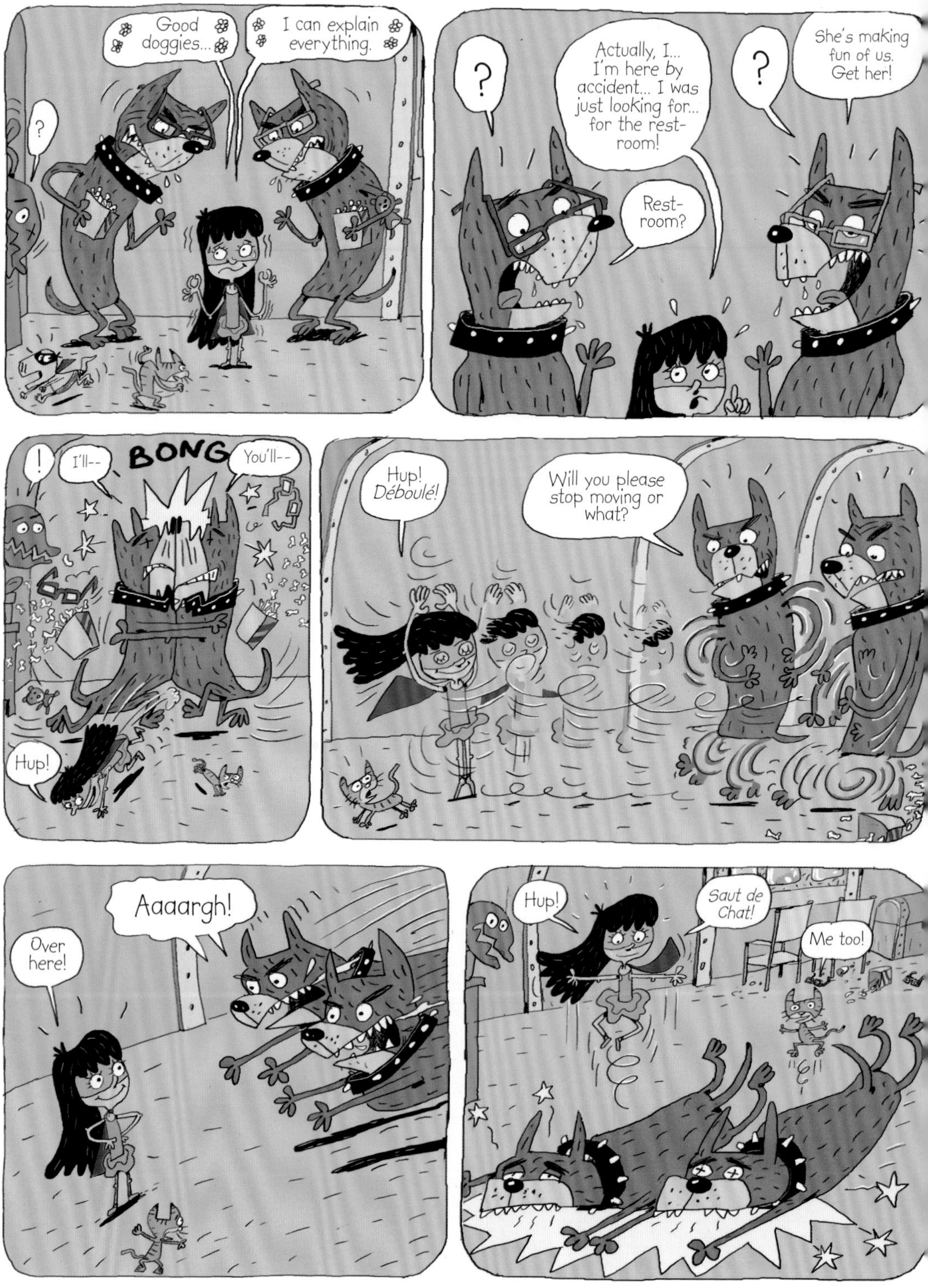
Good doggies...
I can explain everything.
?
?
Actually, I... I'm here by accident... I was just looking for... for the rest-room!
Rest-room?
?
She's making fun of us. Get her!
!
I'll--
BONG
You'll--
Hup!
Hup! Déboulé!
Will you please stop moving or what?
Aaaargh!
Over here!
Hup!
Saut de Chat!
Me too!

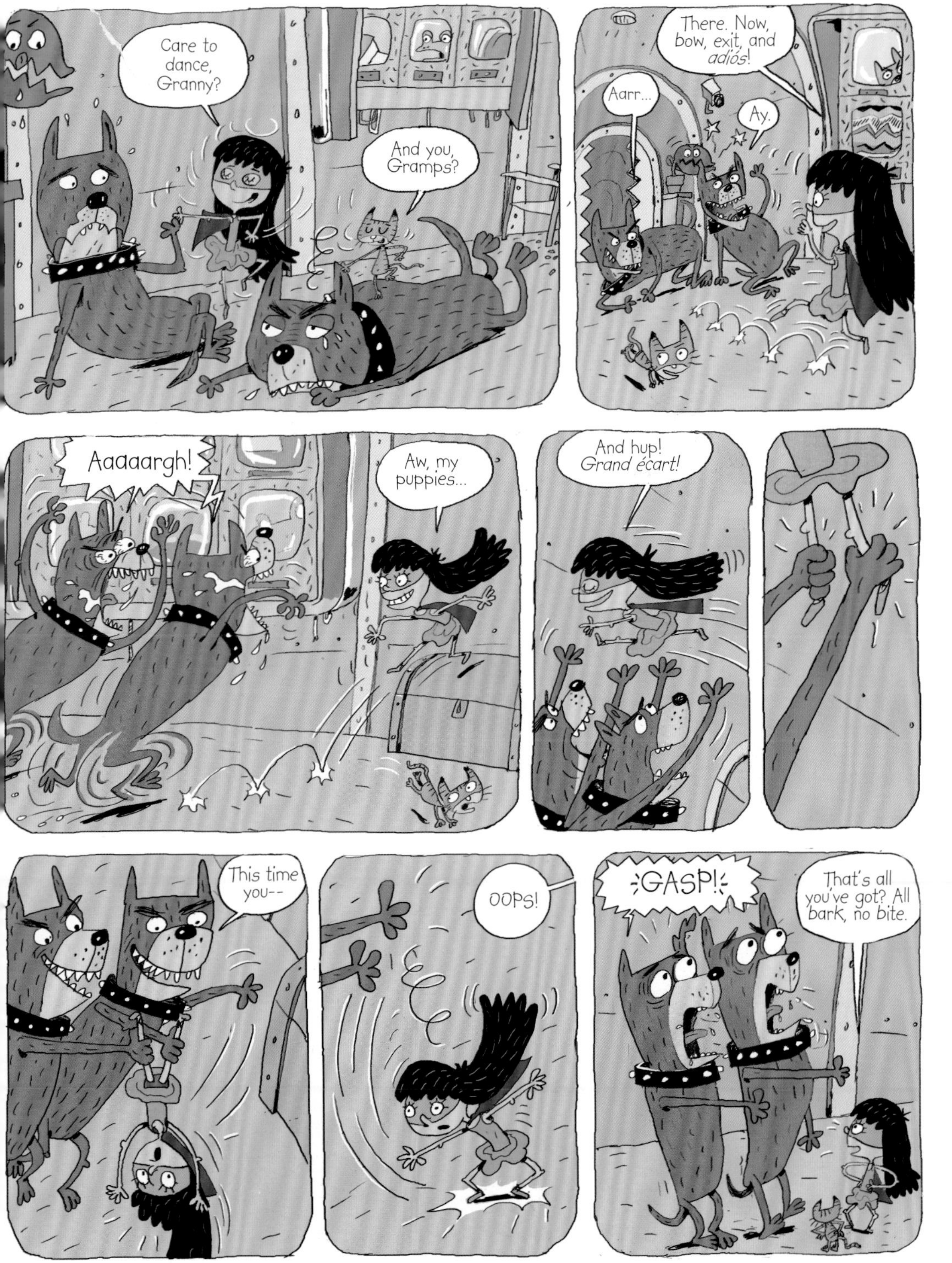
Care to dance, Granny?
And you, Gramps?
There. Now, bow, exit, and *adiós*!
Aarr...
Ay.
Aaaaargh!
Aw, my puppies...
And hup! *Grand écart*!
This time you--
OOPS!
GASP!
That's all you've got? All bark, no bite.

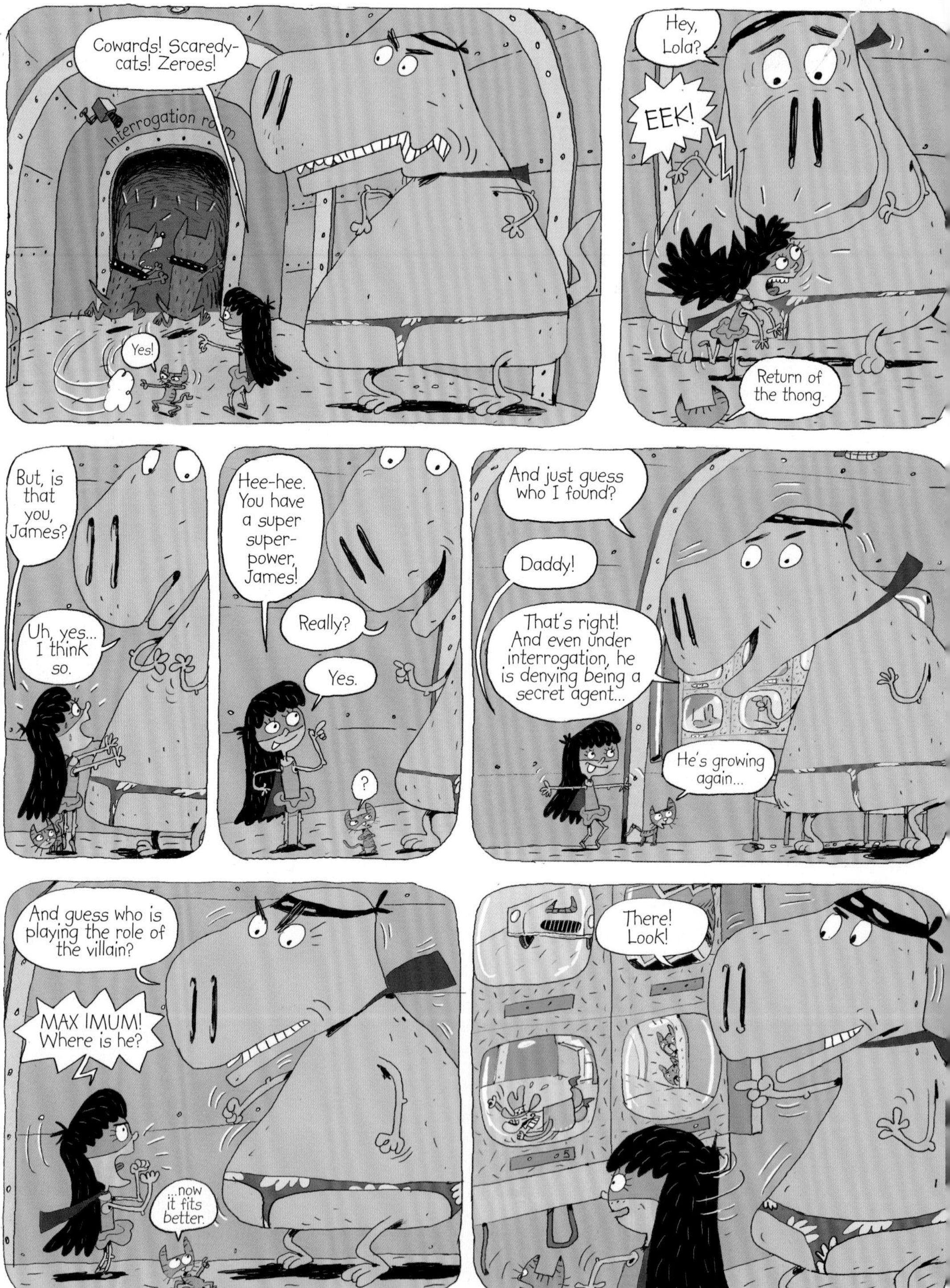
Cowards! Scaredy-cats! Zeroes!
Interrogation room
Yes!
Hey, Lola?
EEK!
Return of the thong.
But, is that you, James?
Uh, yes... I think so.
Hee-hee. You have a super super-power, James!
Really?
Yes.
?
And just guess who I found?
Daddy!
That's right! And even under interrogation, he is denying being a secret agent...
He's growing again...
And guess who is playing the role of the villain?
MAX IMUM! Where is he?
...now it fits better.
There! Look!

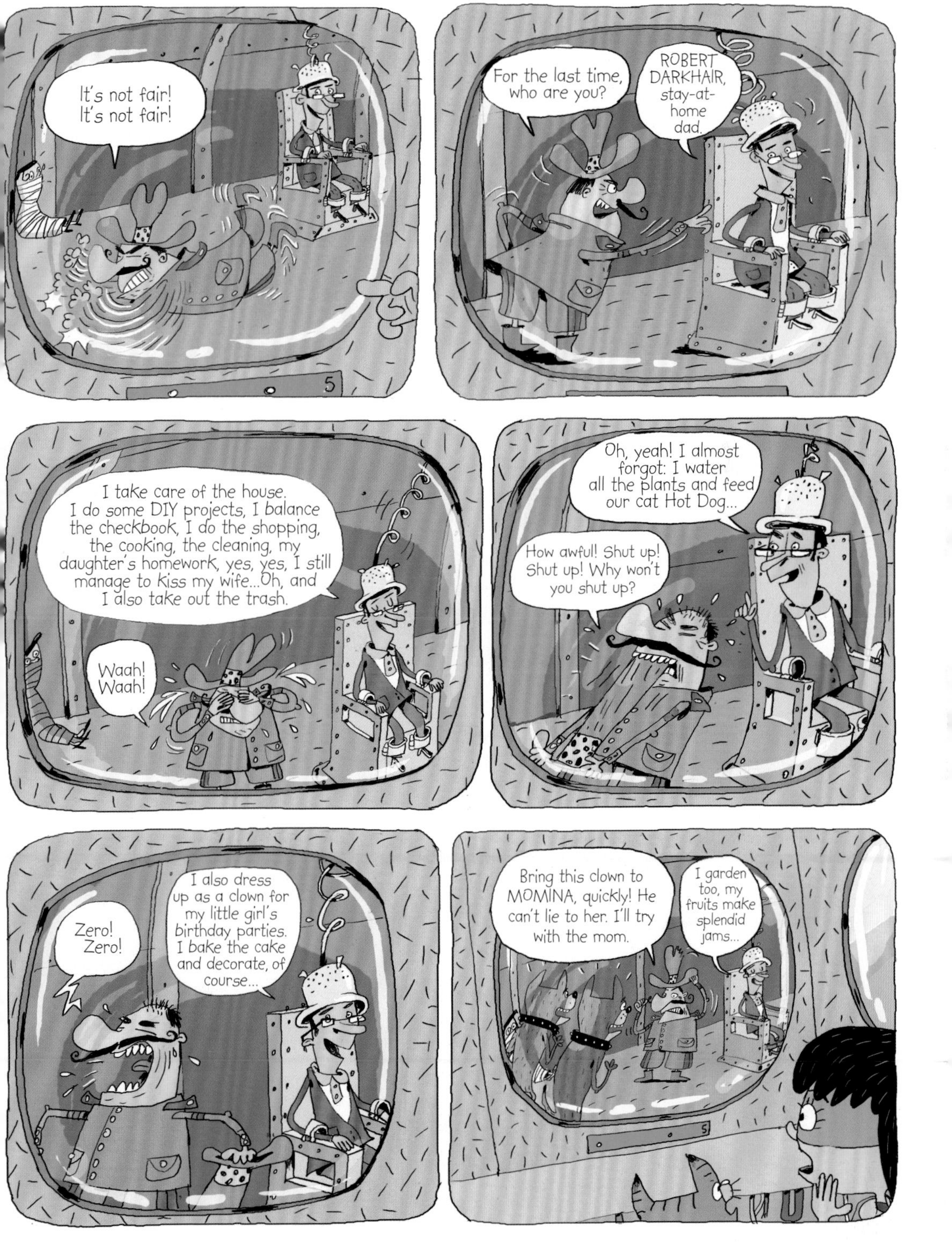
It's not fair! It's not fair!
For the last time, who are you?
ROBERT DARKHAIR, stay-at-home dad.
I take care of the house. I do some DIY projects, I balance the checkbook, I do the shopping, the cooking, the cleaning, my daughter's homework, yes, yes, I still manage to kiss my wife...Oh, and I also take out the trash.
Waah! Waah!
Oh, yeah! I almost forgot: I water all the plants and feed our cat Hot Dog...
How awful! Shut up! Shut up! Why won't you shut up?
Zero! Zero!
I also dress up as a clown for my little girl's birthday parties. I bake the cake and decorate, of course...
Bring this clown to MOMINA, quickly! He can't lie to her. I'll try with the mom.
I garden too, my fruits make splendid jams...

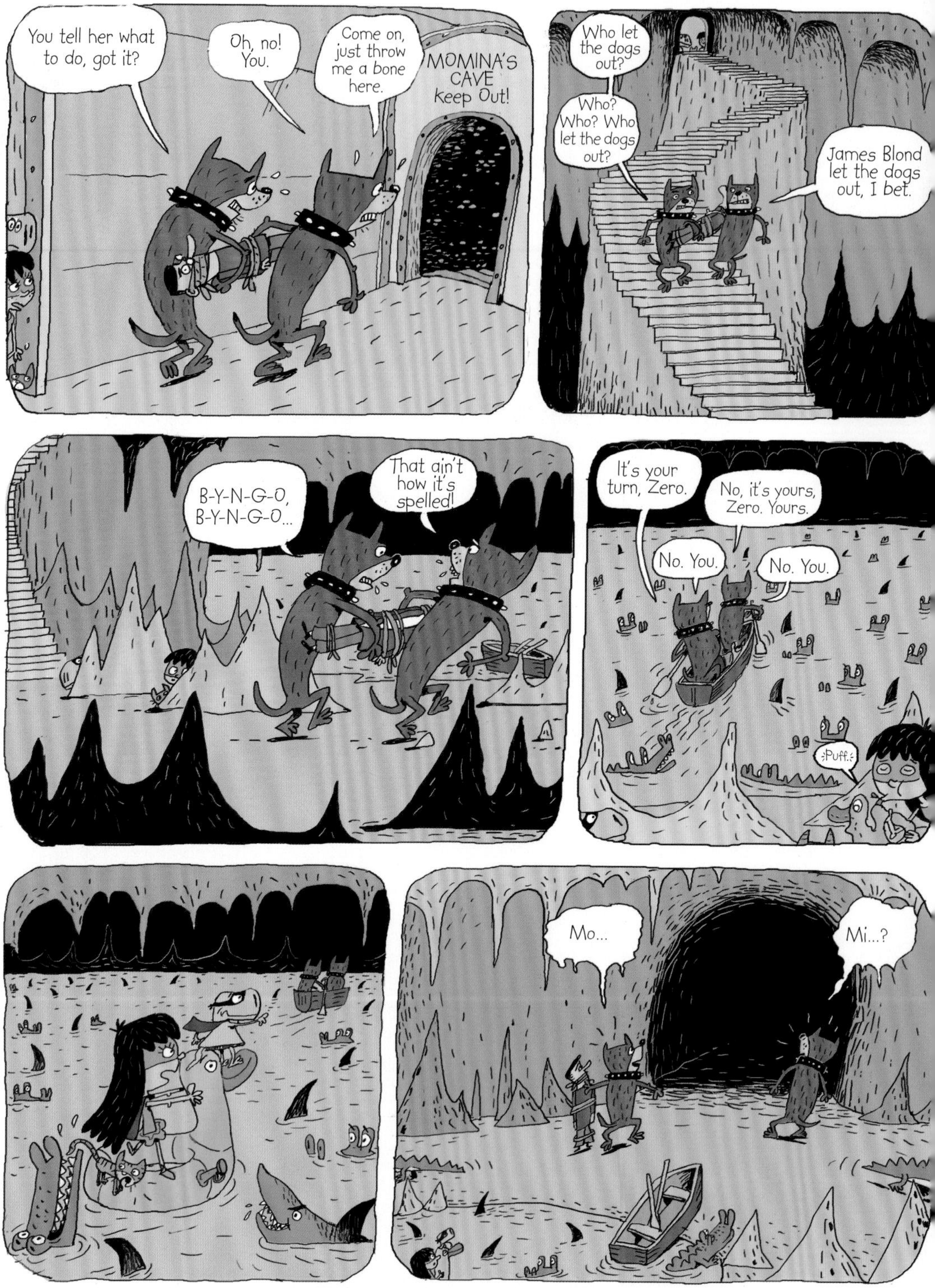
You tell her what to do, got it?
Oh, no! You.
Come on, just throw me a bone here.
MOMINA'S CAVE Keep Out!
Who let the dogs out?
Who? Who? Who let the dogs out?
James Blond let the dogs out, I bet.
B-Y-N-G-O, B-Y-N-G-O...
That ain't how it's spelled!
It's your turn, Zero.
No, it's yours, Zero. Yours.
No. You.
No. You.
Puff
Mo...
Mi...?

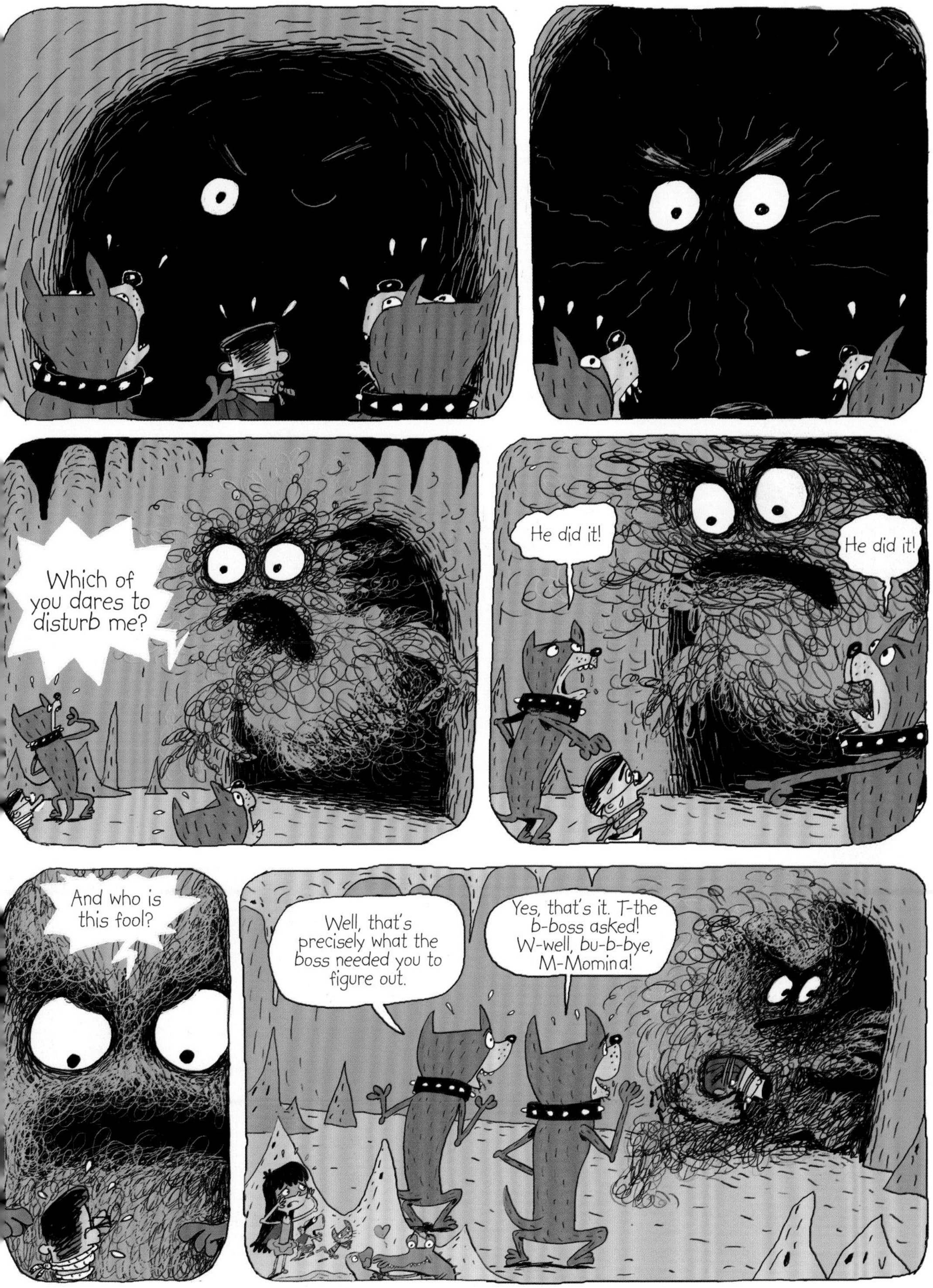
Which of you dares to disturb me?
He did it!
He did it!
And who is this fool?
Well, that's precisely what the boss needed you to figure out.
Yes, that's it. T-the b-boss asked! W-well, bu-b-bye, M-Momina!

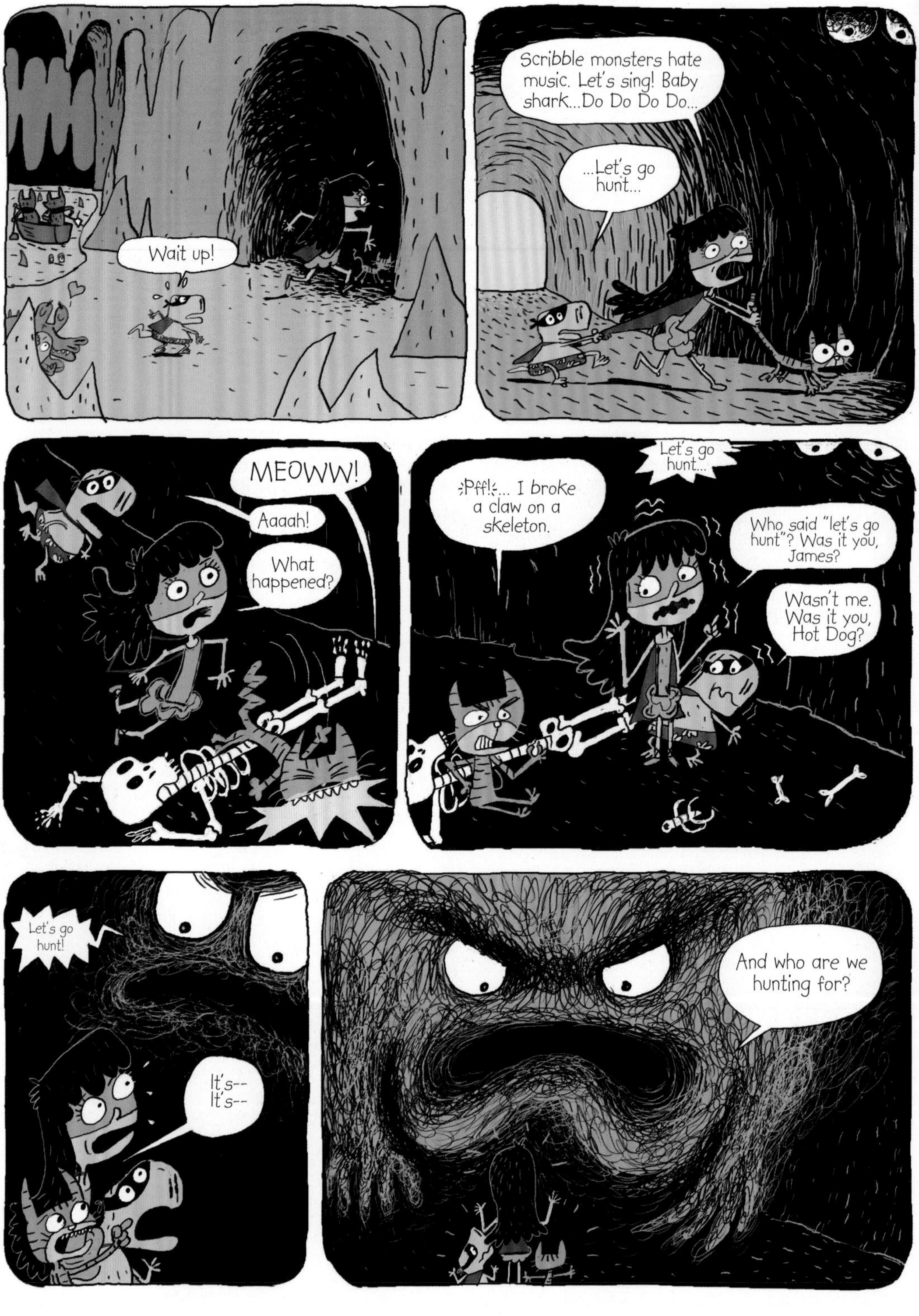
Wait up!
Scribble monsters hate music. Let's sing! Baby shark...Do Do Do Do...
...Let's go hunt...
MEOWW!
Aaaah!
What happened?
Let's go hunt...
Pff!... I broke a claw on a skeleton.
Who said "let's go hunt"? Was it you, James?
Wasn't me. Was it you, Hot Dog?
Let's go hunt!
It's--
It's--
And who are we hunting for?

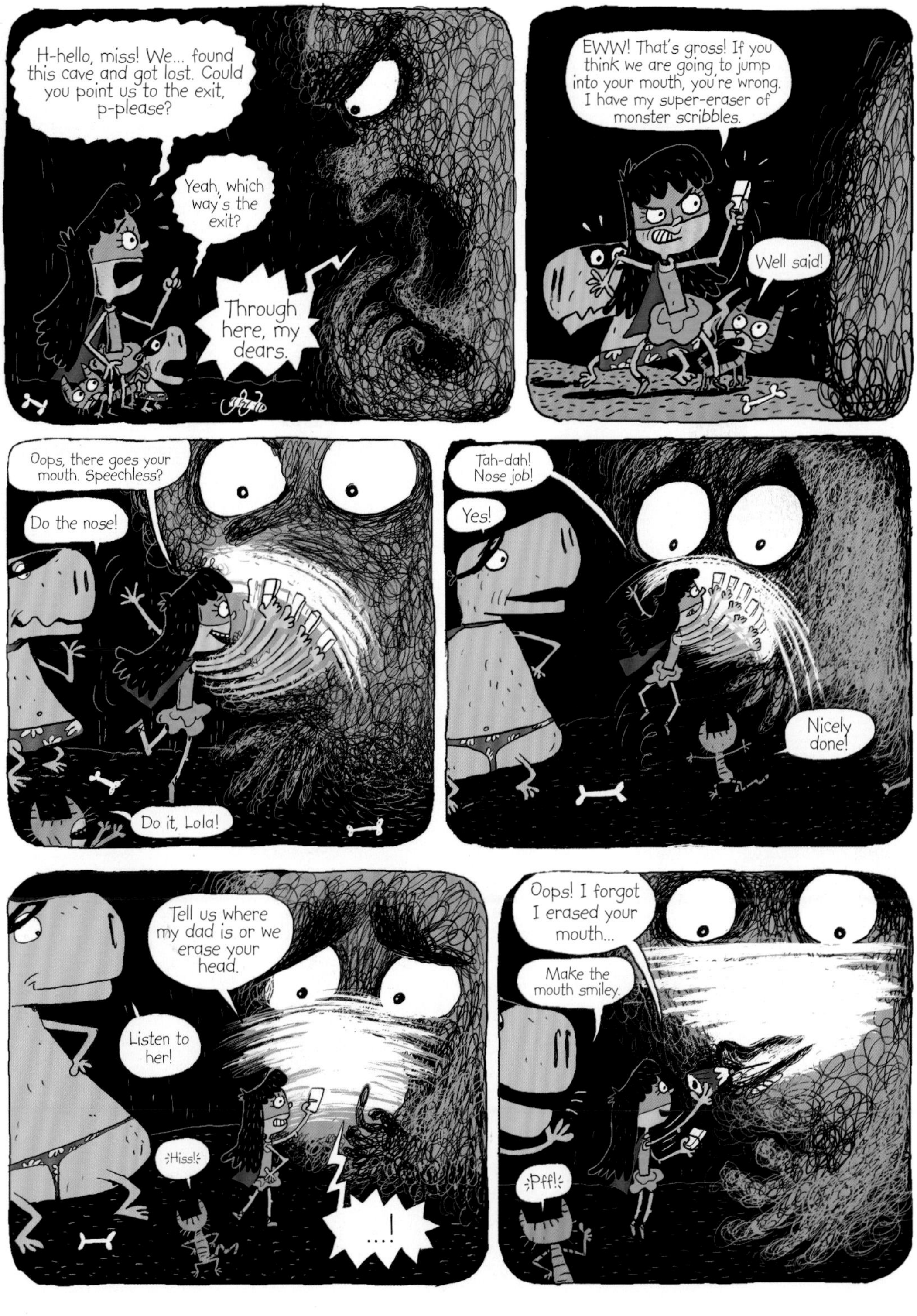
H-hello, miss! We... found this cave and got lost. Could you point us to the exit, p-please?
Yeah, which way's the exit?
Through here, my dears.
EWW! That's gross! If you think we are going to jump into your mouth, you're wrong. I have my super-eraser of monster scribbles.
Well said!
Oops, there goes your mouth. Speechless?
Do the nose!
Do it, Lola!
Tah-dah! Nose job!
Yes!
Nicely done!
Tell us where my dad is or we erase your head.
Listen to her!
Hiss!
...!
Oops! I forgot I erased your mouth...
Make the mouth smiley.
Pff!

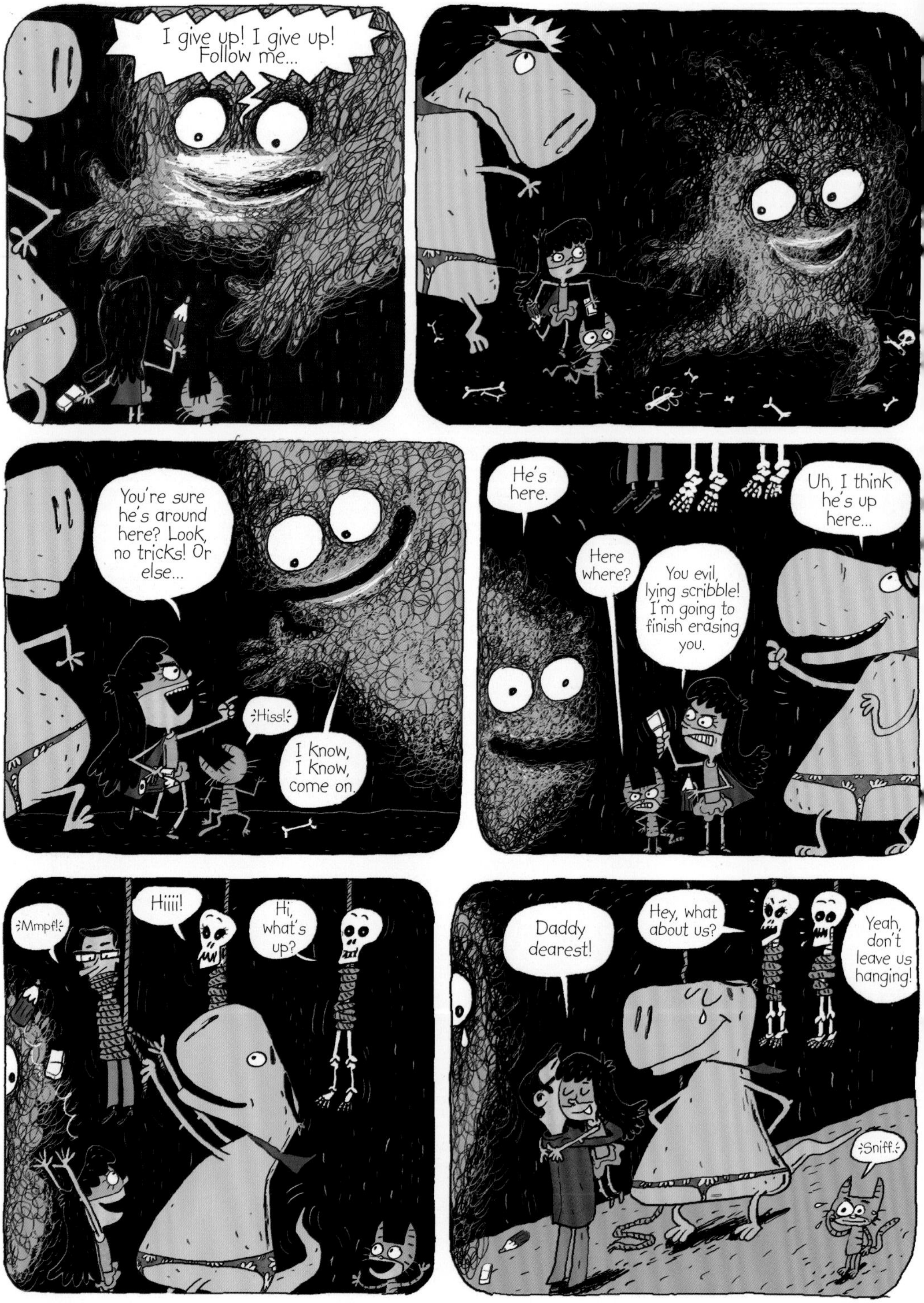
I give up! I give up! Follow me...
You're sure he's around here? Look, no tricks! Or else...
Hiss!
I know, I know, come on.
He's here.
Here where?
You evil, lying scribble! I'm going to finish erasing you.
Uh, I think he's up here...
Mmpf!
Hiiii!
Hi, what's up?
Daddy dearest!
Hey, what about us?
Yeah, don't leave us hanging!
Sniff.

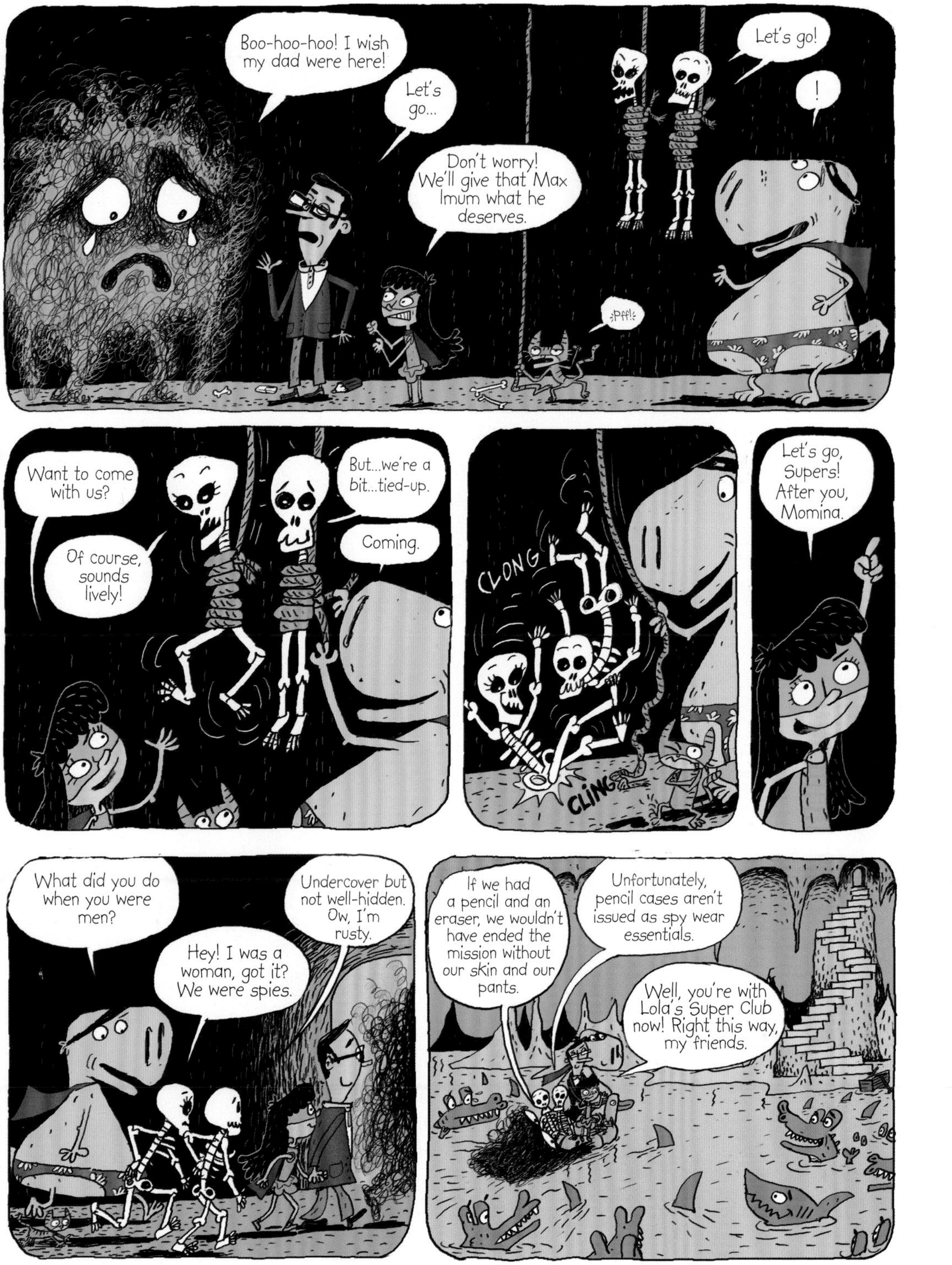
Boo-hoo-hoo! I wish my dad were here!
Let's go...
Don't worry! We'll give that Max Imum what he deserves.
Pff!
Let's go!
!
Want to come with us?
Of course, sounds lively!
But...we're a bit...tied-up.
Coming.
CLONG
CLING
Let's go, Supers! After you, Momina.
What did you do when you were men?
Hey! I was a woman, got it? We were spies.
Undercover but not well-hidden. Ow, I'm rusty.
If we had a pencil and an eraser, we wouldn't have ended the mission without our skin and our pants.
Unfortunately, pencil cases aren't issued as spy wear essentials.
Well, you're with Lola's Super Club now! Right this way, my friends.

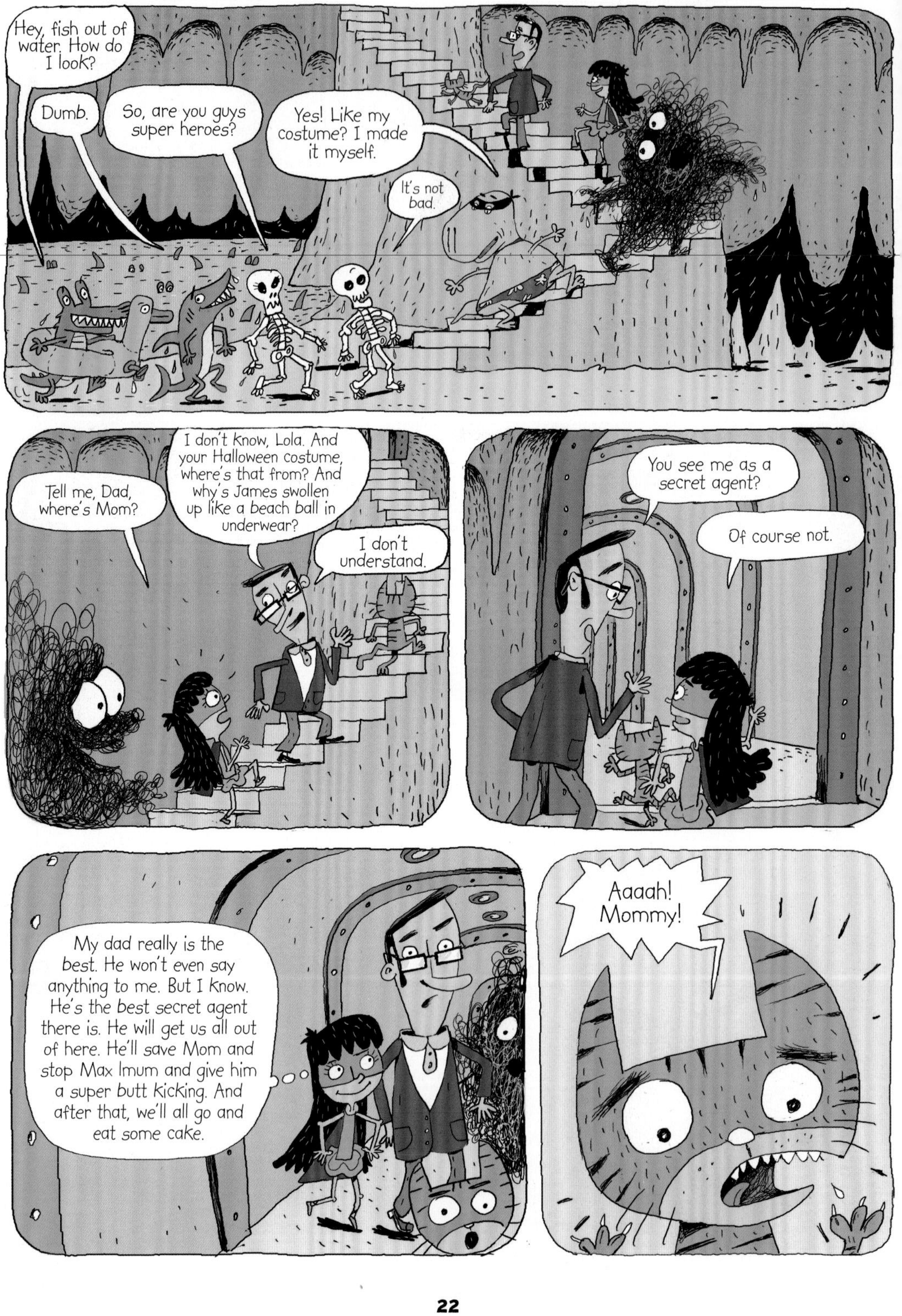
Hey, fish out of water. How do I look?
Dumb.
So, are you guys super heroes?
Yes! Like my costume? I made it myself.
It's not bad.
Tell me, Dad, where's Mom?
I don't know, Lola. And your Halloween costume, where's that from? And why's James swollen up like a beach ball in underwear?
I don't understand.
You see me as a secret agent?
Of course not.
My dad really is the best. He won't even say anything to me. But I know. He's the best secret agent there is. He will get us all out of here. He'll save Mom and stop Max Imum and give him a super butt kicking. And after that, we'll all go and eat some cake.
Aaaah! Mommy!

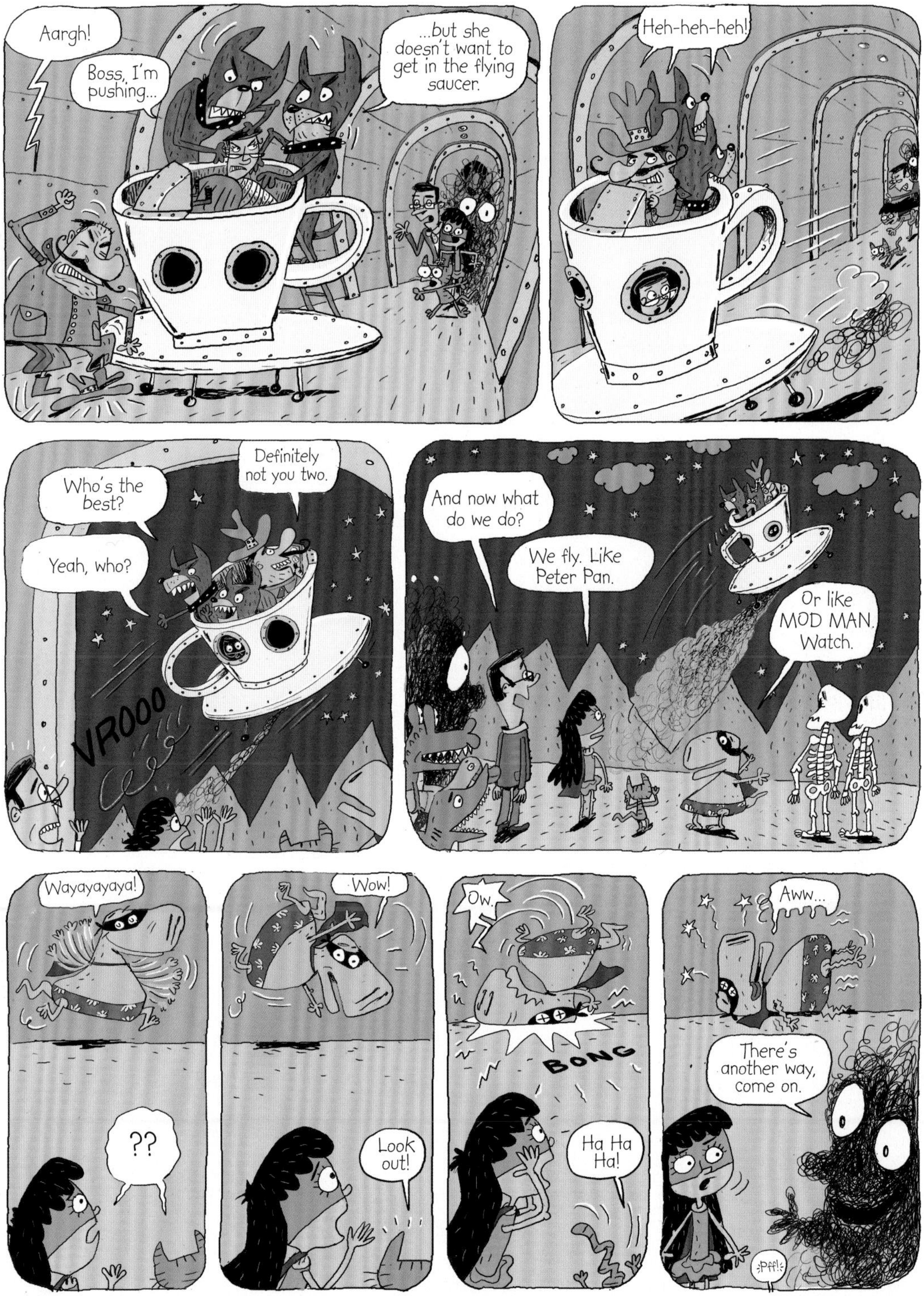
Aargh!
Boss, I'm pushing...
...but she doesn't want to get in the flying saucer.
Heh-heh-heh!
Who's the best?
Definitely not you two.
Yeah, who?
VROOO
And now what do we do?
We fly. Like Peter Pan.
Or like MOD MAN. Watch.
Wayayayaya!
??
Wow!
Look out!
Ow.
BONG
Ha Ha Ha!
Aww...
There's another way, come on.
Pff!

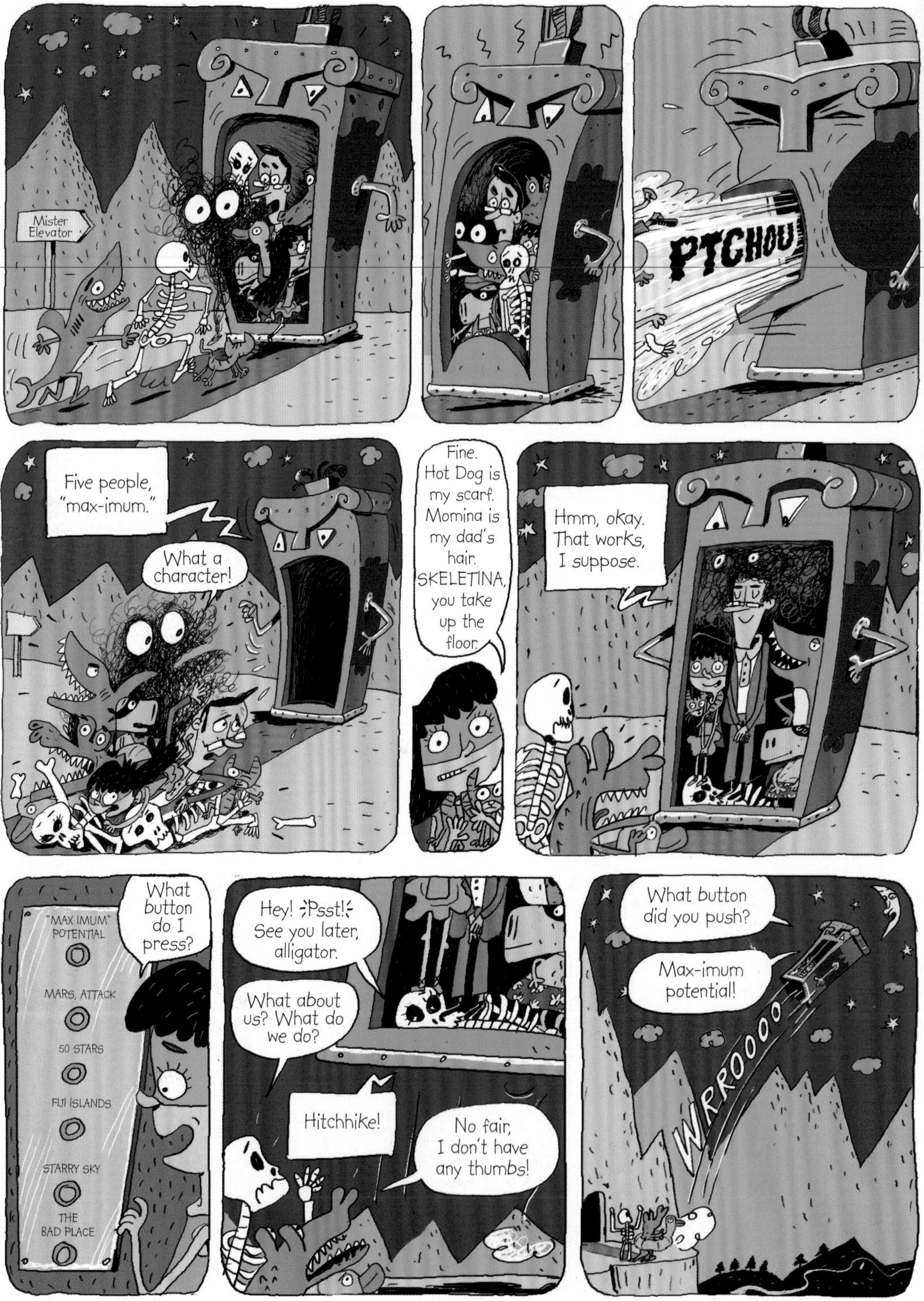
Mister Elevator
PTCHOU
Five people, "max-imum."
What a character!
Fine. Hot Dog is my scarf. Momina is my dad's hair. SKELETINA, you take up the floor.
Hmm, okay. That works, I suppose.
"MAX IMUM" POTENTIAL
MARS, ATTACK
50 STARS
FIJI ISLANDS
STARRY SKY
THE BAD PLACE
What button do I press?
Hey! Psst! See you later, alligator.
What about us? What do we do?
Hitchhike!
No fair, I don't have any thumbs!
What button did you push?
Max-imum potential!
WRROOOO

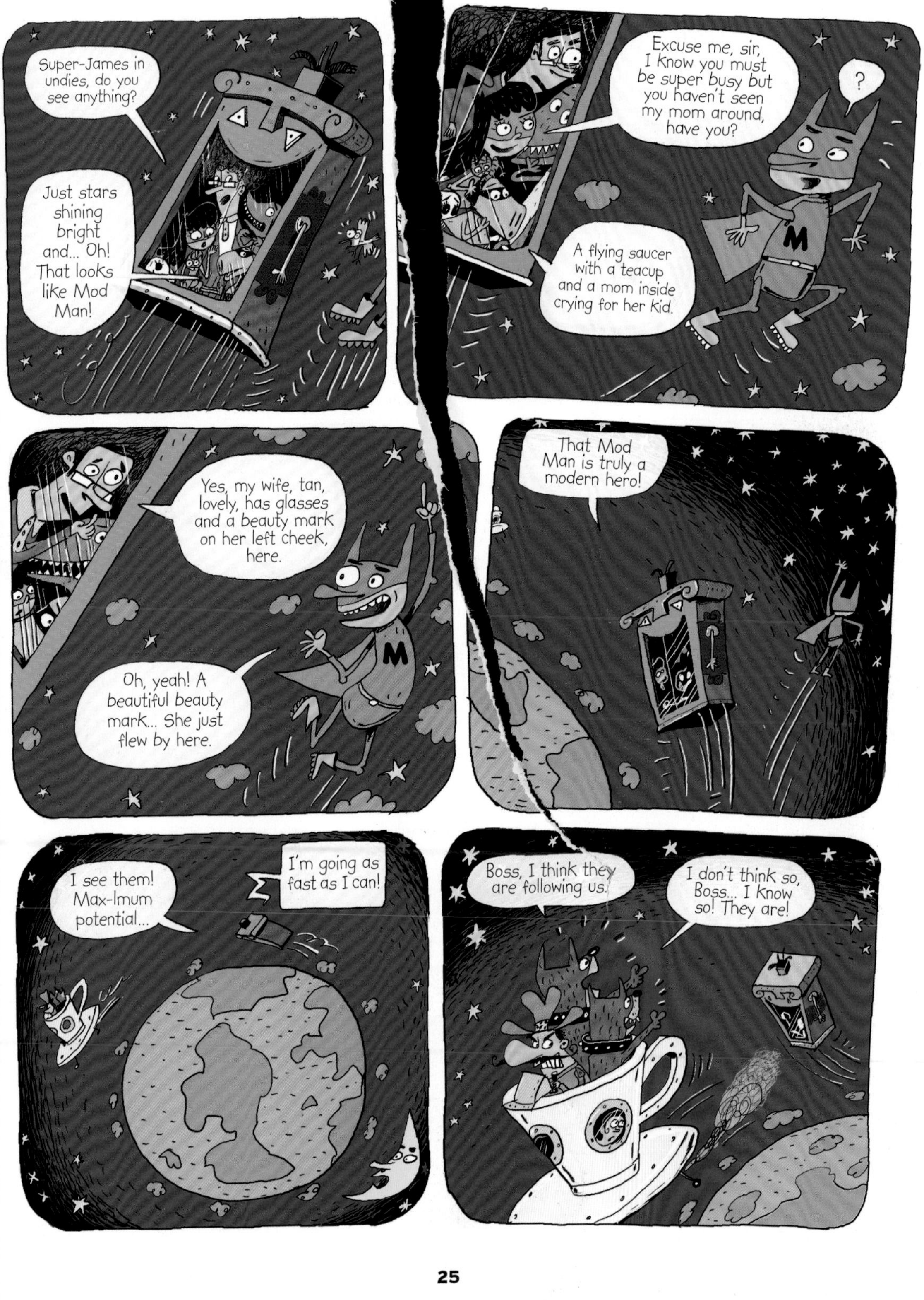

Super-James in undies, do you see anything?
Just stars shining bright and... Oh! That looks like Mod Man!
Excuse me, sir, I know you must be super busy but you haven't seen my mom around, have you?
?
A flying saucer with a teacup and a mom inside crying for her kid.
Yes, my wife, tan, lovely, has glasses and a beauty mark on her left cheek, here.
Oh, yeah! A beautiful beauty mark... She just flew by here.
That Mod Man is truly a modern hero!
I see them! Max-Imum potential...
I'm going as fast as I can!
Boss, I think they are following us.
I don't think so, Boss... I know so! They are!

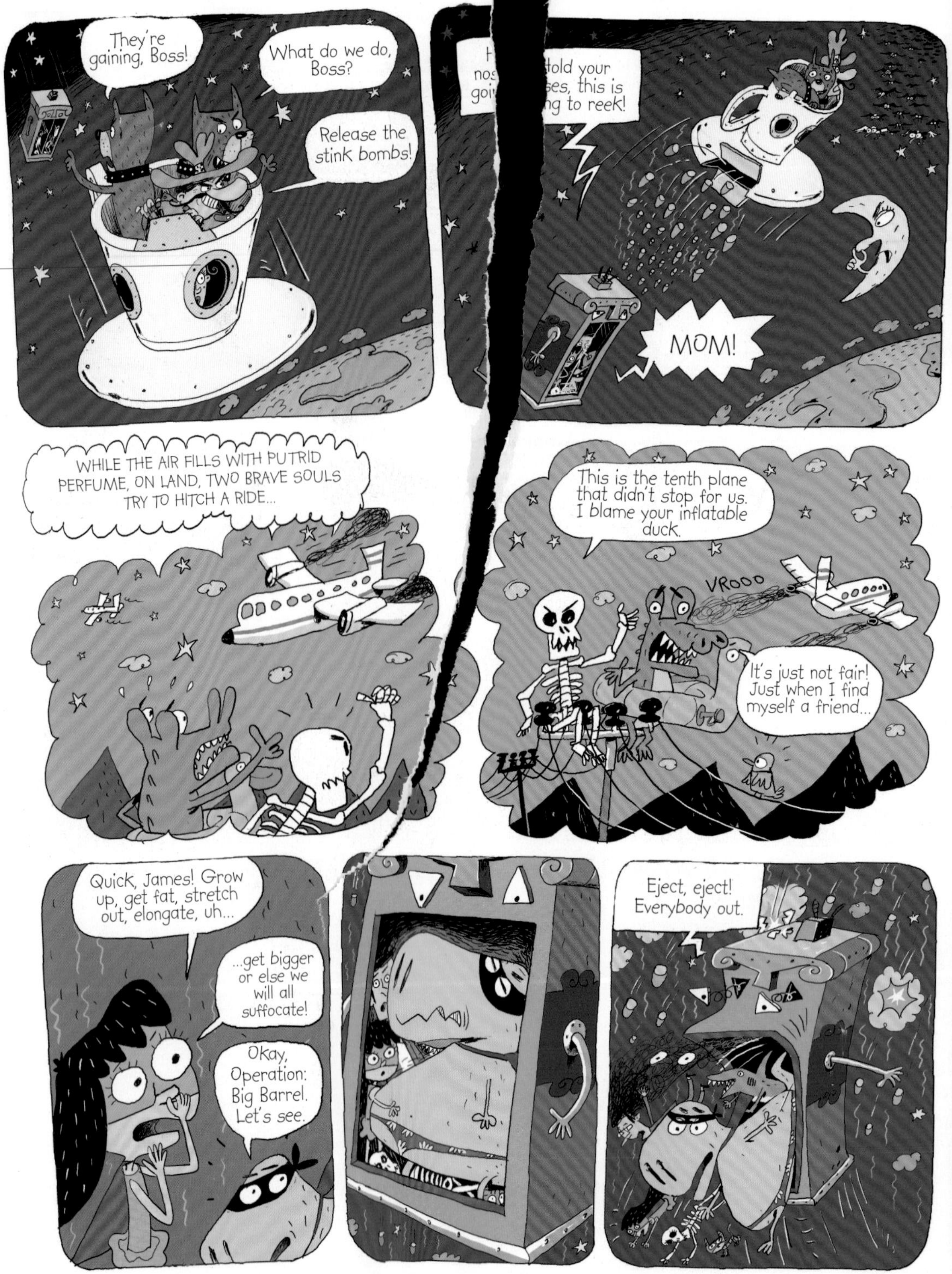

They're gaining, Boss!
What do we do, Boss?
Release the stink bombs!
H told your
nos ses, this is
goi ng to reek!
MOM!
WHILE THE AIR FILLS WITH PUTRID PERFUME, ON LAND, TWO BRAVE SOULS TRY TO HITCH A RIDE...
This is the tenth plane that didn't stop for us. I blame your inflatable duck.
VROOO
It's just not fair! Just when I find myself a friend...
Quick, James! Grow up, get fat, stretch out, elongate, uh...
...get bigger or else we will all suffocate!
Okay, Operation: Big Barrel. Let's see.
Eject, eject! Everybody out.

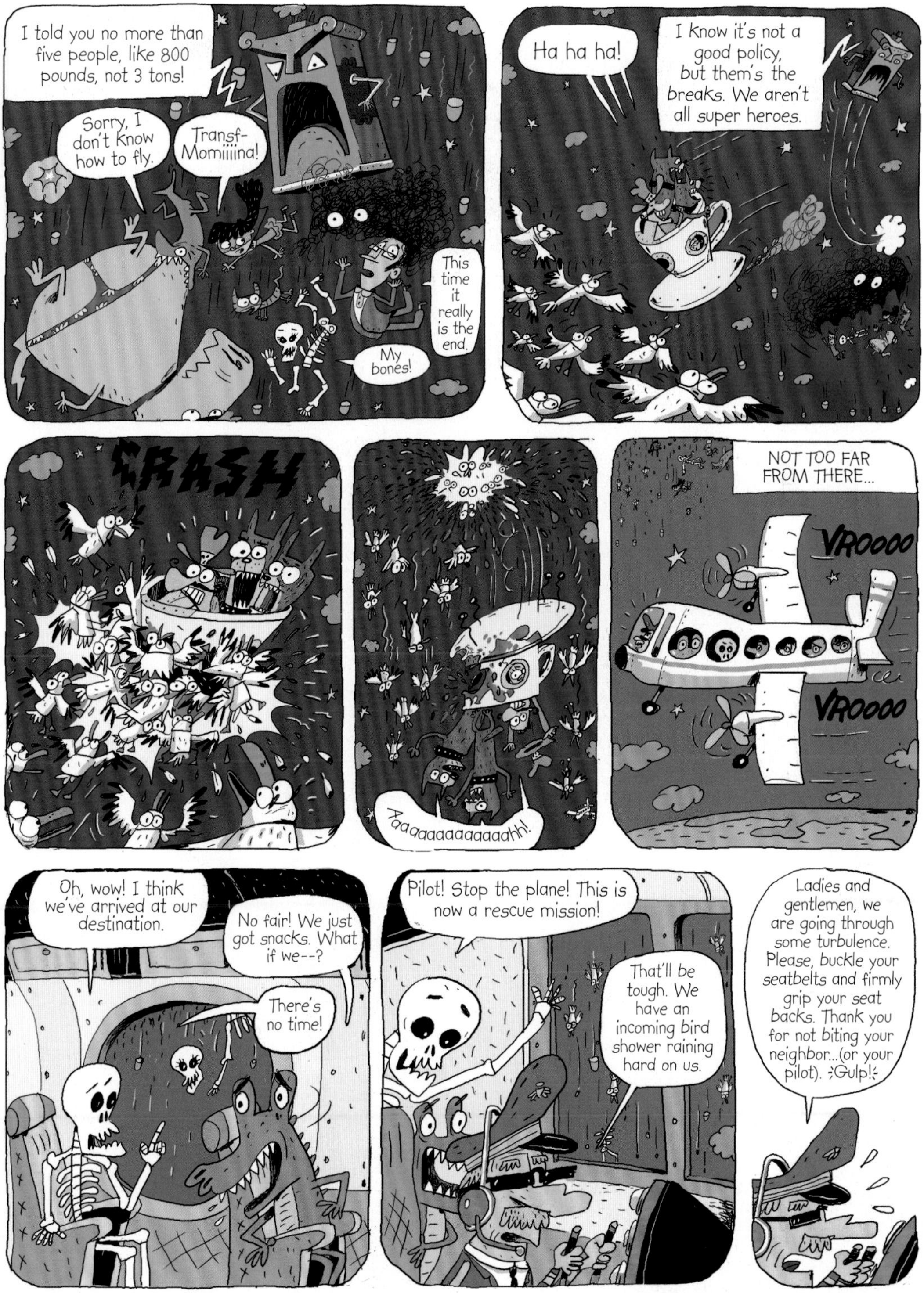
I told you no more than five people, like 800 pounds, not 3 tons!
Sorry, I don't know how to fly.
Transf-Momiiiina!
This time it really is the end.
My bones!
Ha ha ha!
I know it's not a good policy, but them's the breaks. We aren't all super heroes.
CRASH
Aaaaaaaaaaaaaahh!
NOT TOO FAR FROM THERE...
VROOOO
VROOOO
Oh, wow! I think we've arrived at our destination.
No fair! We just got snacks. What if we--?
There's no time!
Pilot! Stop the plane! This is now a rescue mission!
That'll be tough. We have an incoming bird shower raining hard on us.
Ladies and gentlemen, we are going through some turbulence. Please, buckle your seatbelts and firmly grip your seat backs. Thank you for not biting your neighbor...(or your pilot). Gulp!

SHPOUF
PFFFF
SHPLOP
PFUITT
SHPOOF
SHLAAA
PUFF
PUPF
PFOFF
WOOUUF
Yahoo!
Boss! We made it, Boss! Look!
Shut it, cretins!
Untie me, would you, dear?
Snif! How beautiful!
Mom!
My love...
That cloud! Drop us off there.
Or perhaps it's cotton given the size and number of people on it.
It's not fair.
We'll risk crashing down but, hey...
WOOOUUUFF
SSSSHHAIIIIIIII

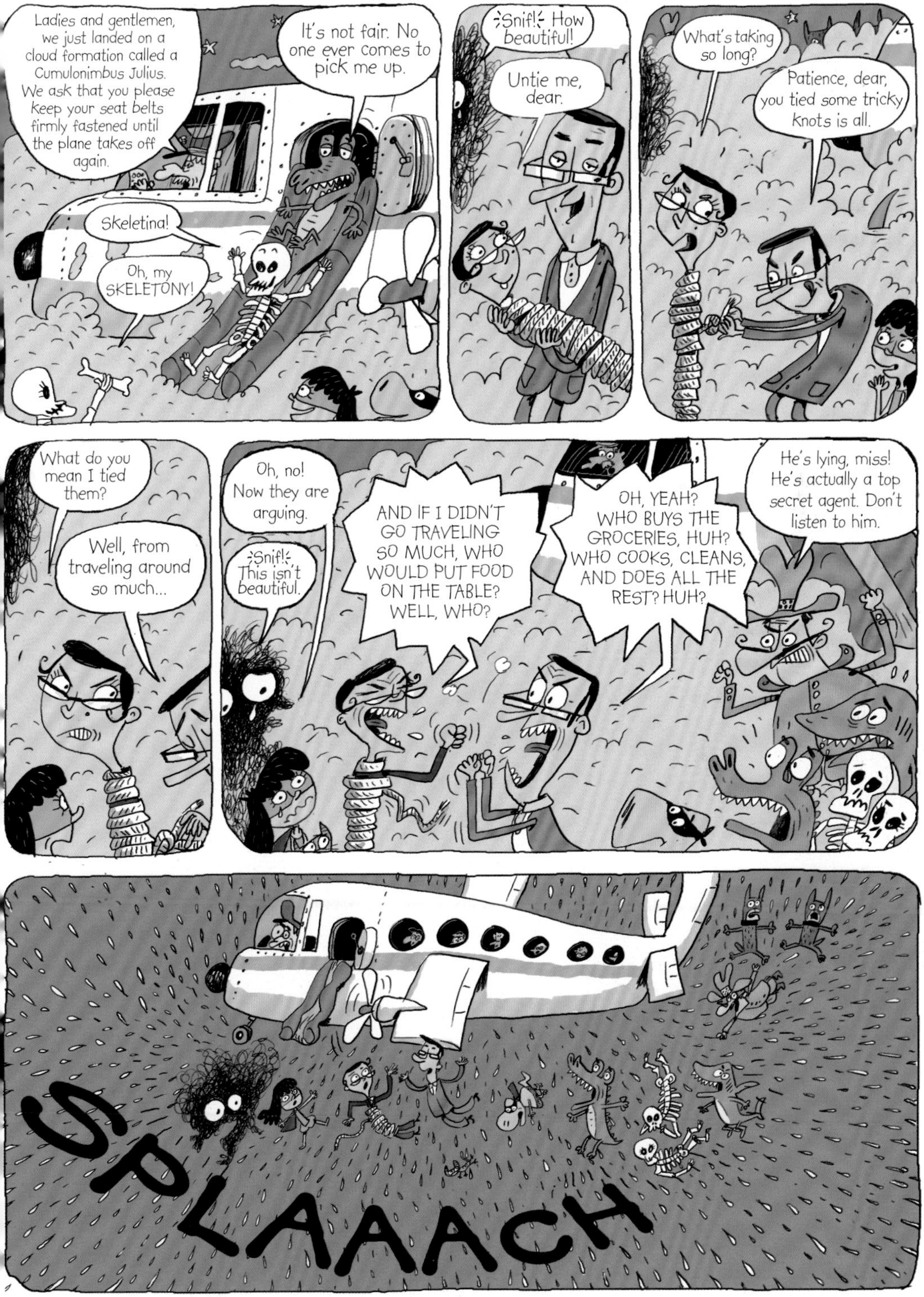
Ladies and gentlemen, we just landed on a cloud formation called a Cumulonimbus Julius. We ask that you please keep your seat belts firmly fastened until the plane takes off again.
It's not fair. No one ever comes to pick me up.
Skeletina!
Oh, my SKELETONY!
Snif! How beautiful!
Untie me, dear.
What's taking so long?
Patience, dear, you tied some tricky knots is all.
What do you mean I tied them?
Well, from traveling around so much...
Oh, no! Now they are arguing.
Snif! This isn't beautiful.
AND IF I DIDN'T GO TRAVELING SO MUCH, WHO WOULD PUT FOOD ON THE TABLE? WELL, WHO?
OH, YEAH? WHO BUYS THE GROCERIES, HUH? WHO COOKS, CLEANS, AND DOES ALL THE REST? HUH?
He's lying, miss! He's actually a top secret agent. Don't listen to him.
SPLAAACH

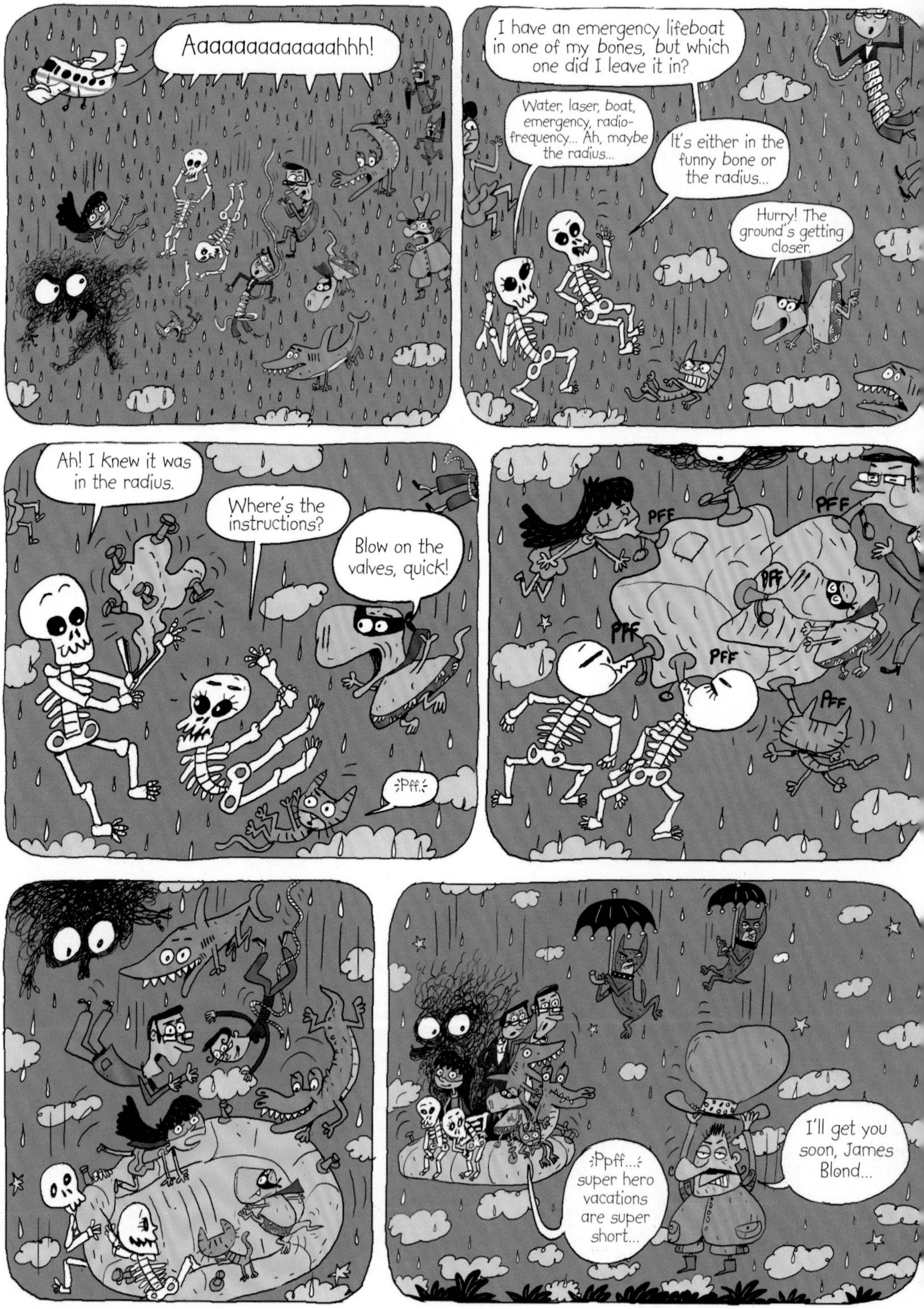
Aaaaaaaaaaaaahhh!
I have an emergency lifeboat in one of my bones, but which one did I leave it in?
Water, laser, boat, emergency, radio-frequency... Ah, maybe the radius...
It's either in the funny bone or the radius...
Hurry! The ground's getting closer.
Ah! I knew it was in the radius.
Where's the instructions?
Blow on the valves, quick!
Pff.
PFF
PFF
PFF
PFF
PFF
PFF
Ppff... super hero vacations are super short...
I'll get you soon, James Blond...

Oh, dear...

I love you too.

;Oof!;

Oof!

Aaaaaaaaaaahhh!

WZiiiiiiiiiiiiiiiiii

Psiiii

Psiii

Psiii

Biiii

Here we go again.

No fair. My monkey is in love with me.

Haha!

Hi, friends!

JUNGLOR! You see we're just dealing with some monkey business, nothing super urgent.

You've arrived at the island of Notondamap, inhabited by snakes who wear hypnotic glasses, flies that bite, and mosquitos who work at the Nite Nite Slumber Company. There's also a tiger who eats everything named CHOMPYALEG and myself. And my wife, JUANA, and our monkey children.

What about us? What about us?

You two as well. This way, my friends. Let's hit the beach.

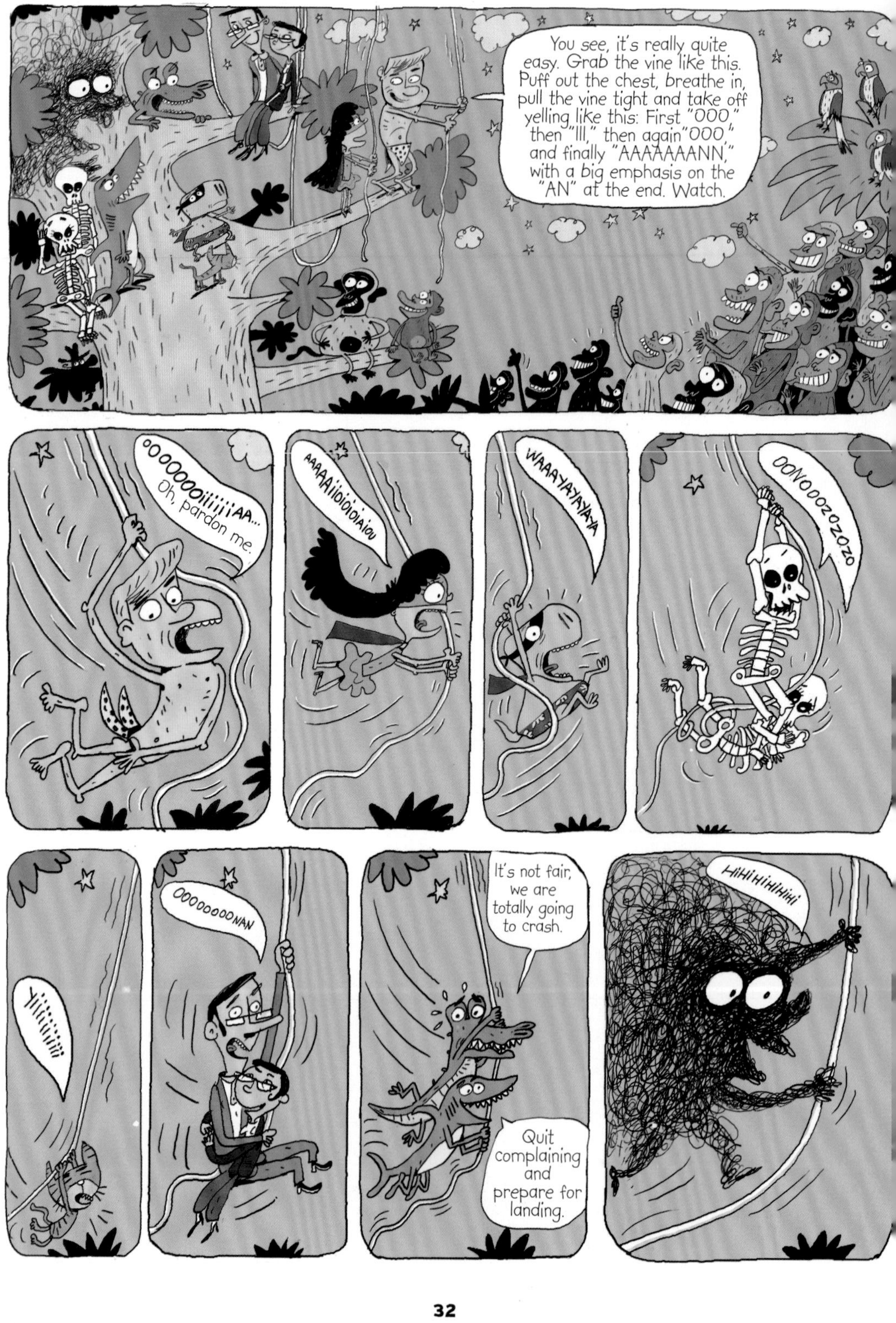
You see, it's really quite easy. Grab the vine like this. Puff out the chest, breathe in, pull the vine tight and take off yelling like this: First "OOO," then "III," then again "OOO," and finally "AAAAAAANN," with a big emphasis on the "AN" at the end. Watch.
oOOOOOOiiiiiiAA... Oh, pardon me.
AAAAAAiioioioiAiou
WAAAYAYAYAYAYA
OONOOOZOZOZO
Yiiiiiiiiii
OOOOOOOONAN
It's not fair, we are totally going to crash.
Quit complaining and prepare for landing.
HIHIHIHIHIHI

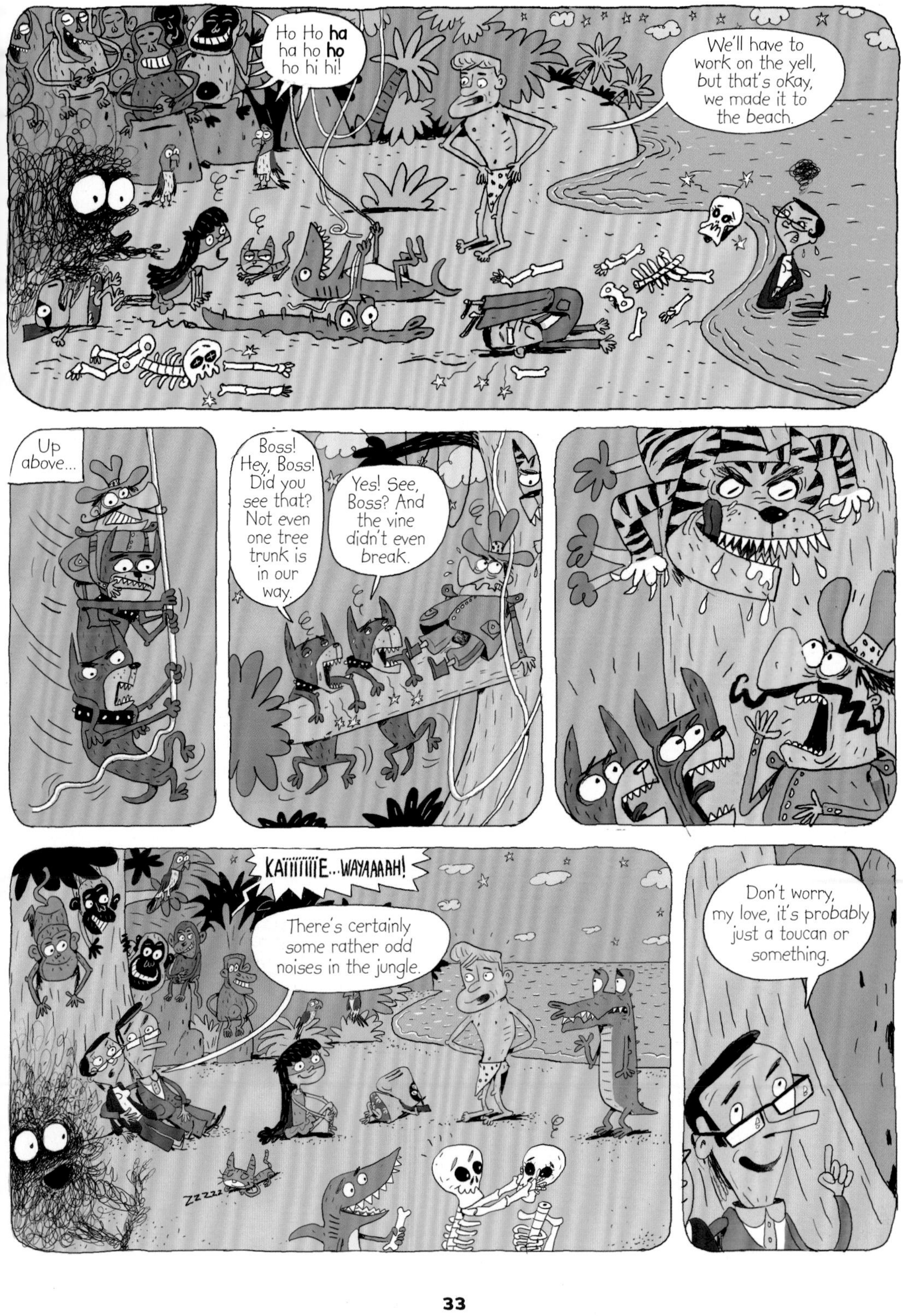
Ho Ho ha ha ho ho ho hi hi!
We'll have to work on the yell, but that's okay, we made it to the beach.
Up above...
Boss! Hey, Boss! Did you see that? Not even one tree trunk is in our way.
Yes! See, Boss? And the vine didn't even break.
KAÏÏÏÏÏÏE...WAYAAAAH!
There's certainly some rather odd noises in the jungle.
ZZZZZ
Don't worry, my love, it's probably just a toucan or something.

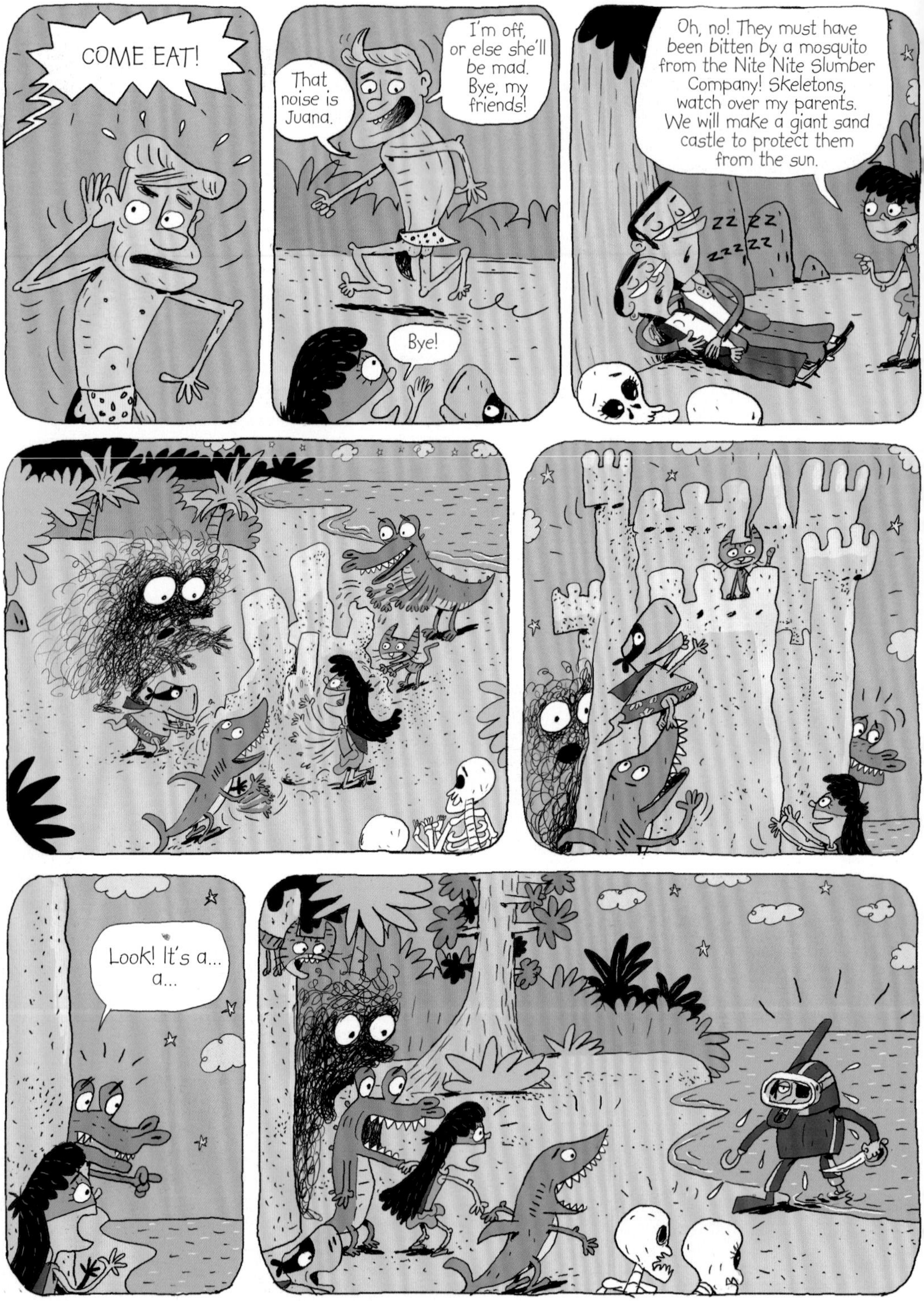
COME EAT!
That noise is Juana.
I'm off, or else she'll be mad. Bye, my friends!
Bye!
Oh, no! They must have been bitten by a mosquito from the Nite Nite Slumber Company! Skeletons, watch over my parents. We will make a giant sand castle to protect them from the sun.
ZZZ ZZ ZZZZ ZZ
Look! It's a... a...

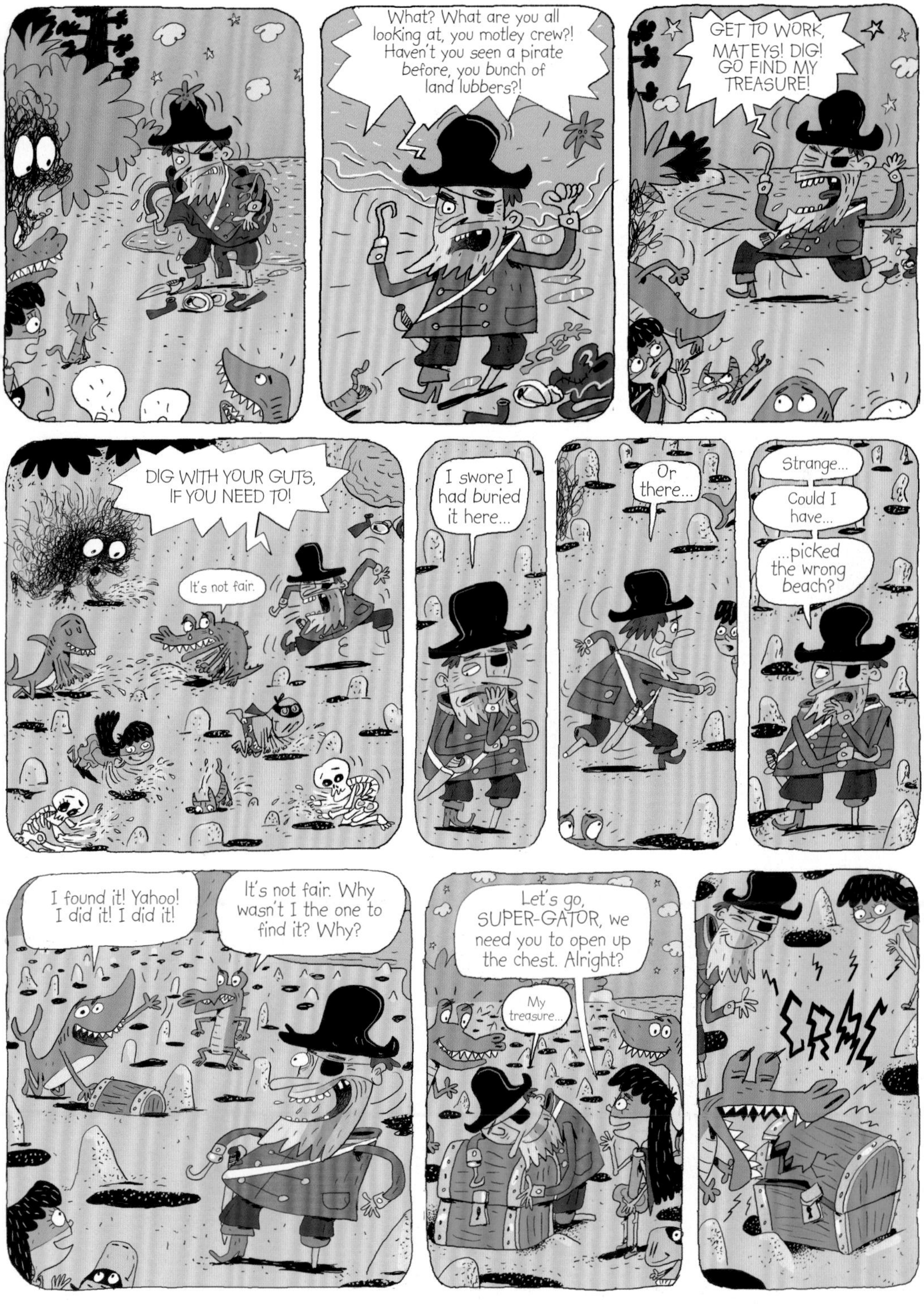
What? What are you all looking at, you motley crew?! Haven't you seen a pirate before, you bunch of land lubbers?!
GET TO WORK, MATEYS! DIG! GO FIND MY TREASURE!
DIG WITH YOUR GUTS, IF YOU NEED TO!
It's not fair.
I swore I had buried it here...
Or there...
Strange...
Could I have...
...picked the wrong beach?
I found it! Yahoo! I did it! I did it!
It's not fair. Why wasn't I the one to find it? Why?
Let's go, SUPER-GATOR, we need you to open up the chest. Alright?
My treasure...
CRAC

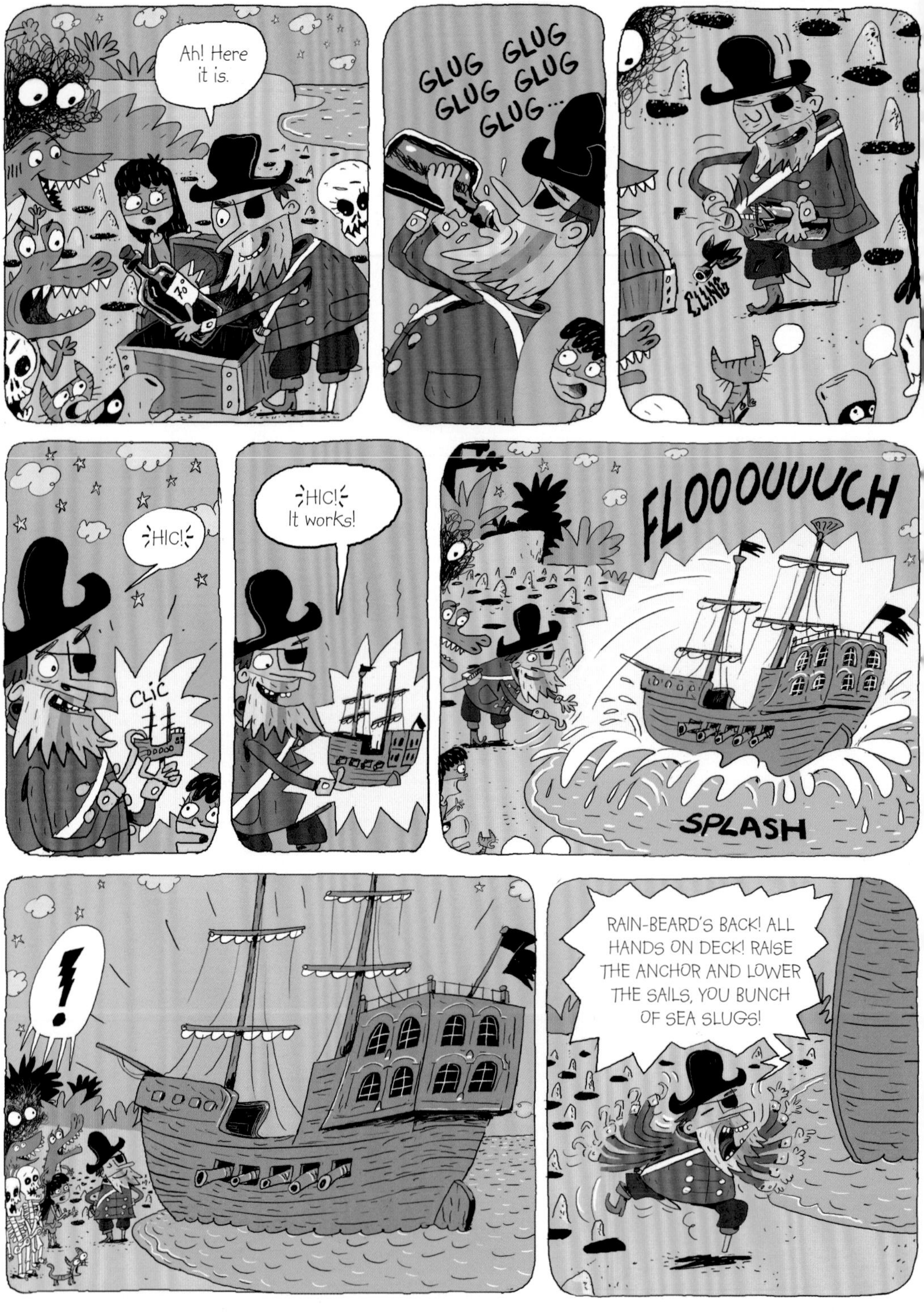
Ah! Here it is.
GLUG GLUG GLUG GLUG GLUG...
CLING
HIC!
CLIC
HIC! It works!
FLOOOUUUCH
SPLASH
!
RAIN-BEARD'S BACK! ALL HANDS ON DECK! RAISE THE ANCHOR AND LOWER THE SAILS, YOU BUNCH OF SEA SLUGS!

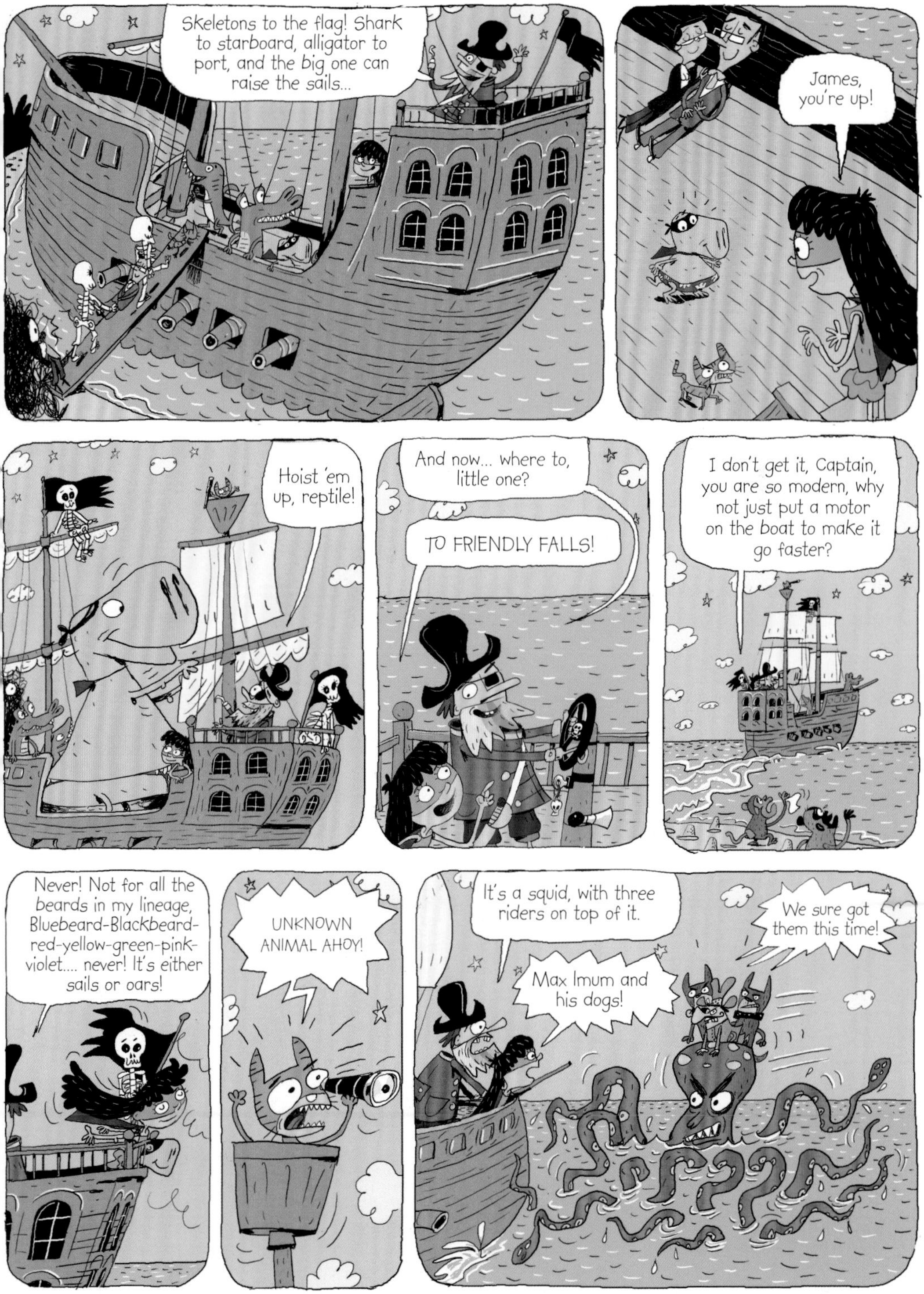
Skeletons to the flag! Shark to starboard, alligator to port, and the big one can raise the sails...
James, you're up!
Hoist 'em up, reptile!
And now... where to, little one?
TO FRIENDLY FALLS!
I don't get it, Captain, you are so modern, why not just put a motor on the boat to make it go faster?
Never! Not for all the beards in my lineage, Bluebeard-Blackbeard-red-yellow-green-pink-violet.... never! It's either sails or oars!
UNKNOWN ANIMAL AHOY!
It's a squid, with three riders on top of it.
Max Imum and his dogs!
We sure got them this time!

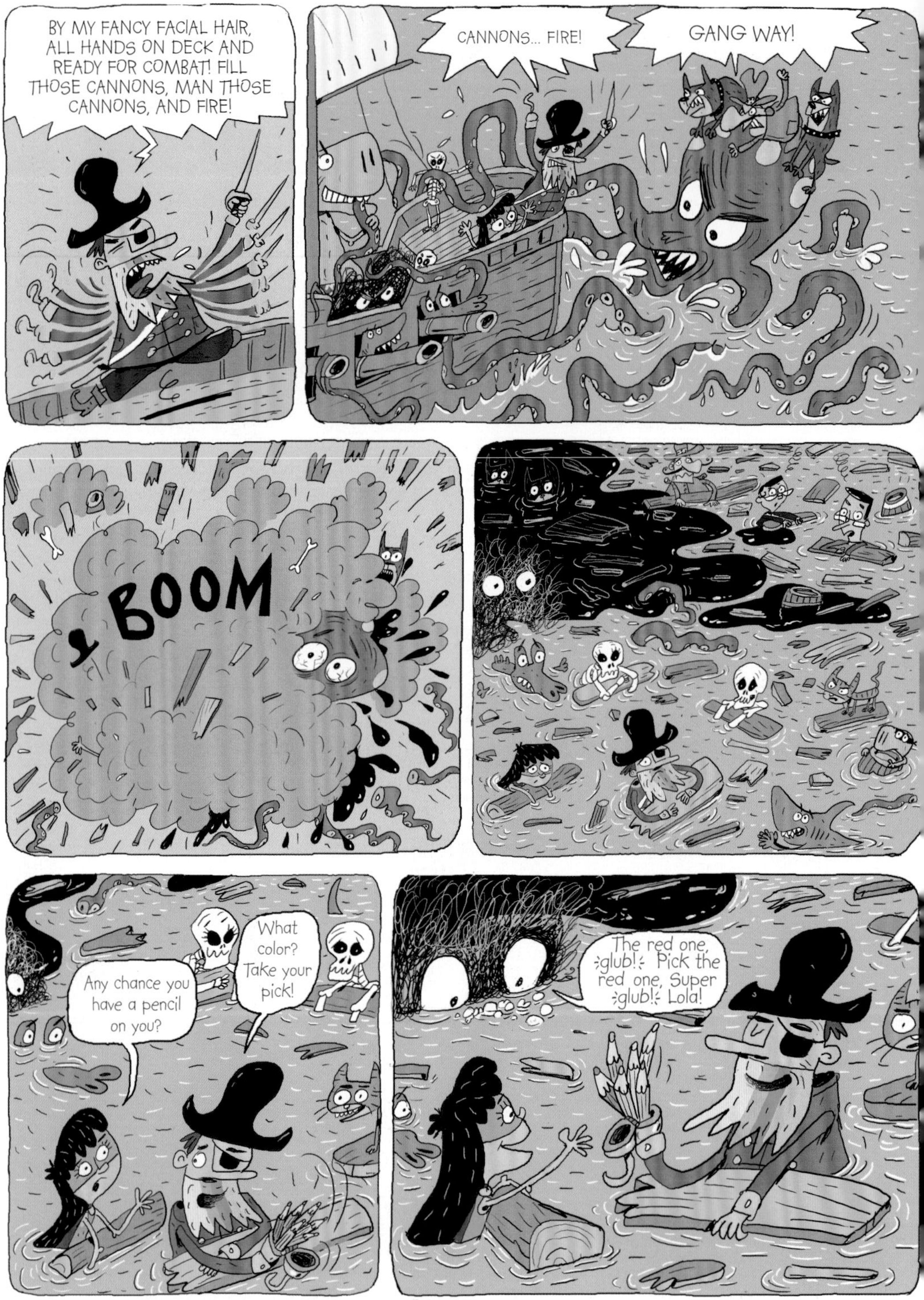

BY MY FANCY FACIAL HAIR, ALL HANDS ON DECK AND READY FOR COMBAT! FILL THOSE CANNONS, MAN THOSE CANNONS, AND FIRE!
CANNONS... FIRE!
GANG WAY!
BOOM
Any chance you have a pencil on you?
What color? Take your pick!
The red one, glub! Pick the red one, Super glub! Lola!

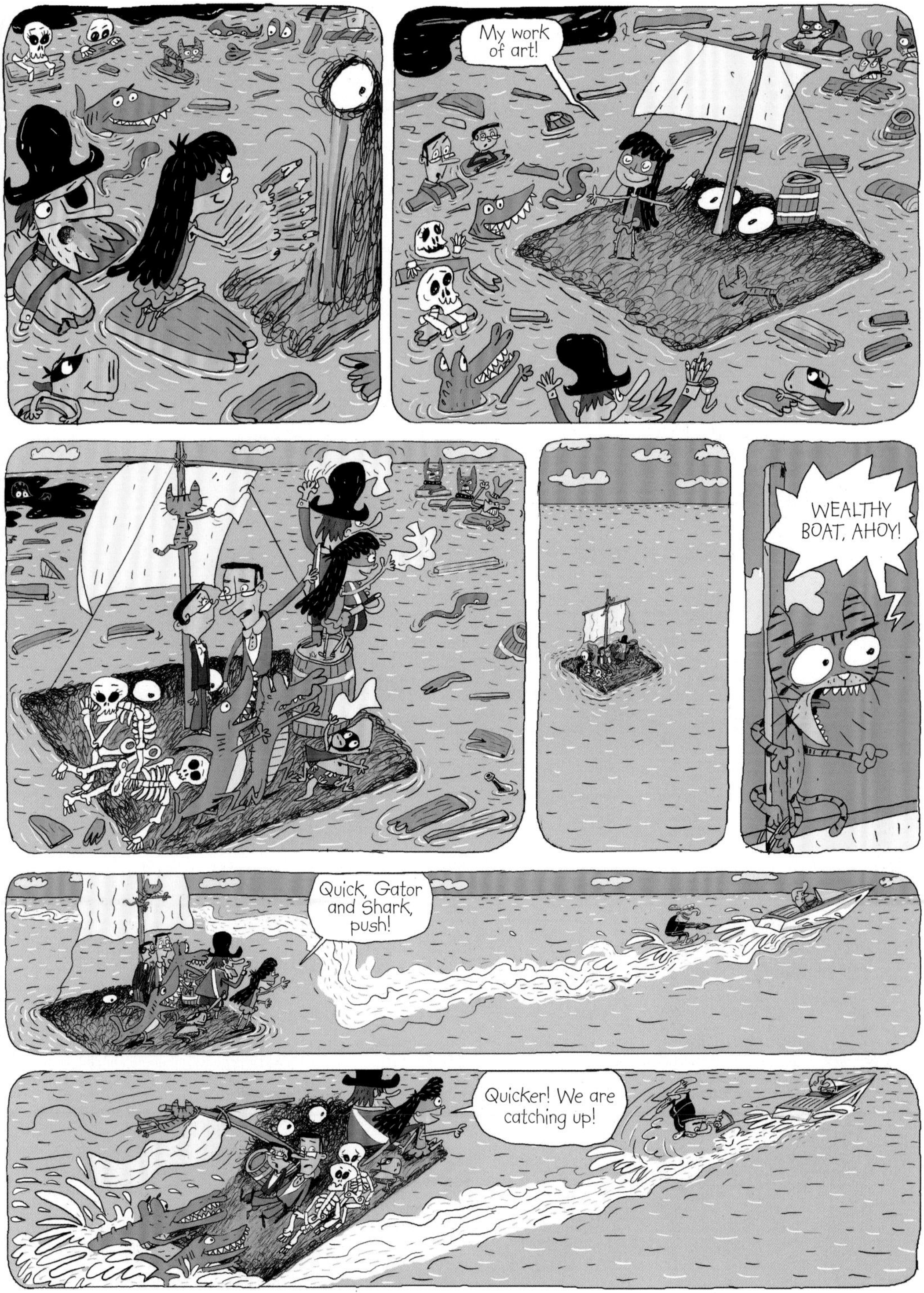
My work of art!
WEALTHY BOAT, AHOY!
Quick, Gator and Shark, push!
Quicker! We are catching up!

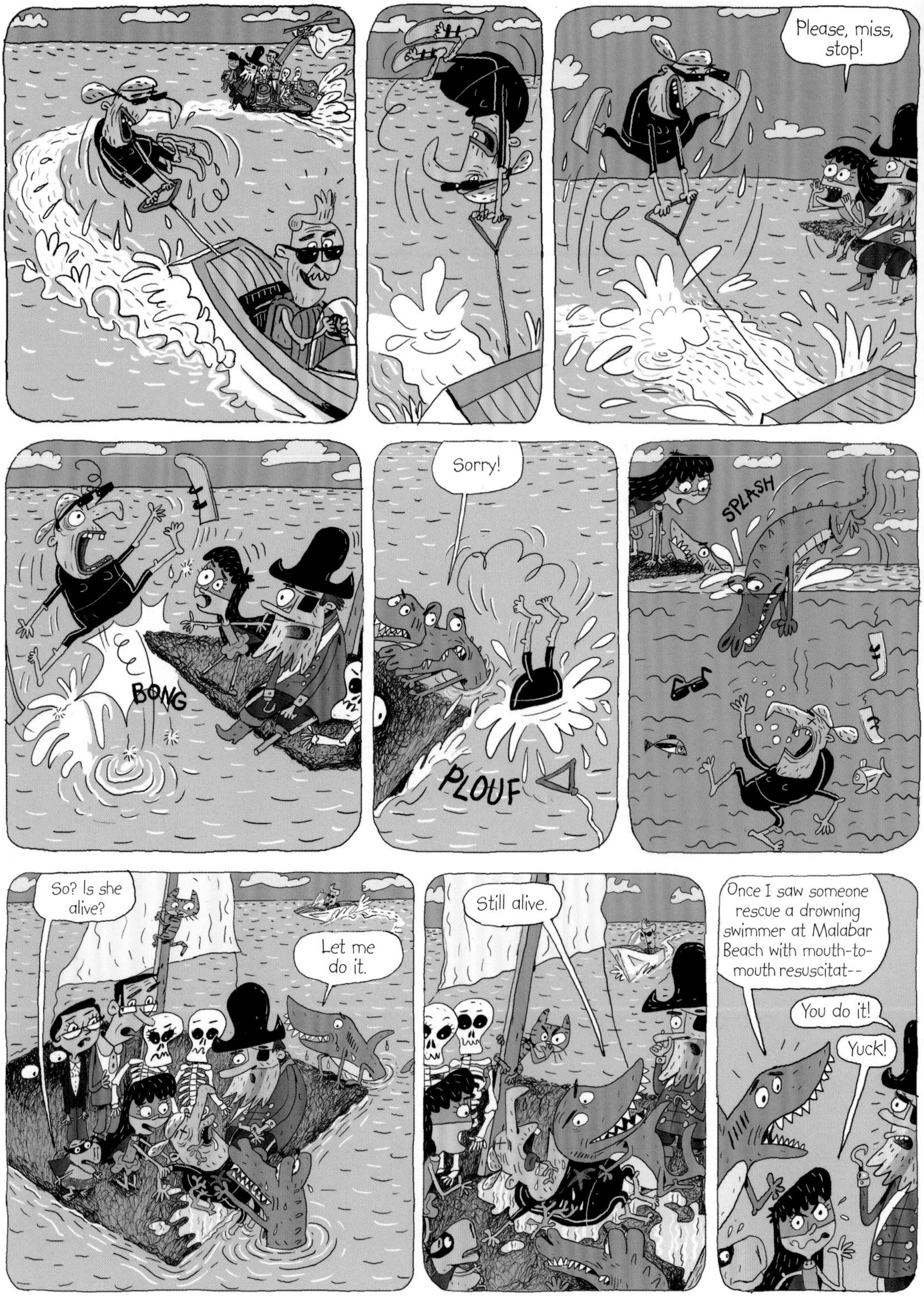
Please, miss, stop!
BONG
Sorry!
PLOUF
SPLASH
So? Is she alive?
Let me do it.
Still alive.
Once I saw someone rescue a drowning swimmer at Malabar Beach with mouth-to-mouth resuscitat--
You do it!
Yuck!

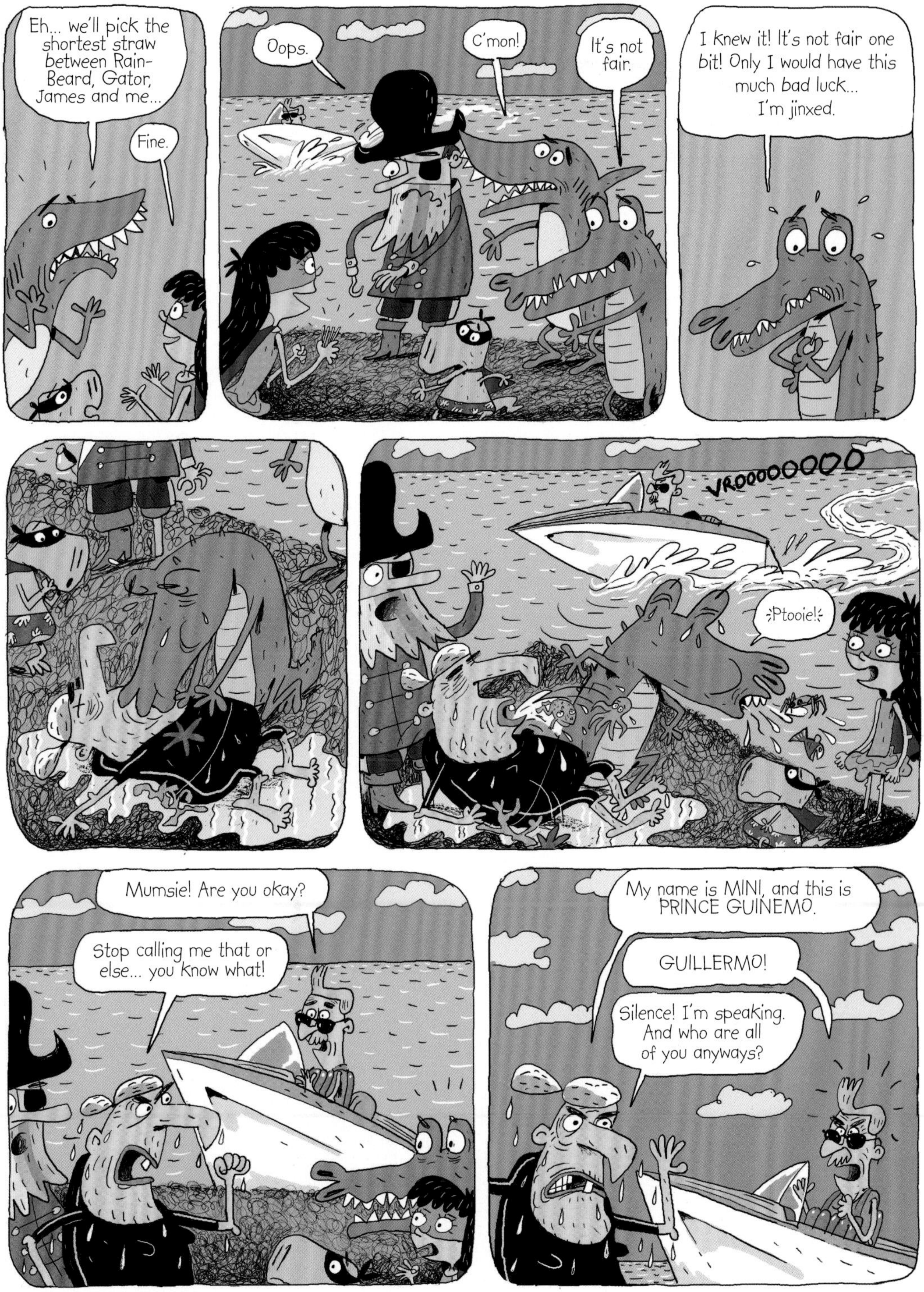
Eh... we'll pick the shortest straw between Rain-Beard, Gator, James and me...
Fine.
Oops.
C'mon!
It's not fair.
I knew it! It's not fair one bit! Only I would have this much bad luck... I'm jinxed.
VROOOOOOOOO
Ptooie!
Mumsie! Are you okay?
Stop calling me that or else... you know what!
My name is MINI, and this is PRINCE GUINEMO.
GUILLERMO!
Silence! I'm speaking. And who are all of you anyways?

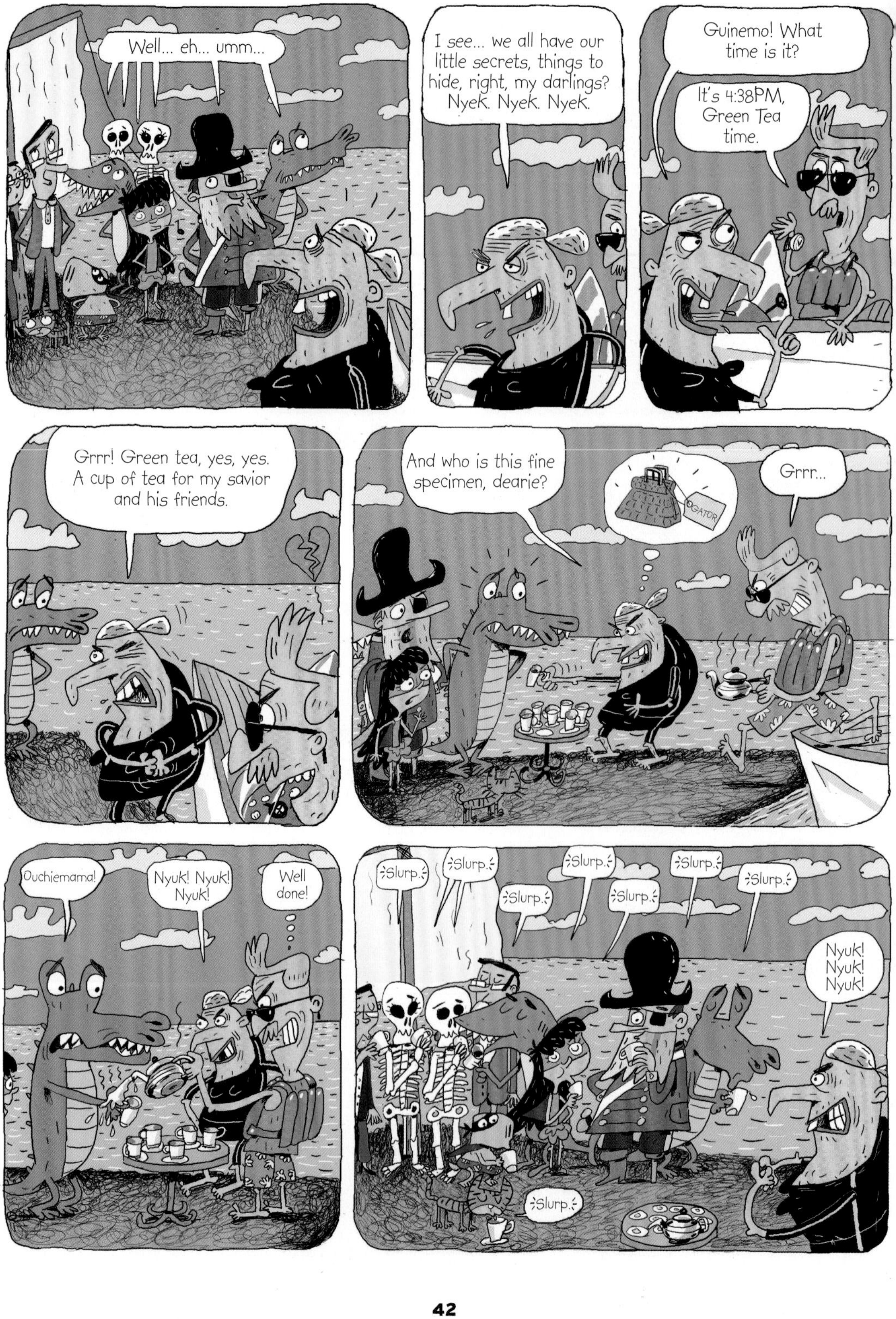
Well... eh... umm...
I see... we all have our little secrets, things to hide, right, my darlings? Nyek. Nyek. Nyek.
Guinemo! What time is it?
It's 4:38PM, Green Tea time.
Grrr! Green tea, yes, yes. A cup of tea for my savior and his friends.
And who is this fine specimen, dearie?
GATOR
Grrr...
Ouchiemama!
Nyuk! Nyuk! Nyuk!
Well done!
Slurp.
Slurp.
Slurp.
Slurp.
Slurp.
Slurp.
Slurp.
Nyuk! Nyuk! Nyuk!
Slurp.

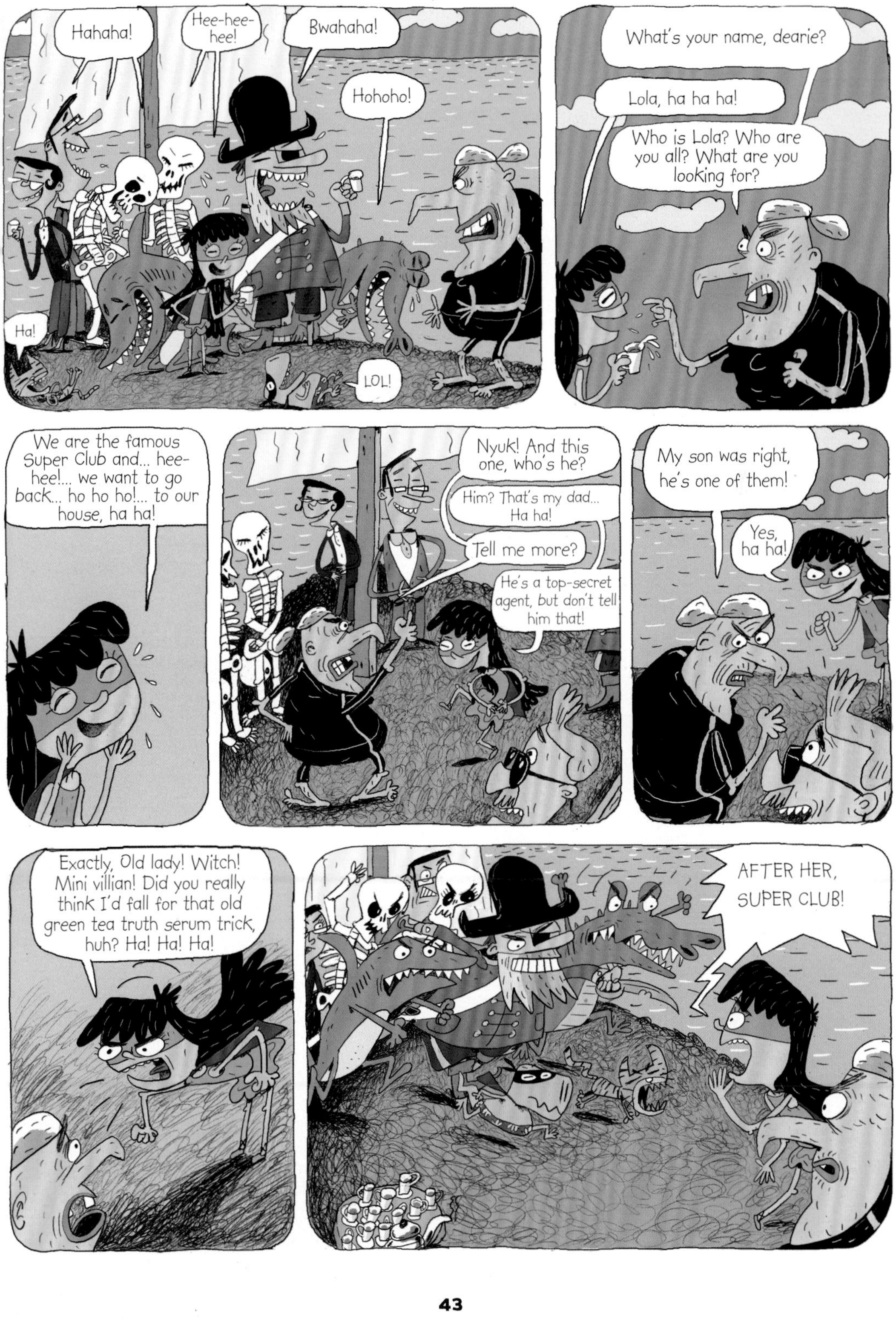
Hahaha!
Hee-hee-hee!
Bwahaha!
Hohoho!
Ha!
LOL!
What's your name, dearie?
Lola, ha ha ha!
Who is Lola? Who are you all? What are you looking for?
We are the famous Super Club and... hee-hee!... we want to go back... ho ho ho!... to our house, ha ha!
Nyuk! And this one, who's he?
Him? That's my dad... Ha ha!
Tell me more?
He's a top-secret agent, but don't tell him that!
My son was right, he's one of them!
Yes, ha ha!
Exactly, Old lady! Witch! Mini villian! Did you really think I'd fall for that old green tea truth serum trick, huh? Ha! Ha! Ha!
AFTER HER, SUPER CLUB!

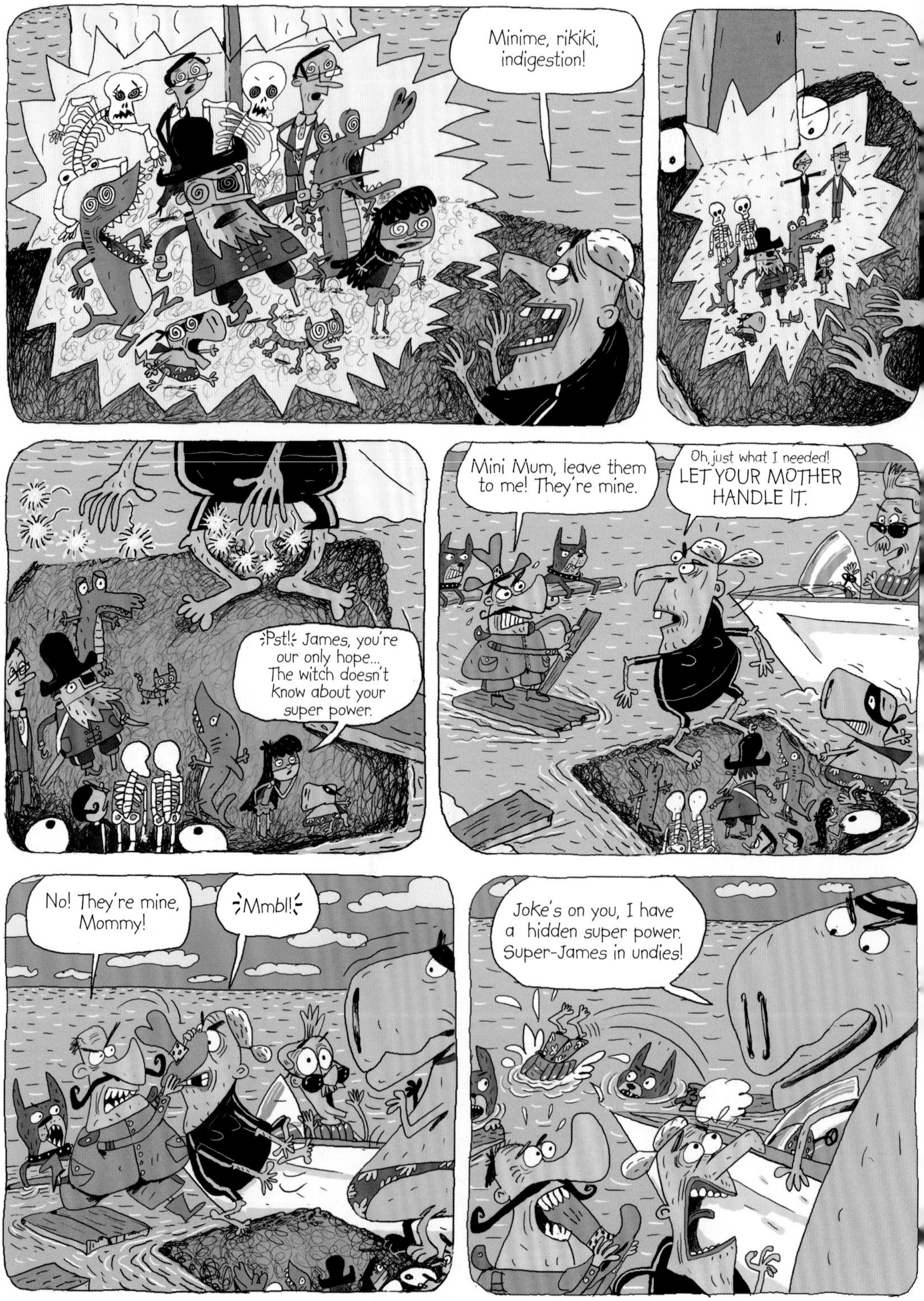
Minime, rikiki, indigestion!
Pst! James, you're our only hope... The witch doesn't know about your super power.
Mini Mum, leave them to me! They're mine.
Oh, just what I needed! LET YOUR MOTHER HANDLE IT.
No! They're mine, Mommy!
Mmbl!
Joke's on you, I have a hidden super power. Super-James in undies!

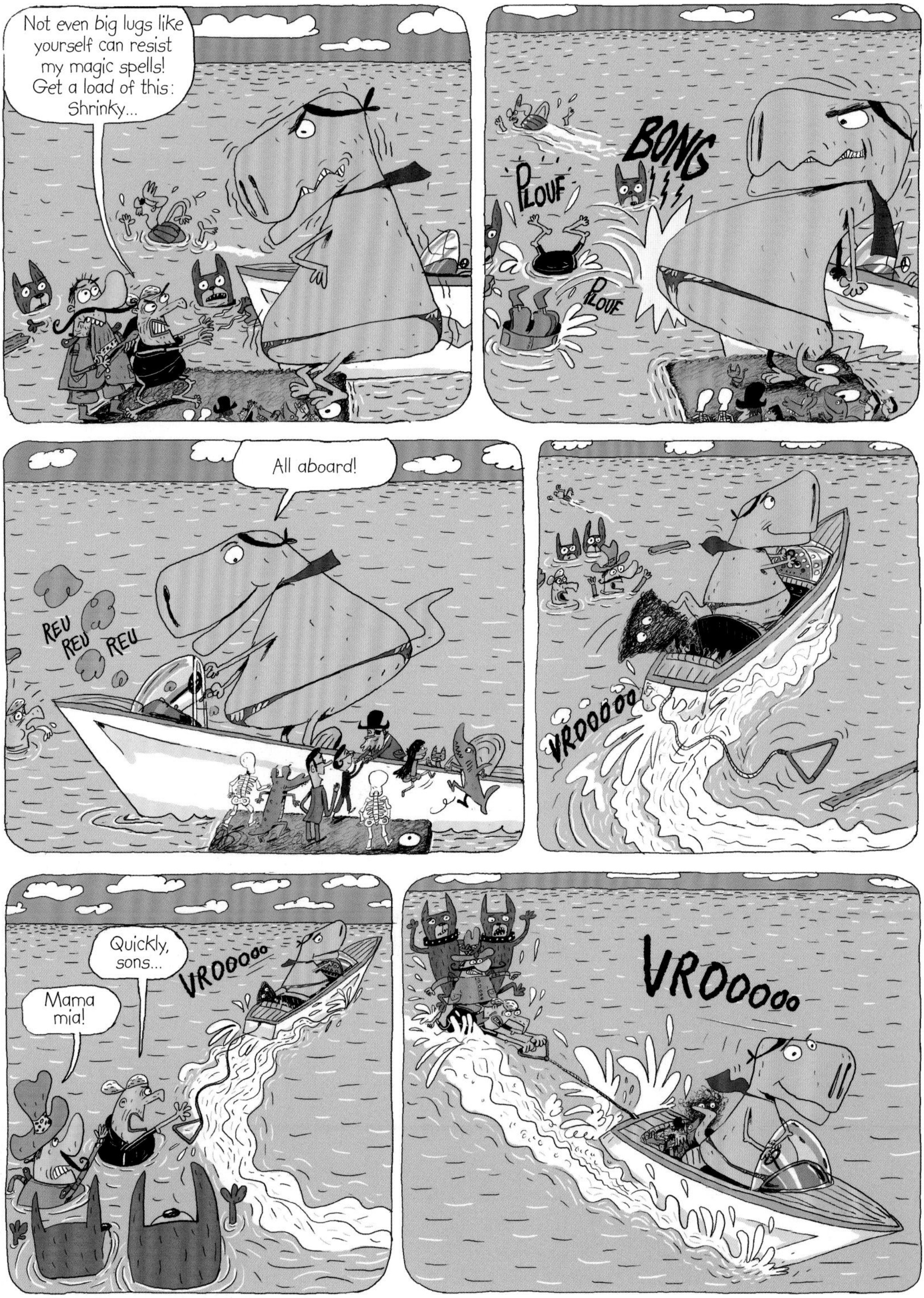
Not even big lugs like yourself can resist my magic spells! Get a load of this: Shrinky...
PLOUF
BONG
PLOUF
All aboard!
REU
REU
REU
VROOOOO
Quickly, sons...
Mama mia!
VROOooo
VROOooo

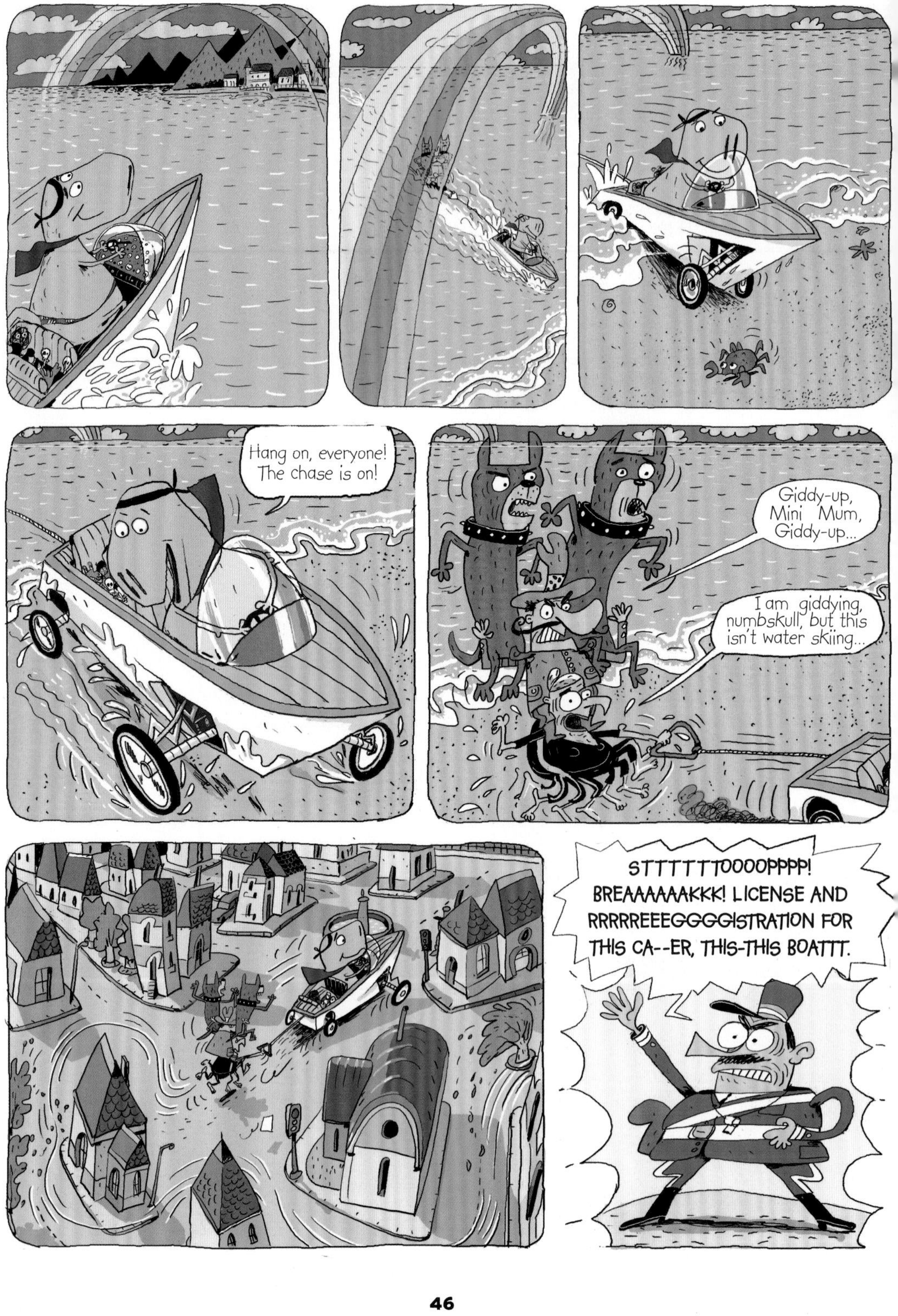
Hang on, everyone! The chase is on!
Giddy-up, Mini Mum, Giddy-up...
I am giddying, numbskull, but this isn't water skiing...
STTTTTTOOOOPPPP! BREAAAAAAKKK! LICENSE AND RRRRREEEGGGGISTRATION FOR THIS CA--ER, THIS-THIS BOATTT.

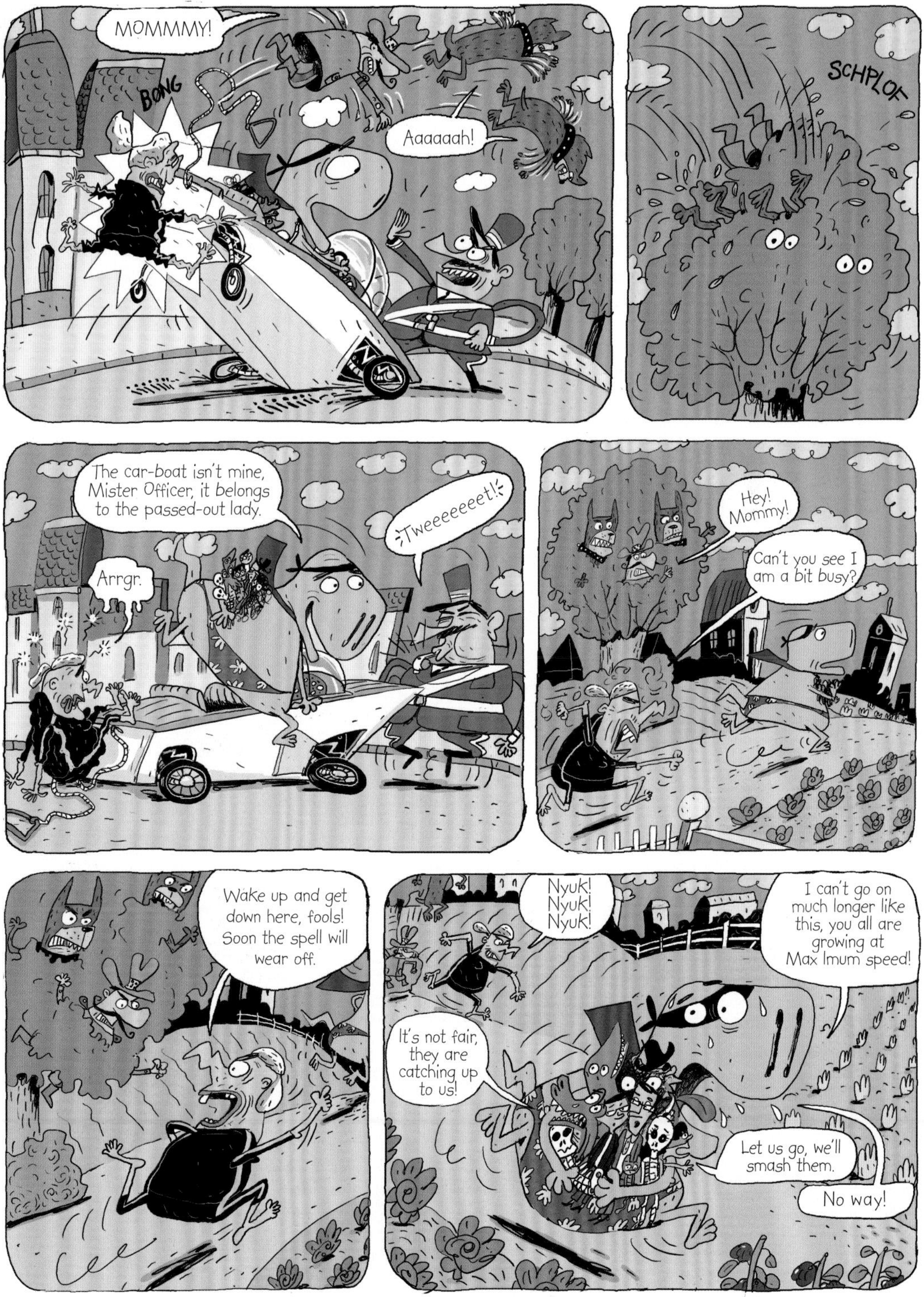
MOMMMY!
BONG
Aaaaaah!
SCHPLOF
The car-boat isn't mine, Mister Officer, it belongs to the passed-out lady.
Tweeeeeeet!
Arrgr.
Hey! Mommy!
Can't you see I am a bit busy?
Wake up and get down here, fools! Soon the spell will wear off.
Nyuk! Nyuk! Nyuk!
I can't go on much longer like this, you all are growing at Max Imum speed!
It's not fair, they are catching up to us!
Let us go, we'll smash them.
No way!

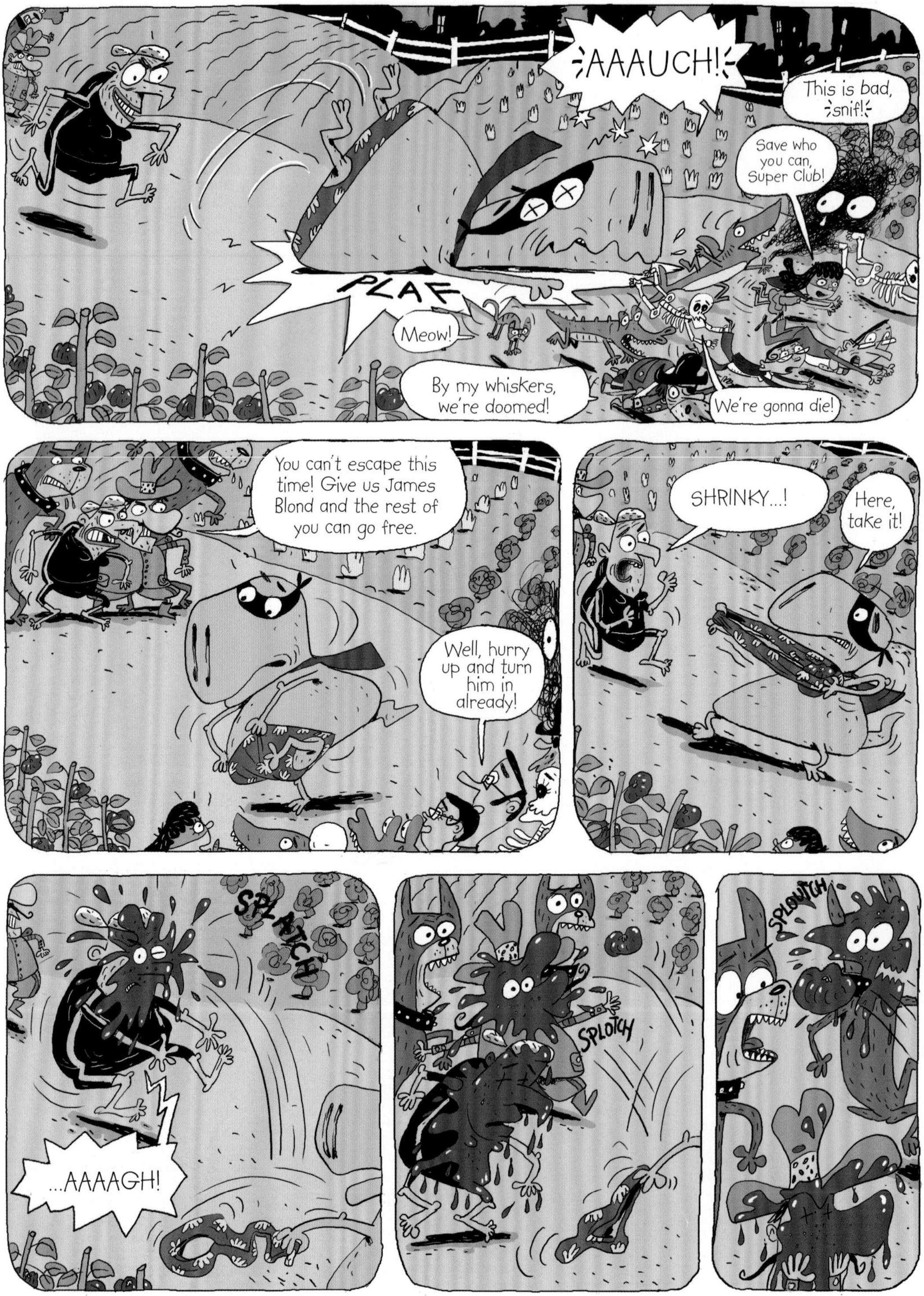
PLAF
AAAUCH!
This is bad, snif!
Save who you can, Super Club!
Meow!
By my whiskers, we're doomed!
We're gonna die!
You can't escape this time! Give us James Blond and the rest of you can go free.
Well, hurry up and turn him in already!
SHRINKY...!
Here, take it!
SPLATCH
...AAAAGH!
SPLOTCH
SPLOUTCH

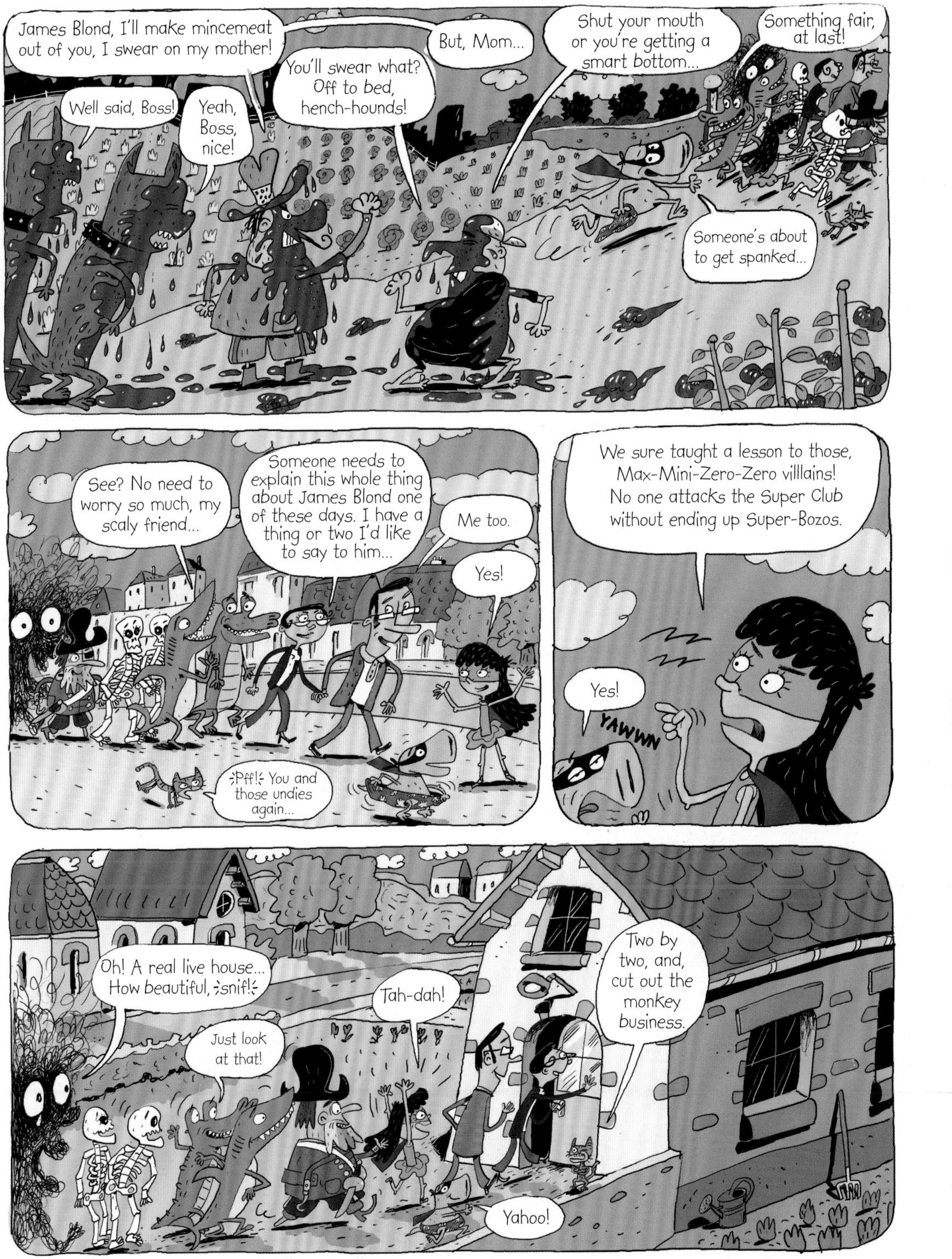

James Blond, I'll make mincemeat out of you, I swear on my mother!
Well said, Boss!
Yeah, Boss, nice!
You'll swear what? Off to bed, hench-hounds!
But, Mom...
Shut your mouth or you're getting a smart bottom...
Something fair, at last!
Someone's about to get spanked...
See? No need to worry so much, my scaly friend...
Someone needs to explain this whole thing about James Blond one of these days. I have a thing or two I'd like to say to him...
Me too.
Yes!
;Pff!; You and those undies again...
We sure taught a lesson to those, Max-Mini-Zero-Zero villlains! No one attacks the Super Club without ending up Super-Bozos.
Yes!
YAWWN
Oh! A real live house... How beautiful, ;snif!;
Just look at that!
Tah-dah!
Two by two, and, cut out the monkey business.
Yahoo!

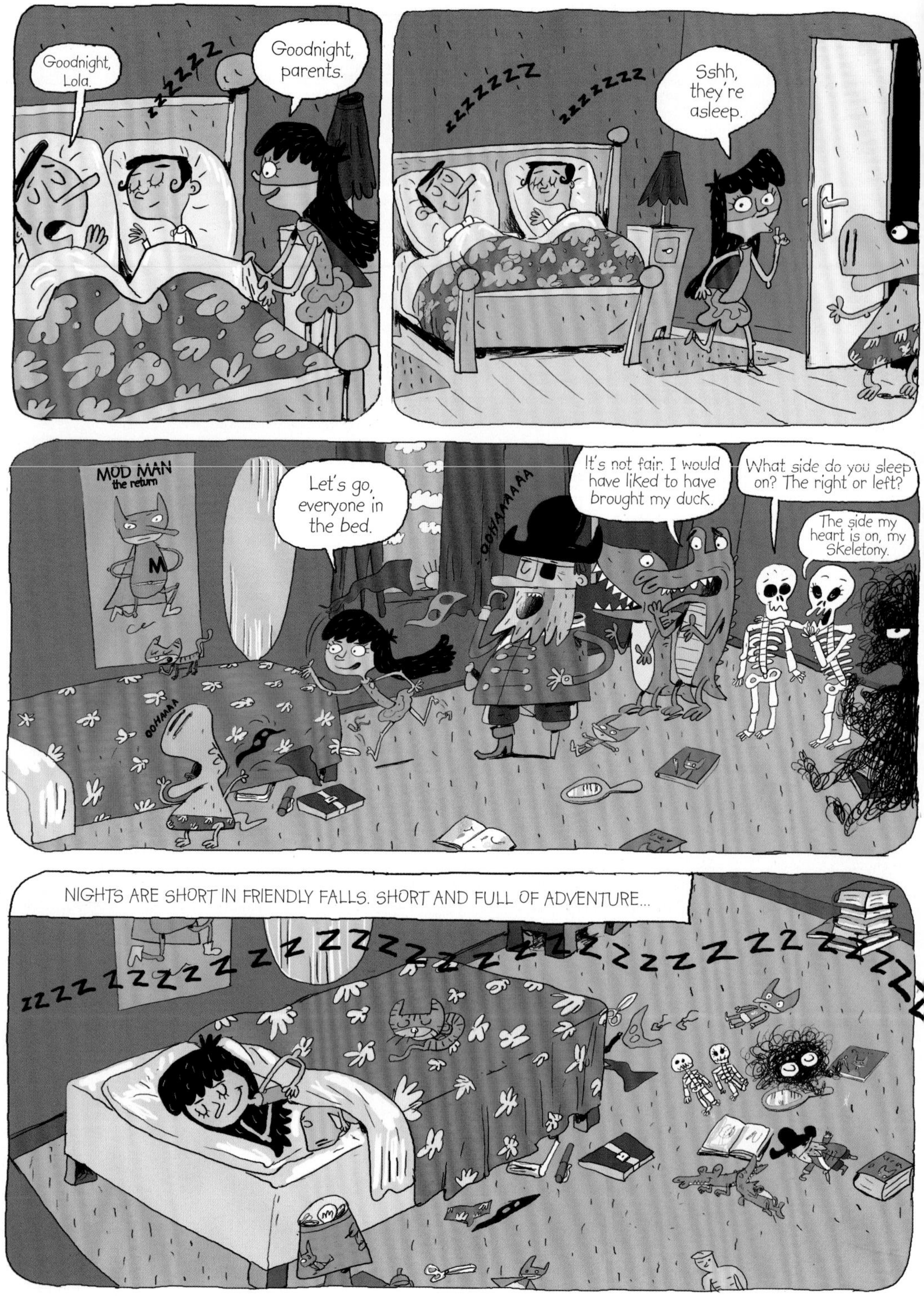
Goodnight, Lola.
Goodnight, parents.
Sshh, they're asleep.
MOD MAN the return
Let's go, everyone in the bed.
It's not fair. I would have liked to have brought my duck.
What side do you sleep on? The right or left?
The side my heart is on, my Skeletony.
NIGHTS ARE SHORT IN FRIENDLY FALLS. SHORT AND FULL OF ADVENTURE...

-Pierre Fouillet-2011-

ZZZZZZZZZZ ZZZZZZZZZZZZZZ

Lola's SUPER CLUB

MY MOM IS LOST IN TIME

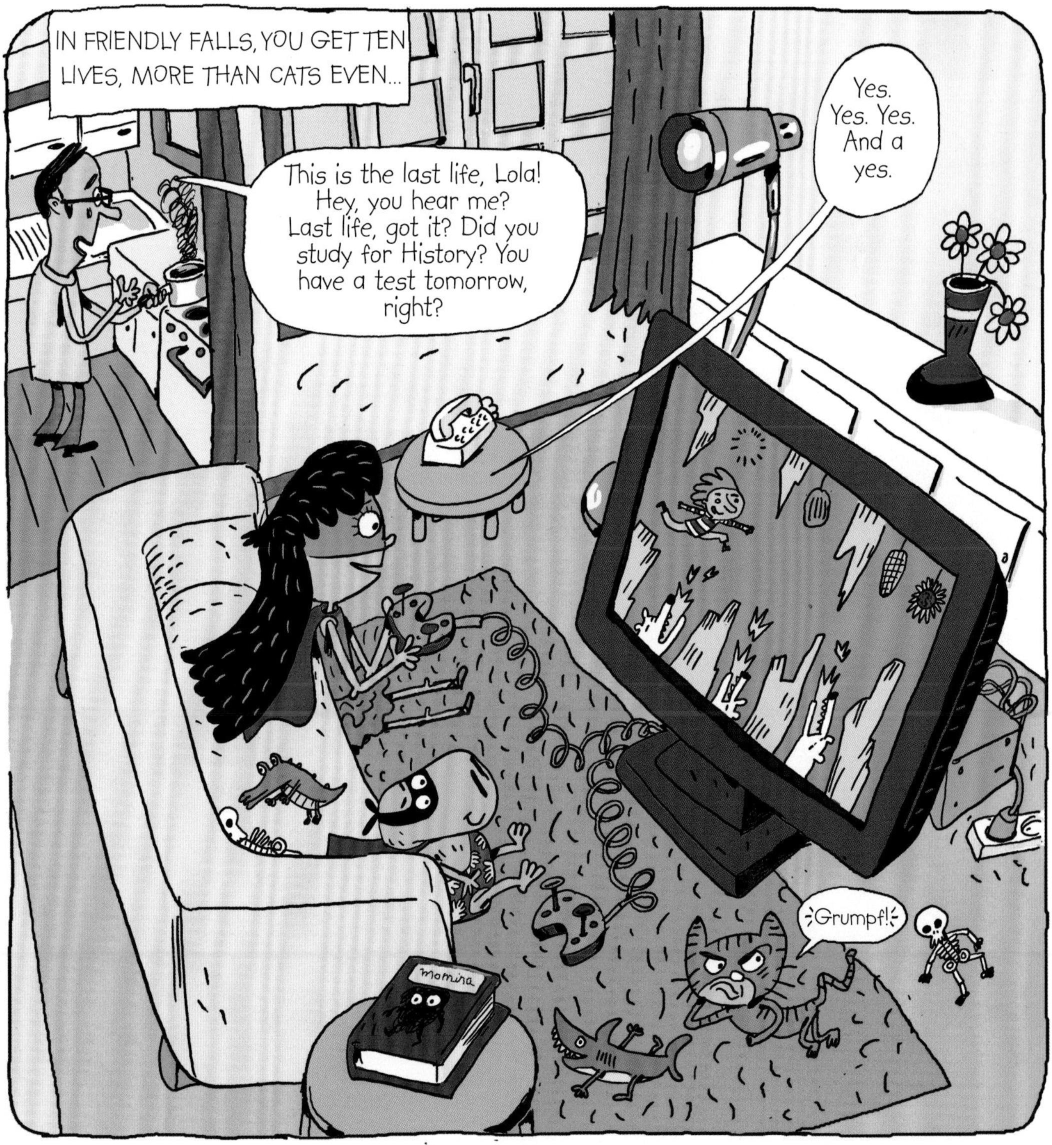

IN FRIENDLY FALLS, YOU GET TEN LIVES, MORE THAN CATS EVEN...
This is the last life, Lola! Hey, you hear me? Last life, got it? Did you study for History? You have a test tomorrow, right?
Yes. Yes. Yes. And a yes.
Grumpf!
momira

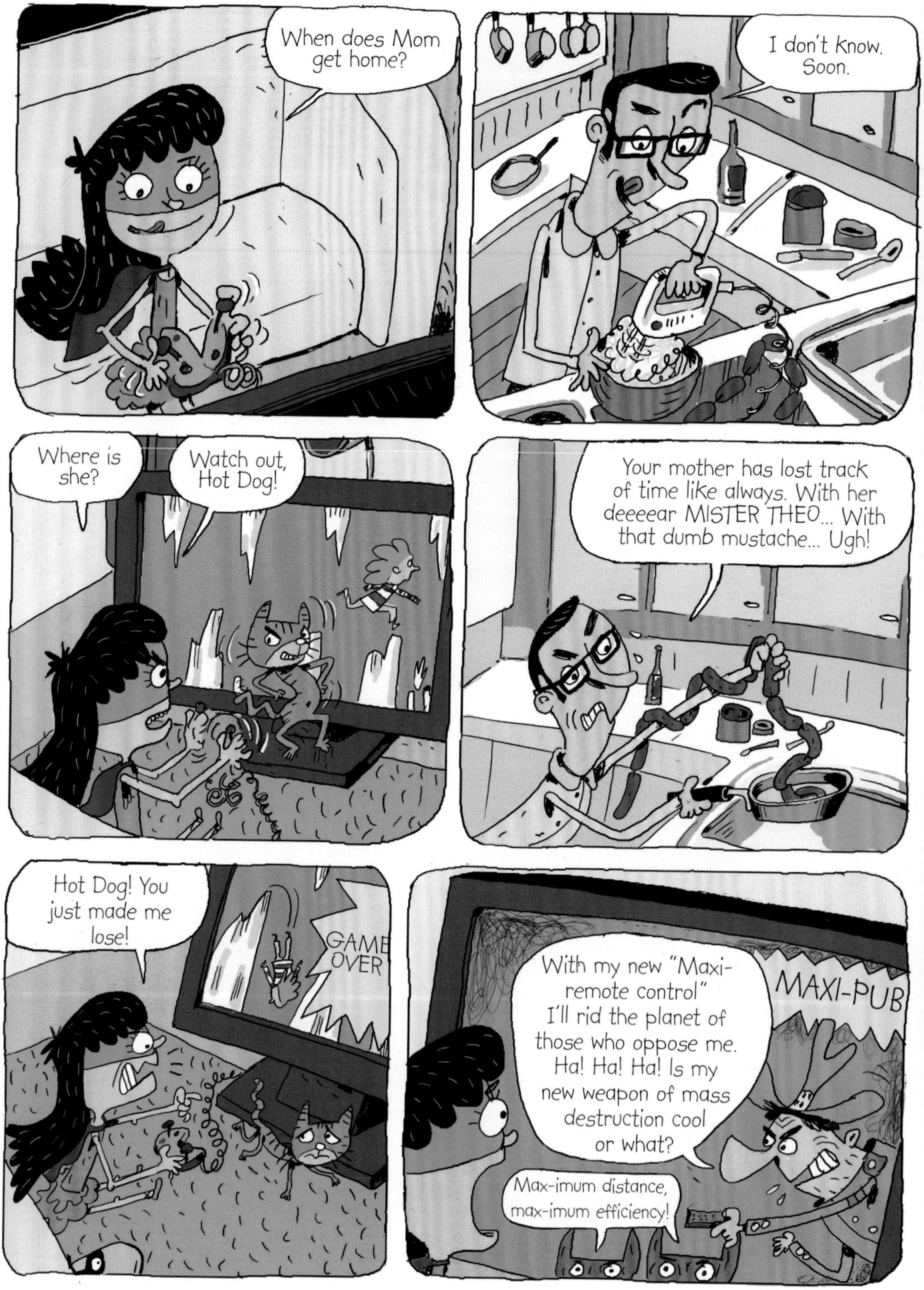
When does Mom get home?
I don't know. Soon.
Where is she?
Watch out, Hot Dog!
Your mother has lost track of time like always. With her deeeear MISTER THEO... With that dumb mustache... Ugh!
Hot Dog! You just made me lose!
GAME OVER
MAXI-PUB
With my new "Maxi-remote control" I'll rid the planet of those who oppose me. Ha! Ha! Ha! Is my new weapon of mass destruction cool or what?
Max-imum distance, max-imum efficiency!

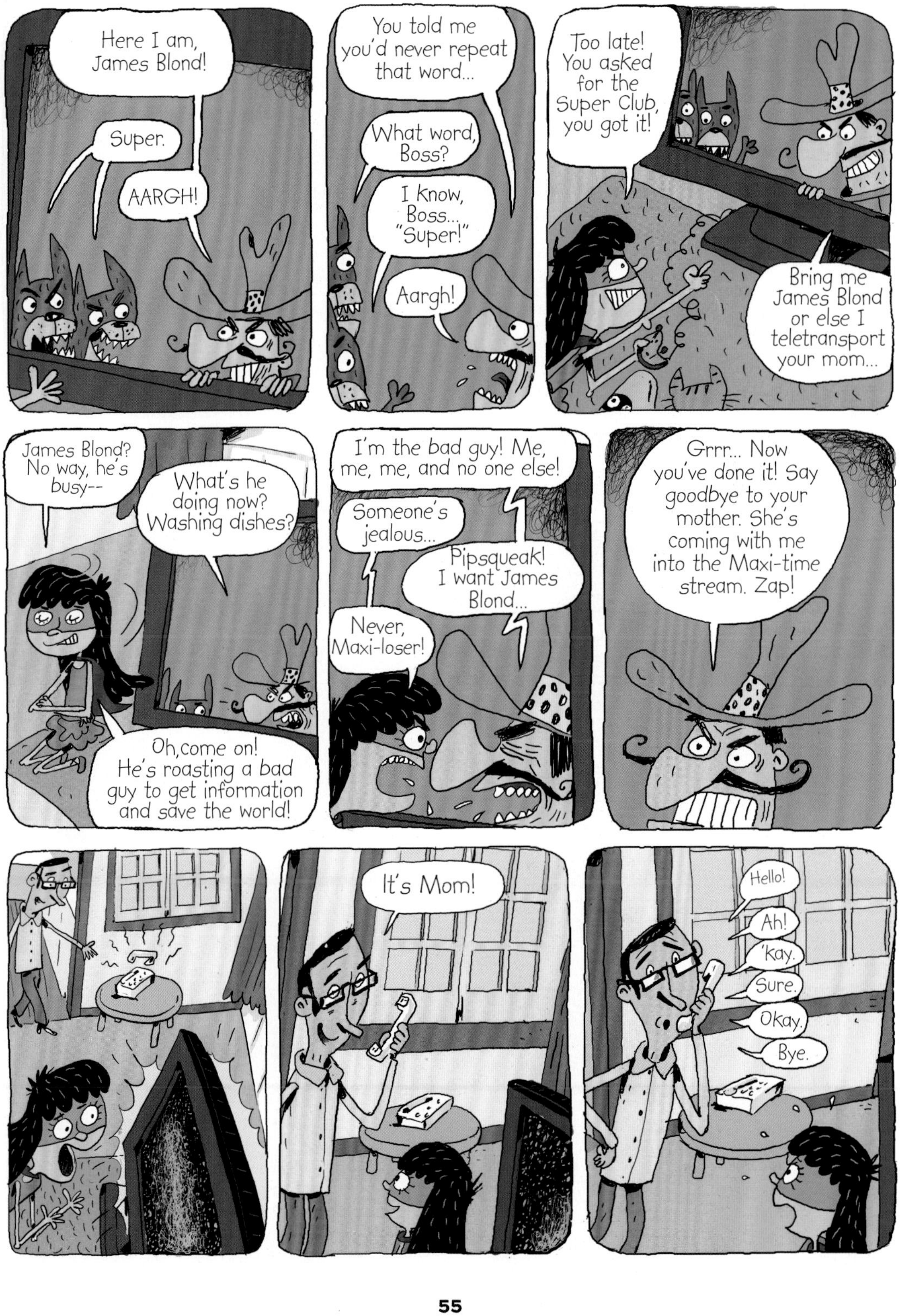
Here I am, James Blond!
Super.
AARGH!
You told me you'd never repeat that word...
What word, Boss?
I know, Boss... "Super!"
Aargh!
Too late! You asked for the Super Club, you got it!
Bring me James Blond or else I teletransport your mom...
James Blond? No way, he's busy--
What's he doing now? Washing dishes?
Oh, come on! He's roasting a bad guy to get information and save the world!
I'm the *bad guy!* Me, me, me, and no one else!
Someone's jealous...
Pipsqueak! I want James Blond...
Never, Maxi-loser!
Grrr... Now you've done it! Say goodbye to your mother. She's coming with me into the Maxi-time stream. Zap!
It's Mom!
Hello!
Ah!
'Kay.
Sure.
Okay.
Bye.

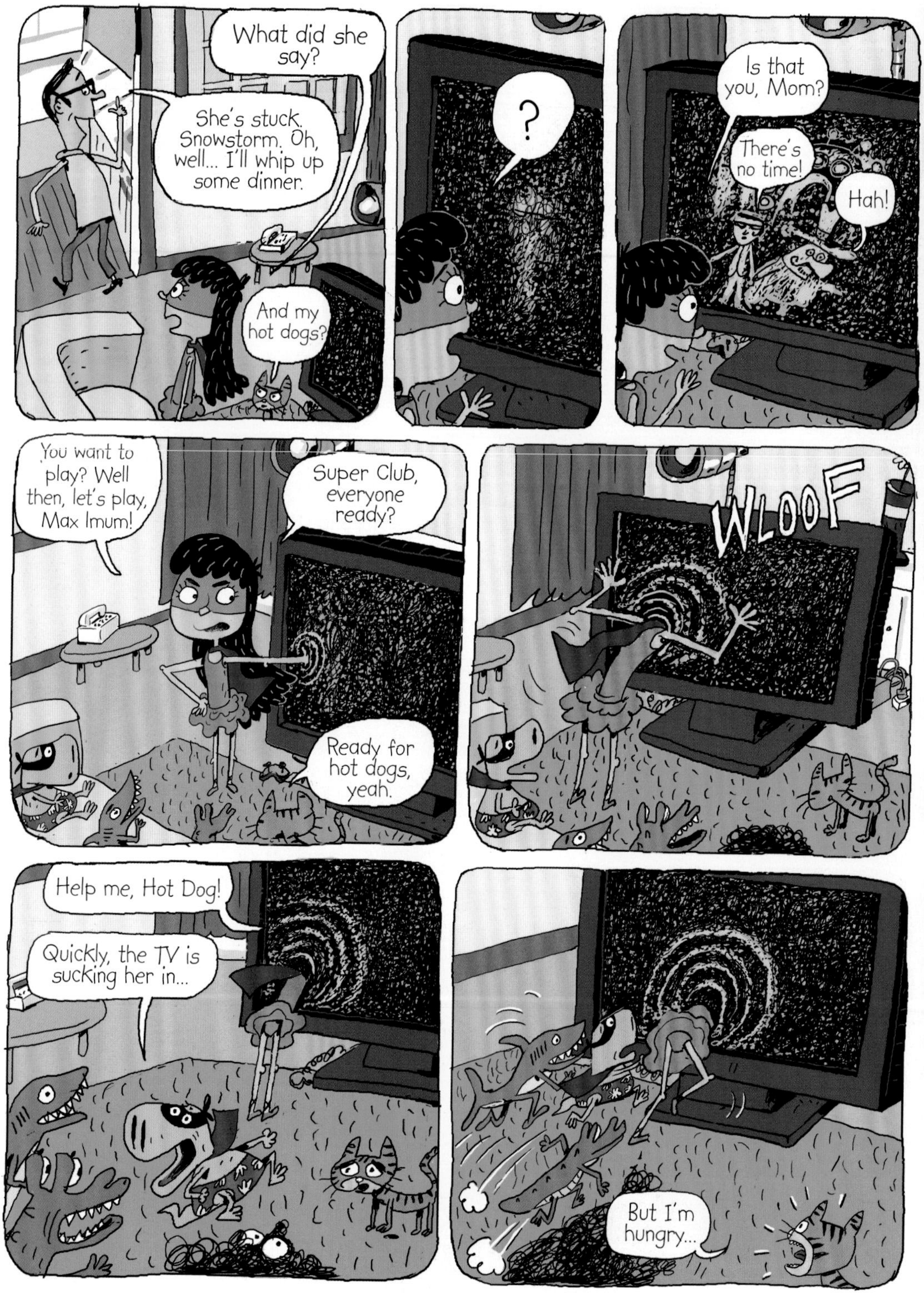
What did she say?
She's stuck. Snowstorm. Oh, well... I'll whip up some dinner.
And my hot dogs?
?
Is that you, Mom?
There's no time!
Hah!
You want to play? Well then, let's play, Max Imum!
Super Club, everyone ready?
Ready for hot dogs, yeah.
WLOOF
Help me, Hot Dog!
Quickly, the TV is sucking her in...
But I'm hungry...

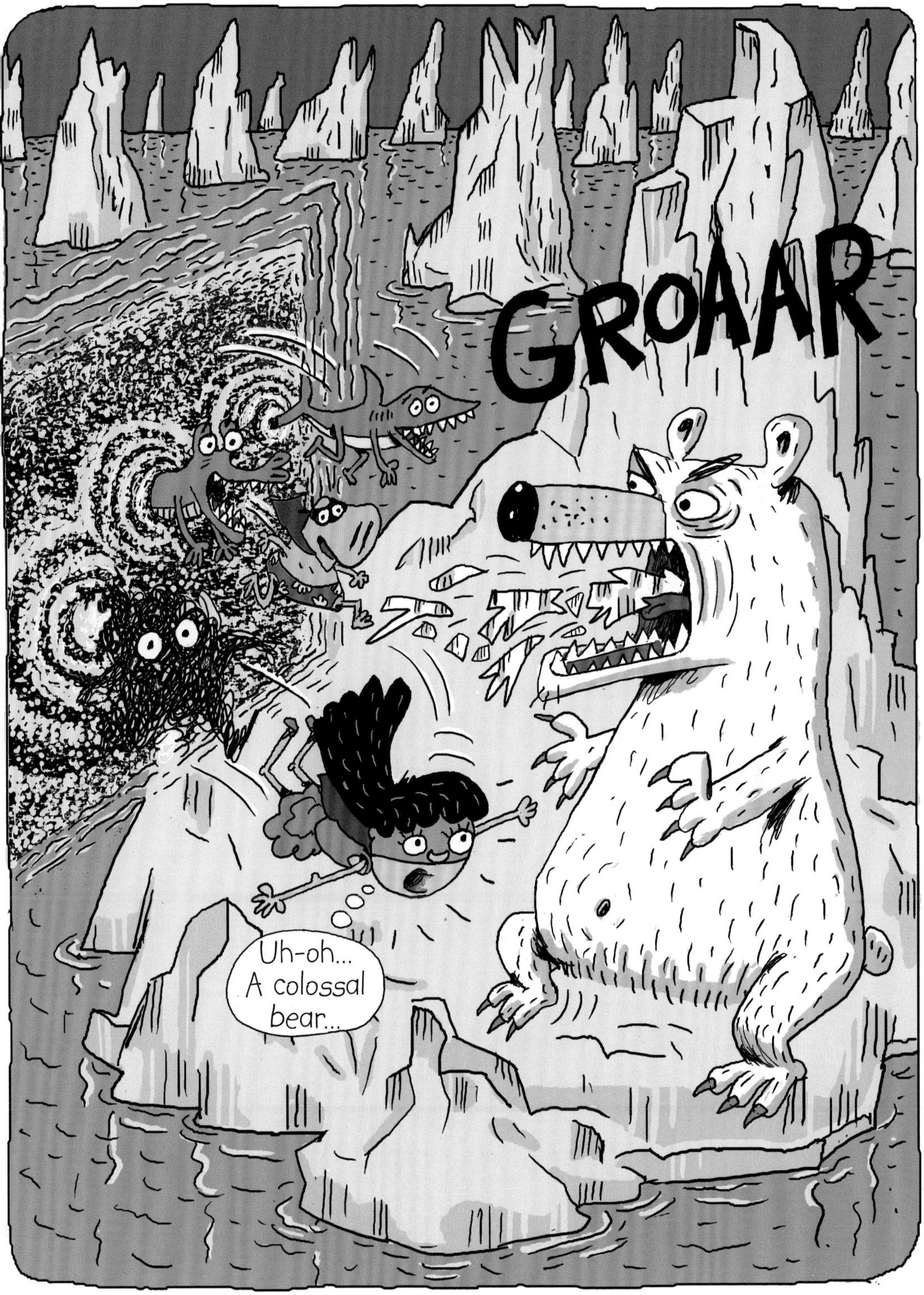
GROAAR
Uh-oh...
A colossal
bear...

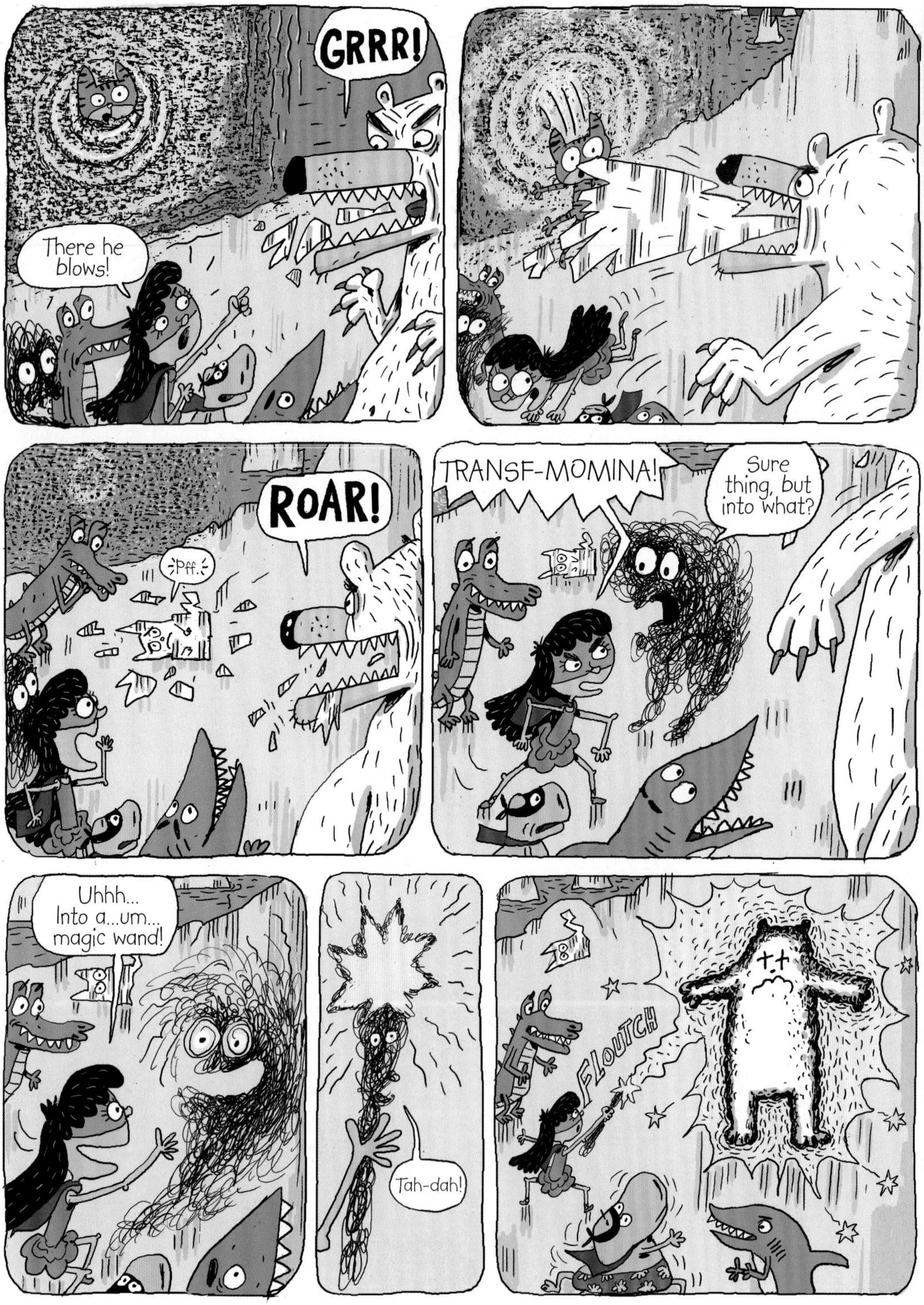
GRRR!
There he blows!
ROAR!
Pff.
TRANSF-MOMINA!
Sure thing, but into what?
Uhhh... Into a...um... magic wand!
Tah-dah!
FLOUTCH

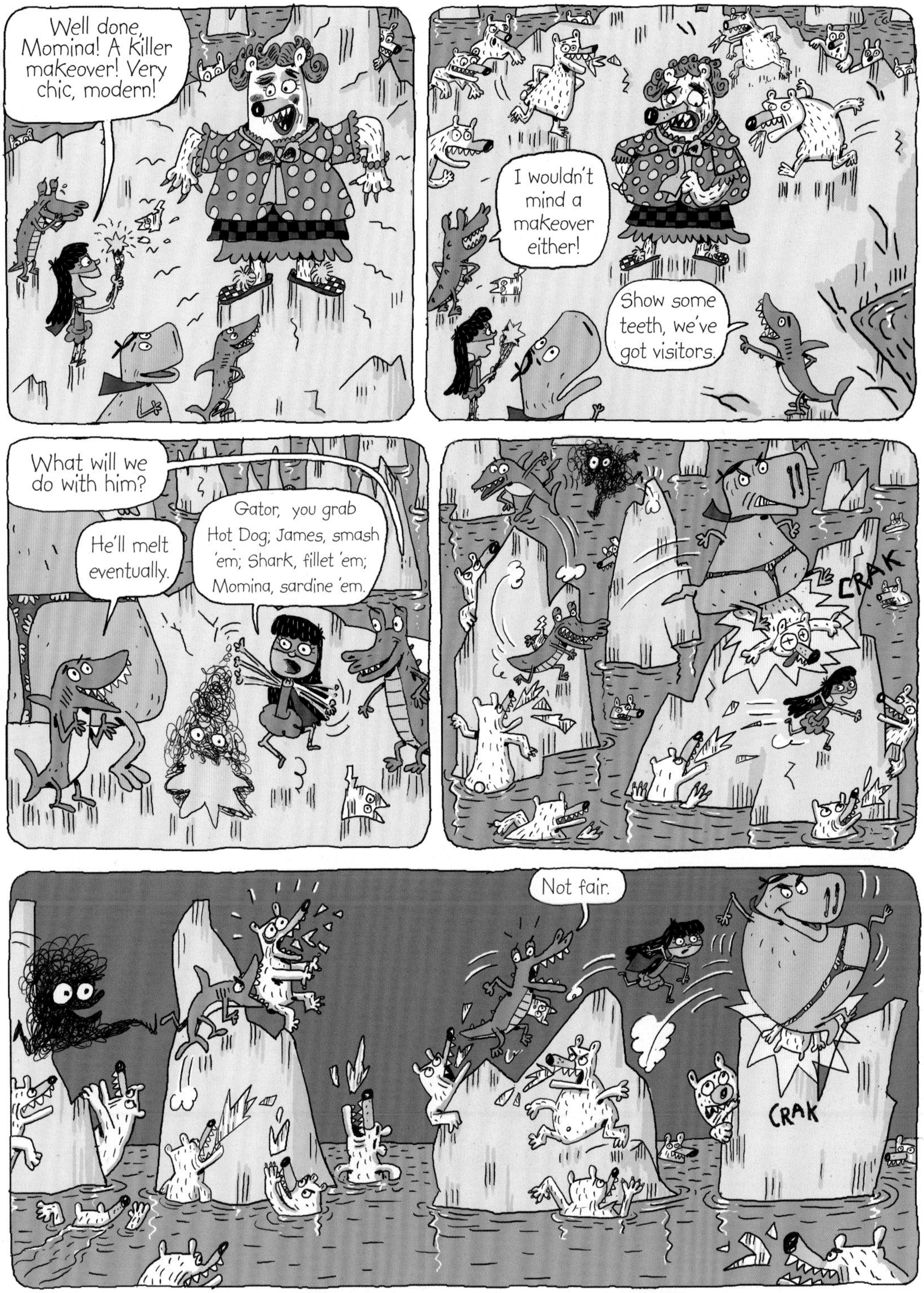

Well done, Momina! A killer makeover! Very chic, modern!
I wouldn't mind a makeover either!
Show some teeth, we've got visitors.
What will we do with him?
He'll melt eventually.
Gator, you grab Hot Dog; James, smash 'em; Shark, fillet 'em; Momina, sardine 'em.
CRAK
Not fair.
CRAK

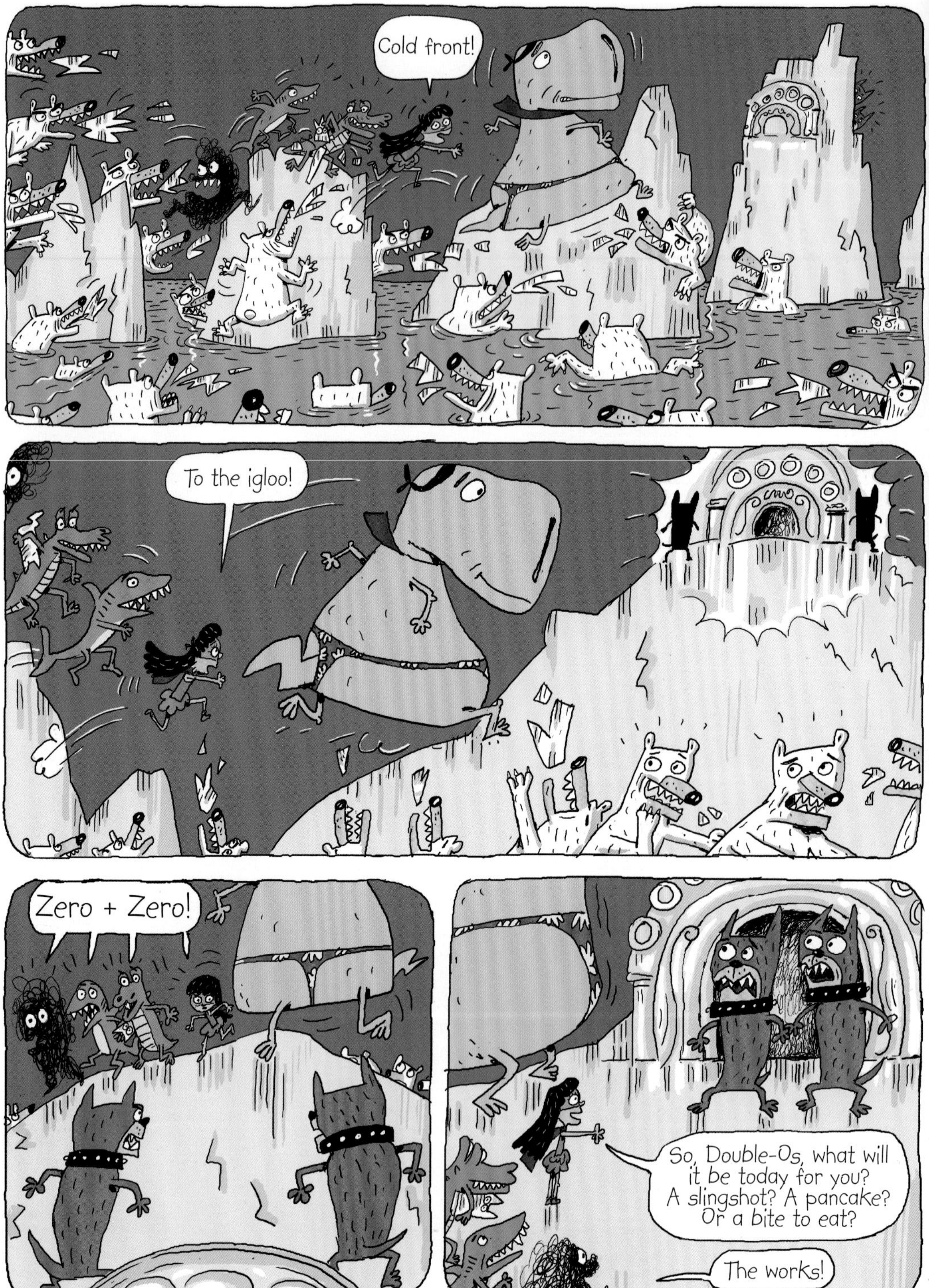
Cold front!
To the igloo!
Zero + Zero!
So, Double-Os, what will it be today for you? A slingshot? A pancake? Or a bite to eat?
The works!

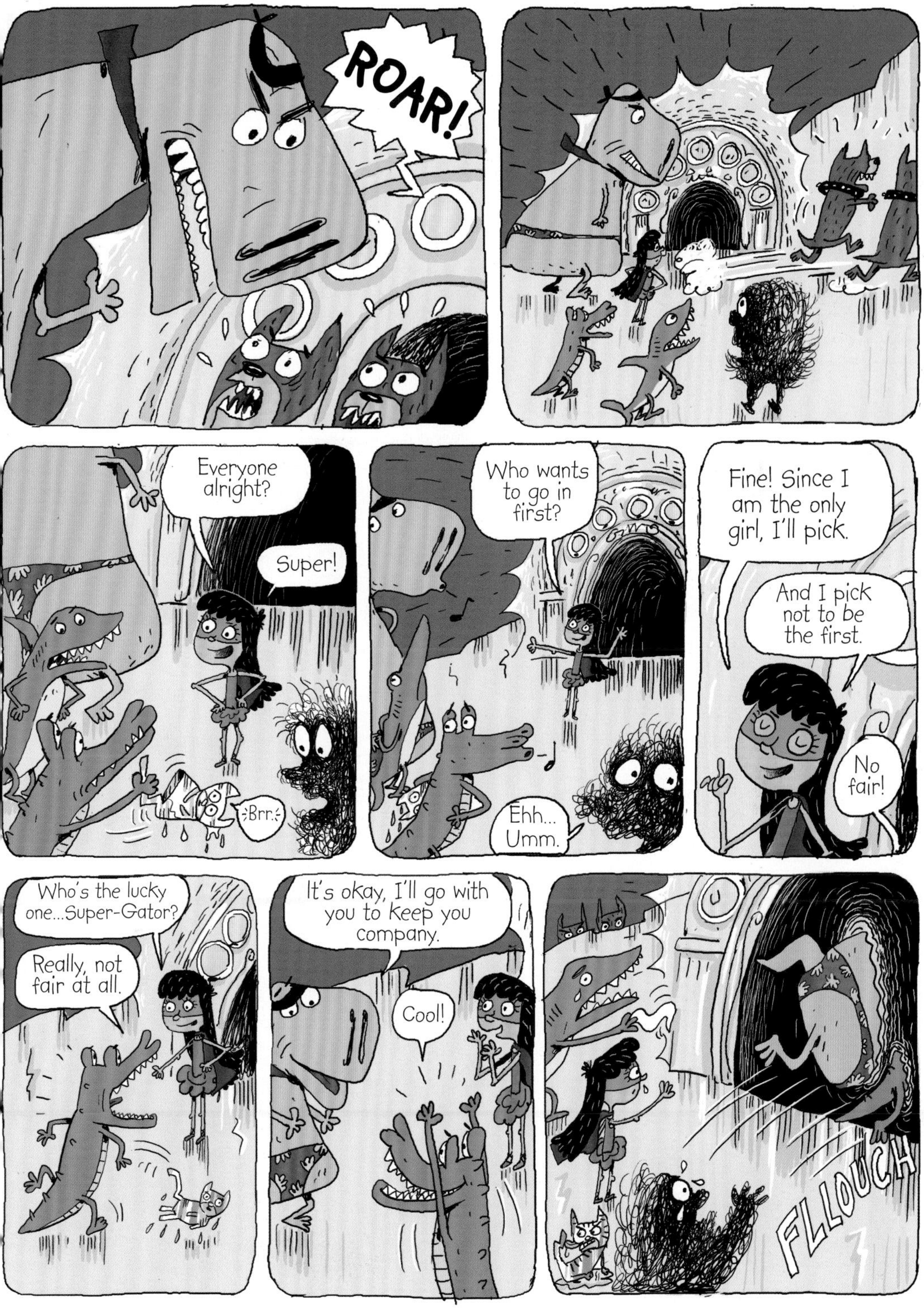
ROAR!
Everyone alright?
Super!
Brr.
Who wants to go in first?
Ehh... Umm.
Fine! Since I am the only girl, I'll pick.
And I pick not to be the first.
No fair!
Who's the lucky one...Super-Gator?
Really, not fair at all.
It's okay, I'll go with you to keep you company.
Cool!
FLLOUCH

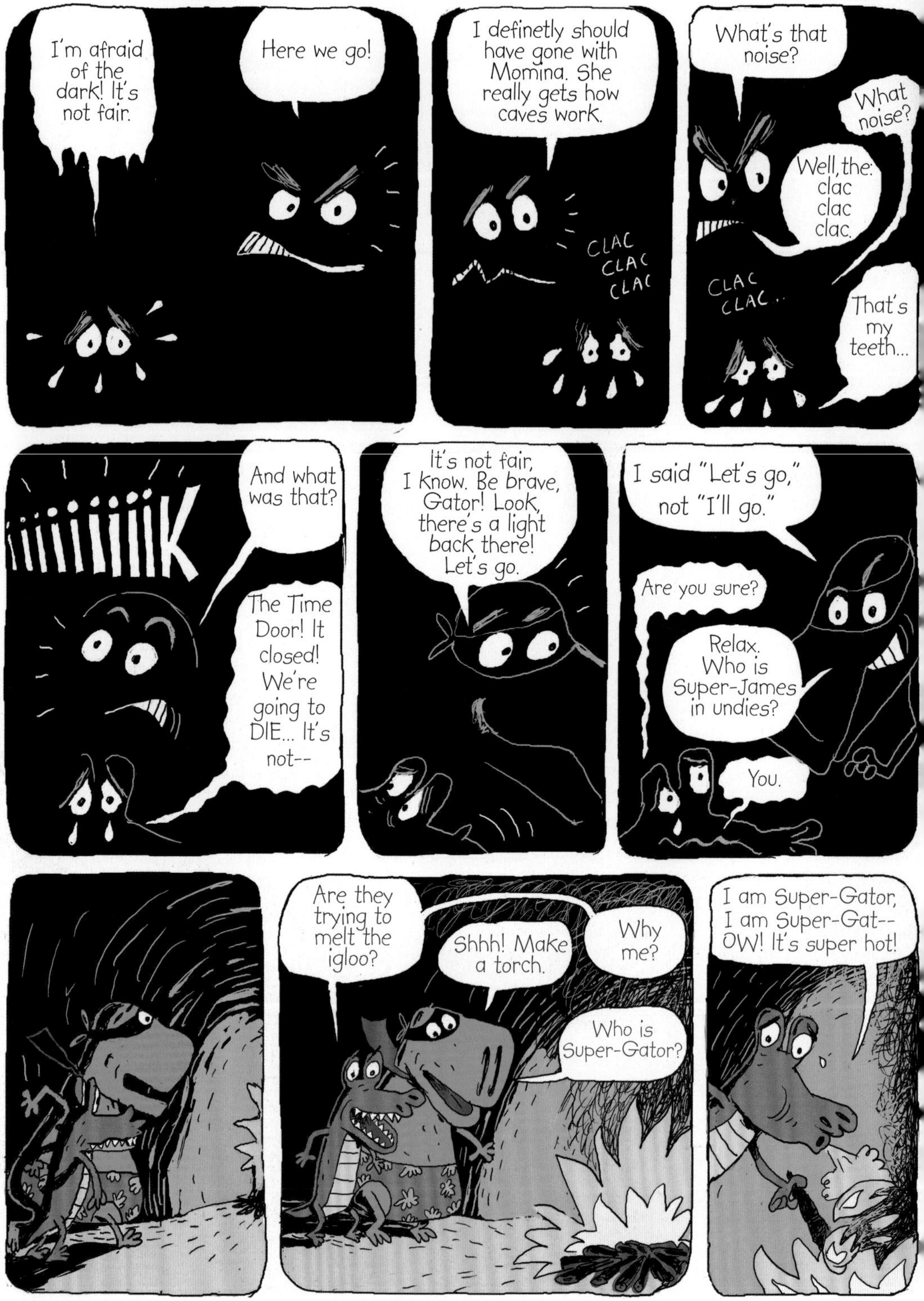

I'm afraid of the dark! It's not fair.
Here we go!
I definetly should have gone with Momina. She really gets how caves work.
CLAC CLAC CLAC
What's that noise?
What noise?
Well, the: clac clac clac.
CLAC CLAC...
That's my teeth...
iiiiiiiiiK
And what was that?
The Time Door! It closed! We're going to DIE... It's not--
It's not fair, I know. Be brave, Gator! Look, there's a light back there! Let's go.
I said "Let's go," not "I'll go."
Are you sure?
Relax. Who is Super-James in undies?
You.
Are they trying to melt the igloo?
Shhh! Make a torch.
Why me?
Who is Super-Gator?
I am Super-Gator, I am Super-Gat-- OW! It's super hot!

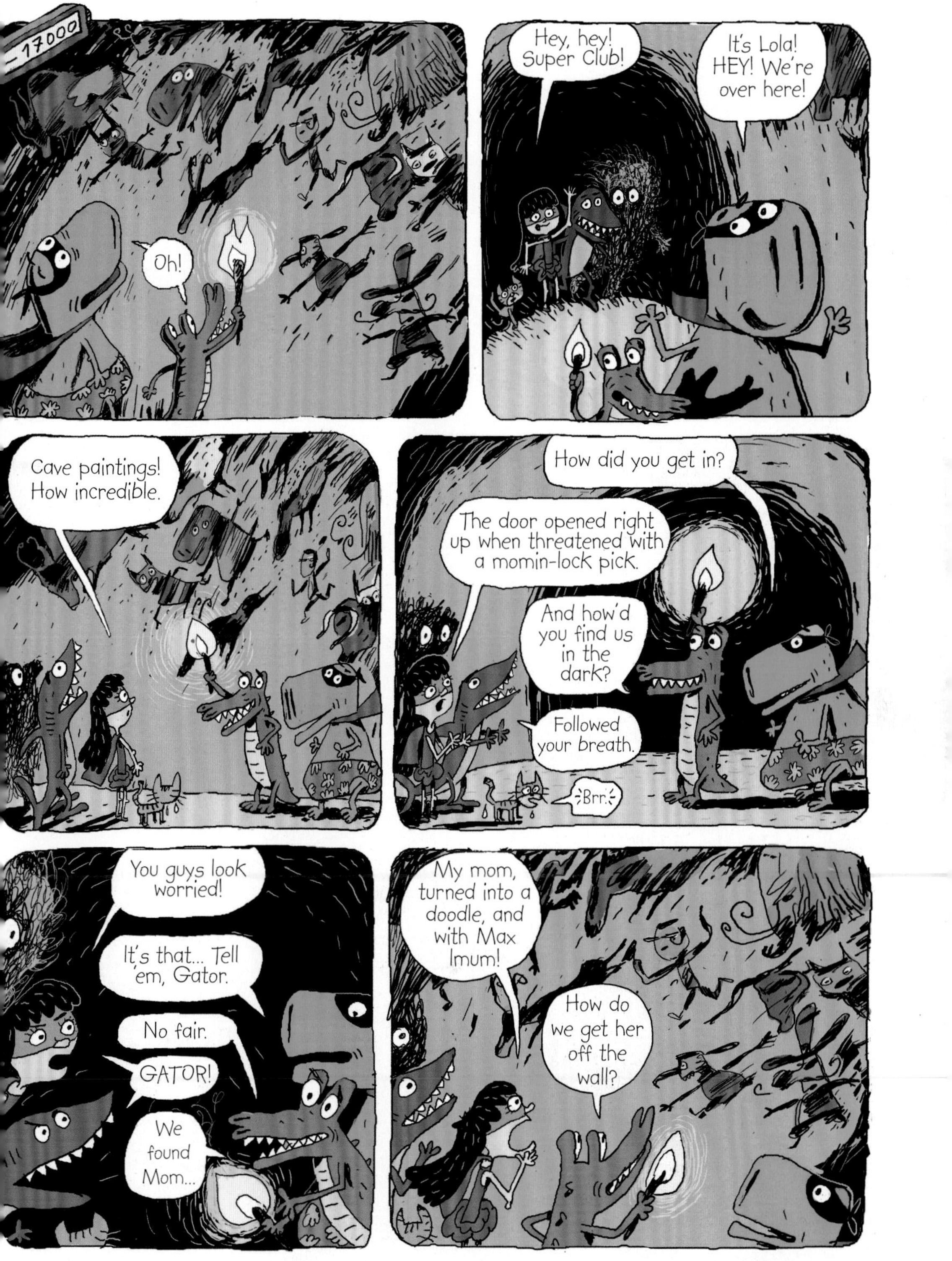
-17000
Oh!
Hey, hey! Super Club!
It's Lola! HEY! We're over here!
Cave paintings! How incredible.
How did you get in?
The door opened right up when threatened with a momin-lock pick.
And how'd you find us in the dark?
Followed your breath.
Brr.
You guys look worried!
It's that... Tell 'em, Gator.
No fair.
GATOR!
We found Mom...
My mom, turned into a doodle, and with Max Imum!
How do we get her off the wall?

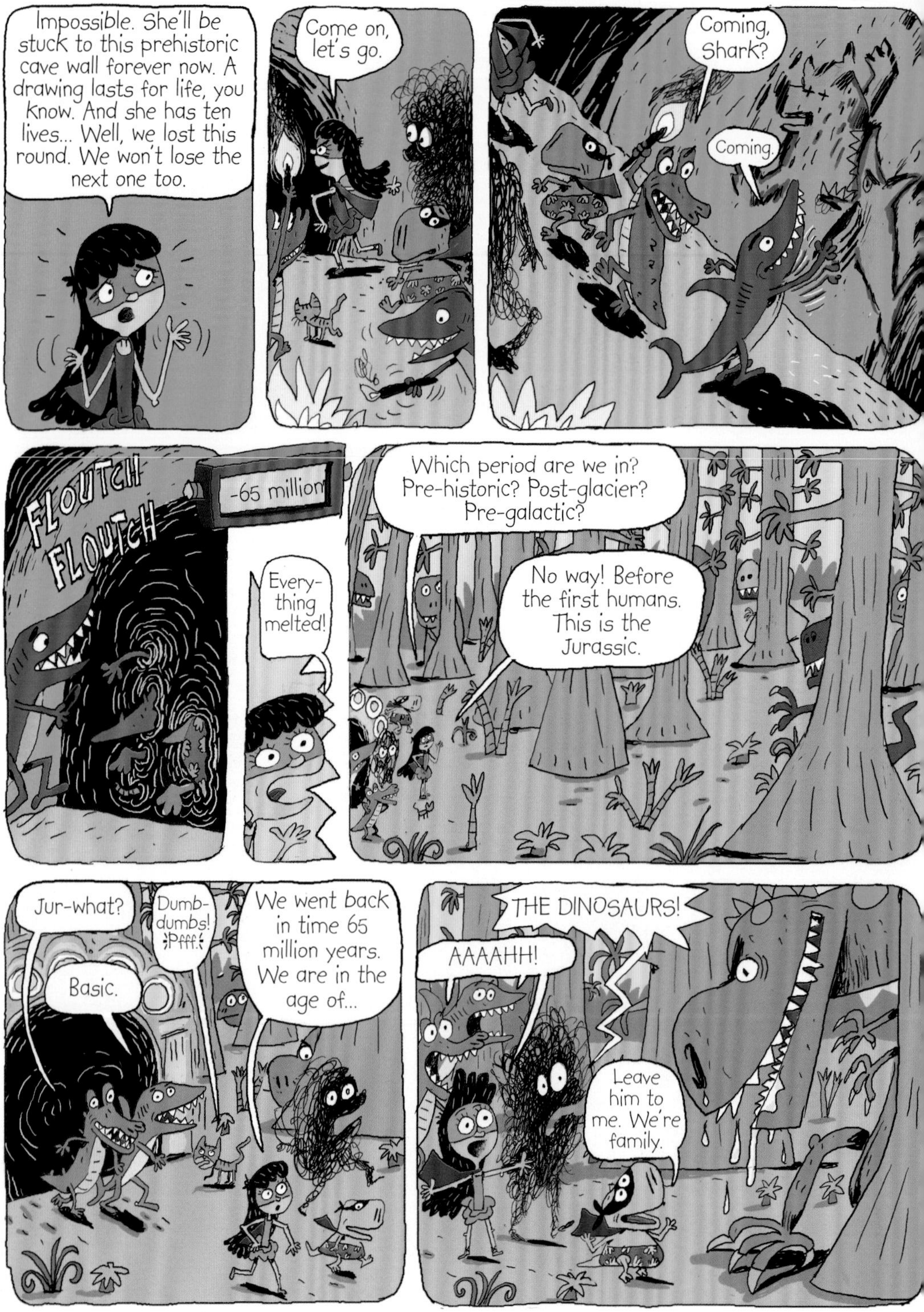

Impossible. She'll be stuck to this prehistoric cave wall forever now. A drawing lasts for life, you know. And she has ten lives... Well, we lost this round. We won't lose the next one too.
Come on, let's go.
Coming, Shark?
Coming.
FLOUTCH
FLOUTCH
-65 million
Every-thing melted!
Which period are we in? Pre-historic? Post-glacier? Pre-galactic?
No way! Before the first humans. This is the Jurassic.
Jur-what?
Basic.
Dumb-dumbs! Pfff.
We went back in time 65 million years. We are in the age of...
THE DINOSAURS!
AAAAHH!
Leave him to me. We're family.

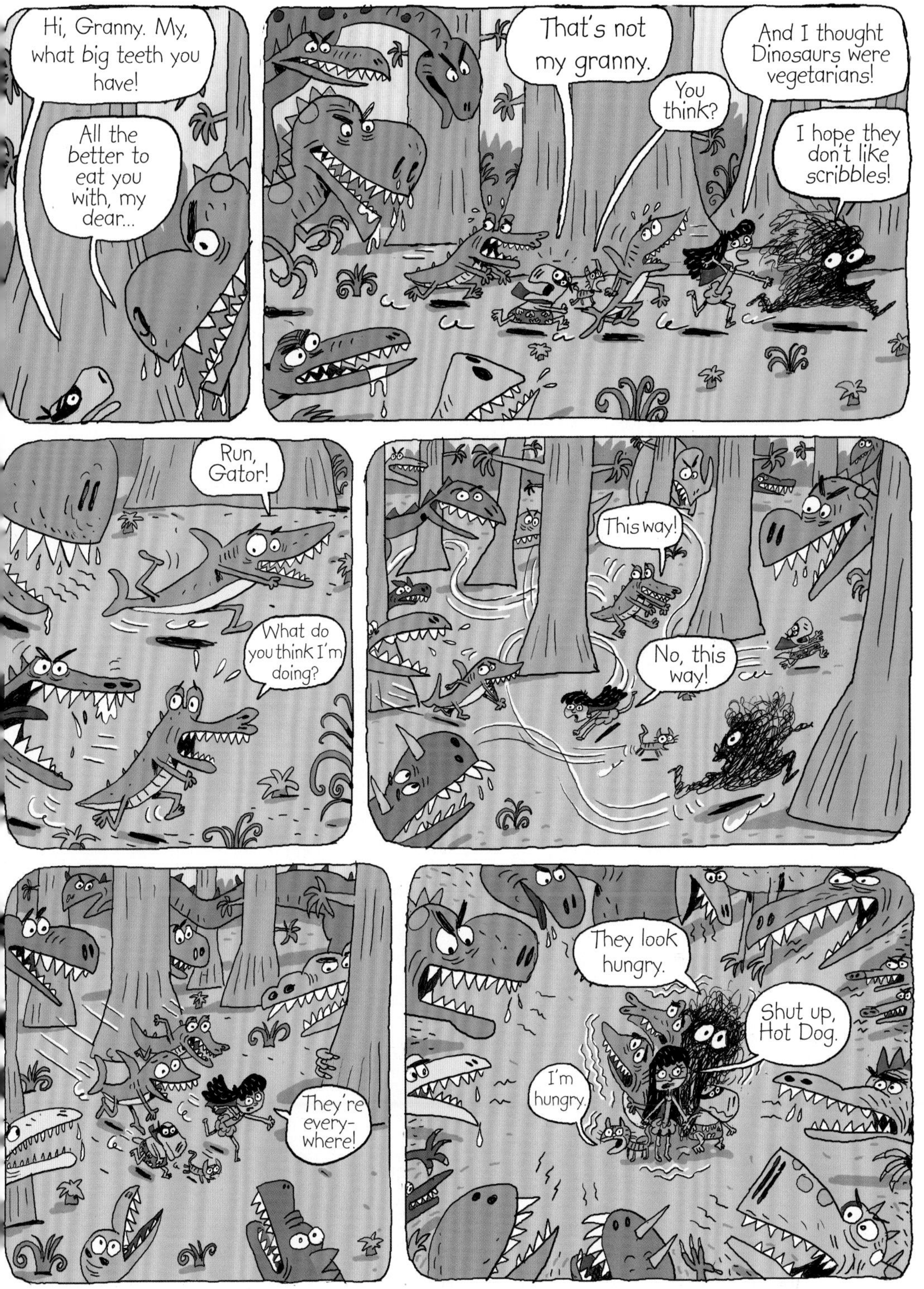
Hi, Granny. My, what big teeth you have!
All the better to eat you with, my dear...
That's not my granny.
You think?
And I thought Dinosaurs were vegetarians!
I hope they don't like scribbles!
Run, Gator!
What do you think I'm doing?
This way!
No, this way!
They're every-where!
They look hungry.
Shut up, Hot Dog.
I'm hungry.

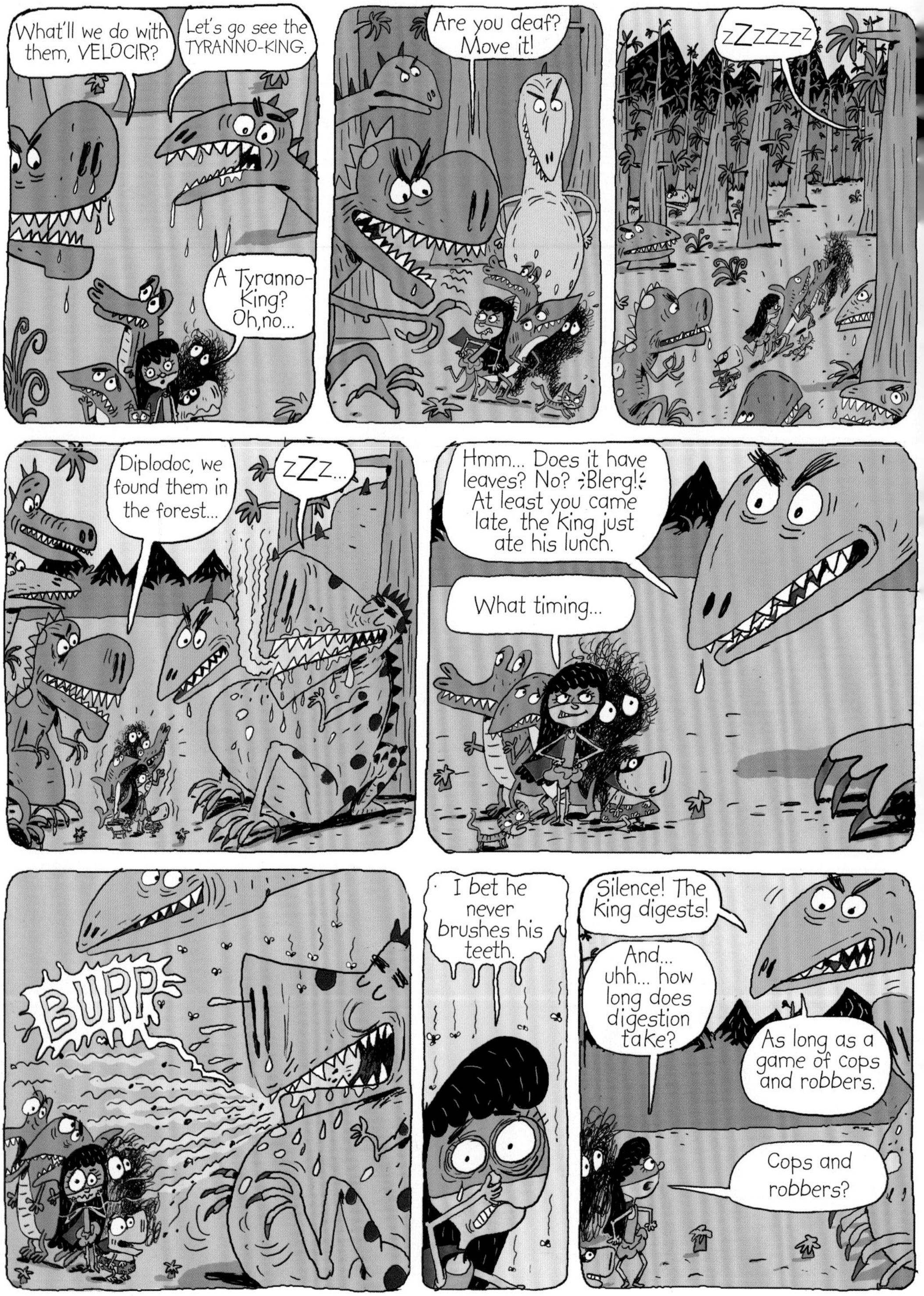
What'll we do with them, VELOCIR?
Let's go see the TYRANNO-KING.
A Tyranno-King? Oh, no...
Are you deaf? Move it!
zZZZZZZ
Diplodoc, we found them in the forest...
zZZ...
Hmm... Does it have leaves? No? Blerg! At least you came late, the King just ate his lunch.
What timing...
BURP
I bet he never brushes his teeth.
Silence! The King digests!
And... uhh... how long does digestion take?
As long as a game of cops and robbers.
Cops and robbers?

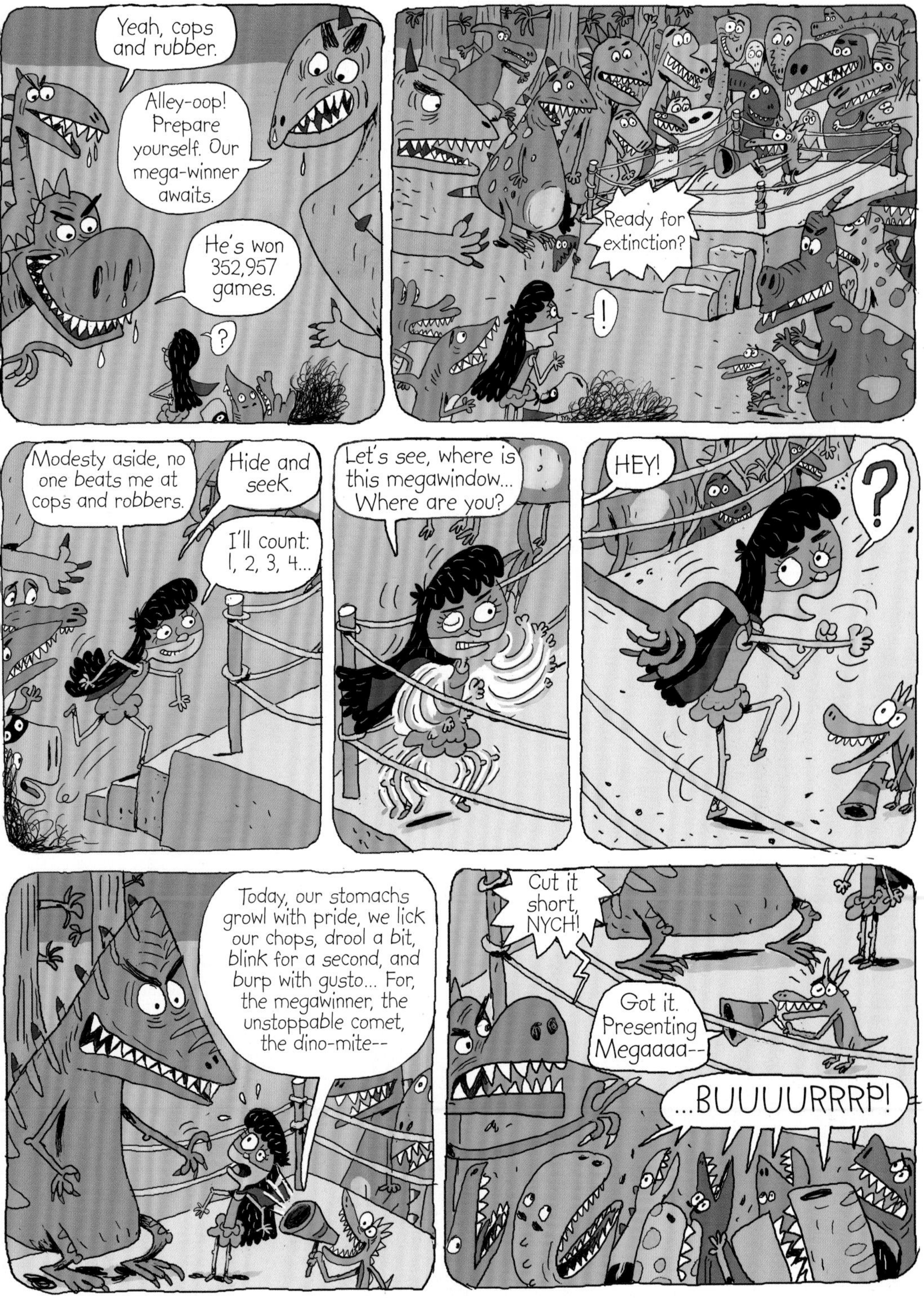

Yeah, cops and rubber.
Alley-oop! Prepare yourself. Our mega-winner awaits.
He's won 352,957 games.
?
Ready for extinction?
!
Modesty aside, no one beats me at cops and robbers.
Hide and seek.
I'll count: 1, 2, 3, 4...
Let's see, where is this megawindow... Where are you?
HEY!
?
Today, our stomachs growl with pride, we lick our chops, drool a bit, blink for a second, and burp with gusto... For, the megawinner, the unstoppable comet, the dino-mite--
Cut it short, NYCH!
Got it. Presenting Megaaaa--
...BUUUURRRP!

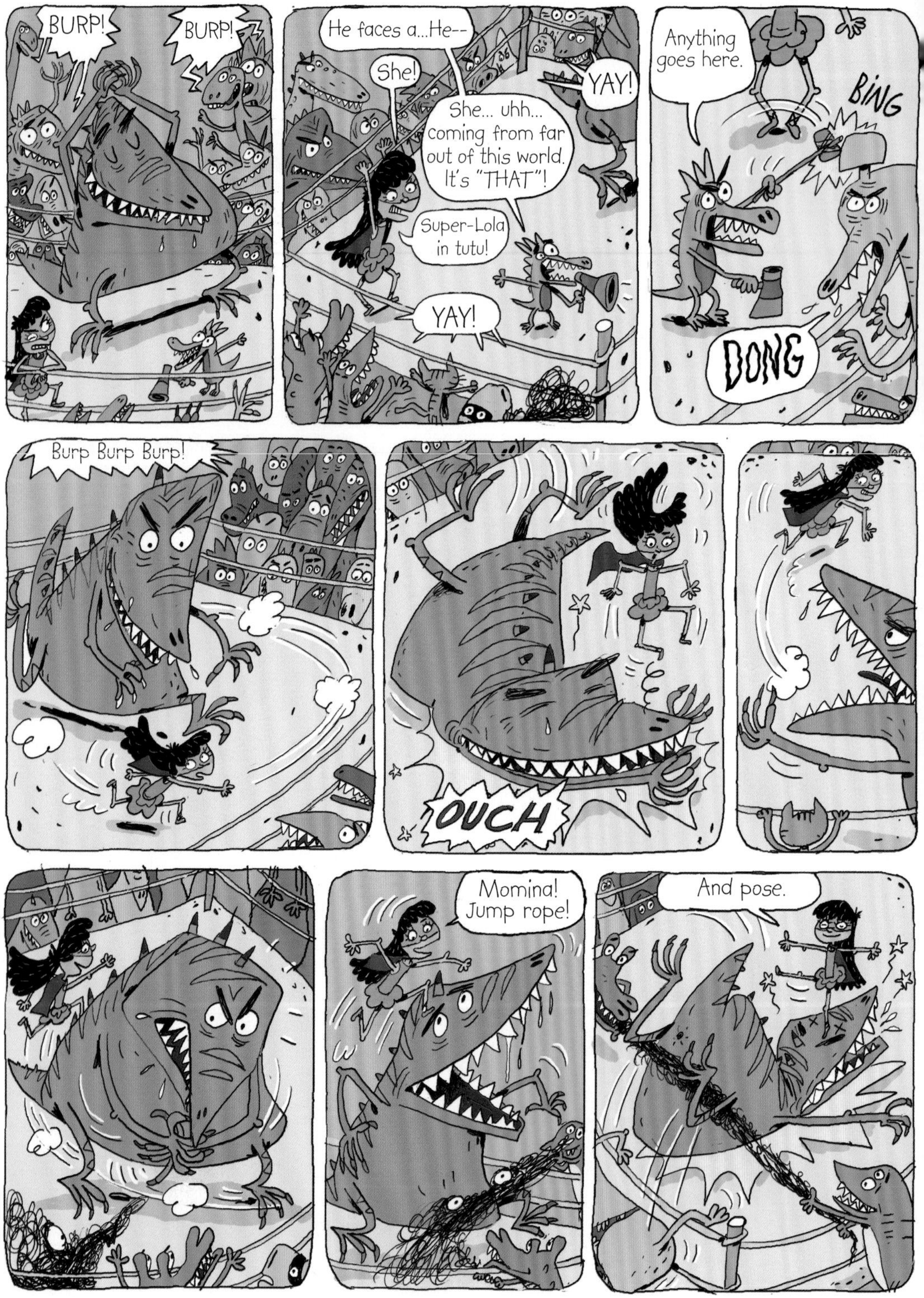
BURP!
BURP!
He faces a...He--
She!
She... uhh... coming from far out of this world. It's "THAT"!
Super-Lola in tutu!
YAY!
YAY!
Anything goes here.
BING
DONG
Burp Burp Burp!
OUCH
Momina! Jump rope!
And pose.

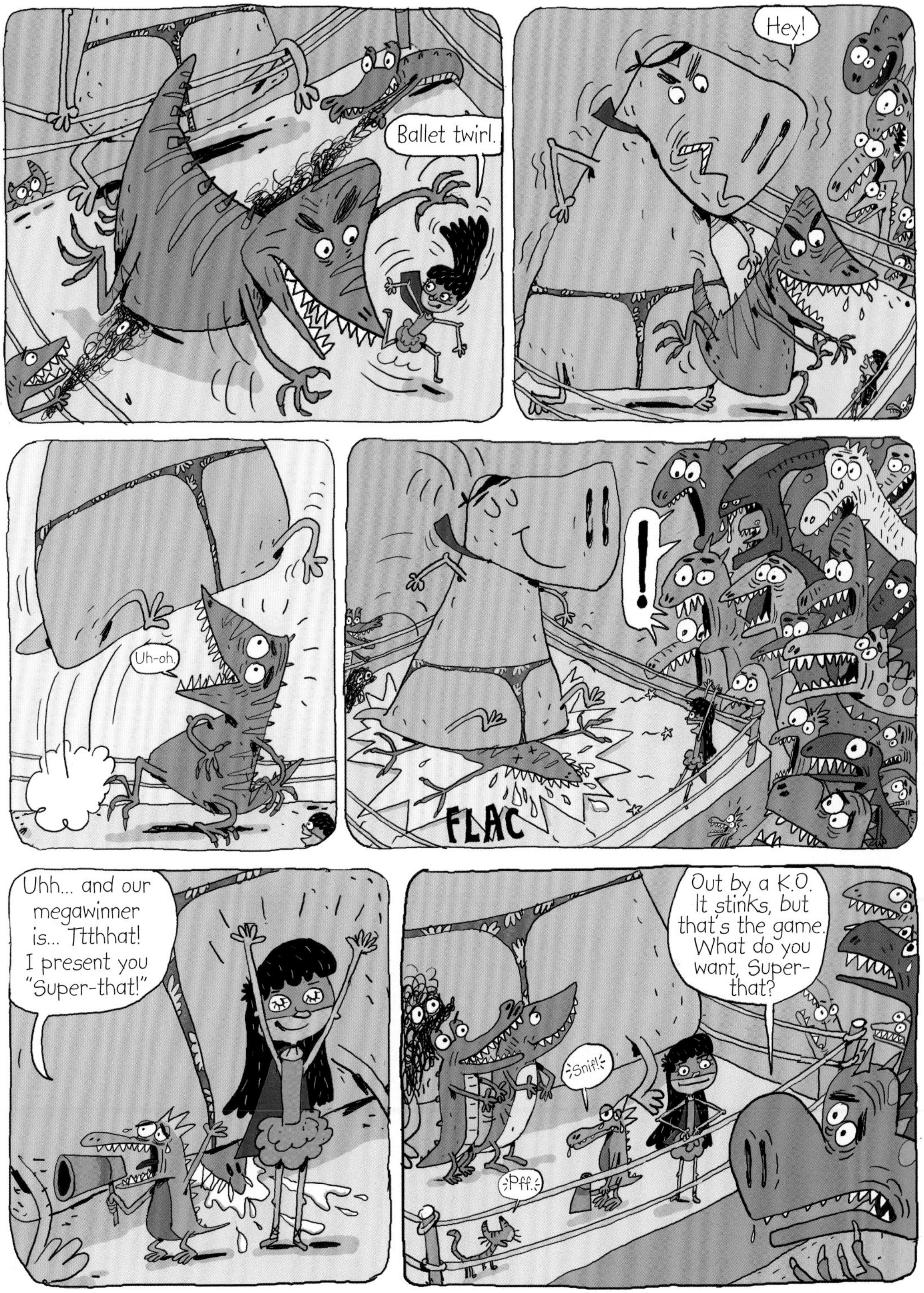
Ballet twirl.
Hey!
Uh-oh.
!
FLAC
Uhh... and our megawinner is... Ttthhat! I present you "Super-that!"
Out by a K.O. It stinks, but that's the game. What do you want, Super-that?
Snif!
Pff.

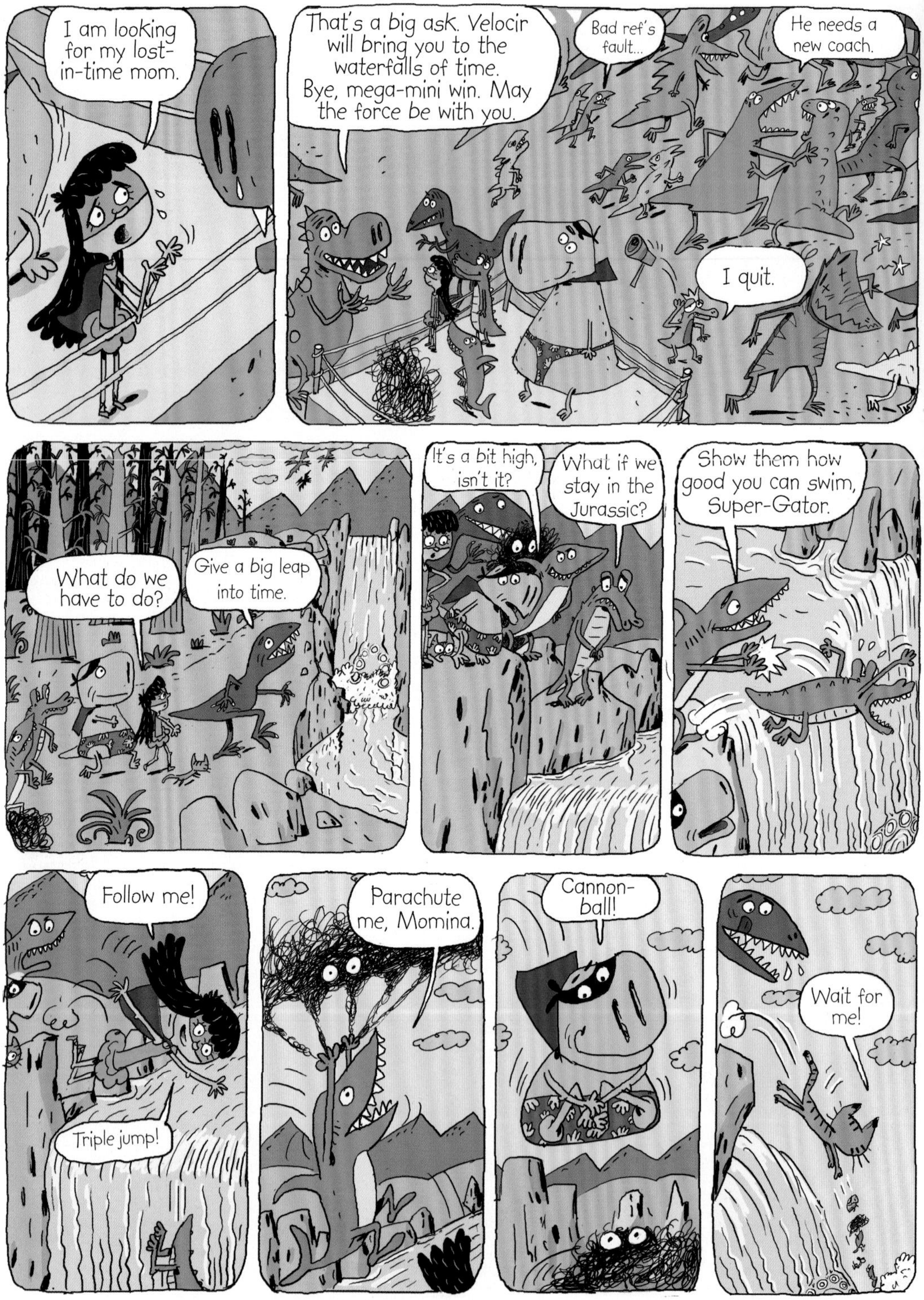
I am looking for my lost-in-time mom.
That's a big ask. Velocir will bring you to the waterfalls of time. Bye, mega-mini win. May the force be with you.
Bad ref's fault...
He needs a new coach.
I quit.
What do we have to do?
Give a big leap into time.
It's a bit high, isn't it?
What if we stay in the Jurassic?
Show them how good you can swim, Super-Gator.
Follow me!
Triple jump!
Parachute me, Momina.
Cannon-ball!
Wait for me!

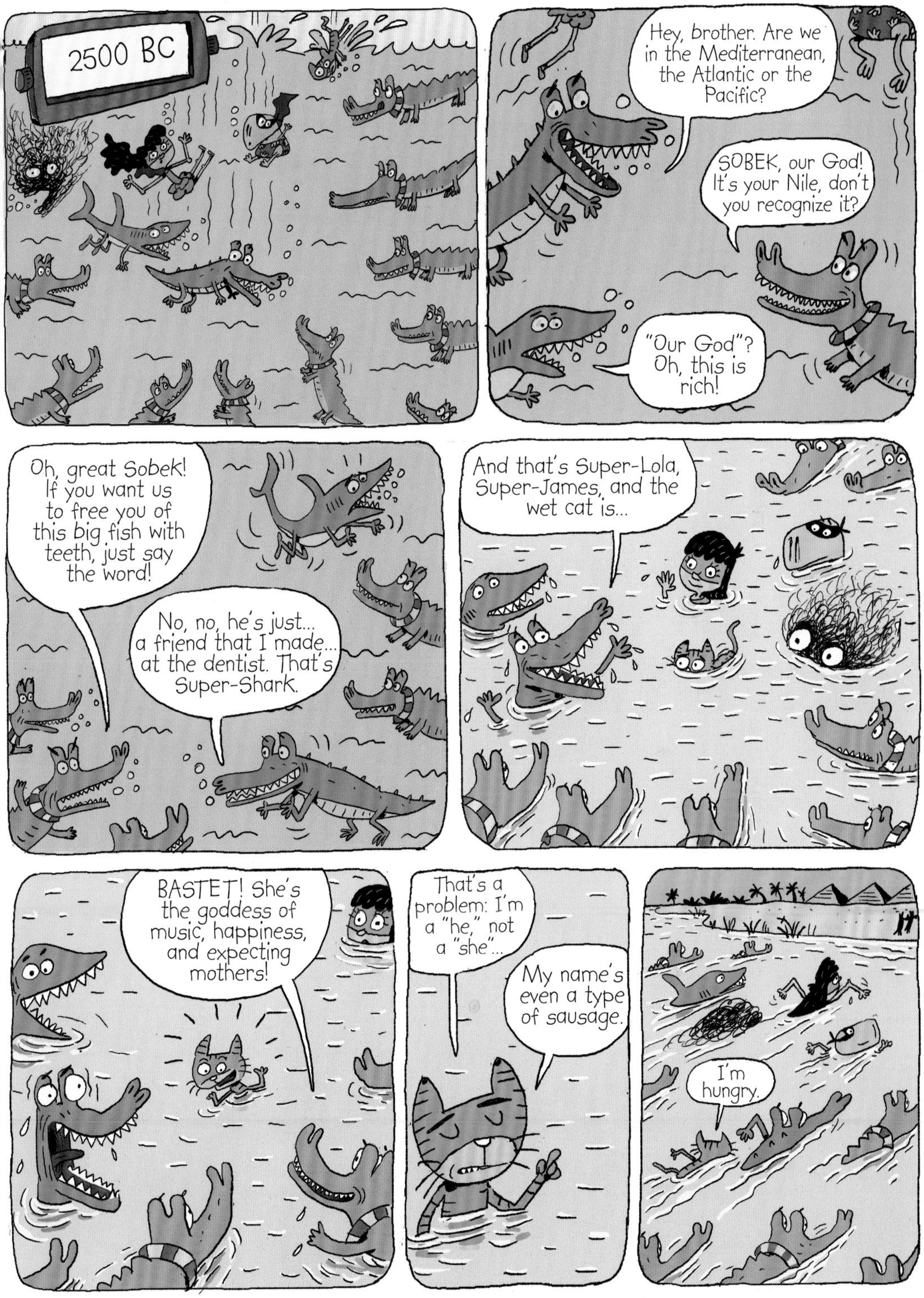
2500 BC
Hey, brother. Are we in the Mediterranean, the Atlantic or the Pacific?
SOBEK, our God! It's your Nile, don't you recognize it?
"Our God"? Oh, this is rich!
Oh, great Sobek! If you want us to free you of this big fish with teeth, just say the word!
No, no, he's just... a friend that I made... at the dentist. That's Super-Shark.
And that's Super-Lola, Super-James, and the wet cat is...
BASTET! She's the goddess of music, happiness, and expecting mothers!
That's a problem: I'm a "he," not a "she"...
My name's even a type of sausage.
I'm hungry.

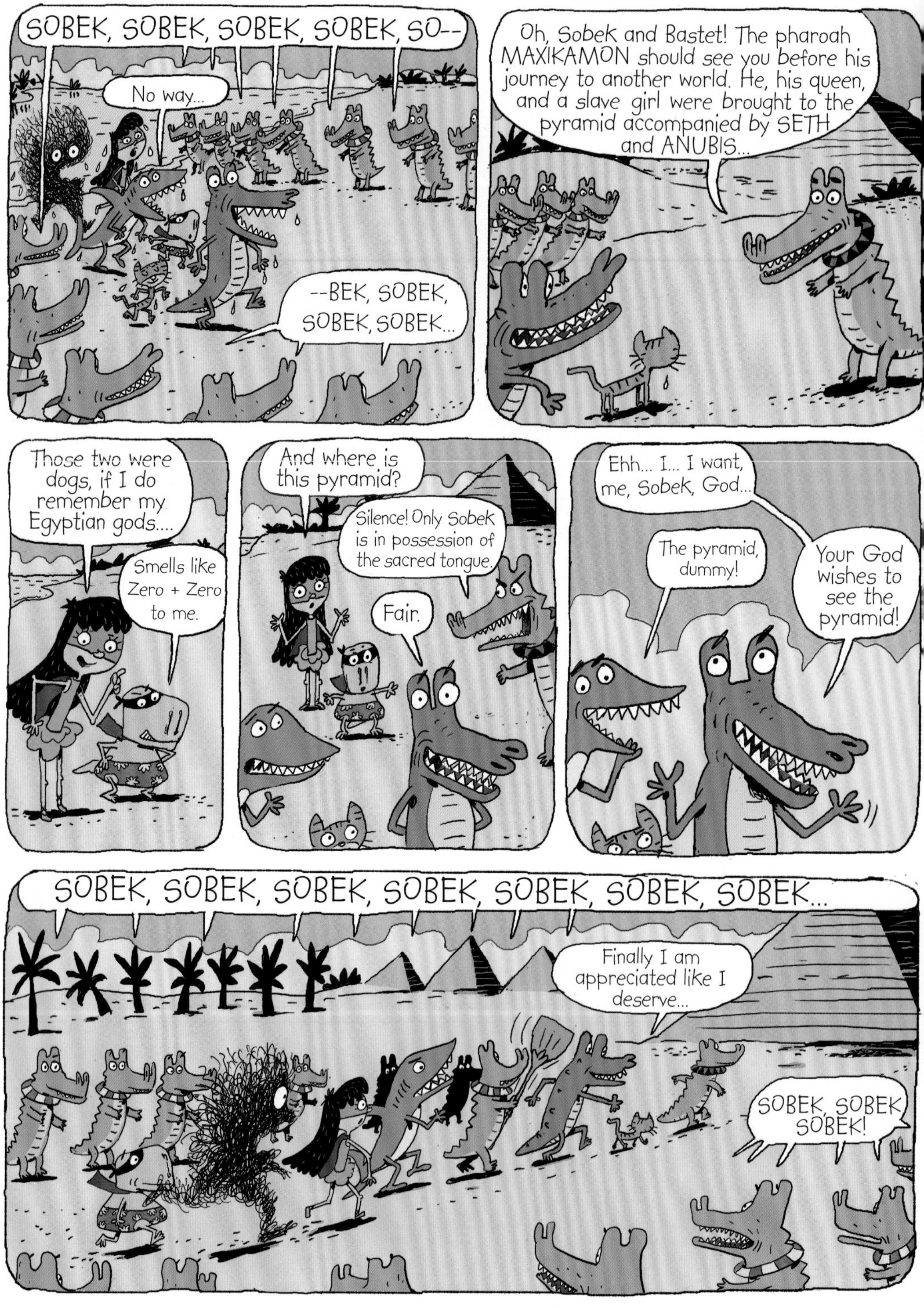
SOBEK, SOBEK, SOBEK, SOBEK, SO--
No way...
--BEK, SOBEK, SOBEK, SOBEK...
Oh, Sobek and Bastet! The pharoah MAXIKAMON should see you before his journey to another world. He, his queen, and a slave girl were brought to the pyramid accompanied by SETH and ANUBIS...
Those two were dogs, if I do remember my Egyptian gods....
Smells like Zero + Zero to me.
And where is this pyramid?
Silence! Only Sobek is in possession of the sacred tongue.
Fair.
Ehh... I... I want, me, Sobek, God...
The pyramid, dummy!
Your God wishes to see the pyramid!
SOBEK, SOBEK, SOBEK, SOBEK, SOBEK, SOBEK, SOBEK...
Finally I am appreciated like I deserve...
SOBEK, SOBEK SOBEK!

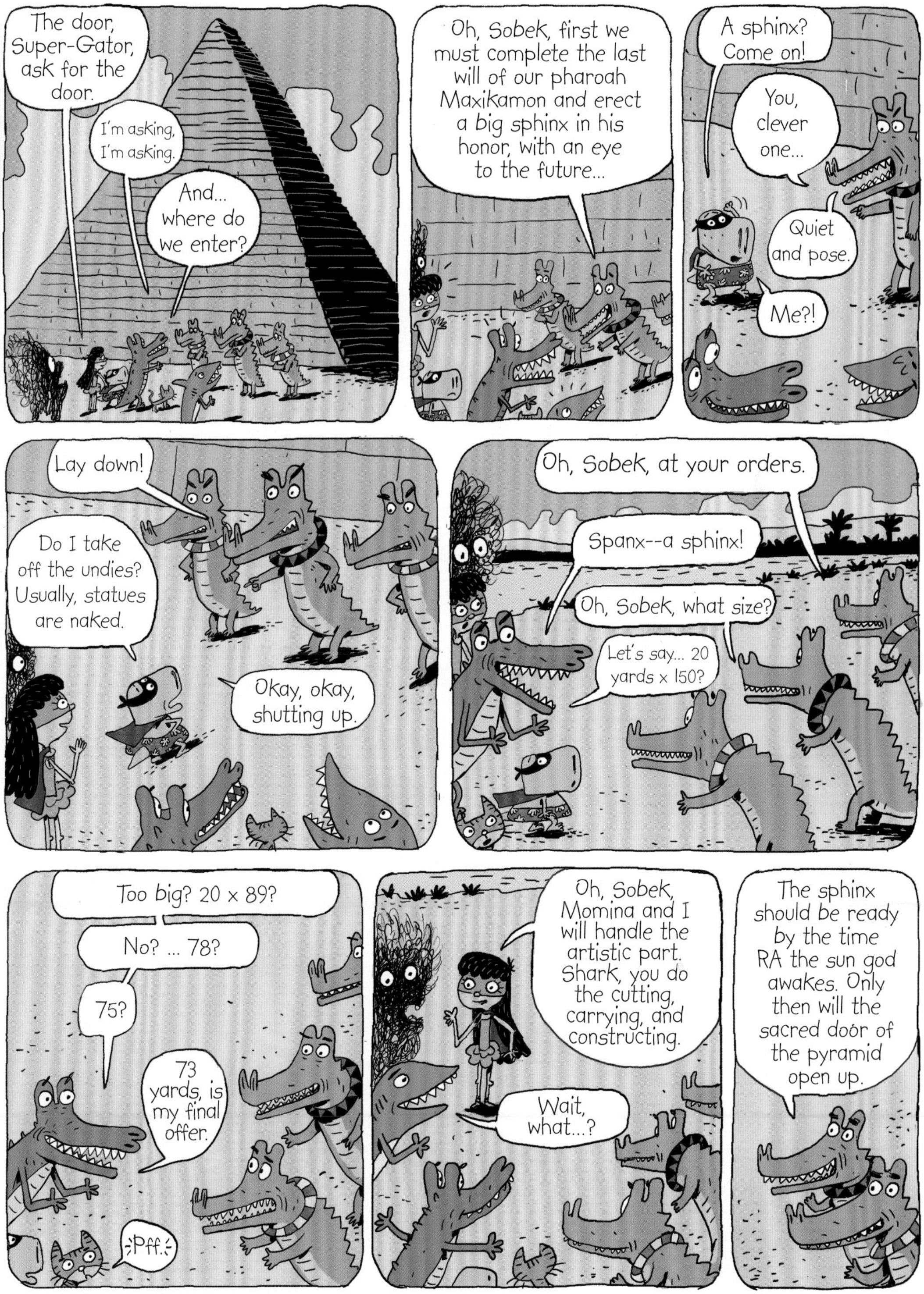
The door, Super-Gator, ask for the door.
I'm asking, I'm asking.
And... where do we enter?
Oh, Sobek, first we must complete the last will of our pharoah Maxikamon and erect a big sphinx in his honor, with an eye to the future...
A sphinx? Come on!
You, clever one...
Quiet and pose.
Me?!
Lay down!
Do I take off the undies? Usually, statues are naked.
Okay, okay, shutting up.
Oh, Sobek, at your orders.
Spanx--a sphinx!
Oh, Sobek, what size?
Let's say... 20 yards x 150?
Too big? 20 x 89?
No? ... 78?
75?
73 yards, is my final offer.
Pff.
Oh, Sobek, Momina and I will handle the artistic part. Shark, you do the cutting, carrying, and constructing.
Wait, what...?
The sphinx should be ready by the time RA the sun god awakes. Only then will the sacred door of the pyramid open up.

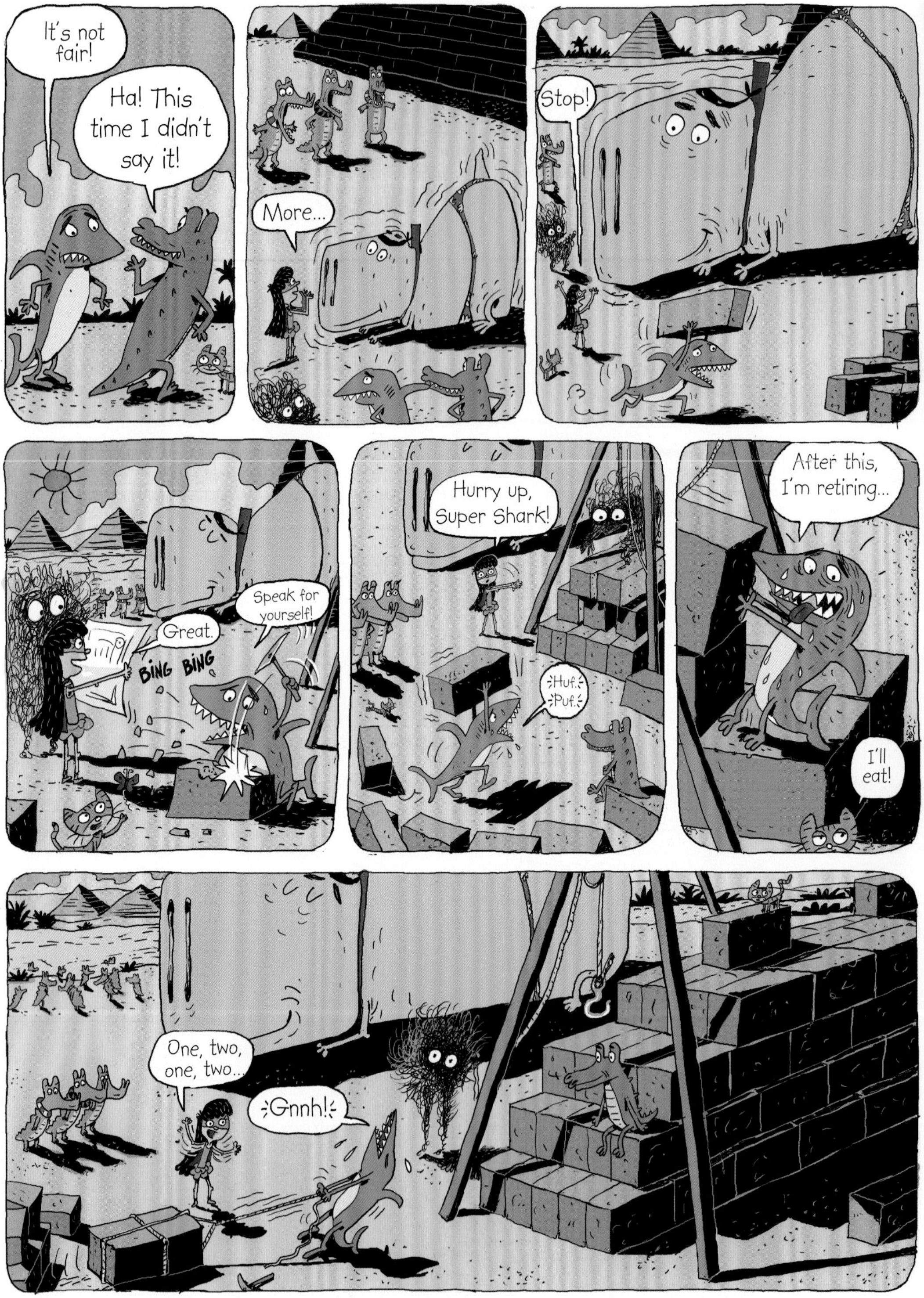
It's not fair!
Ha! This time I didn't say it!
More...
Stop!
Great.
BING BING
Speak for yourself!
Hurry up, Super Shark!
Huf. Puf.
After this, I'm retiring...
I'll eat!
One, two, one, two...
Gnnh!

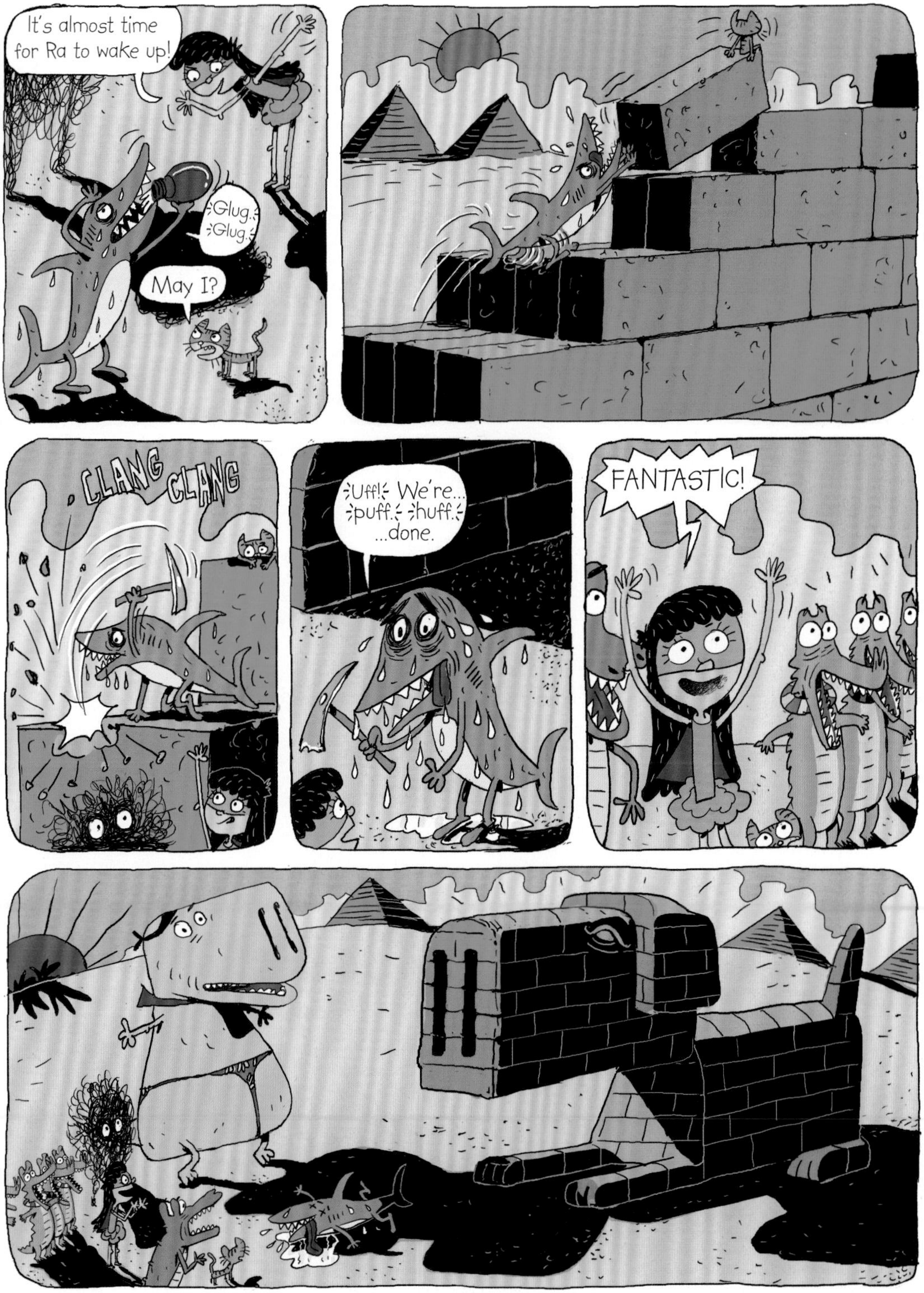

It's almost time for Ra to wake up!
Glug. Glug.
May I?
CLANG CLANG
Uff! We're... puff. huff. ...done.
FANTASTIC!

Oh, Sobek, do you hear the faint rumbles? That is the divine slumber of Ra. It is time! Follow me!

RRRRRRRRRRRRRR RRRRRRRRRRR

RRRRRRRRRRRRRRRRRR

CLAC

Oh, Sobek, be careful. There are 333 steps to the vault of the pharoah and his queen. It is a bad omen to skip even one.

110, 111, 112, 113...

334... 334?! It's not fair!

Any problem, Oh, Sobek?

Nnno.

Well then, let's continue...

76

Well, well, well, look who we've found.

Some respect? I'm the god of death!

Yeah. And respect the god of war too...

Jackals!

Oh, Sobek, Maxikamon and his queen are ready for their big trip.

Mom!

Mummy!

Give them the go ahead, we've got this.

Okay, got it.

Godly, Sobek.

?

BRRRRR

But... But... the... py-py... the-the pyra... The pyra-ra... The pyramid is... Ah, mo... moo.. ah! Moving. The pyramid is tumbling down! We're toast... I'll die hungry!

BRRRRR

BRRRRRRRRRRRRRBRRRRRRRRRBRRRRRRRRRR

...rats! Take cover, Supers!

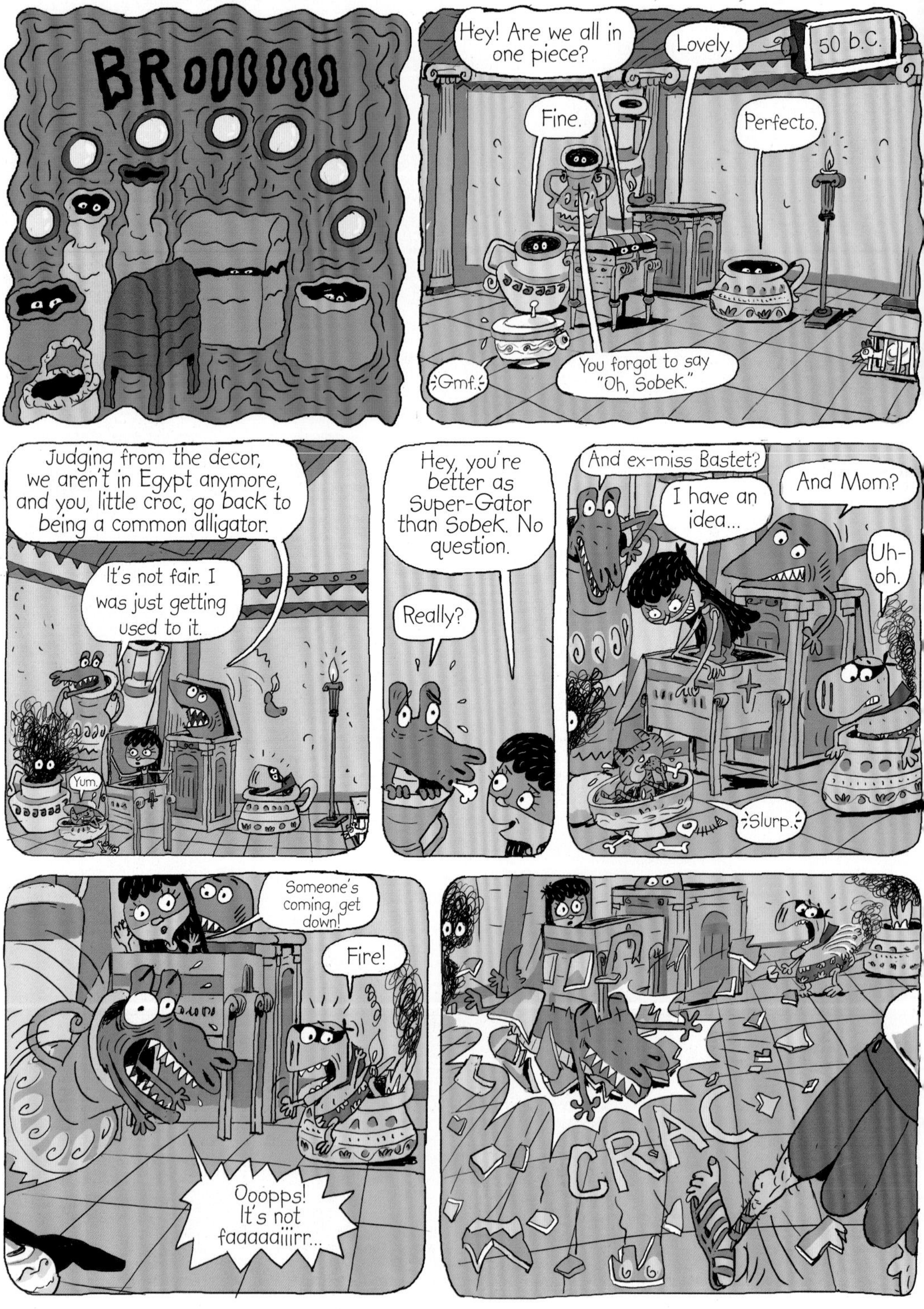
BROOOOOO
Hey! Are we all in one piece?
Lovely.
50 b.C.
Fine.
Perfecto.
Gmf.
You forgot to say "Oh, Sobek."
Judging from the decor, we aren't in Egypt anymore, and you, little croc, go back to being a common alligator.
It's not fair. I was just getting used to it.
Yum.
Hey, you're better as Super-Gator than Sobek. No question.
Really?
And ex-miss Bastet?
I have an idea...
And Mom?
Uh-oh.
Slurp.
Someone's coming, get down!
Fire!
Ooopps! It's not faaaaaiiirr...
CRAC

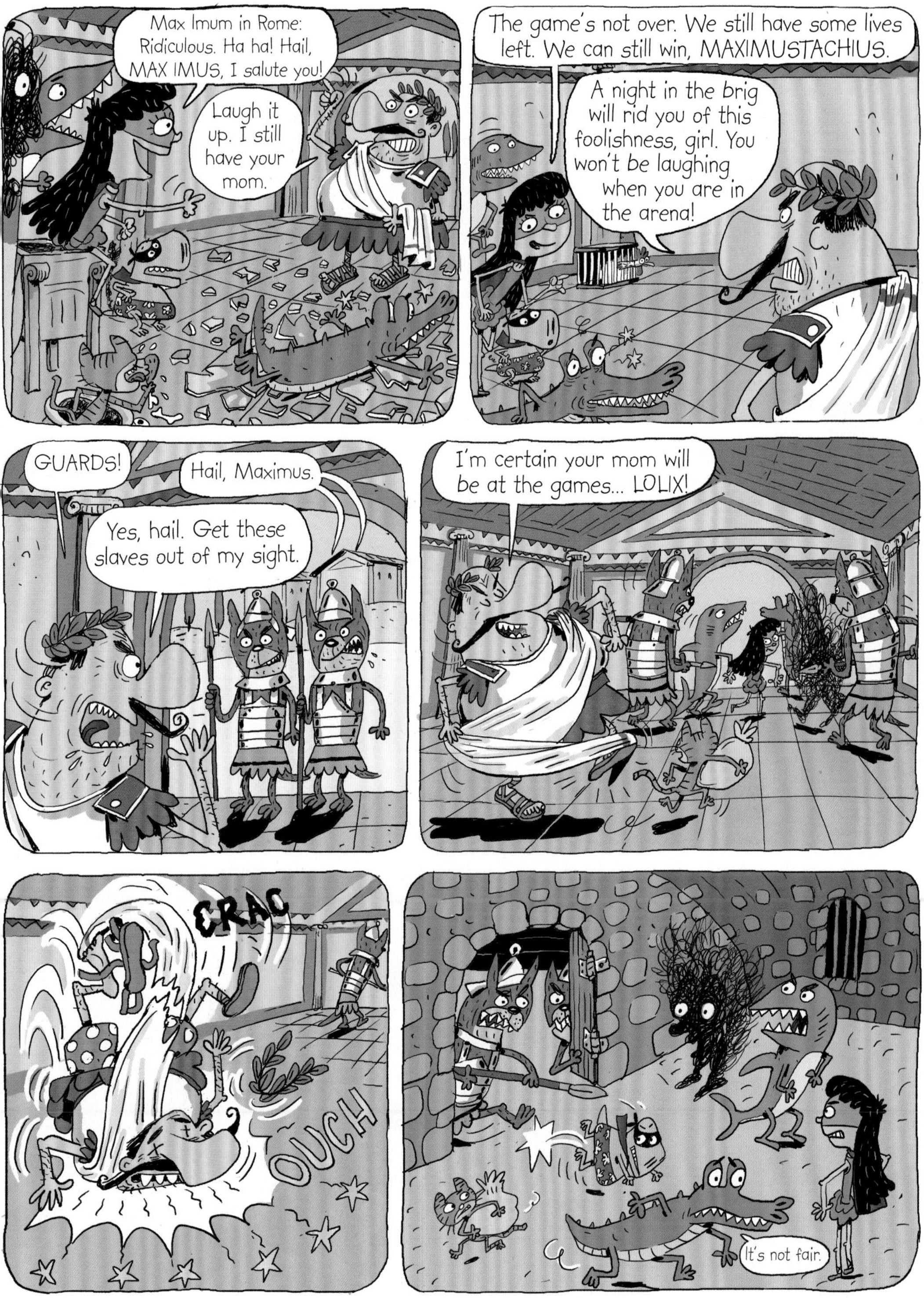

Max Imum in Rome: Ridiculous. Ha ha! Hail, MAX IMUS, I salute you!
Laugh it up. I still have your mom.
The game's not over. We still have some lives left. We can still win, MAXIMUSTACHIUS.
A night in the brig will rid you of this foolishness, girl. You won't be laughing when you are in the arena!
GUARDS!
Hail, Maximus.
Yes, hail. Get these slaves out of my sight.
I'm certain your mom will be at the games... LOLIX!
CRAC
OUCH
It's not fair.

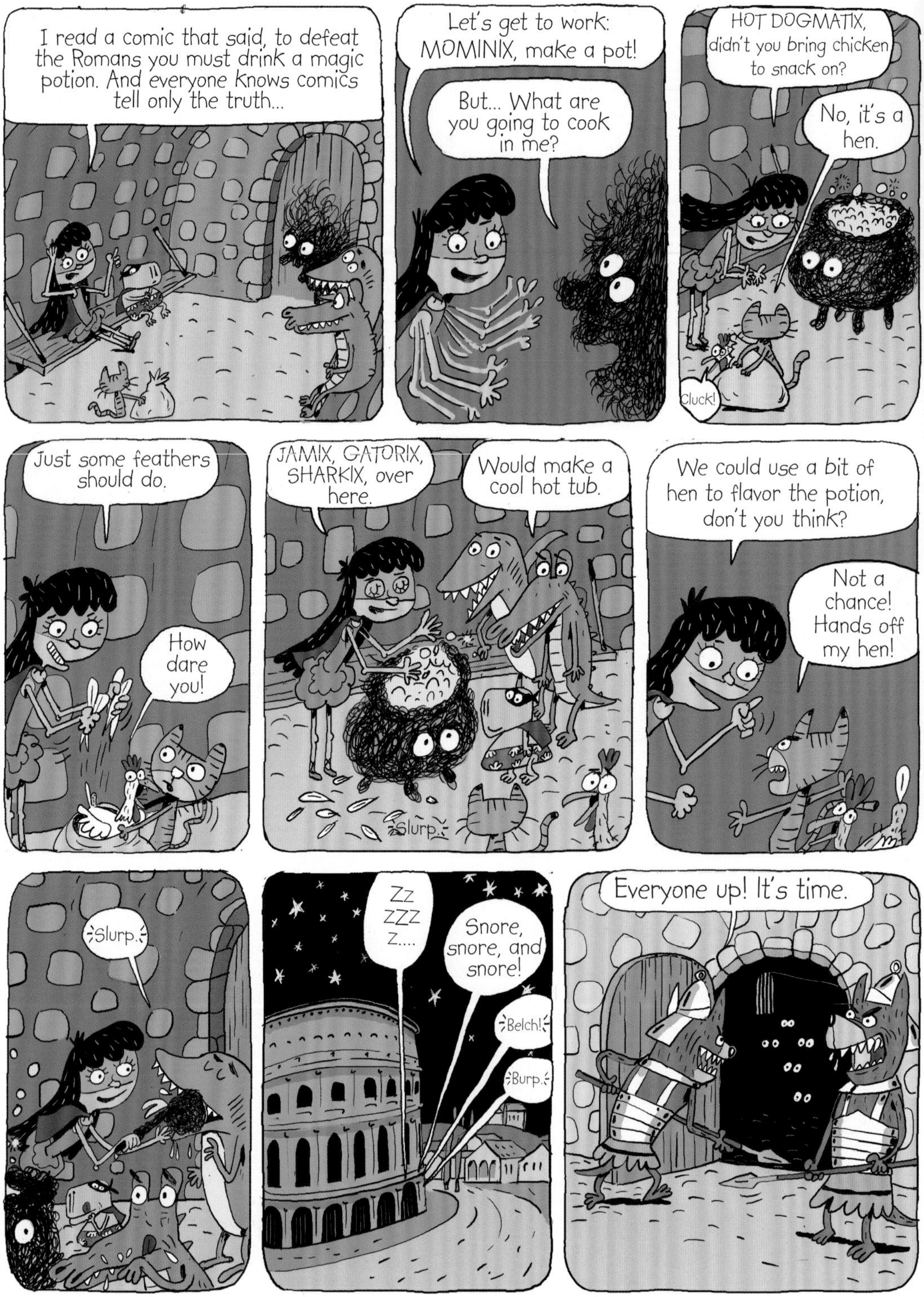
I read a comic that said, to defeat the Romans you must drink a magic potion. And everyone knows comics tell only the truth...
Let's get to work: MOMINIX, make a pot!
But... What are you going to cook in me?
HOT DOGMATIX, didn't you bring chicken to snack on?
No, it's a hen.
Cluck!
Just some feathers should do.
How dare you!
JAMIX, GATORIX, SHARKIX, over here.
Would make a cool hot tub.
Slurp
We could use a bit of hen to flavor the potion, don't you think?
Not a chance! Hands off my hen!
!
Slurp.
Zz
ZZZ
Z....
Snore, snore, and snore!
Belch!
Burp.
Everyone up! It's time.

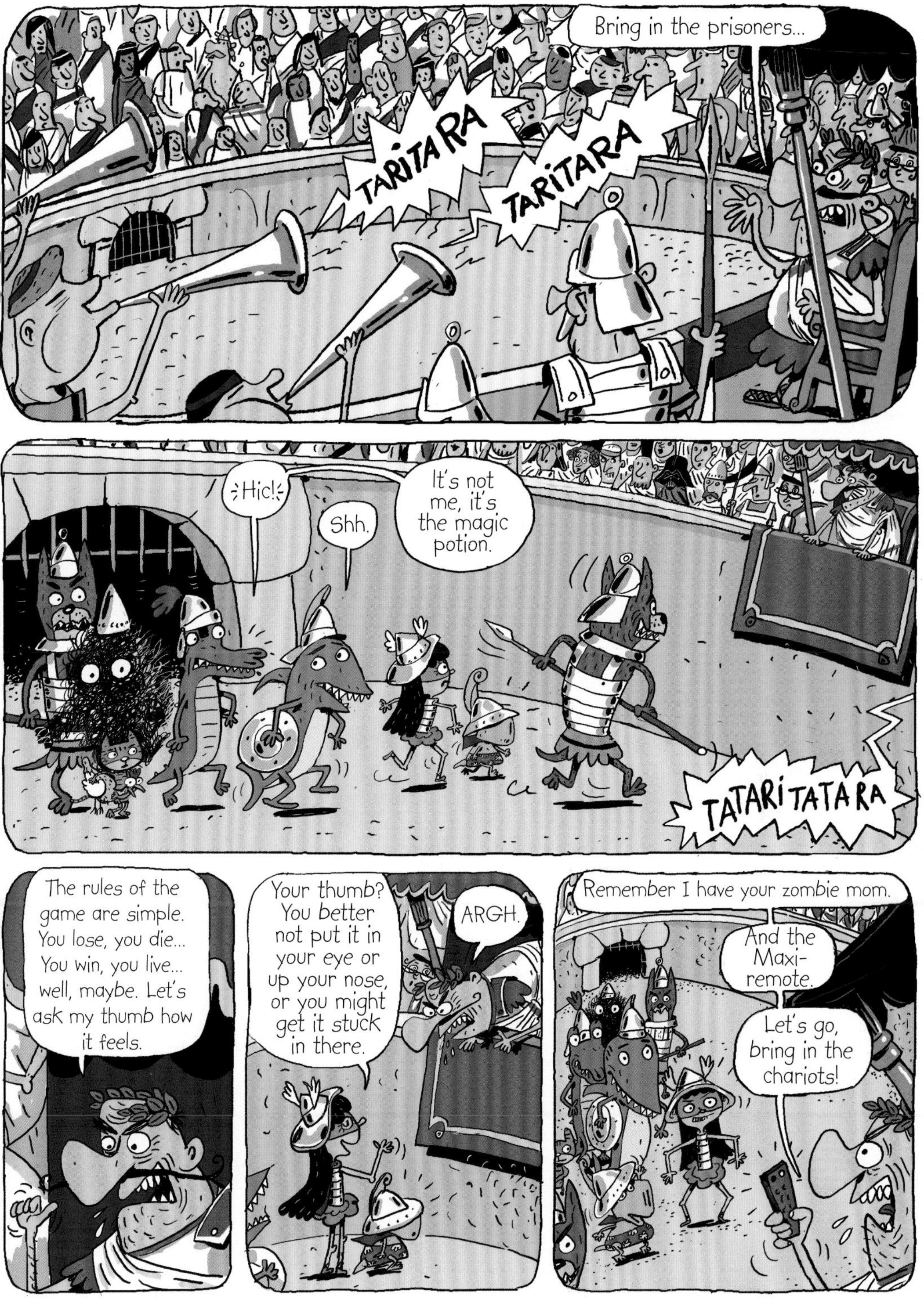
Bring in the prisoners...
TARITARA
TARITARA
Hic!
Shh.
It's not me, it's the magic potion.
TATARITATARA
The rules of the game are simple. You lose, you die... You win, you live... well, maybe. Let's ask my thumb how it feels.
Your thumb? You better not put it in your eye or up your nose, or you might get it stuck in there.
ARGH.
Remember I have your zombie mom.
And the Maxi-remote.
Let's go, bring in the chariots!

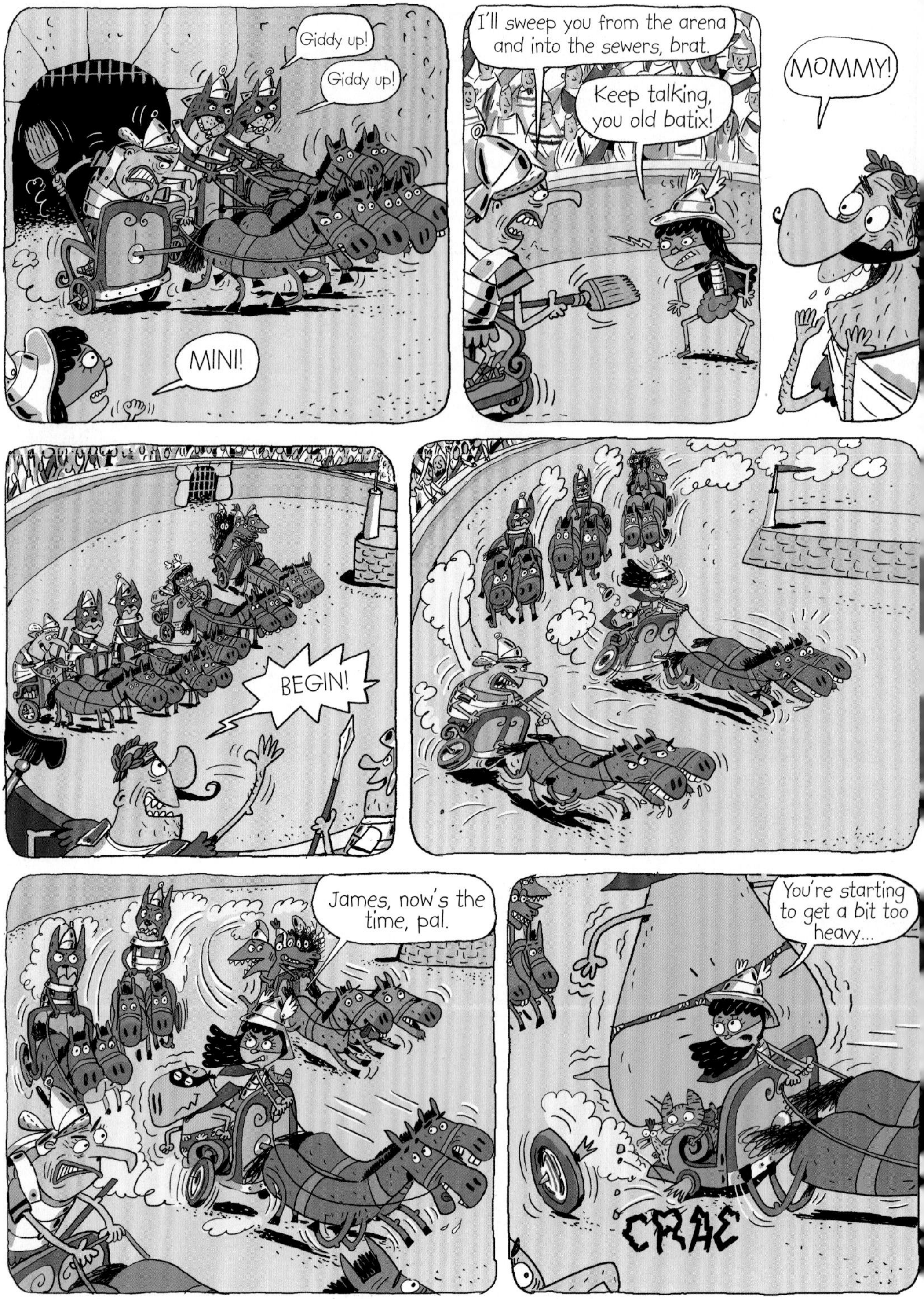
Giddy up!
Giddy up!
MINI!
I'll sweep you from the arena and into the sewers, brat.
Keep talking, you old batix!
MOMMY!
BEGIN!
James, now's the time, pal.
You're starting to get a bit too heavy...
CRAC

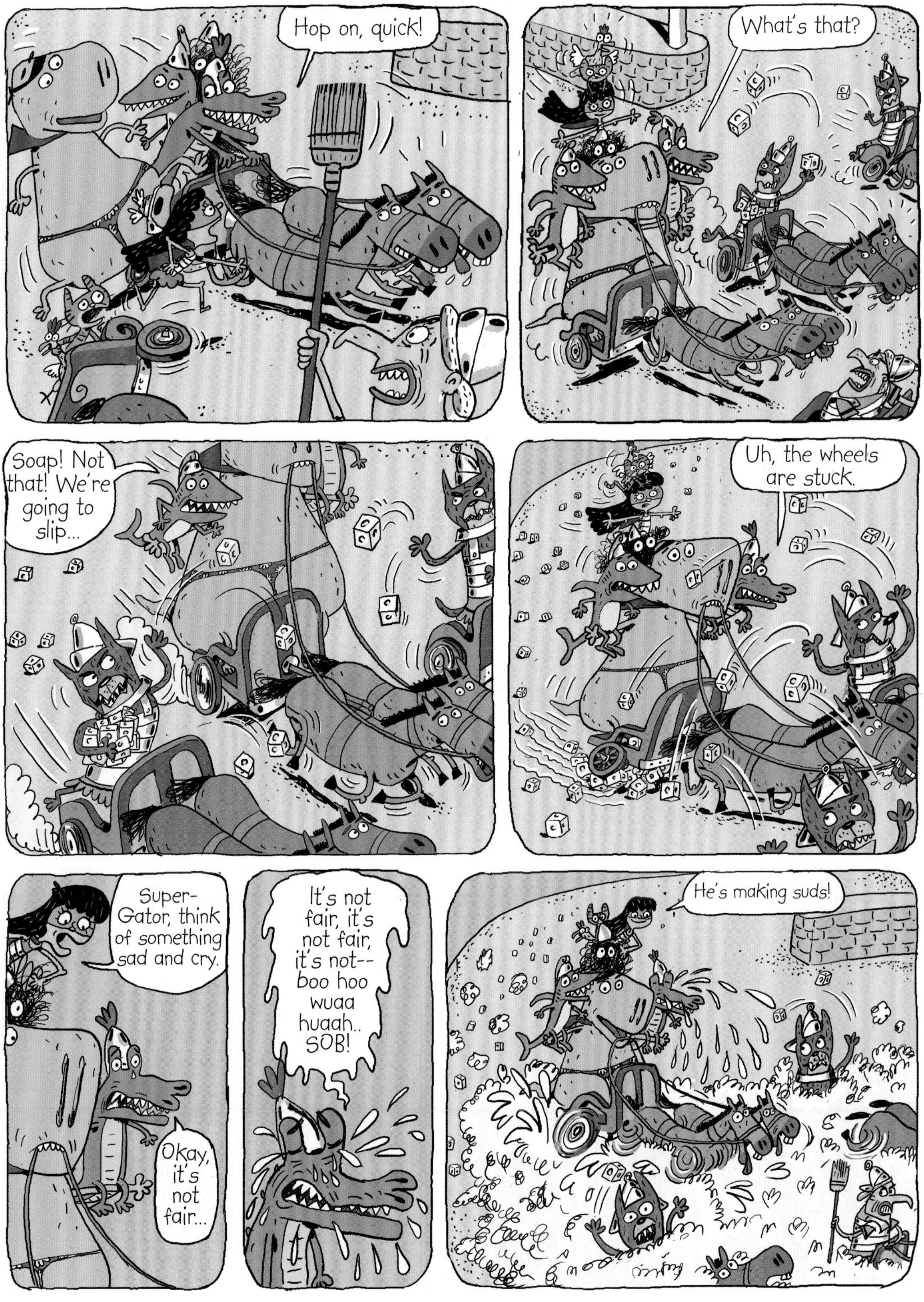

Hop on, quick!
What's that?
Soap! Not that! We're going to slip...
Uh, the wheels are stuck.
Super-Gator, think of something sad and cry.
Okay, it's not fair...
It's not fair, it's not fair, it's not-- boo hoo wuaa huaah.. SOB!
He's making suds!

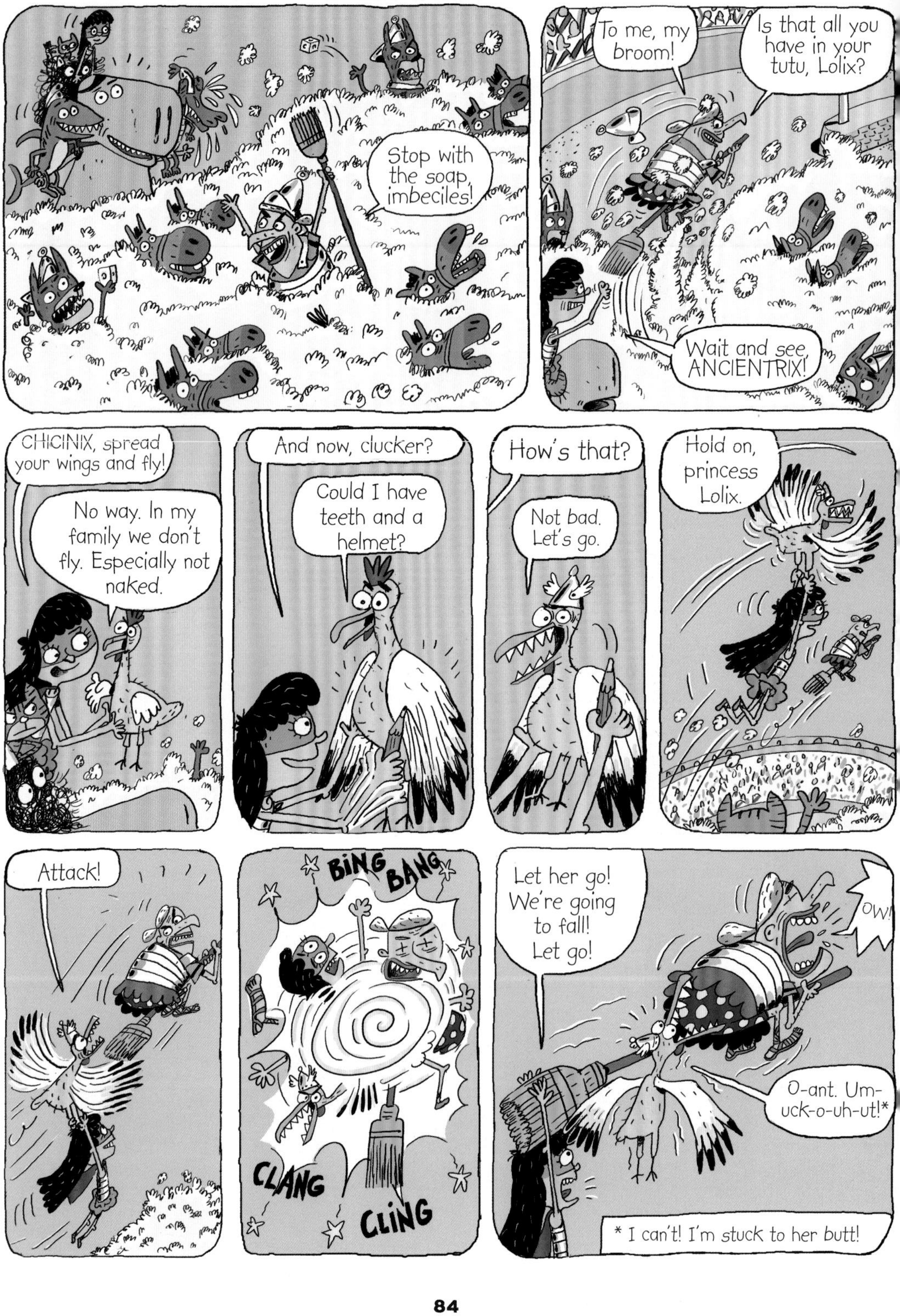

Stop with the soap, imbeciles!
To me, my broom!
Is that all you have in your tutu, Lolix?
Wait and see, ANCIENTRIX!
CHICINIX, spread your wings and fly!
No way. In my family we don't fly. Especially not naked.
And now, clucker?
Could I have teeth and a helmet?
How's that?
Not bad. Let's go.
Hold on, princess Lolix.
Attack!
BING
BANG
CLANG
CLING
Let her go! We're going to fall! Let go!
OW!
O-ant. Um-uck-o-uh-ut!*
* I can't! I'm stuck to her butt!

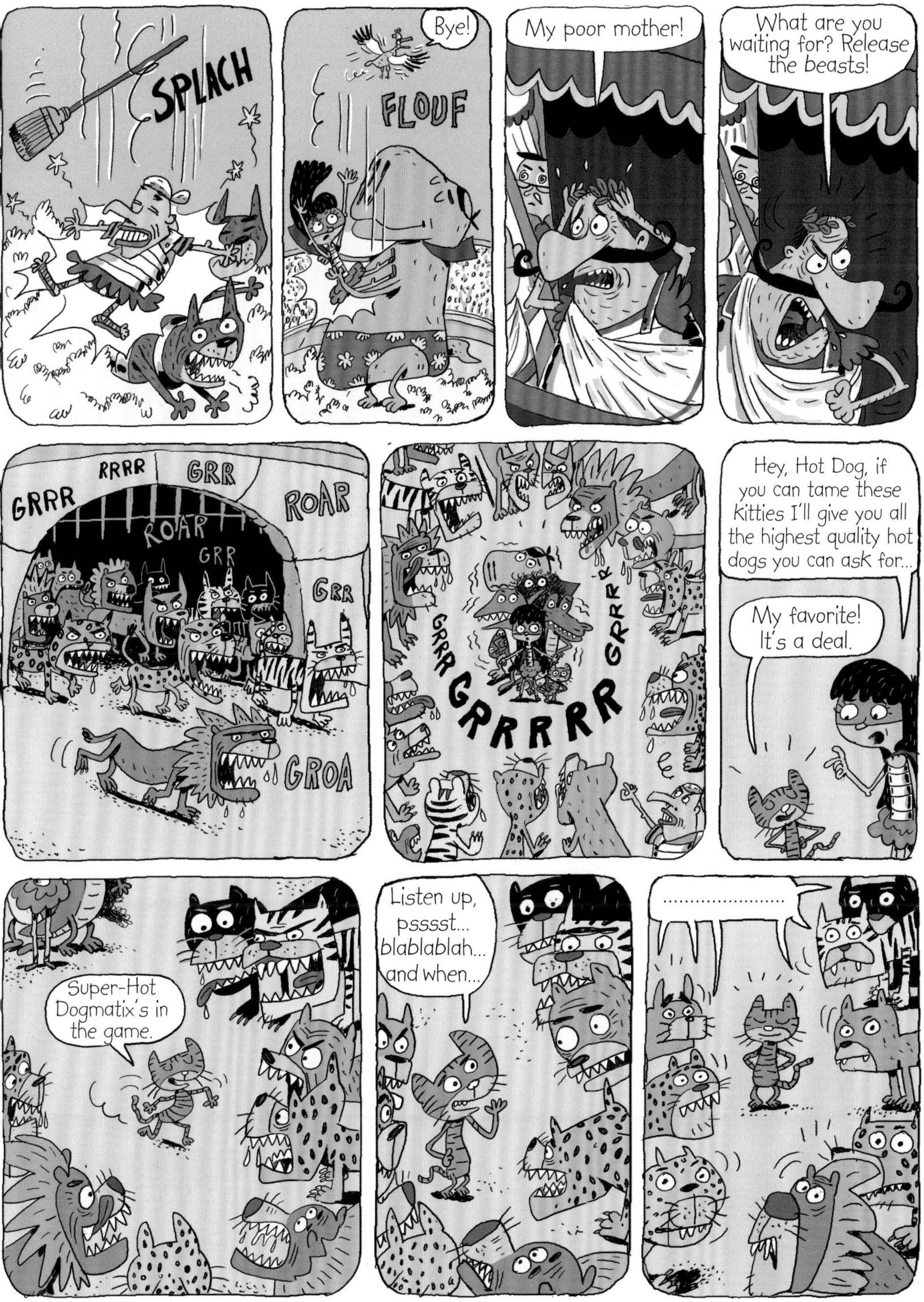
SPLACH
Bye!
FLOUF
My poor mother!
What are you waiting for? Release the beasts!
GRRR
RRRR
GRR
ROAR
ROAR
GRR
GRR
GROA
GRRR
GRRRRRR
GRRRR
Hey, Hot Dog, if you can tame these Kitties I'll give you all the highest quality hot dogs you can ask for...
My favorite! It's a deal.
Super-Hot Dogmatix's in the game.
Listen up, psssst... blablablah... and when...
....

HO HO!

Hehehe!

BWUA HA HA!

HA HA HA!

Hee! Hee!

HU HU HU HU!

Heh! Heh!

HAAH!

What are you doing? Attack! Rip them to shreds, finish them, annihilate them, pulverize them!

Death, death!

He always like this?

Ha ha! Yup. He fell in here as a baby a lot.

Enough jokes. Now let go of my mom, I won.

ZAP

Never! You won the right to advance to the next level, is all.

ZAP

Mom!

Follow me, Super Club!

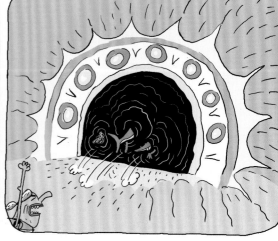

86

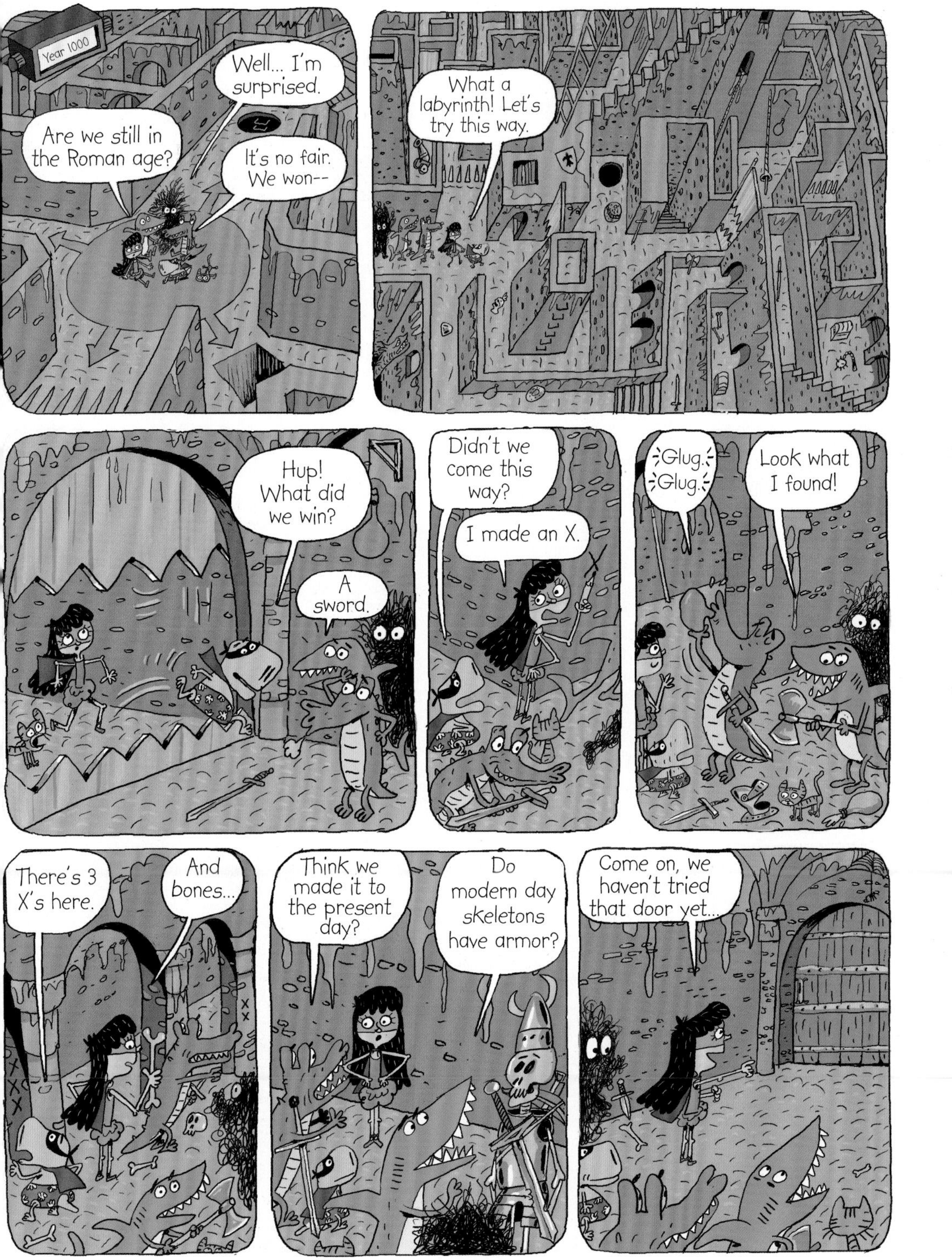
Year 1000
Well... I'm surprised.
Are we still in the Roman age?
It's no fair. We won--
What a labyrinth! Let's try this way.
Hup! What did we win?
A sword.
Didn't we come this way?
I made an X.
Glug. Glug.
Look what I found!
There's 3 X's here.
And bones...
Think we made it to the present day?
Do modern day skeletons have armor?
Come on, we haven't tried that door yet...

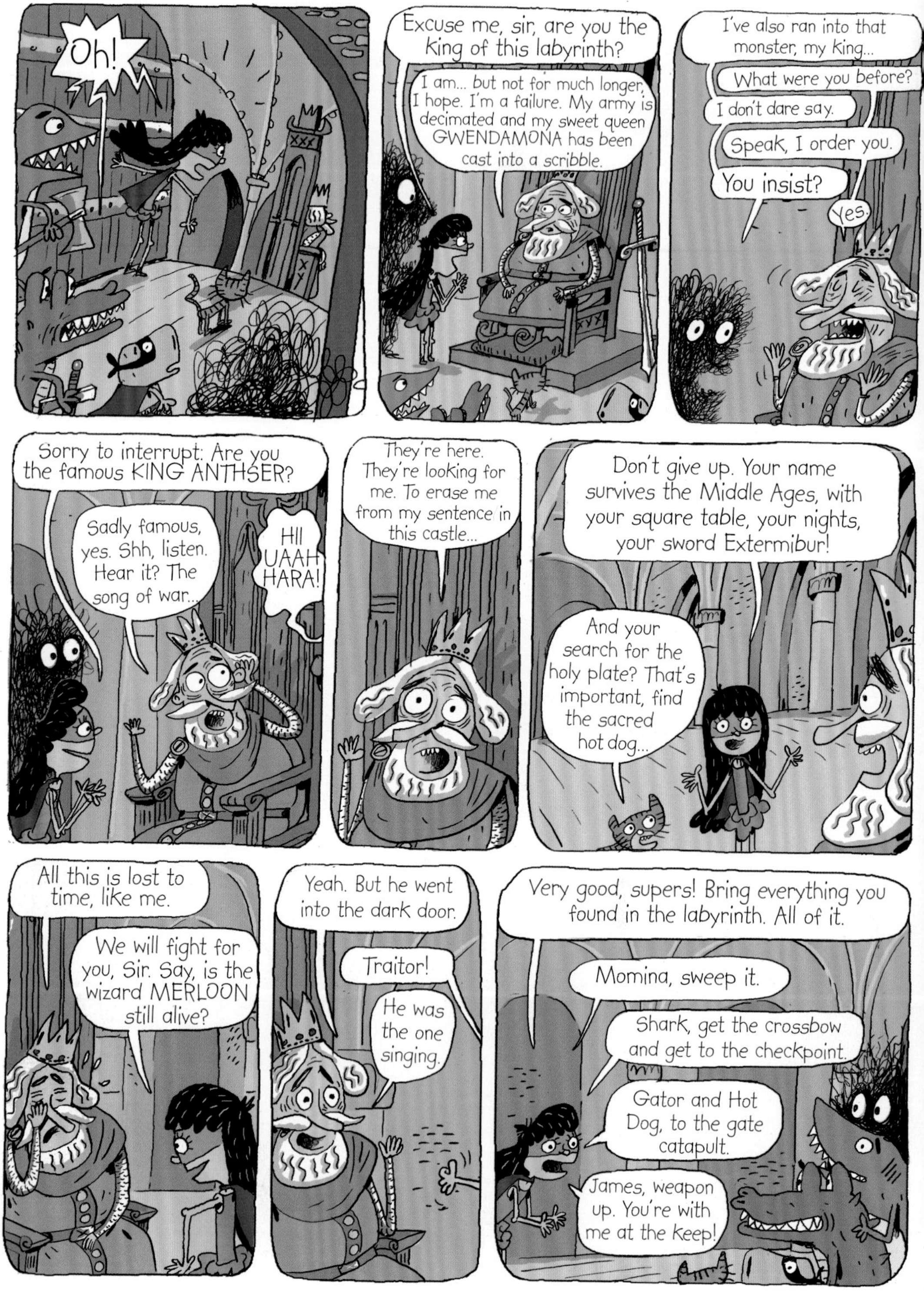
Oh!
Excuse me, sir, are you the King of this labyrinth?
I am... but not for much longer, I hope. I'm a failure. My army is decimated and my sweet queen GWENDAMONA has been cast into a scribble.
I've also ran into that monster, my King...
What were you before?
I don't dare say.
Speak, I order you.
You insist?
Yes.
Sorry to interrupt: Are you the famous KING ANTHSER?
Sadly famous, yes. Shh, listen. Hear it? The song of war...
HII UAAH HARA!
They're here. They're looking for me. To erase me from my sentence in this castle...
Don't give up. Your name survives the Middle Ages, with your square table, your nights, your sword Extermibur!
And your search for the holy plate? That's important, find the sacred hot dog...
All this is lost to time, like me.
We will fight for you, Sir. Say, is the wizard MERLOON still alive?
Yeah. But he went into the dark door.
Traitor!
He was the one singing.
Very good, supers! Bring everything you found in the labyrinth. All of it.
Momina, sweep it.
Shark, get the crossbow and get to the checkpoint.
Gator and Hot Dog, to the gate catapult.
James, weapon up. You're with me at the keep!

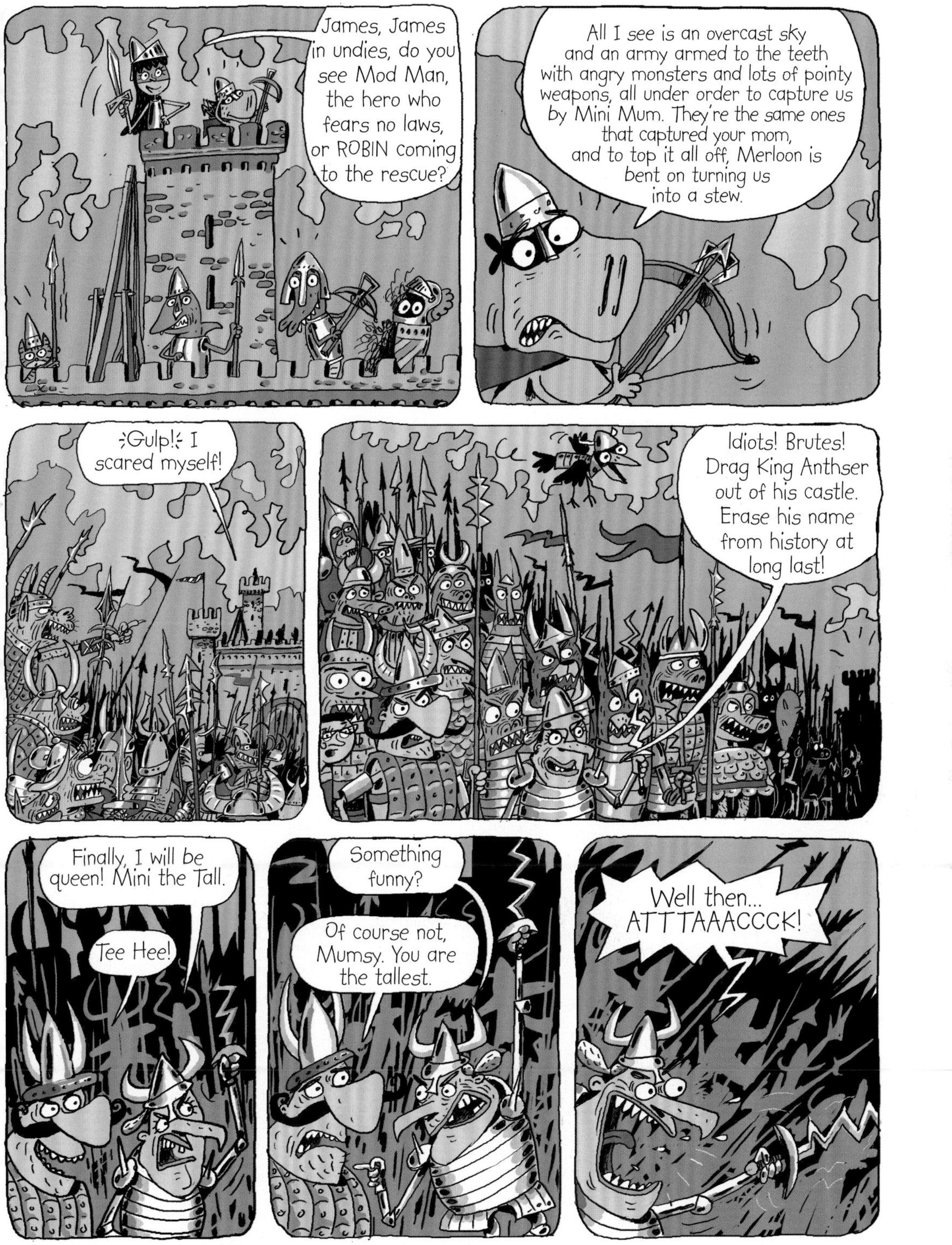
James, James in undies, do you see Mod Man, the hero who fears no laws, or ROBIN coming to the rescue?
All I see is an overcast sky and an army armed to the teeth with angry monsters and lots of pointy weapons, all under order to capture us by Mini Mum. They're the same ones that captured your mom, and to top it all off, Merloon is bent on turning us into a stew.
Gulp! I scared myself!
Idiots! Brutes! Drag King Anthser out of his castle. Erase his name from history at long last!
Finally, I will be queen! Mini the Tall.
Tee Hee!
Something funny?
Of course not, Mumsy. You are the tallest.
Well then... ATTTAAACCCK!

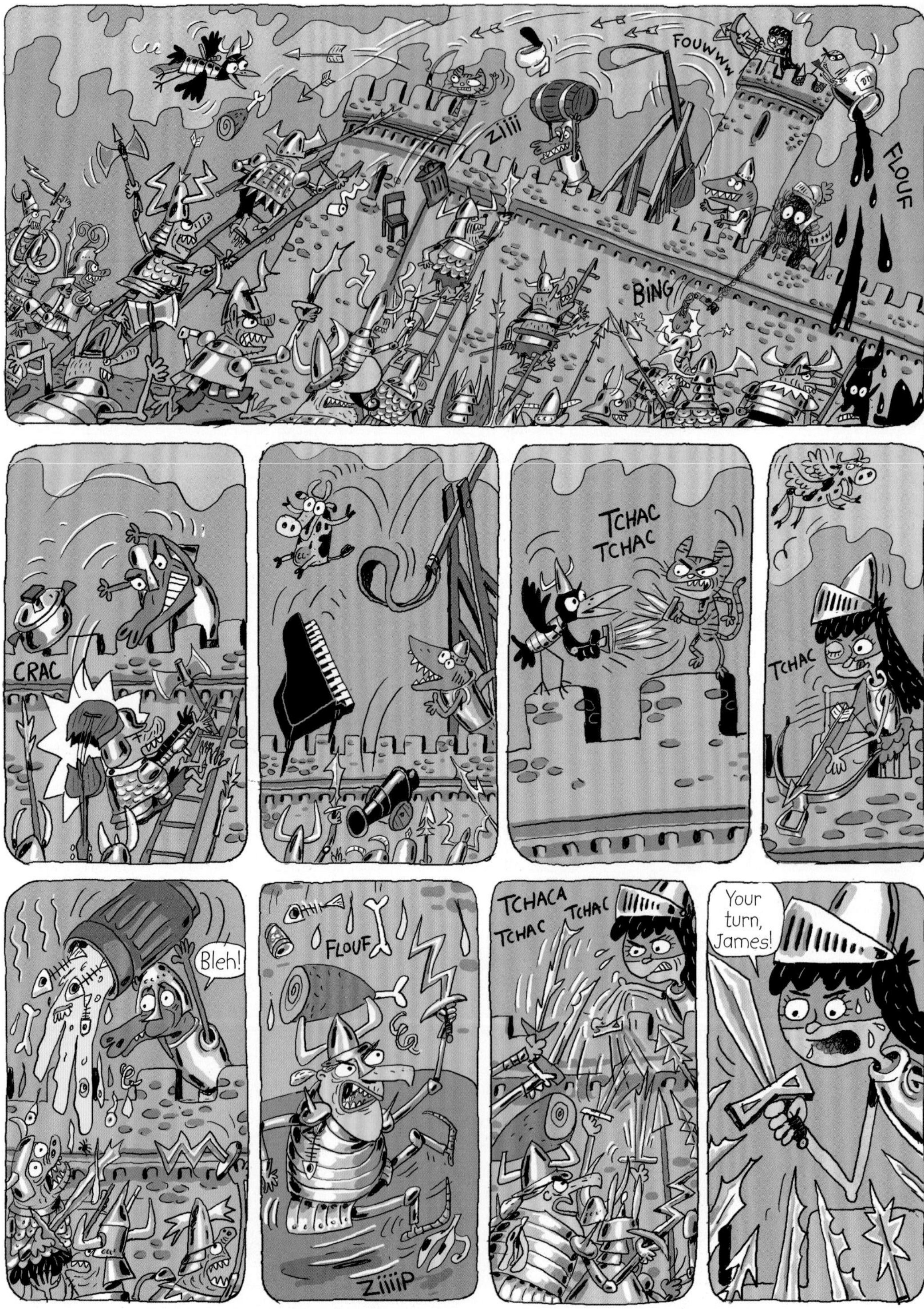

FOUWWW
Ziiii
FLOUF
BING
CRAC
TCHAC
TCHAC
TCHAC
Bleh!
FLOUF
ZiiiiP
TCHACA
TCHAC
TCHAC
Your turn, James!

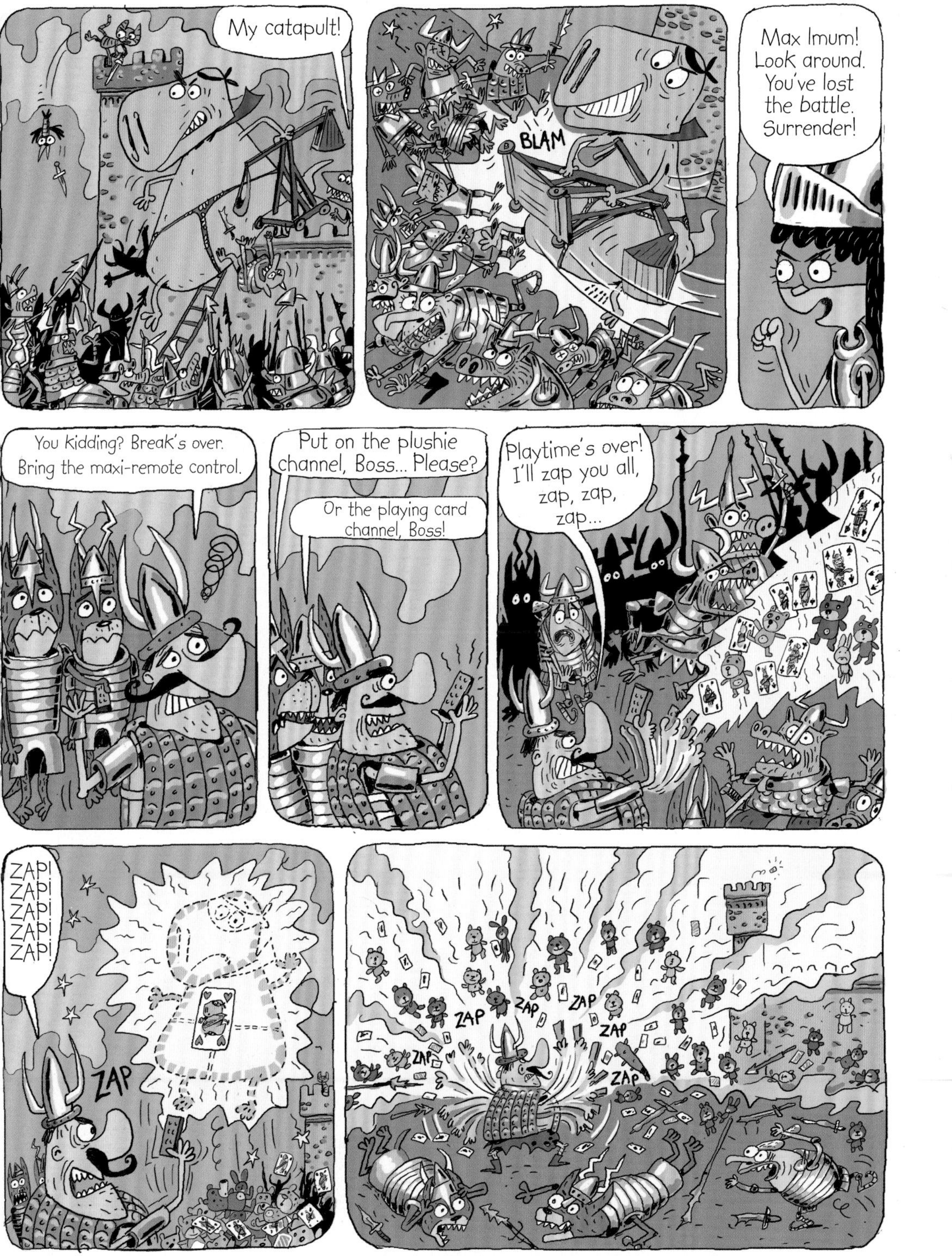
My catapult!
BLAM
Max Imum! Look around. You've lost the battle. Surrender!
You kidding? Break's over. Bring the maxi-remote control.
Put on the plushie channel, Boss... Please?
Or the playing card channel, Boss!
Playtime's over! I'll zap you all, zap, zap, zap...
ZAP! ZAP! ZAP! ZAP! ZAP!
ZAP
ZAP
ZAP
ZAP
ZAP
ZAP
ZAP

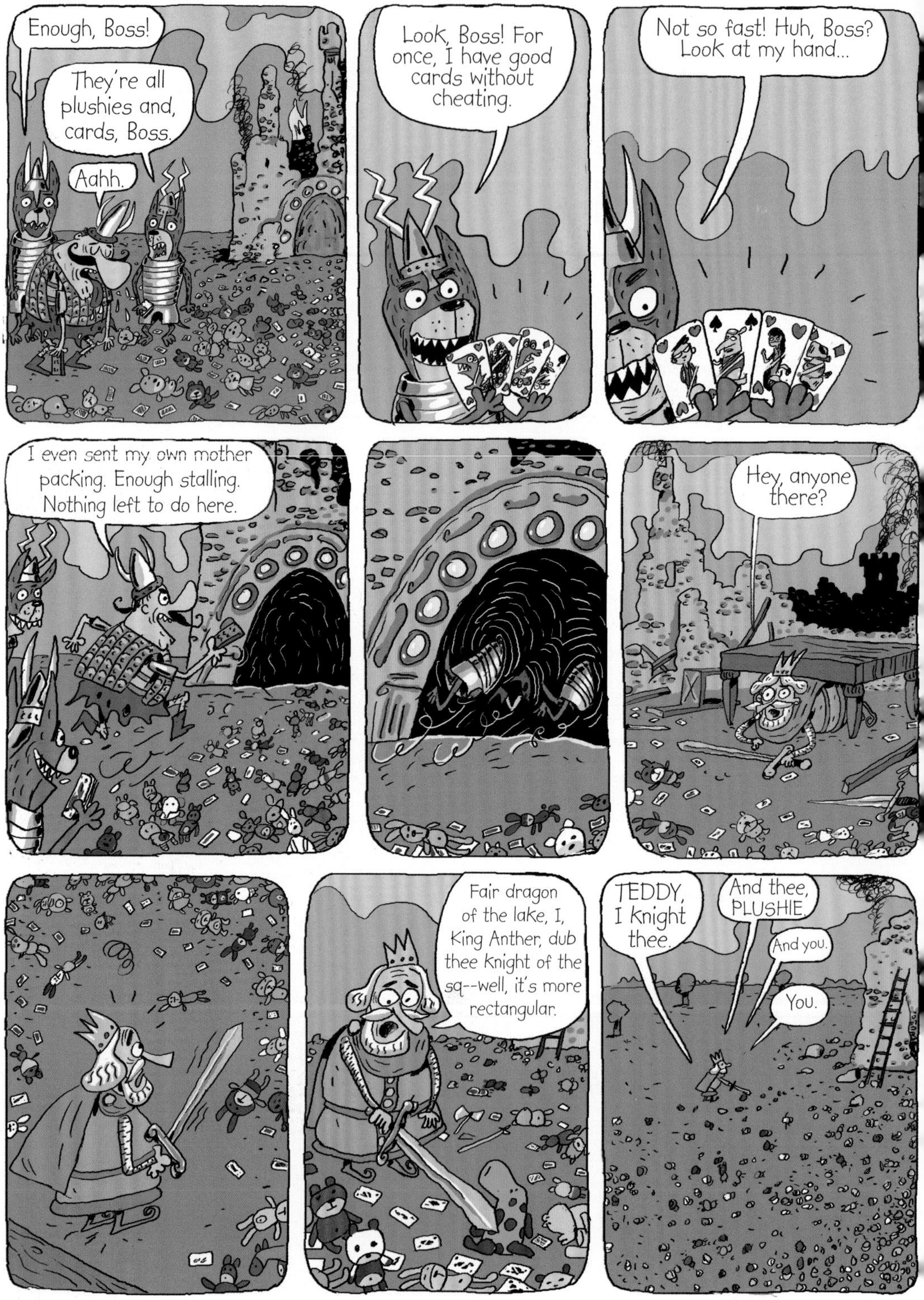
Enough, Boss!
They're all plushies and, cards, Boss.
Aahh.
Look, Boss! For once, I have good cards without cheating.
Not so fast! Huh, Boss? Look at my hand...
I even sent my own mother packing. Enough stalling. Nothing left to do here.
Hey, anyone there?
Fair dragon of the lake, I, King Anther, dub thee knight of the sq--well, it's more rectangular.
TEDDY, I knight thee.
And thee, PLUSHIE.
And you.
You.

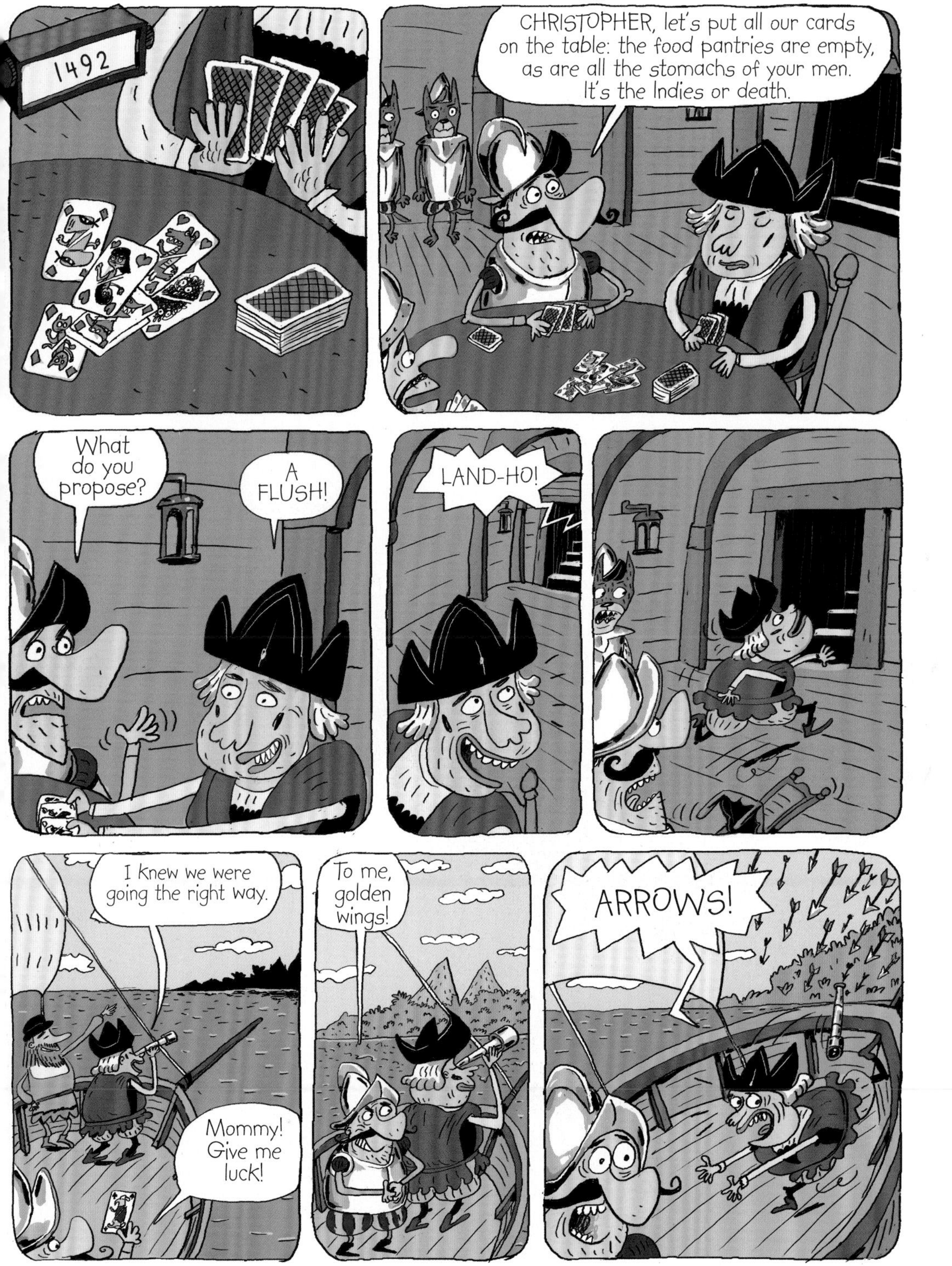
1492
CHRISTOPHER, let's put all our cards on the table: the food pantries are empty, as are all the stomachs of your men. It's the Indies or death.
What do you propose?
A FLUSH!
LAND-HO!
I knew we were going the right way.
Mommy! Give me luck!
To me, golden wings!
ARROWS!

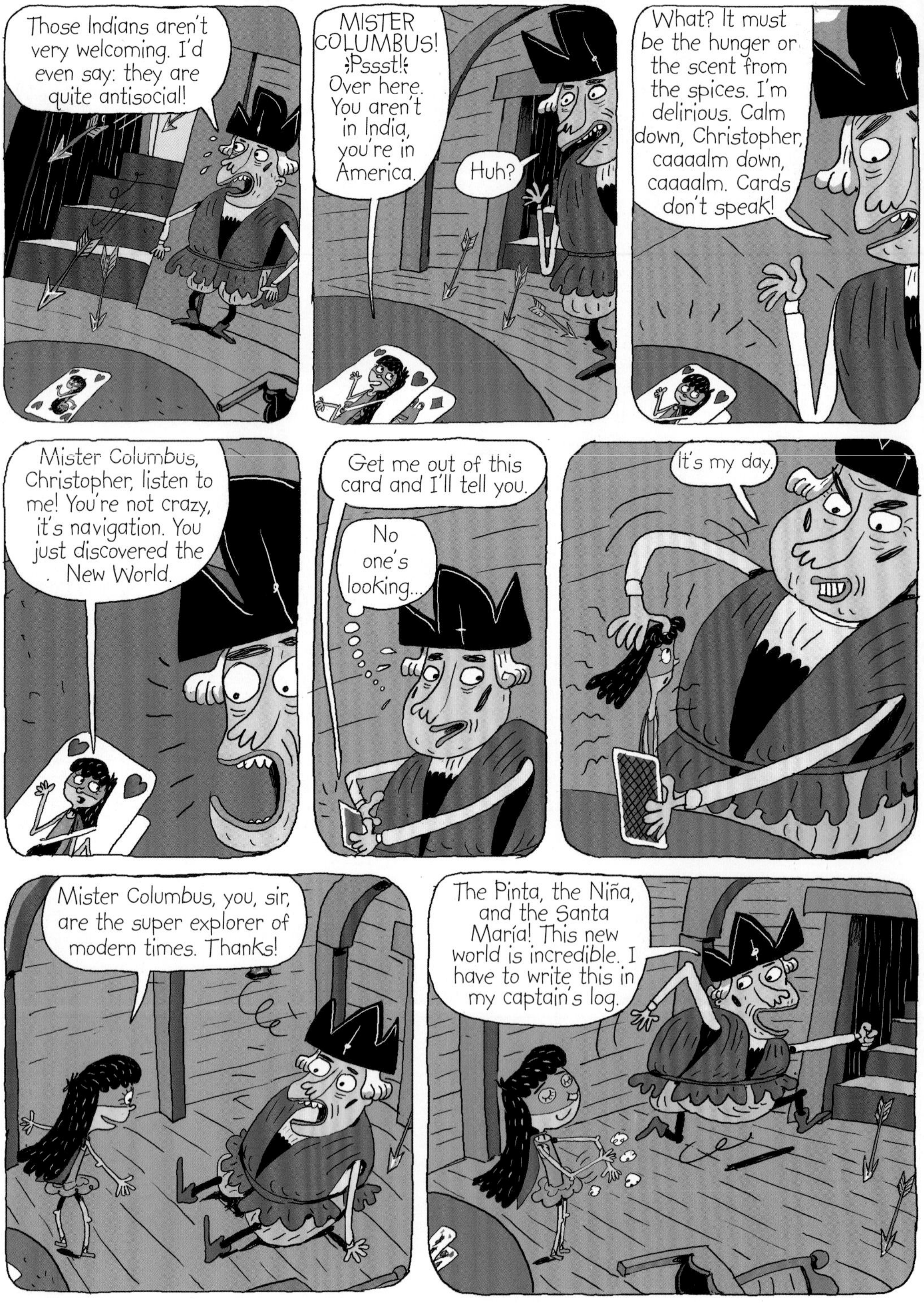

Those Indians aren't very welcoming. I'd even say: they are quite antisocial!
MISTER COLUMBUS! Pssst! Over here. You aren't in India, you're in America.
Huh?
What? It must be the hunger or the scent from the spices. I'm delirious. Calm down, Christopher, caaaalm down, caaaalm. Cards don't speak!
Mister Columbus, Christopher, listen to me! You're not crazy, it's navigation. You just discovered the New World.
Get me out of this card and I'll tell you.
No one's looking...
It's my day.
Mister Columbus, you, sir, are the super explorer of modern times. Thanks!
The Pinta, the Niña, and the Santa María! This new world is incredible. I have to write this in my captain's log.

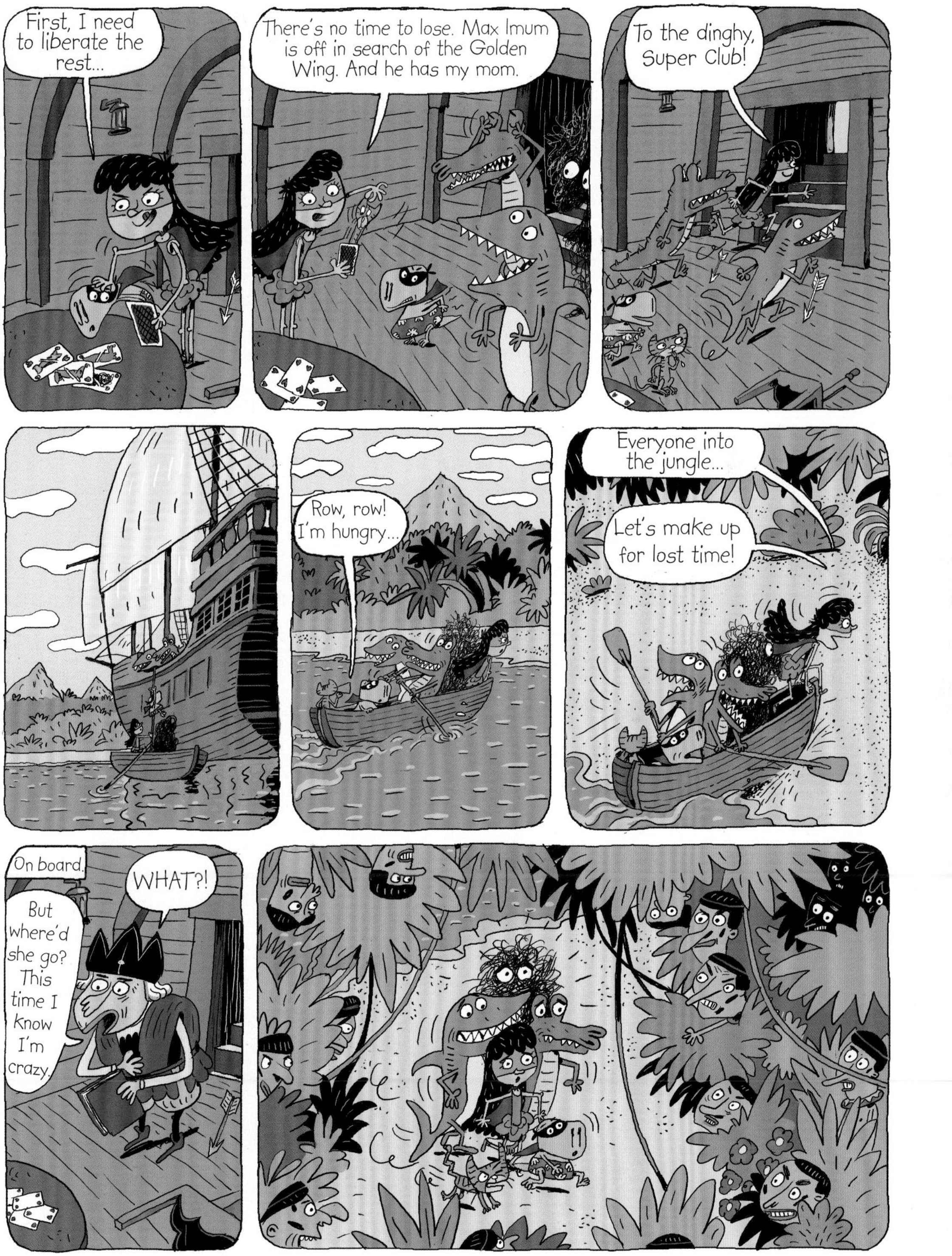
First, I need to liberate the rest...
There's no time to lose. Max Imum is off in search of the Golden Wing. And he has my mom.
To the dinghy, Super Club!
Row, row! I'm hungry...
Everyone into the jungle...
Let's make up for lost time!
On board.
WHAT?!
But where'd she go? This time I know I'm crazy.

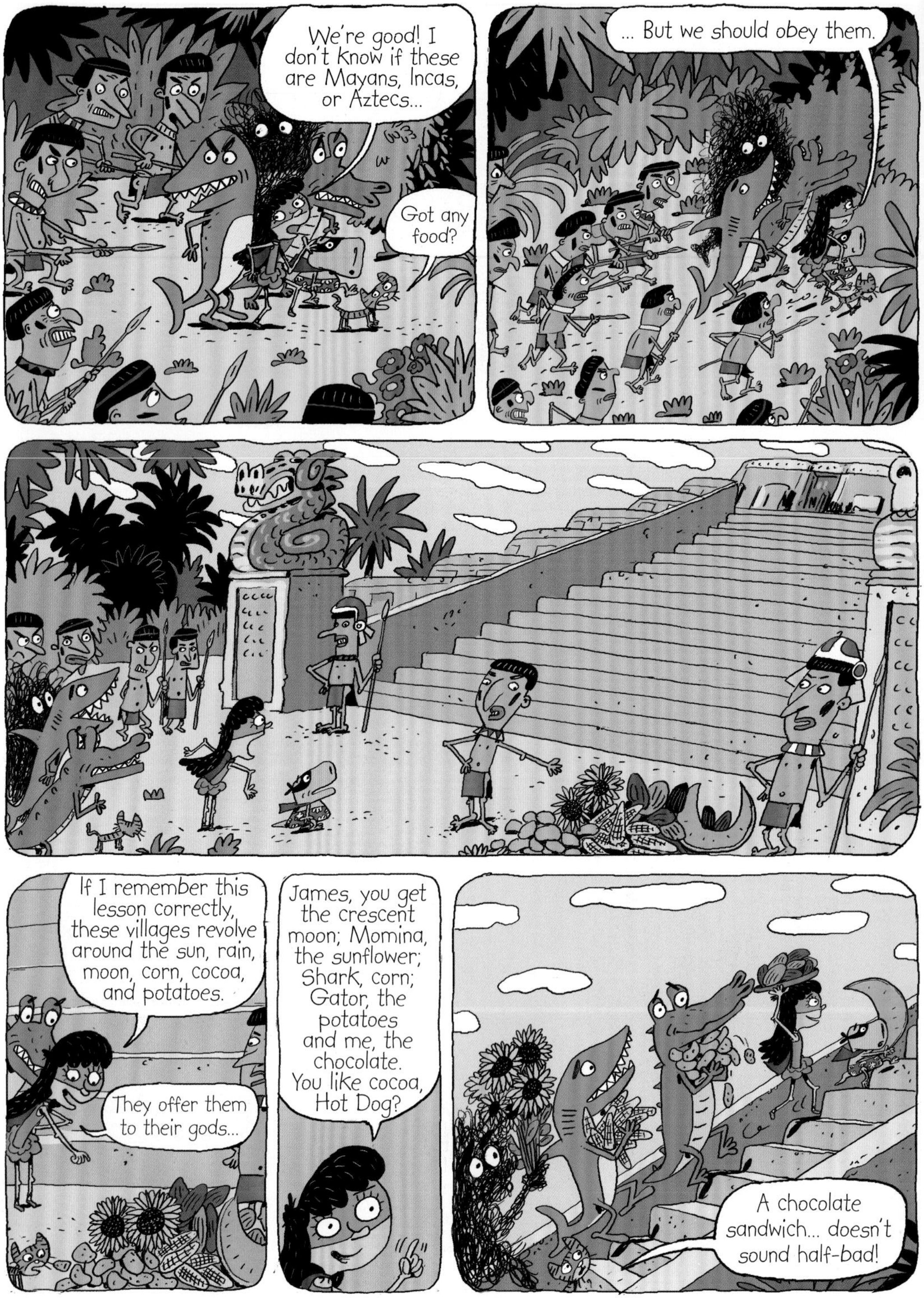
We're good! I don't know if these are Mayans, Incas, or Aztecs...
Got any food?
... But we should obey them.
If I remember this lesson correctly, these villages revolve around the sun, rain, moon, corn, cocoa, and potatoes.
They offer them to their gods...
James, you get the crescent moon; Momina, the sunflower; Shark, corn; Gator, the potatoes and me, the chocolate. You like cocoa, Hot Dog?
A chocolate sandwich... doesn't sound half-bad!

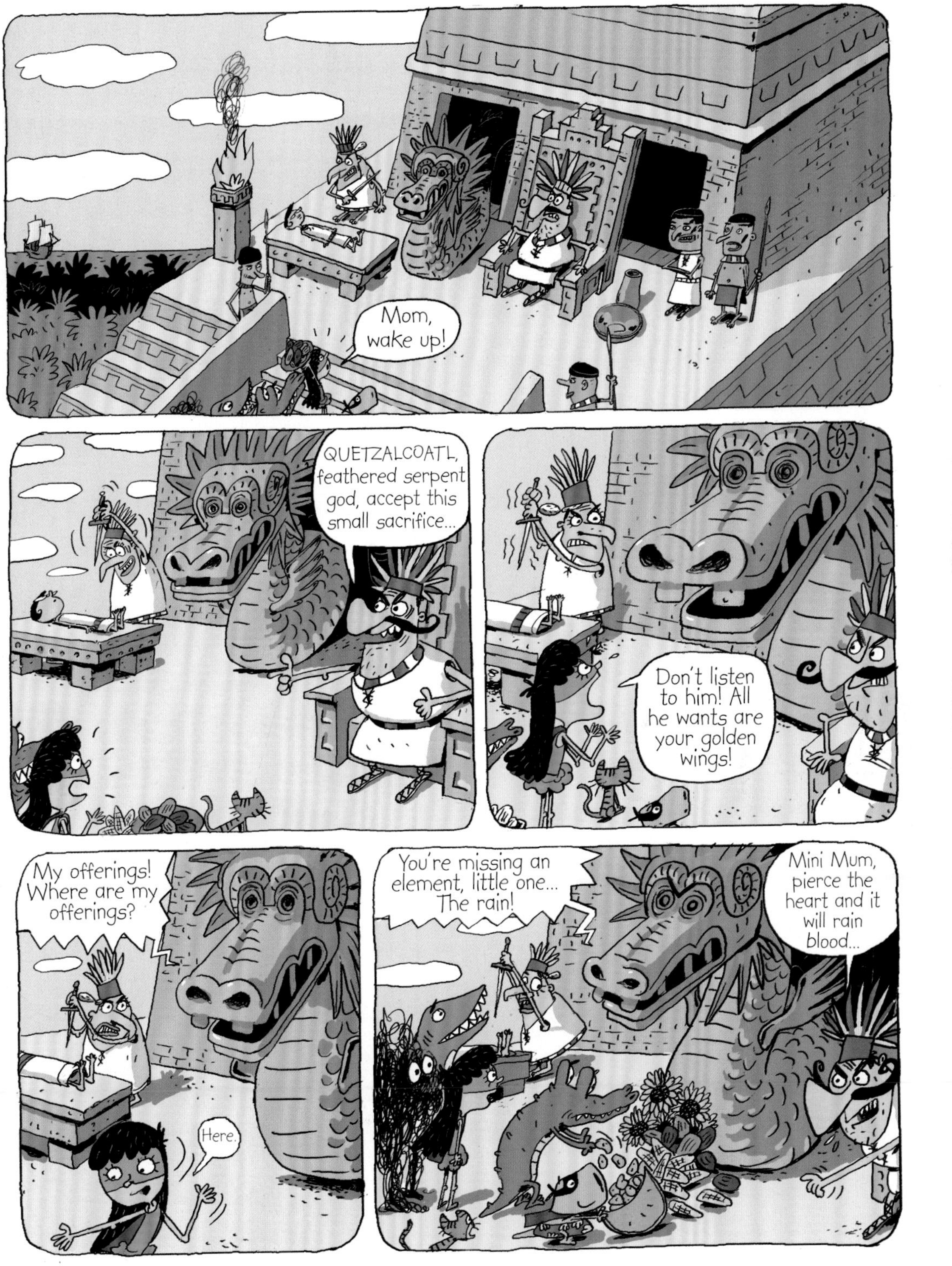
Mom, wake up!
QUETZALCOATL, feathered serpent god, accept this small sacrifice...
Don't listen to him! All he wants are your golden wings!
My offerings! Where are my offerings?
Here.
You're missing an element, little one... The rain!
Mini Mum, pierce the heart and it will rain blood...

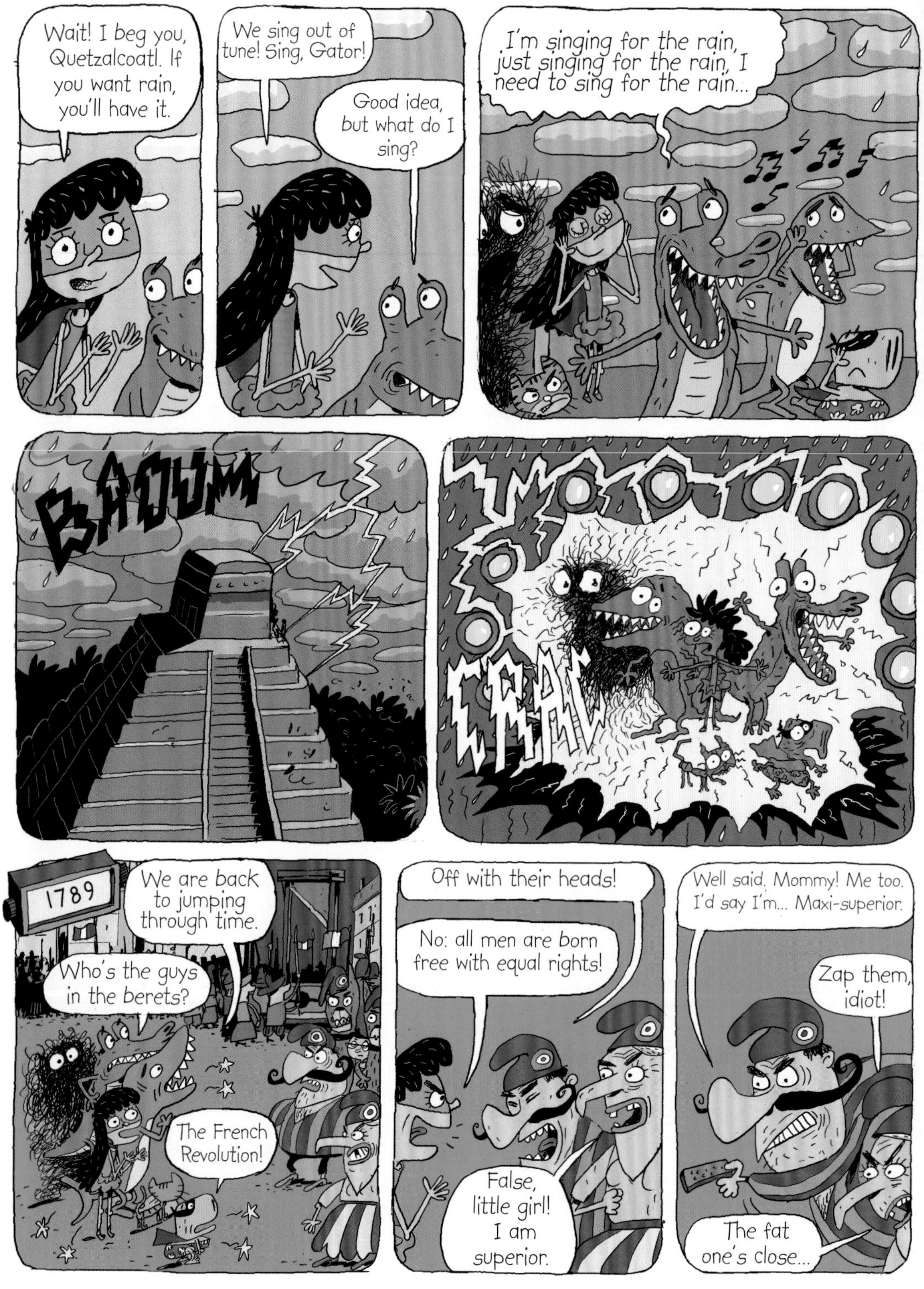
Wait! I beg you, Quetzalcoatl. If you want rain, you'll have it.
We sing out of tune! Sing, Gator!
Good idea, but what do I sing?
I'm singing for the rain, just singing for the rain, I need to sing for the rain...
BAOUM
CRAC
1789
We are back to jumping through time.
Who's the guys in the berets?
The French Revolution!
Off with their heads!
No: all men are born free with equal rights!
False, little girl! I am superior.
Well said, Mommy! Me too. I'd say I'm... Maxi-superior.
Zap them, idiot!
The fat one's close...

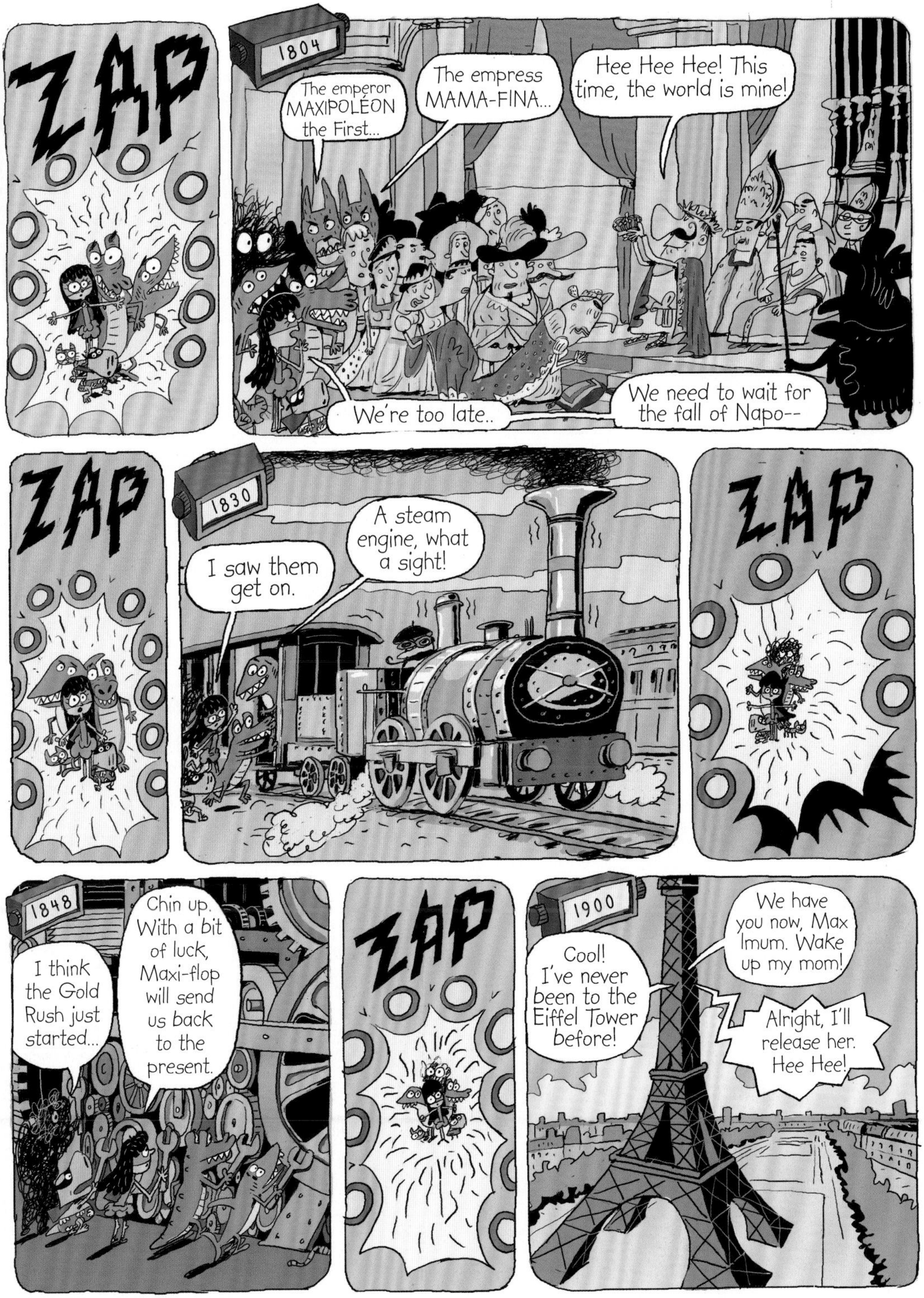
ZAP
1804
The emperor MAXIPOLÉON the First...
The empress MAMA-FINA...
Hee Hee Hee! This time, the world is mine!
We're too late..
We need to wait for the fall of Napo--
ZAP
1830
I saw them get on.
A steam engine, what a sight!
ZAP
1848
I think the Gold Rush just started...
Chin up. With a bit of luck, Maxi-flop will send us back to the present.
ZAP
1900
Cool! I've never been to the Eiffel Tower before!
We have you now, Max Imum. Wake up my mom!
Alright, I'll release her. Hee Hee!

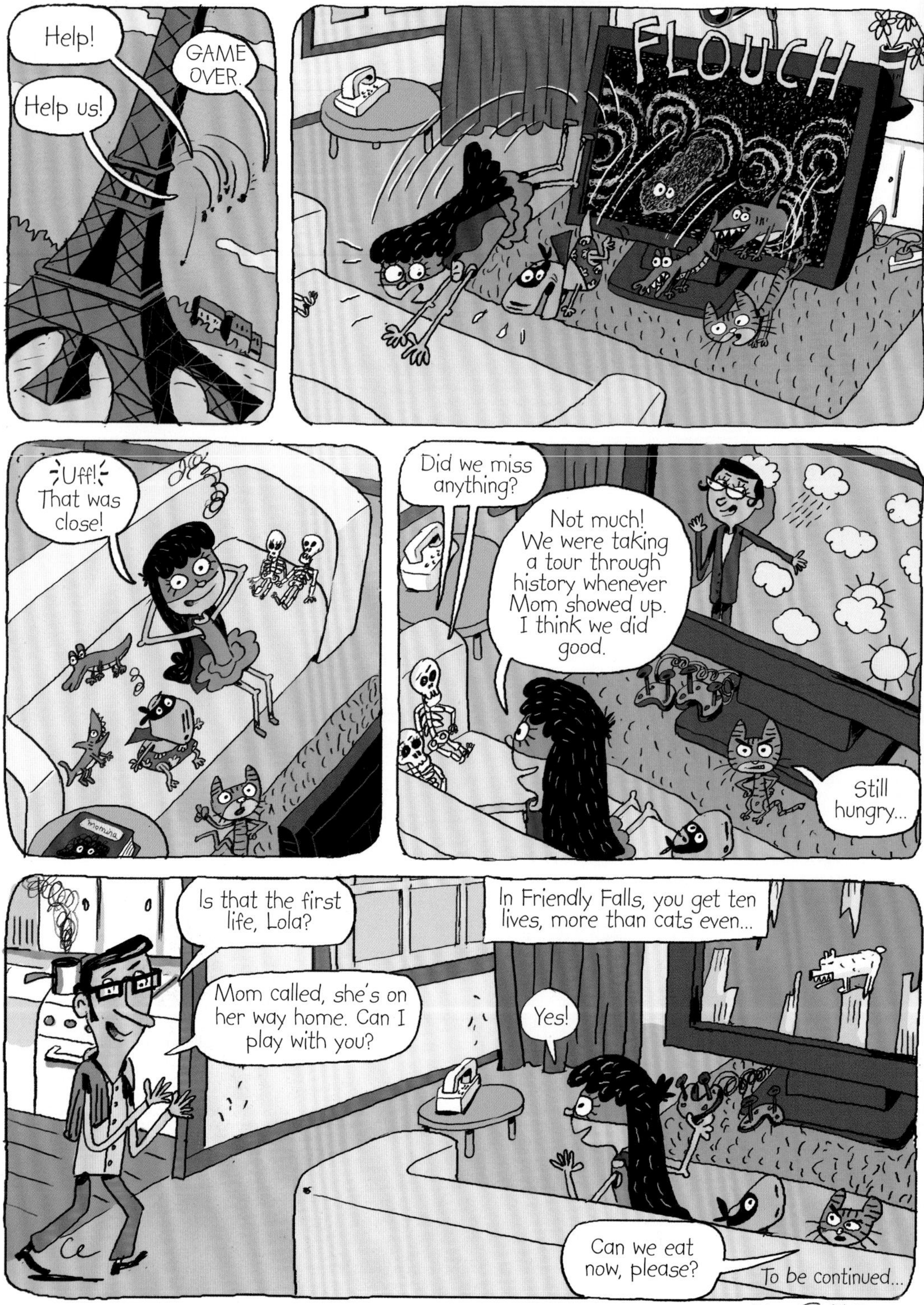
Help!
Help us!
GAME OVER.
FLOUCH
Uff! That was close!
Did we miss anything?
Not much! We were taking a tour through history whenever Mom showed up. I think we did good.
Still hungry...
Is that the first life, Lola?
In Friendly Falls, you get ten lives, more than cats even...
Mom called, she's on her way home. Can I play with you?
Yes!
Can we eat now, please?
To be continued...

Pierre Fouillet 2012

WATCH OUT FOR PAPERCUTZ

Welcome to LOLA'S SUPER CLUB #1 "My Dad is a Super Secret Agent," by Christine Beigel and Pierre Fouillet, from Papercutz—those mere mortals dedicated to publishing great graphic novels for all ages. I'm Jim Salicrup, the Editor-in-Chief and person who is about to tell you about some Papercutz graphic novels you may enjoy if you loved LOLA'S SUPER CLUB...

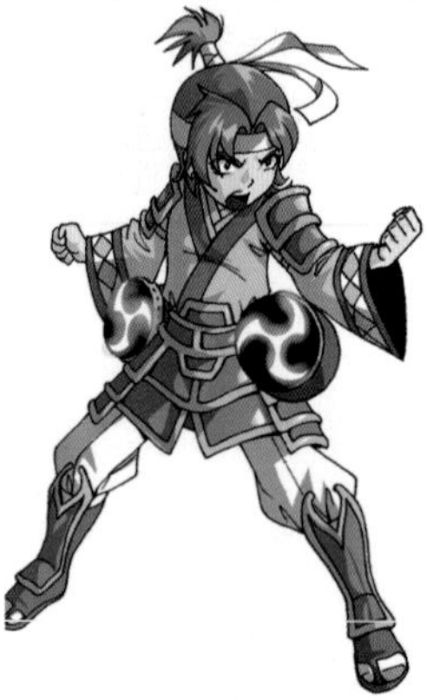

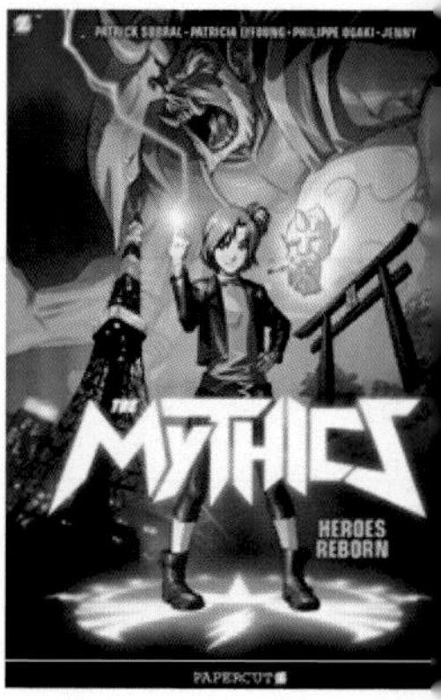

MYTHICS
HEROES REBORN
PAPERCUTZ

But first we must ask ourselves, is Lola a true super-hero or just a girl with a very active imagination? If you believe Lola and her friends are the real deal, you might really like THE MYTHICS, the Papercutz graphic novel series about six children who are called upon by their god-like ancestors to battle an ancient evil that has returned to Earth. In THE MYTHICS #1 "Heroes Reborn," by Patrick Sobral, Patricia Lyfoung, Philippe Ogaki, Jenny, and Dara, you'll meet the first three of the six heroes: Yuko, a Japanese schoolgirl in a rock band, who has electrical powers; Amir, a recently-orphaned young Egyptian boy who must take over his family's successful business, whose powers are derived from the sun and the moon; and a young opera hopeful, Abigail, whose voice also becomes her super power. These children all suddenly find themselves in unreal situations, granted great powers, and having to battle powerful foes to save their cities. Hey, it's not always fun and games being a super-hero. Spoiler Alert: Quetzalcoatl, who we see on page 97, appears in THE MYTHICS #2.

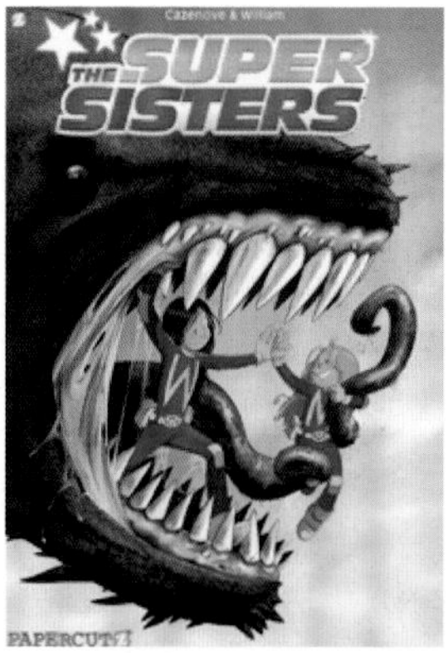

Cazenove & William
THE SUPER SISTERS
PAPERCUTZ

But if you think Lola's adventures are just imaginary tales she dreams up, you may also enjoy THE SISTERS by Cazenove and William, the Papercutz graphic novel series about Wendy and Maureen, who lead fairly ordinary lives driving each other crazy, but then they also imagine themselves as the Super Sisters and have all sorts of real-life inspired adventures. These mini-adventures are so popular within their already super popular series, that an entire graphic novel has been created by Cazenove and William devoted exclusively to their super-hero fantasies, Naturally it's called THE SUPER SISTERS, and there's a super-secret sneak peek of one of the stories in a few pages...

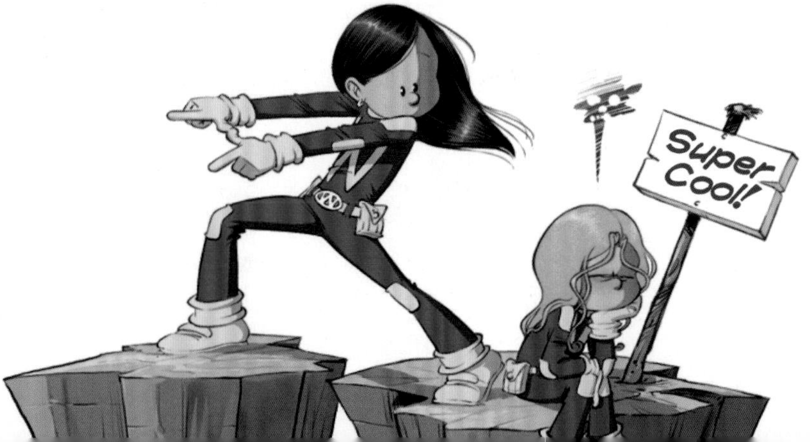

Super Cool!

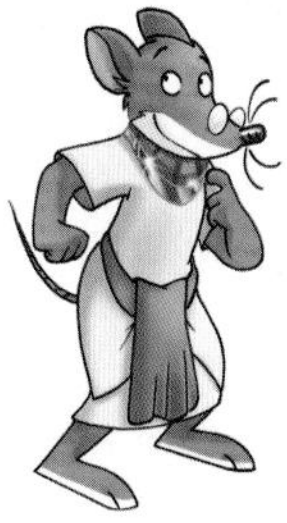

There's also another aspect of Lola's adventures that we witnessed in the second story in this graphic novel, that's where Lola and her super-friends travel through time. This is a very popular concept in several Papercutz graphic novel series. Perhaps our most experienced time-traveler is Geronimo Stilton, the editor-in-chief of the *Rodent's Gazette*. Geronimo has hopped in the Speedrat countless times to save the future, by protecting the past from his enemies, the Pirate Cats. Oh, in case you didn't know, Geronimo's a mouse. The talking kind who lives in New Mouse City. Yet his world is remarkably similar to ours, especially regarding major historic events. It's just a lot mousier. Check out the special excerpt from GERONOMO STILTON #2 starting on page 109.

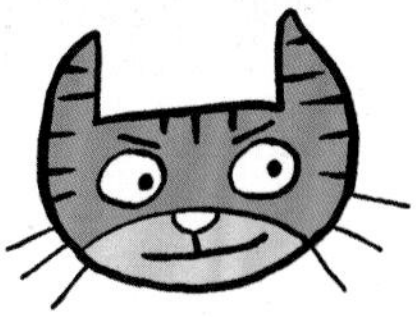

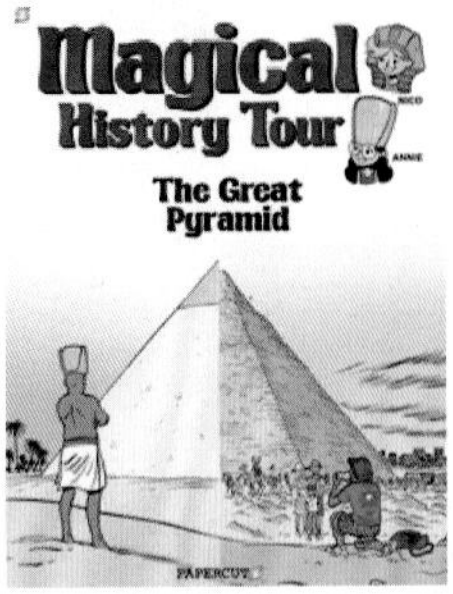
Magical
History Tour
NICO
ANNIE
The Great
Pyramid
PAPERCUTZ

For a somewhat more human experience through time, may we suggest the premiere volume of the newest Papercutz graphic novel series, MAGICAL HISTORY TOUR #1 "The Great Pyramid" by Fabrice Erre and Sylvain Savoia? Within its pages Nico and Annie will be your guide through important events in history. Usually each volume focuses on one major event or time period and their aren't any nasty super-villains trying to disrupt everything. And unlike Lola's rushed trip through time, in this series you get to linger a bit.

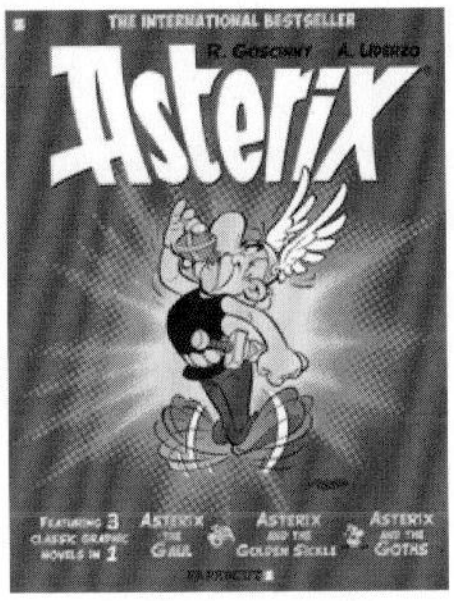
THE INTERNATIONAL BESTSELLER
R. GOSCINNY A. UDERZO
Asterix

When Lola landed in 50 BC, some of you may have gotten the inside gags based on one of the best-selling comics series in the world, ASTERIX. That's the comic Lola refers to when she says "to defeat the Romans you must drink a magic potion." If you're not already a fan of ASTERIX, the little Gaul who gains super-strength from a magic potion that helps him battle the Romans, then you're in luck! Papercutz has recently started publishing all new translations of the classic comics series by Goscinny and Uderzo, and it's your opportunity to not only meet the real "Dogmatix," but to experience one of the greatest graphic novel series ever created.

We saved the best news for last. I'm happy to announce you are now officially a member of LOLA'S SUPER CLUB! As you know the membership requirements are super-tough: you have to have either a super power or an imagination. You know what you have. We hope you enjoyed LOLA'S SUPER CLUB #1 and that you'll be back for #2 "My Substitute Teacher is a Witch," as it won't be any fun without you!

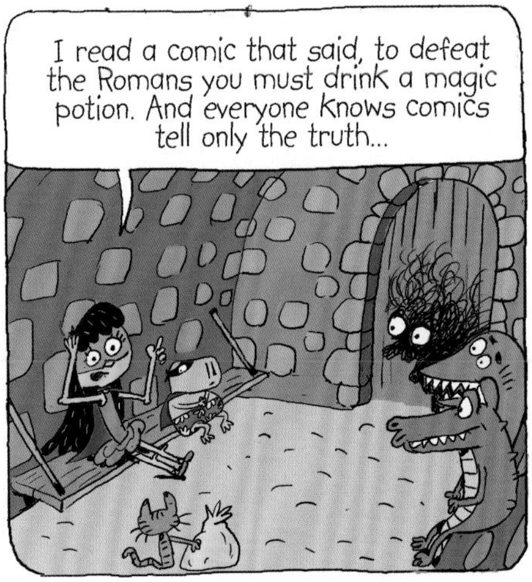
I read a comic that said, to defeat the Romans you must drink a magic potion. And everyone knows comics tell only the truth...

Thanks!

Jim

STAY IN TOUCH!

EMAIL: salicrup@papercutz.com
WEB: papercutz.com
TWITTER: @papercutzgn
INSTAGRAM: @papercutzgn
FACEBOOK: PAPERCUTZGRAPHICNOVELS
FAN MAIL: Papercutz, 160 Broadway, Suite 700, East Wing New York, NY 10038

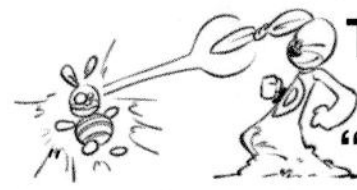

Take off with Maureen and Wendy as they use their imagination to become THE SUPER SISTERS In this special preview...

"The Time When Maureen Wasn't Allowed to Have a Laser..."

THE ALIENS HAD BURST ONTO ASTERIA WITHOUT ADVANCE WARNING. LUCKILY WE SUPER SISTERS WERE THERE TO DEFEND OUR FRIENDS.

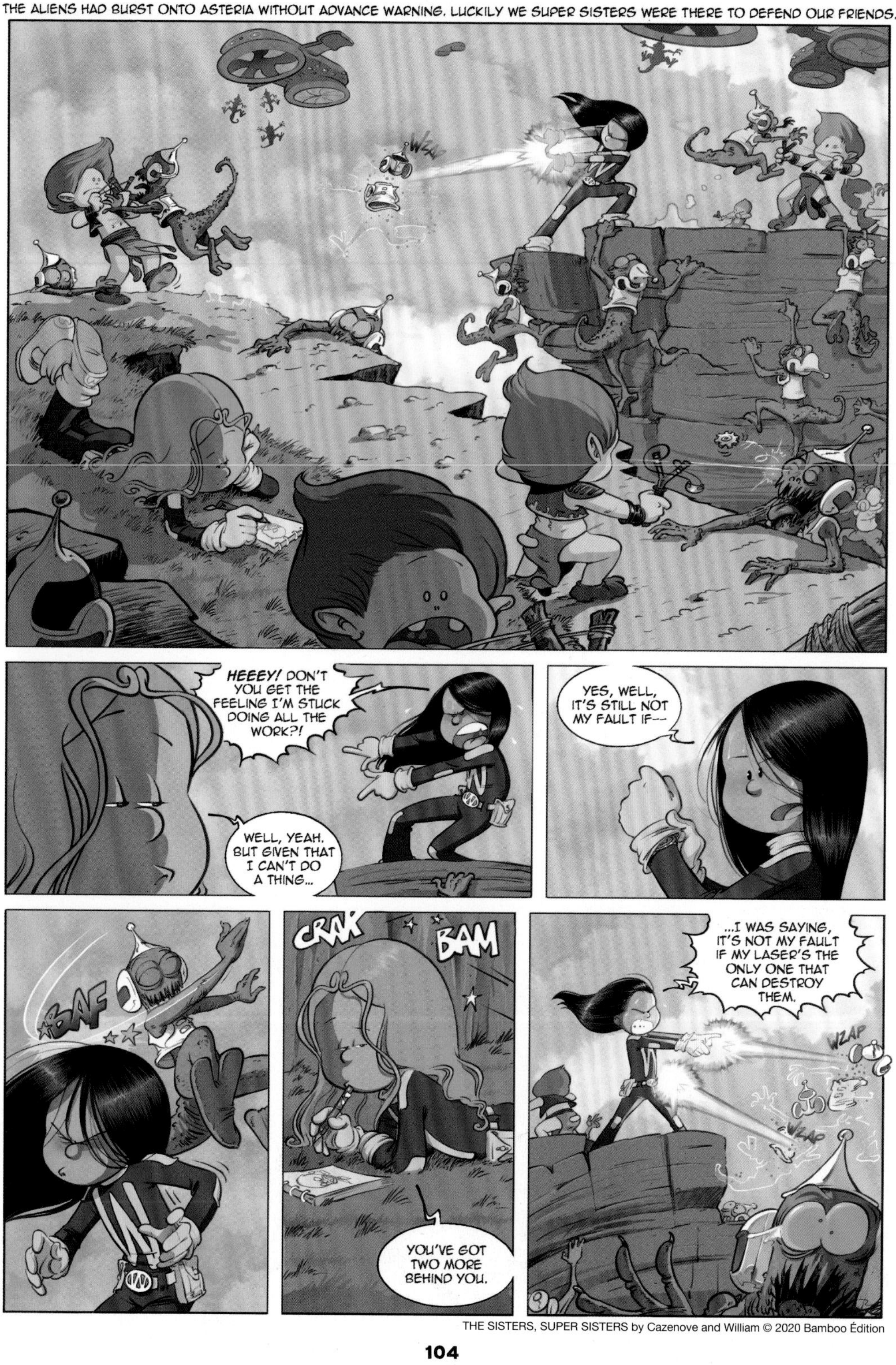

HEEEY! DON'T YOU GET THE FEELING I'M STUCK DOING ALL THE WORK?!
WELL, YEAH. BUT GIVEN THAT I CAN'T DO A THING...
YES, WELL, IT'S STILL NOT MY FAULT IF--
BAF
CRAK
BAM
YOU'VE GOT TWO MORE BEHIND YOU.
...I WAS SAYING, IT'S NOT MY FAULT IF MY LASER'S THE ONLY ONE THAT CAN DESTROY THEM.
WZAP
WZAP

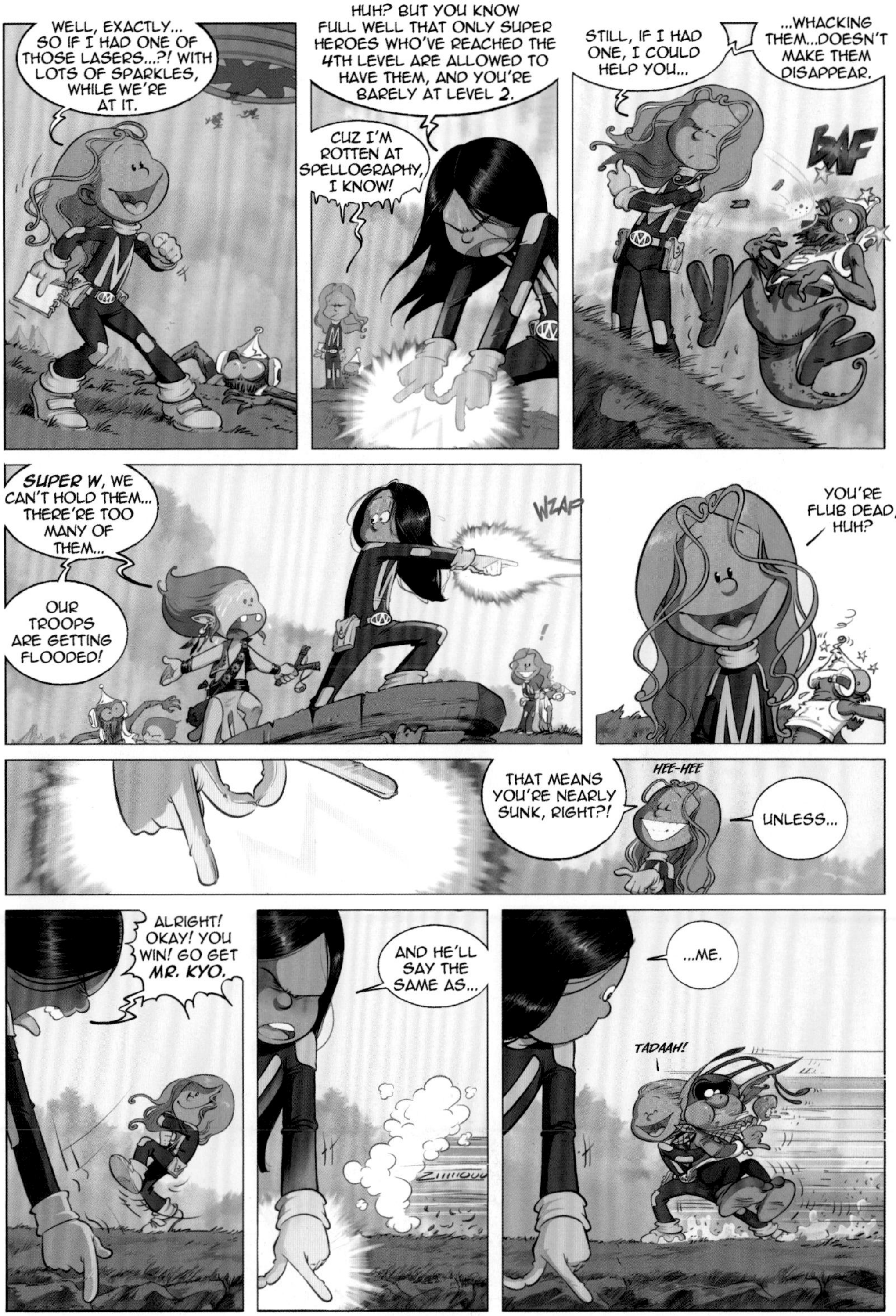
WELL, EXACTLY... SO IF I HAD ONE OF THOSE LASERS...?! WITH LOTS OF SPARKLES, WHILE WE'RE AT IT.
HUH? BUT YOU KNOW FULL WELL THAT ONLY SUPER HEROES WHO'VE REACHED THE 4TH LEVEL ARE ALLOWED TO HAVE THEM, AND YOU'RE BARELY AT LEVEL 2.
CUZ I'M ROTTEN AT SPELLOGRAPHY, I KNOW!
STILL, IF I HAD ONE, I COULD HELP YOU...
...WHACKING THEM...DOESN'T MAKE THEM DISAPPEAR.
BAF
SUPER W, WE CAN'T HOLD THEM... THERE'RE TOO MANY OF THEM...
OUR TROOPS ARE GETTING FLOODED!
WZAP
YOU'RE FLUB DEAD, HUH?
THAT MEANS YOU'RE NEARLY SUNK, RIGHT?!
HEE-HEE
UNLESS...
ALRIGHT! OKAY! YOU WIN! GO GET MR. KYO.
AND HE'LL SAY THE SAME AS...
...ME.
TADAAH!

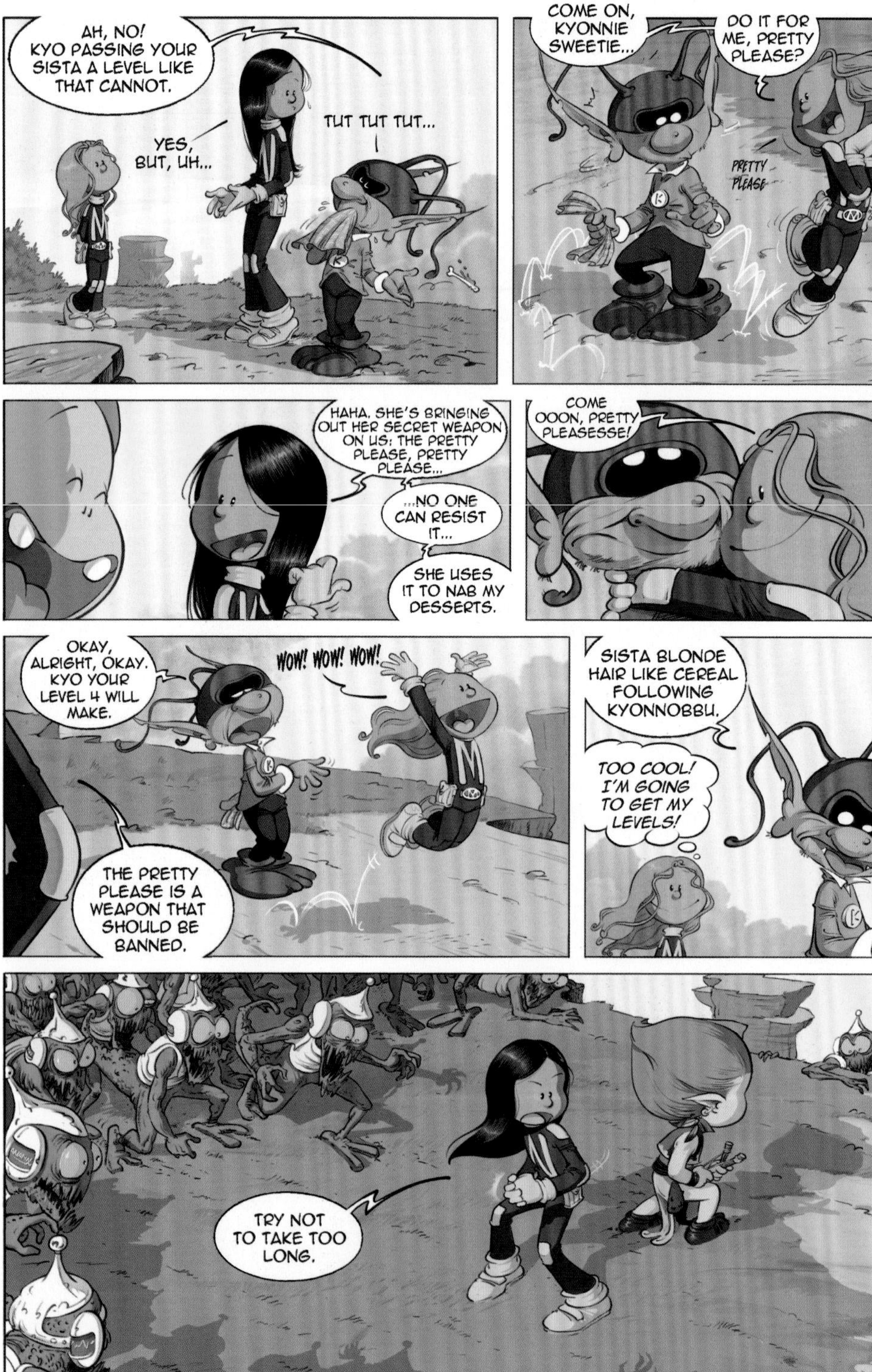
AH, NO! KYO PASSING YOUR SISTA A LEVEL LIKE THAT CANNOT.
YES, BUT, UH...
TUT TUT TUT...
COME ON, KYONNIE SWEETIE...
DO IT FOR ME, PRETTY PLEASE?
PRETTY PLEASE
PRETTY PLEASE
HAHA. SHE'S BRINGING OUT HER SECRET WEAPON ON US: THE PRETTY PLEASE, PRETTY PLEASE...
...NO ONE CAN RESIST IT...
SHE USES IT TO NAB MY DESSERTS.
COME OOON, PRETTY PLEASESSE!
OKAY, ALRIGHT, OKAY. KYO YOUR LEVEL 4 WILL MAKE.
WOW! WOW! WOW!
THE PRETTY PLEASE IS A WEAPON THAT SHOULD BE BANNED.
SISTA BLONDE HAIR LIKE CEREAL FOLLOWING KYONNOBBU.
TOO COOL! I'M GOING TO GET MY LEVELS!
TRY NOT TO TAKE TOO LONG.

SEVERAL SUPER GIANT STEPS AWAY...

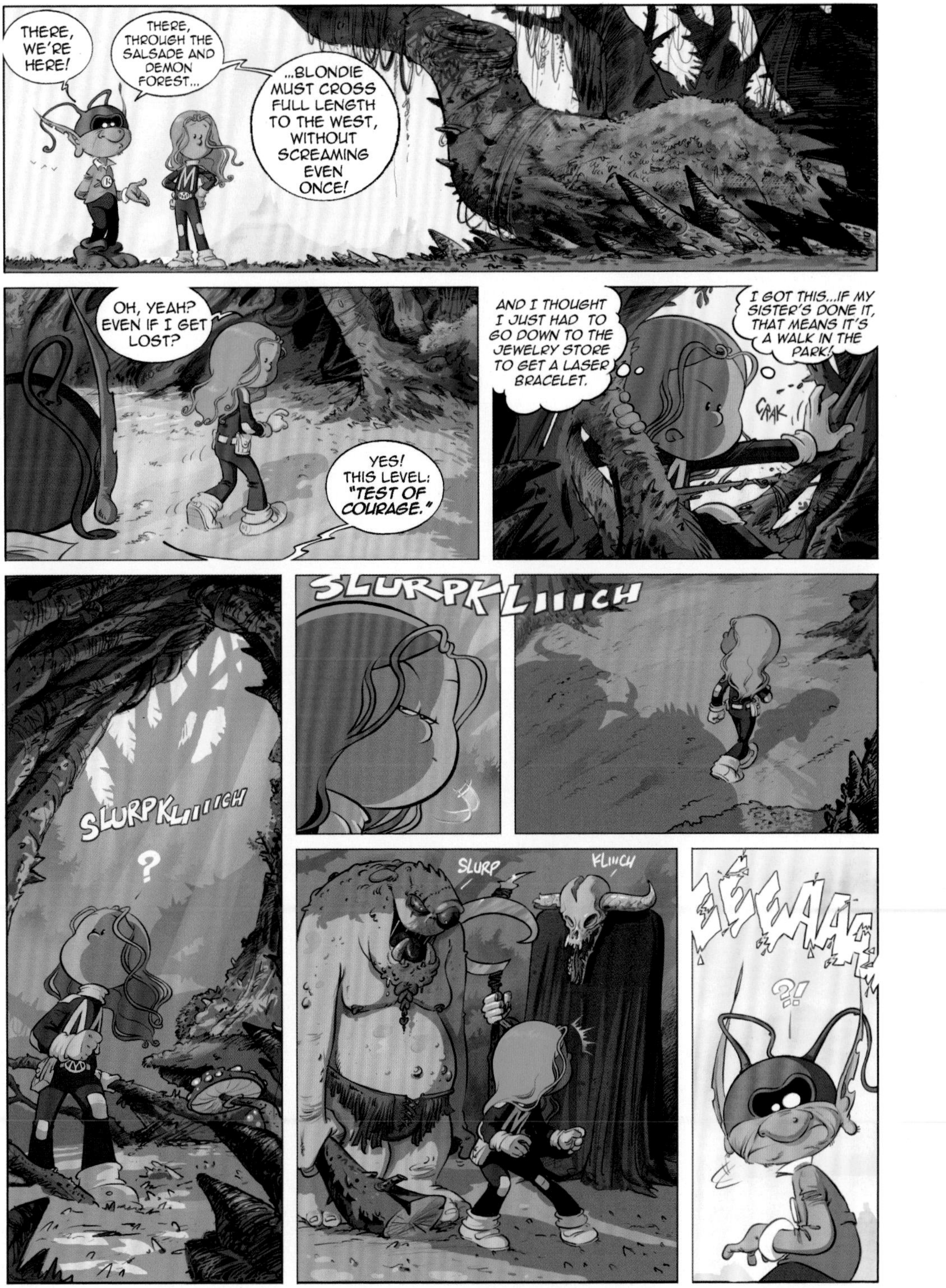
THERE, WE'RE HERE!
THERE, THROUGH THE SALSADE AND DEMON FOREST...
...BLONDIE MUST CROSS FULL LENGTH TO THE WEST, WITHOUT SCREAMING EVEN ONCE!
OH, YEAH? EVEN IF I GET LOST?
YES! THIS LEVEL: "TEST OF COURAGE."
AND I THOUGHT I JUST HAD TO GO DOWN TO THE JEWELRY STORE TO GET A LASER BRACELET.
I GOT THIS...IF MY SISTER'S DONE IT, THAT MEANS IT'S A WALK IN THE PARK!
CRAK
SLURPKLIIICH
SLURPKLIIICH
?
SLURP
KLIICH
?!

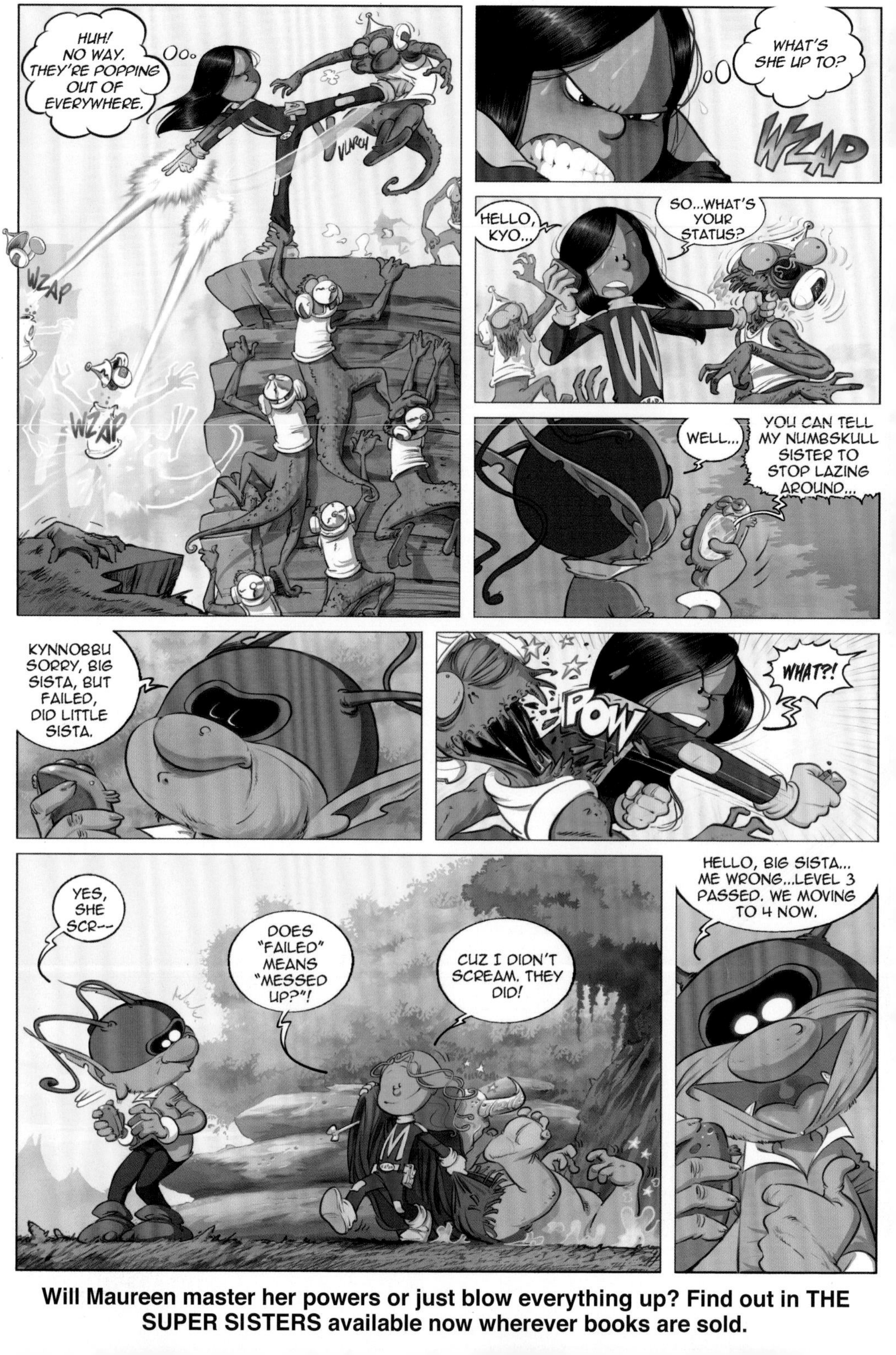
HUH! NO WAY. THEY'RE POPPING OUT OF EVERYWHERE.
VLARCH
WZAP
WZAP
WHAT'S SHE UP TO?
WZAP
HELLO, KYO...
SO...WHAT'S YOUR STATUS?
WELL...
YOU CAN TELL MY NUMBSKULL SISTER TO STOP LAZING AROUND...
KYNNOBBU SORRY, BIG SISTA, BUT FAILED, DID LITTLE SISTA.
POW
WHAT?!
YES, SHE SCR---
DOES "FAILED" MEANS "MESSED UP?"!
CUZ I DIDN'T SCREAM. THEY DID!
HELLO, BIG SISTA... ME WRONG...LEVEL 3 PASSED. WE MOVING TO 4 NOW.

Will Maureen master her powers or just blow everything up? Find out in THE SUPER SISTERS available now wherever books are sold.

Catch a ride to Ancient Egypt with GERONIMO STILTON in this special excerpt of GERONIMO STILTON #2 "The Secret of the Sphinx"...

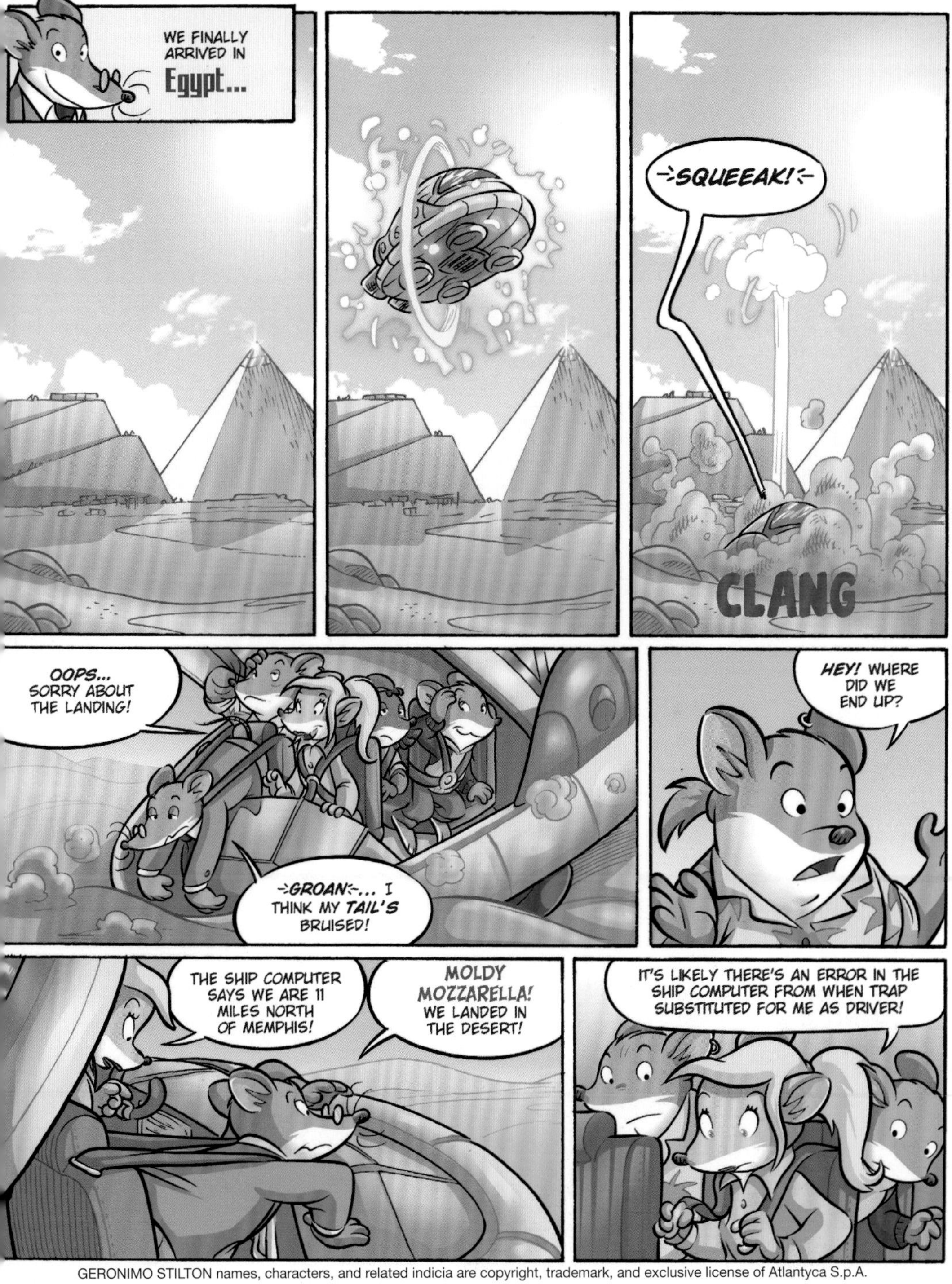

WE FINALLY ARRIVED IN Egypt...
-SQUEEAK!-
CLANG
OOPS... SORRY ABOUT THE LANDING!
-GROAN-... I THINK MY TAIL'S BRUISED!
HEY! WHERE DID WE END UP?
THE SHIP COMPUTER SAYS WE ARE 11 MILES NORTH OF MEMPHIS!
MOLDY MOZZARELLA! WE LANDED IN THE DESERT!
IT'S LIKELY THERE'S AN ERROR IN THE SHIP COMPUTER FROM WHEN TRAP SUBSTITUTED FOR ME AS DRIVER!

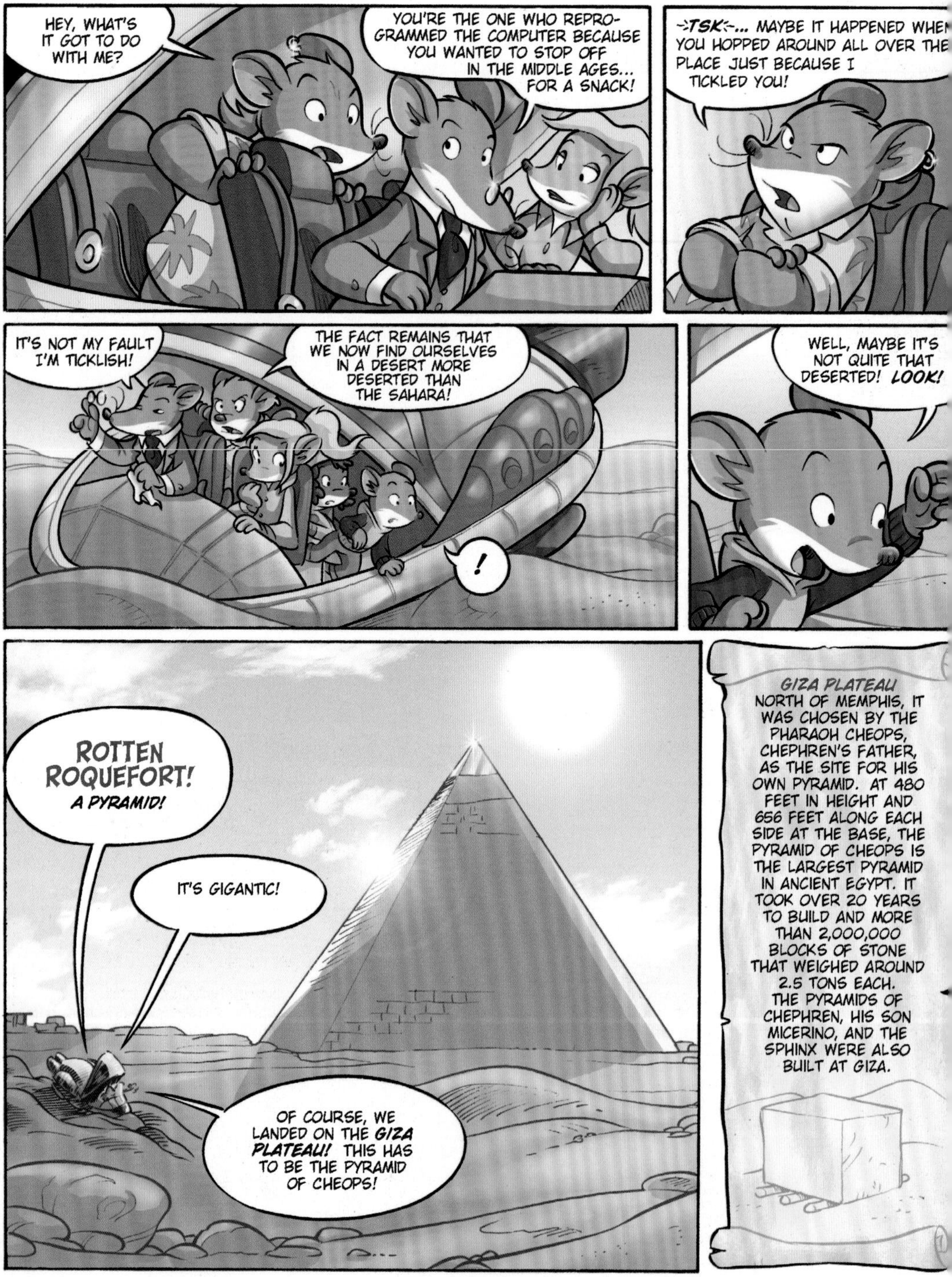
HEY, WHAT'S IT GOT TO DO WITH ME?
YOU'RE THE ONE WHO REPROGRAMMED THE COMPUTER BECAUSE YOU WANTED TO STOP OFF IN THE MIDDLE AGES... FOR A SNACK!
TSK... MAYBE IT HAPPENED WHEN YOU HOPPED AROUND ALL OVER THE PLACE JUST BECAUSE I TICKLED YOU!
IT'S NOT MY FAULT I'M TICKLISH!
THE FACT REMAINS THAT WE NOW FIND OURSELVES IN A DESERT MORE DESERTED THAN THE SAHARA!
!
WELL, MAYBE IT'S NOT QUITE THAT DESERTED! LOOK!
ROTTEN ROQUEFORT! A PYRAMID!
IT'S GIGANTIC!
OF COURSE, WE LANDED ON THE GIZA PLATEAU! THIS HAS TO BE THE PYRAMID OF CHEOPS!
GIZA PLATEAU
NORTH OF MEMPHIS, IT WAS CHOSEN BY THE PHARAOH CHEOPS, CHEPHREN'S FATHER, AS THE SITE FOR HIS OWN PYRAMID. AT 480 FEET IN HEIGHT AND 656 FEET ALONG EACH SIDE AT THE BASE, THE PYRAMID OF CHEOPS IS THE LARGEST PYRAMID IN ANCIENT EGYPT. IT TOOK OVER 20 YEARS TO BUILD AND MORE THAN 2,000,000 BLOCKS OF STONE THAT WEIGHED AROUND 2.5 TONS EACH. THE PYRAMIDS OF CHEPHREN, HIS SON MICERINO, AND THE SPHINX WERE ALSO BUILT AT GIZA.

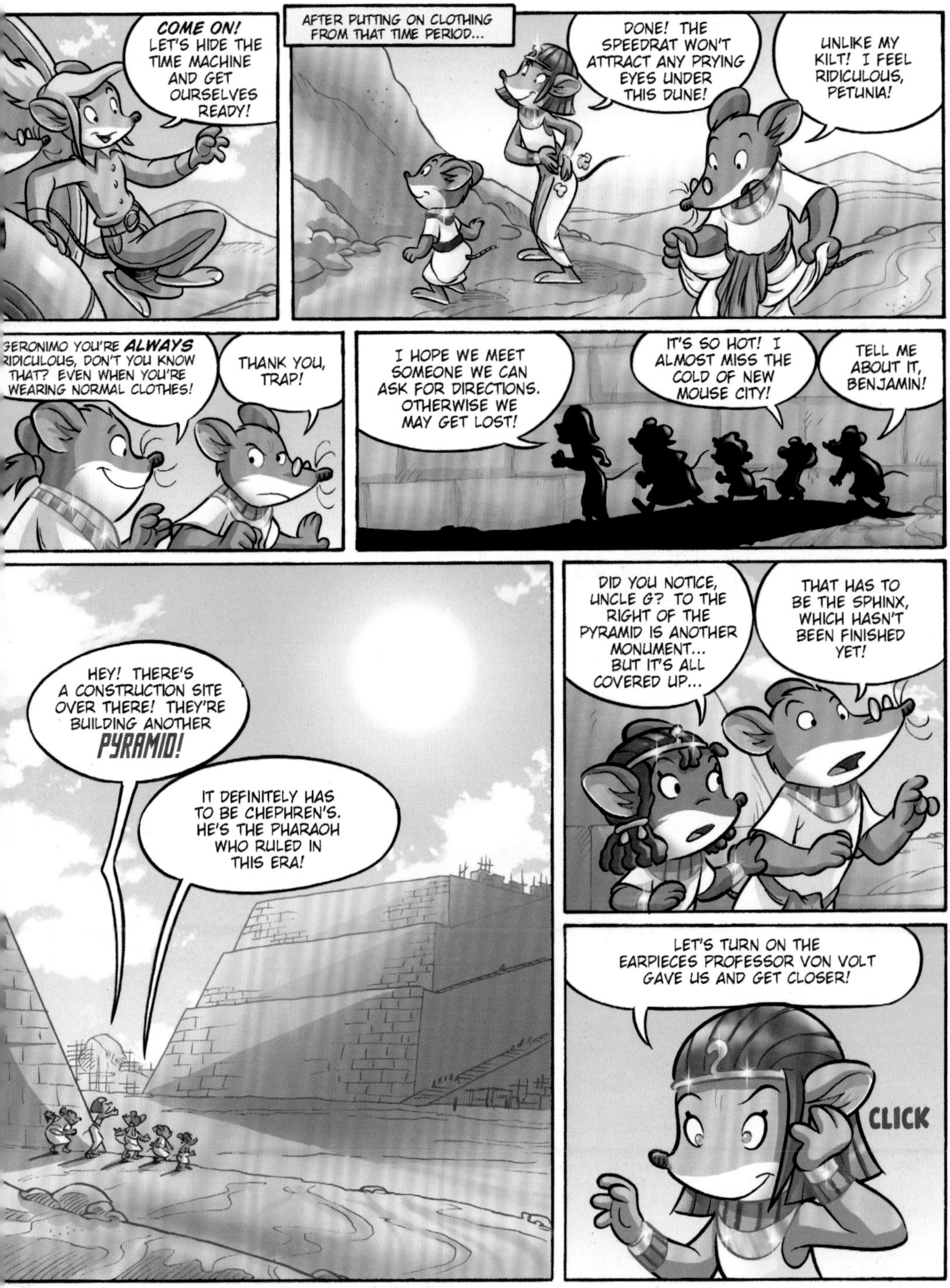
COME ON! LET'S HIDE THE TIME MACHINE AND GET OURSELVES READY!
AFTER PUTTING ON CLOTHING FROM THAT TIME PERIOD...
DONE! THE SPEEDRAT WON'T ATTRACT ANY PRYING EYES UNDER THIS DUNE!
UNLIKE MY KILT! I FEEL RIDICULOUS, PETUNIA!
GERONIMO YOU'RE ALWAYS RIDICULOUS, DON'T YOU KNOW THAT? EVEN WHEN YOU'RE WEARING NORMAL CLOTHES!
THANK YOU, TRAP!
I HOPE WE MEET SOMEONE WE CAN ASK FOR DIRECTIONS. OTHERWISE WE MAY GET LOST!
IT'S SO HOT! I ALMOST MISS THE COLD OF NEW MOUSE CITY!
TELL ME ABOUT IT, BENJAMIN!
HEY! THERE'S A CONSTRUCTION SITE OVER THERE! THEY'RE BUILDING ANOTHER PYRAMID!
IT DEFINITELY HAS TO BE CHEPHREN'S. HE'S THE PHARAOH WHO RULED IN THIS ERA!
DID YOU NOTICE, UNCLE G? TO THE RIGHT OF THE PYRAMID IS ANOTHER MONUMENT... BUT IT'S ALL COVERED UP...
THAT HAS TO BE THE SPHINX, WHICH HASN'T BEEN FINISHED YET!
LET'S TURN ON THE EARPIECES PROFESSOR VON VOLT GAVE US AND GET CLOSER!
CLICK

nearth more historical findings with Geronimo and friends in GERONIMO STILTON #2 "The Secret of the Sphinx"available wherever fine books are sold.

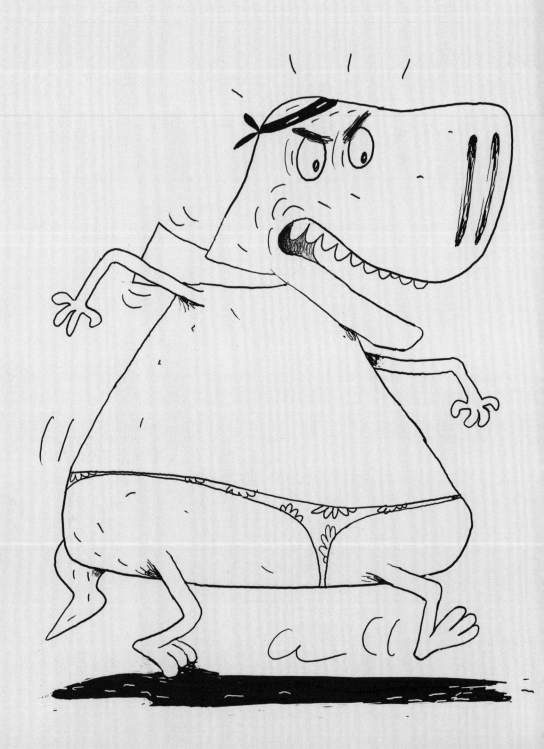